A MAJOR BLOCKBUSTING NOVEL OF
LETHAL POWER POLITICS

With THE FORTY-FIRST THIEF, Edward A. Pollitz steps
straight into the first rank of today's bestselling thriller
writers alongside such internationally famous names as Len
Deighton, Robert Ludlum and Frederick Forsyth.

Here is a big, major novel of international power politics –
with the emphasis on 'power' in more than one sense – that
moves at such a breathtaking pace that the reader will find
it difficult to put down once he has started on the compul-
sively exciting story. It moves between the secret conference
rooms of the White House and American Big Business,
horrific scenes of carnage on the French Riviera, tightrope-
tense confrontations between the U.S. Armed Forces and
hostile powers, a coup in an oil-rich Arab state and a secret
hideout where the finishing touches are being put to the research on a device that will liberate the Western world from
the tyranny of oil for ever...

Combining outstanding powers of exciting storytelling with
a staggeringly expert knowledge of the intricacies of top-
level politics and big business, Edward A. Pollitz Jr. has
created a stunning story of international violence and intrigue sure to appeal to hundreds of thousands of readers
eager for prime quality excitement.

D1392153

Edward A. Pollitz

The Forty-first Thief

Panther

Granada Publishing Limited
Published in 1976 by Panther Books Ltd
Frogmore, St Albans, Herts AL2 2NF
Reprinted 1977

First published in Great Britain by Hart-Davis,
MacGibbon Ltd in 1975
Copyright © 1975 by Edward A. Pollitz Jr.
Made and printed in Great Britain by
Richard Clay (The Chaucer Press) Ltd
Bungay, Suffolk
Set in Linotype Pilgrim

Many people have gone to Persia
and stood in front of rocks saying, 'Open Sesame,'
but always they have been disappointed

ALI BABA AND THE FORTY THIEVES

One

Pascal Lambert opened one dark eye and looked up across the brilliant sand as the girl emerged from the water. She raised her face to the August sun and swept her hands through her hair. The slight breeze hardened the nipples of her breasts, still conical in adolescence.

Pascal closed his eye and ground his hips into the mat on which he was stretched. His tongue darted out to lick at the film of perspiration and salt that had gathered on his upper lip. He had been watching the girl all afternoon. She lay on a mattress not far from his own, next to her parents. He arched his shoulders and casually moved the hair from his forehead. She was lying on her back, her head facing away from him. He tried to catch a glimpse of the few strands of pubic hair that escaped her bikini.

It was nearly four-thirty, and he knew that soon he must go home. Home to Arthur Edelman and his moodiness and his pudgy body and his little-old-lady ways, his incomprehensible papers and equations and his stupid little counting machine. Pascal sighed. Well, Arthur was certainly generous. He saw that Pascal had plenty of spending money and the best clothes from the good boutiques, a reasonable exchange for his services, and for the occasional strange errand he asked Pascal to run.

Pascal enjoyed dressing well in the skin-tight clothes which favored his girl-slim six-foot body. His thin clean-shaven face with its pointed nose was saved from a feral look by enormous liquid brown eyes framed by long curling lashes.

His towel in hand, Pascal rose and turned, his back to the water, and walked toward the changing cabins near the bar, drawing appreciative glances from men and women. He opened the bamboo swinging door and let it shut lightly behind him. He backed against the wall of the four-foot-square enclosure and dropped the towel to the sand beneath his feet. He lowered his bathing suit to the floor, leaned against the wall and closed his eyes. Thinking of the girl, he began to stroke himself rhythmically. So intense was his gratification that he hardly felt the slight breeze as the door of the cabin opened.

The dark heavy-set middle-aged man cursed to himself in an odd tongue. Using the white cotton gloves clenched in his hand to wipe his thigh, he strode purposefully but without hurrying from the changing cabin to his motorcycle in the parking lot behind the beach. He stuffed his gloves into the bag at the back of the bike, started it and drove off, waving to the attendant as he passed up the dirt road. When he arrived at the intersection where the road became paved and turned toward St. Tropez, three miles distant, and away from the private beach called Moorea, he allowed himself a small smile and a casual swipe at his black mustache.

The hot sand burning the bottom of his feet, Donald Hamilton walked awkwardly away from the bar, and the dozen people who lounged along the twenty-foot expanse looking out over the white sand which sloped downward fifty yards to wave tops glistening in the late afternoon sun, stretching to the horizon, beyond which Africa lay unseen.

He reached up to scratch at his hair, graying at thirty-seven. The scalp under the military cut prickled with perspiration. His dark eyes squinted above high sunburned cheekbones as he picked his way among the mattresses, with their bare-breasted girls and relaxed men. He started to lie down, changed his mind and picked up his towel. His butt itched with salt and the sand in his bathing suit. He brushed ruefully at the pot which had begun to grow on his otherwise fit body. He stood for a moment and glanced again at the bar and the restaurant building a hundred feet to its left. The rectangular tables at which lunch was served stood empty, their umbrellas folded limply above them, casting shadows on the narrow concrete floor.

He headed toward the shower at the back of the beach, to the right of the restaurant, wet himself with fresh water and went into a changing cabin to wipe himself dry, before returning for the last hour or two of sunlight.

Emerging from the cabin, Hamilton closed the door behind him and leaned his broad shoulders against it. His Adam's apple bobbed in his throat as he struggled to control his churning stomach. His face sought the warmth of the sun.

He took a deep breath, then glancing about quickly, edged the door open and looked in again. The thin strip of sunlight admitted by the crack in the door shone on the body of a young man. It was almost erect, the eyes wide and staring in horror. It was pinned to the back wall by what looked to be a skewer with a wooden handle, thrust with great strength through the hollow of the throat. His genitals had been cut off and stuffed into his bulging mouth.

Hamilton turned his head and slammed the door, fighting nausea again. He wiped at his face with the towel. He spotted a board near a tree a few feet away and propped it against the door at an angle, jamming the base into the sand. He marched past the bar and the restaurant building to the office at the far end and knocked on the door.

'Oui, entrez.'

'You speak English, don't you?'

'Yes, monsieur. What can I do for you?' The patron smiled, gray hair curling above a deeply tanned face, his body muscular in a bathing suit.

Hamilton blinked twice, as though to clear his vision, swallowed and said, 'I think you'd better call the police. There's a dead man in one of your cabins. I just found him.'

The patron half rose from his chair, his face twisted in alarm. 'Mon Dieu, are you sure that he's dead? I should call a doctor first, or the emergency squad.' He reached for the phone.

Hamilton put his hand on the patron's arm. 'Don't bother. Somebody killed him. He's all cut to pieces. It isn't very pretty.'

The patron slumped back into his chair. 'Merde. If someone else finds him . . .'

'I blocked the door with a piece of wood. It looks like it's out of order or something. Now you'd better call the cops.'

Late afternoon traffic streamed heavily both to and from St. Tropez as bathers vacated the beaches, and diners and night revelers poured into town. It took the two officers in the white uniforms of the Côte d'Azur almost half an hour to reach the beach restaurant.

Neither officer spoke English, and Hamilton waited quietly as the middle-aged man in the bathing suit explained in French, gesturing occasionally in his direction.

The younger of the two put his hand firmly on Hamilton's arm. 'Allons, monsieur . . . Je veux voir ce que vous avez trouvé.'

The restaurateur started to translate, but Hamilton shook his head in agreement, rose and started out of the door. He led both officers across the sand to the cabin, followed by a few curious stares from the guests at the now sparsely populated bar and beach, while the patron stayed behind, his head in his hands.

White-faced and shaken, the younger officer replaced the board. Wordlessly, the three of them walked back to the office. A naval clock on the wall tolled once. It was six-thirty. The older policeman called the station and spoke with the officer in charge.

When he hung up, he turned to the proprietor and said, 'He has asked us to wait here, M. Levesque, and asked that you detain your staff as well.' Levesque rose slowly, his shoulders stooped, and left the office. 'And you, M. Hamilton, we would ask you to wait as well. Comprenez?'

'Oui. Je comprends.'

Forty minutes later, the last dregs of day draining from the sky, the red ambulance of the Sapeurs-pompiers pulled into the parking lot, followed by a black and white Renault in which the Chief Inspector of St. Tropez rode, in slacks and sport shirt on his Saturday off. He was tall and tanned, with a curiously long, rather good-looking face. He seemed to Hamilton to be in his early forties. He spoke good, if stilted, English.

Inspector Riez strode to the cabin, looked inside and said unemotionally to the doctor who had accompanied the ambulance, 'Clean that up as best you can. Put it on a stretcher covered with a blanket, and have it brought out to the front of the restaurant so that we can get an identification if possible. And especially,' he gestured, 'fix the face.' Then he turned back to a uniformed officer. 'Du Long, take pictures. Don't bother with any of the other nonsense, prints and all that. There won't be anything.'

The moon was reflected in the calm Mediterranean across the sand that separated the concrete strip in front of the restaurant from the water by the time the remains of Pascal Lambert were in the ambulance.

'Of course, M. Levesque, every effort will be made to keep the matter in proportion. But there is no way that I can keep this matter from the press.'

'Mon Dieu, it's terrible for me, Inspector Riez. The middle of the haute saison! Is it at least all right to have the cabin cleaned up?'

The inspector frowned. 'Who knows, perhaps the publicity will do you some good. But by all means, have it cleaned up.'

The proprietor pointed to two of the boys sitting on chairs around the dining tables and motioned them toward the cabin. When they hesitated, he threw up his hands and led the way himself.

Hamilton turned to Claudie, the mop-headed bartender, and said, 'How about making me a drink?'

'Déjà fait,' he said, trotting off behind the bar to mix a Scotch and soda. It was Claudie who had remembered that the fag, 'la petite pédale,' who had got himself dismembered, was named Pascal.

'Inspector, can I buy you a drink?' Hamilton asked.

'Very kind of you, M. Hamilton, but not during working hours.' He looked down at his casual attire and smiled deprecatingly. 'Well, I think that we can call it a night. There is nothing left to be done here. Du Long, tell these people that they can go home, or whatever.'

'May I go too, Inspector?'

'Certainly, M. Hamilton, I don't wish to detain you any longer than necessary. Naturally, there will be an inquest at which you must be present.'

Hamilton made a sour face. 'When will that be, Inspector?'

'Tomorrow, I am sure. This will upset your vacation plans?'

'I'm not here on vacation, Inspector. And it may well upset my plans. I live in Toulon, you see.'

Somewhat surprised, the Inspector asked, 'What are you doing here then?'

'I'm an architect. My firm is cooperating on the building of the Hôtel La Boudrague,' he pointed vaguely over his shoulder, 'across the bay in Ste. Maxime. I'm in charge of project coordination. I've been here for about three months. Normally, I'm at the job site, but tomorrow is supposed to be an office day. We have a meeting. And then there is the question of where to stay. I'm sure the hotels are booked solid.'

Inspector Riez nodded, paused, then said, 'I think that I can probably get you a room at the Byblos for the night. In a matter as unpleasant as this one – your having found the cadaver – I am sure that you can see that your presence is most important. If you could see your way to make a phone

14

call. To postpone the meeting. Perhaps you are under time pressure. You will not be staying in France much longer?'

Defeated, Hamilton sighed and shook his head. 'All right, Inspector. I'll call someone at the office to postpone the meeting.' He smiled a little and went on, 'I'd like to get on with my work, but it'll keep a day, I suppose. The project won't be finished for eight or nine months.'

The Inspector inclined his head in polite thanks and said, 'Very kind of you to cooperate, M. Hamilton. I will take care of the hotel. A real shame, this inconvenience.'

A uniformed officer approached to say that they had accounted for all of the vehicles left in the parking lot, except for a new Honda 750-cc motorcycle.

'Check the registration,' the Inspector said. 'And tell me as soon as you have anything. M. Hamilton, that must have been quite a shock for you, finding him like that.'

'I tell you quite frankly, Inspector, I damn near threw up. And I thought that I'd seen everything in Vietnam.'

'You were in Indo-China?'

'Yes. A year. In Special Forces. Our commandos. I saw some ugly things, but never anything quite like this. Have you?'

'Jamais. I have been a flic for more than thirty years, since the war. Pederasts do terrible things to each other, they have more jalousie than women. But cutting off,' he searched for the word, 'les couilles and the penis ...' His face mirrored his revulsion. He lifted an eyebrow. 'That's something Arabs do. I might ask, I think. Hallo, Claudie. Venez ici, s'il vous plaît.'

The bartender stepped over and handed Hamilton his drink. No, he said, he had not seen any Arabs at the beach. Even in this new day of Arab power, one did not see that sort at Moorea Beach. He paused a moment, 'You know, just the same, there was this dark-haired gosse, Portuguese, I think he was, that I saw with Pascal several times. They went off together, I think, at least once. He was young. Maybe fourteen or fifteen. They come down here like that, young and good-looking to sell their assholes. They can only starve in their villages.'

'Do you remember his name?' the Inspector asked. 'Have you seen him recently?'

'He was here today. He went off with some fat old man with white hair. They are not noted for their fidelity, you know. His name is Pablino.'

The man in the uniform came back again. 'The bike is registered in the name of Pascal Lambert at 4 Rue des Petits Champs, Paris.'

'So,' the Inspector said, 'M. Pascal becomes Pascal Lambert. Perhaps we can find out something more from this Pablino. Du Long, I want you here all day tomorrow. Better come in a bathing suit, or slacks. I don't want Levesque to have a heart attack. Well, M. Hamilton, I'll see you tomorrow at the Gendarmerie. If you are there by ten, that will be plenty of time. I am sorry that I ruined your day and your evening. I will manage with the hotel room. If you have a problem ...' He took out his wallet and removed a card, scribbling on the back of it. 'This is my home number. The number of the station and my private number are on the front.'

Two

Pierre Tombal craned his neck a little as he sat at his desk waiting for Riez. He could see past the obstructing corner of the building next door and out over the harbor of Toulon. Tombal had always thought that the green of the Mediterranean was the color of the eyes of a beautiful woman. Of course, things were not as clear in his field of view as they had been. At fifty-three one does not have quite the vision of one's youth. Ah well, Tombal thought, at least he didn't have to wear glasses to read. He turned to the cardboard folder on his desk. Crimes of violence were not typical of the Department of the Var. Not even in the summer season, when the beaches were packed like a breeding ground for seals.

A tall immaculate uniformed officer knocked and entered, standing at attention before his desk. 'M. le Commissaire, Inspector Riez is outside.'

Tombal mashed the tiny bit of Gauloise in the ashtray and put his burned finger into his mouth. 'Thank you. Please have him come in.' He brushed at the ashes in his lap, straightened his vest over his bulging stomach and stood facing the door.

Riez was dressed in a tan business suit, lighter than his skin. He put out his right hand and smiled. Tombal shook it warmly, cognizant of the missing top joints of the last two fingers, and the familiar greeting, 'Ça va, mon commandant?'

'Ça va toujours, Hervé. How are you? The family? The kids?'

'Fine. I was dragged out of the garden on this matter I sent down to you. Oh, by the way,' Riez handed him a small package, 'Natalie has sent herbes de Provence. You will have soupe au pistou tonight.'

They sat, and Tombal reached out with mahogany-stained fingers to the cigarette pack on the desk. 'I never get enough,' he said.

Riez grinned, a broken tooth marring an otherwise handsome smile. 'Privations of the war, no doubt.'

Tombal nodded at the private joke, waved out the match and asked, 'So what is so important about the removal of one pédale from the public scene?'

'Absolutely nothing. That's why I'm here. That's why I went around Brignoles to get the file to you. It was quite a thorough job for the elimination of one pédale, don't you think?'

'Who took the pictures, Du Long?'

'Yes. The man is a veritable artist at getting the most out of a plain picture.'

'The man seems to have an eye for the angles that show the most blood. Was it really as bad as it looks?'

'Actually, worse. You know from the report. It was done with a brochette from the kitchen. It must have taken tremendous strength.'

'Yes, and accuracy too. He seems to have been very neatly spitted.'

'I can tell you that it took two hands to pull the damn thing out of the wall. The doctor said that it went right through the windpipe and crushed the spinal column as well.'

'So, you have concluded this was no ordinary faggot taking out his revenge on a straying lover. And certainly not at the beach at St. Tropez in August. There is so much switching around. It wouldn't matter to that sort anyway.'

'Exactly. So I come to your doorstep with a crime of passion, or something that looks like one, committed in the wrong place at the wrong time, and in a professional manner.'

'Some people think that passion gives a murderer added strength. We have both seen that, not so, Hervé? But like you, I think that there is more than a tinge of practiced skill involved here. But mon vieux, what can I do here? We have nothing to go on, and a whole summer season of thefts to deal with, and lunatics trying to wipe out the human race from behind the wheels of their cars and speedboats. If they didn't lend us some CRS for the summer down here,' he threw up his hands, 'I am sure that we would all go mad.'

Riez crossed his long legs and studied his highly polished brown shoes. He rubbed the stubs of his fingers, a silent reminder to Tombal of the grenade Riez had plucked from the ground next to Tombal's head thirty-three years earlier. It had exploded several feet from Riez, tearing off the ends of his fingers and leaving other scars on the chest and stomach, hidden beneath the tan suit. Had Riez not acted, instead of there being a fat aging Commissaire de Police, Brigade Criminelle, there would be a Rue Pierre Tombal somewhere, as there is a Rue Tony Allard, and a Rue François Sibilli, with a sign *Mort Pour La France*.

'I really don't want to make an issue of this, Commissaire. I know that you have a great deal to do, that you are short of personnel, and so forth. But I wondered if I might ask you to devote a little of your time to seeing that the matter is not just dropped in a routine fashion.'

Tombal stubbed out the cigarette he had just lit. 'Alors, Hervé, I'll send someone. I suppose you are looking things over.'

'Yes. Du Long has been at the beach for two days in a bathing suit. That's the kind of duty I never seem to get.'

'You've checked with Paris?'

'Yes. The usual cooperation of the Sûreté for the local Gendarmerie – minimal. We got his address and proper name from his motorcycle registration. He has no record. His term in the Army was totally uneventful.' Riez looked up frowning, as if waiting for an answer.

Tombal sighed. 'I will make some inquiry of the Sûreté myself. Now, let me get back to my work.' He arched his gray brows. 'I'll come down myself tomorrow morning.'

Riez got lightly to his feet, smiling, tugged at his ear,

came to attention and gave a small salute. 'Dinner?'

'If I can stay.'

'The usual?'

'And heavy on the garlic.'

'You grow fat, mon commandant.'

'And old. Now get out.'

Three days after the death of Pascal Lambert, Riez parked his car in front of the police station across from the Prisunic and walked leisurely up the narrow street to the port. He stopped at the window of the little pet shop to look at the puppies and to use the plate glass as a mirror. He was out of uniform, and the bright red sport shirt clung to his too thin form, accentuating the hollow stomach and prominent rib cage. He thought that his ears, a little obvious and pointed, detracted from otherwise regular features. He turned self-consciously and continued down the street.

Despite a lifetime on the Côte d'Azur, Riez never failed to wonder at the beauty and luxury of the yachts, jammed side by side, stern-first against the jetty. For the most part, they flew the flag of Panama or Liberia to indicate their tax-free and non-unionized status, though their transoms, with names carved or painted in gold leaf, indicated a variety of home ports: Cannes, Nice, Hamburg, Bristol. Traditionally, they flew the flag of the host port, in this case France, from a strut on one side, and the flag of the owner's nationality on the other. Of the thirty or forty boats in the harbor, he estimated that more than half were owned by foreigners. A few were rented at from eight thousand to twenty-five thousand dollars per month, from yacht brokers in Cannes and St. Tropez, for the months their owners were either working or enjoying other leisures.

Riez stopped briefly in the middle of the jetty. A broad gangway led twenty feet to the afterdeck of a magnificent ship. She must be sixty meters, Riez thought. *Glen Pool*, Newport, R.I. She flew a French pennant to starboard, and a large American flag from the mast on her superstructure.

Two muscular swarthy sailors sat at the foot of the gang-way, regarding the passers-by. On impulse, Riez crossed the harbor and asked casually, 'How long is she?'

The older sailor rose, squat and powerful, with an elaborate curved mustache reminiscent of Imperial Turkey's Janissary Guards. 'Fifty-five meters,' he said, 'one meter less than the *Belle Simone*,' and then, as an afterthought, 'two meters longer than the *New Horizons*.' The second man stood, taller and more slender in a pair of shorts and a tee shirt imprinted with the name of the boat. 'She goes almost forty knots,' he said. 'She has radar, air conditioning and seventeen guest cabins.'

Odd, Riez thought, both spoke French well, but they were obviously Arabs. There were several hundred thousand in the South of France, emigrants from what was once French North Africa, most doing hand labor. But it was unusual to find them as sailors – and on an American yacht. They were bigger and cleaner than most, though, he thought.

'Who owns this boat? She really is something. The star of the port. I've never seen her here before.'

The guardians of the yachts of St. Tropez boast as much about their owners as about the ships themselves. The sailor with the mustache, Abdul Aboussara, said, 'This boat belongs to Paul Fosburgh.' Then as if to fill a gap created by ignorance, he continued, 'The American millionaire – oil, you know.'

'Yes, I'd heard,' said Riez. 'Well, thank you. She really is lovely.' He turned and crossed the port diagonally, taking another look over his shoulder at the now-seated sailors, then stood before the crowded mass of tables of which Le Senequier consists and chose one in the first row.

A harried-looking uniformed officer hurried by the table, stopped a couple of feet beyond, turned to confirm his first impression, then threw a snappy salute. Riez shook his head slightly and waved the cop away with the back of his hand. A little confused, the cop dropped his salute and hurried on his way. Out of the corner of his eye, Riez saw that the two sailors of the *Glen Pool* were occupied in conversation and probably had not noticed.

A waitress took his order and returned quickly with a glass one-quarter filled with ice and a clear yellow liquid which clouded immediately when she filled the glass with water.

'Casanis. Four francs, monsieur.'

He was on his second drink, rattling the cubes in his glass and looking out over the boats at Ste. Maxime across the bay, when he felt a hand on his shoulder. He looked up and started to rise.

'Stay put, Hervé. Can you get me one too, citron pressé with peppermint. I'm dying of thirst.' Tombal's jowly red-veined face was beaded with perspiration. He sat heavily, tugged at his brown linen trousers which had sagged at his knees, and lifted his paunch a bit with his hands. 'I took the road to Ramatuelle from Toulon, rather than going straight to La Foux. I thought that I would save time because of the traffic. I always think the same thing.' He raised his hands palms up and shrugged. 'And I'm always wrong. My God, those turns. Do you know anything?'

Riez caught the eye of the busy waitress and ordered a drink for both of them before answering. 'No, but I have a thought. I think that whoever killed that pédale is probably still here. Or certainly was the whole night after the murder.'

'Ah. How is that, my friend? One would think that he would run like hell. How about some soupe de poisson?' Tombal asked.

'My God, Pierre, your stomach again. All right. I can wait.' Riez motioned to the waitress.

Tombal put out the cigarette and picked up the spoon almost in the same motion when the waitress brought the dish.

'Very good, the rouille,' motioning at the wooden bowl filled with a malevolent pink paste, 'is very piquante today. Absolutely delicious.'

Riez pulled at his nose impatiently and looked up at the sky.

'I found out a few things,' Tombal said.

'Finally.'

'Pascal Lambert worked for an accounting firm in Paris until two months ago.' He alternated words with spoonfuls of soup. 'Then he started coming in at odd hours, was warned several times after some weeks, but quit before he was cashiered. He had quite a reputation as a ladies' man. In the words of one of the younger secretaries – who by the way regretted his passing – he fucked everything that moved.'

'I can't watch you any longer.' Riez motioned to the waitress again. 'Another ...' Tombal looked up accusingly. 'Two more soupes de poisson and two more drinks. And a large bottle of Badoit mineral water too, please. In any case,' Riez continued, 'it seems strange that the man should have a reputation as a stud in Paris, and at the same time be considered a prize queen down here. That's what Du Long came back with from his paid vacation at Moorea Beach. Poor Du Long, after his two-day holiday, he's back directing traffic in the Place des Lices.'

Tombal wiped his mouth and said, 'That's the penalty for being a cop in a town that has three thousand people in it nine months of the year, and a transient population of three hundred thousand the other three months. How many permanent police are there here in St. Tropez anyway?'

Riez smiled deprecatingly. 'Six, mon commandant. Not including me, of course. If you take into account the cops that the National Police sent down in the summer, the CRS, I have maybe twenty-two or twenty-three. But of course, the ones that they send down here only work a certain number of hours a week. It's really quite a privilege. They bring their wives and families and have that camp up near Grimaud. They're not really interested in getting involved in crimes of violence. The way they look at it, they're down here for the purpose of directing traffic, taking a vacation in the sun with their families and sweeping up the human debris of an occasional road accident.'

'Just the same,' Tombal said, around a piece of crisp bread

and butter, 'there is certainly not much crime in St. Tropez in the summer. Just small burglaries at the villas and at some of the hotels – and a stream of complaints of one kind or another from the camping parks. But what can one expect when people live like animals in a cage? Anyway, I think that it's a miracle that there are not more problems.'

'It's really easy to understand why,' Riez said. 'There are a variety of disadvantages to St. Tropez. Not the least of them is the lousy road system. From five-thirty, or at the latest six o'clock, the traffic getting off the peninsula down that one road to the crossroads at La Foux stands stock-still. It takes about two hours, or even three, to get down that five kilometers, in single file. I often wonder why people would do that and call it a vacation. Yet there are more every year. Because you can't get out of town,' Riez lowered his voice a little, 'the merchants have you by the balls. A carton of twelve bottles of Evian water that costs eleven francs in St. Raphael, thirty kilometers down the coast, costs fifteen francs here. Because the people are trapped. During the day, when there is less traffic and you can drive, they want to be at the beach. When the sun goes down, there's no way out. That's why there is no organized crime here. It's basically a little town. Even with the summer population. The kids come down here and peddle their assholes or their pussies for a few francs or some fancy trinkets in the right quarters,' he waved at the yachts, 'and there is a little smoking and a little hard stuff, but nothing big. The minute something got started, everybody in the world would know.'

Tombal smiled. 'Even us cops?'

'That's why I think that whoever killed Pascal Lambert was still here that night, and could well be here now.'

Tombal put down his spoon and looked seriously at Riez. 'Then why didn't you throw up a roadblock?'

'I thought about that,' Riez said. 'But what good would it have done? How the hell can you check six or eight thousand cars and countless motorcycles when you have six lousy policemen and no idea what you are looking for? My best guess is that the man who did this sat back down on the

24

beach and went back to sunning himself or playing cards or whatever he was doing before.'

Tombal worked on the few remaining croutons. 'I think that you are probably right. The thing that impressed me, on reflection, was the speed with which it must have been done. The man had to be very strong to drive that skewer not only through a human body, but nearly three inches into the matting and wood behind his neck as well. He must have been proficient as hell with a knife, or he would have been completely spattered with blood from his butcher's work. He had to be fast and confident of his skill. How did he know no one would walk in on him? He must have seen Lambert get up and go to the cabin. Then, without being obvious, he had to get the tools, get to the cabin, kill him without making a sound and then carve him up. Then he had to leave unseen. That kind of work is the result of practice. It was all done so neatly. Evidently, it was not the first time that this man has cut off someone's sex organs.'

'I had heard that it was a habit of the Arabs.'

Tombal lit a cigarette and looked up reflectively, then dabbed at his lips with the napkin in his other hand. 'Oh, yes, they did it to each other for centuries, then started on the Israelis during their various wars,' he flicked an ash contemptuously, 'for all the good it did them. But the most famous of all the nut-cutters are the Ethiopians. I read in a book called *The Blue Nile* that during the last century, when the British were sending a punitive expedition against the Emperor Theodore, there was a national complex among the Ethiopian warriors, not that they would be killed, but that they would be captured and that most certainly the enemy would cut off their balls. I suppose they were unaware that British gentlemen did not share their habits and wanted their land – not their balls. There is a tribe in their great desert, the Danakil Depression it is called, that still does ball-cutting. To each other, first and foremost, and to anybody else they can catch unawares. The penis is necessary to give as a bride price to the father of the intended to prove manhood.'

'Quaint,' said Riez, with a sour face. 'Then perhaps we should be looking for an Ethiopian.'

'The thought occurred to me. I think that we shall do just that. Have you had any luck in locating Lambert's local address?'

'No, he must have slept on the beach. I've checked all of the hotel registries for the past two months.'

'Poor Du Long, he must have loved that. You know,' he reached for another cigarette, 'it is possible that the horror of the act was meant to frighten someone. To serve as a warning of the lengths to which our friend the murderer was prepared to go.'

Riez took the money from his wallet to pay the bill that the waitress had placed on the plate before him. 'Very possible.' He looked pained. 'And by the way, I helped Du Long. He only did half of the registries. Now you and I are going to do something together. Lambert must have eaten. He had to have stayed somewhere other than the beach, perhaps a private home. It couldn't have been a hotel, the cards are mandatory. Perhaps he had something delivered to him. I have a picture of him. Let's make the rounds of the merchants.'

Tombal looked at the picture of the face of Pascal Lambert's corpse. 'There were no relatives to notify,' he said. 'He was an orphan and unmarried. But the Sûreté,' he reached a pudgy hand into his pocket, 'were kind enough to provide this picture from his military days. I think that it will be better,' Tombal said, motioning, 'than that portrait of a dead fish.'

'Two-fifteen,' Riez said. 'They should all be open by now.'

The two policemen rose and walked slowly up the quay to begin their search for the late Pascal Lambert's holiday home.

Three

About two hours after Pascal Lambert had died, pinned like a grotesque butterfly to the wall of the changing cabin at Moorea Beach, lengthening shadows streaked the sandy soil behind a house some ten miles distant.

Arthur Edelman looked up at the clock on his desk, then placed his sharpened pencil down in a pile of others on the myriad papers spread before him. He looked westward into the setting sun across the sere hills of the Midi. The olive trees which followed the road at the back edge of the property flashed their semaphore of silver and green in the dwindling light. He was immersed in a particularly critical evaluation of the retentive properties of silica sections with respect to indirect sunlight, rays of the sun partially filtered by cloud cover. But he had been unable to concentrate on his work properly for the past half hour.

His hairless rounded potbelly rumbled at the base of a sunken chest framed by narrow shoulders. He put the back of his hand to his mouth and burped delicately. He squinted a little and strained for the sound of Pascal's new motorcycle. My God, he thought, what if he's hurt himself? I'll never forgive myself. I never should have bought him such a dangerous toy. He smiled with some satisfaction. There were always little fiscal concessions to make with Pascal. After all, he had found that delightful Portuguese boy at the beach. They had had such a lovely luncheon, and then the afternoon. Oh well, was a Honda motorcycle such a grand concession, even if it had a 750-cc engine?

Arthur stretched his thin arms over his head, feeling a little stiff. He had been sitting in virtually the same position since six in the morning. Goodness, almost thirteen hours, he thought. He looked about him and saw the piles of pages filled with formulas and notes in his cramped precise hand. He turned the switch of the little electronic calculator to off and patted it affectionately. A slight stirring below the belt prompted him to stand and move about the room a bit. Oh well, a good day's work done in any case. Closer and closer. Now for a nice dinner, and a quiet evening at home. He walked to the kitchen and tied the pastel printed apron around his waist.

Pascal was fond of the food of the Midi, so Arthur took great pains to prepare the ratatouille properly. Just the right blend of fresh herbs, the wonderful small eggplant, a few green peppers and the incomparable tomatoes, their flavor drawn from the parched earth of Provence. By the time that he had finished and set the pot to cook and had scaled, be-headed and gutted the sardines for grilling, only a sliver of red light remained on the western horizon.

It was nearly eight o'clock, and Arthur, quite disturbed, paced back and forth on the porch, running his hand across his scalp. During the month and a half since Pascal had moved in with him, he had been forgiving of Pascal's minor peccadillos. Arthur even suspected that he went with a woman occasionally. But Pascal was always considerate. He always called.

Feeling the need to replenish his self-esteem, Arthur walked to the desk, took the little key from the chain around his neck and opened the drawer. He looked down at the envelope which bore his name and the words 'Personal' and 'Confidential,' all in script. Enjoying the texture of the creamy off-white Tiffany stationery, he turned it in his hands. Engraved in black on the flap was the legend 'M.G., 767 Fifth Avenue, New York, New York.' He removed the letter and read.

Dear Mr. Edelman,
In response to your most recent correspondence, I am well aware of your desire to keep the nature of your work as confidential as possible. I am equally desirous of maintaining the utmost secrecy. We are both, I believe, aware of what the

impact of your efforts could be, not only on the company, but on the business and political climate of the country as well. However, I am at a considerable disadvantage in not being able to keep in regular contact with you. As per our agreement, these efforts are known only to myself and two other persons here, Mr. Coughtry, our Senior Vice President for Research and Development, and Mr. Hultz, our Senior Executive Vice President. These men were hand-picked for their positions by me, and I place in them the utmost faith. We have the first three segments of the project in a safe-deposit box which must be opened by the three of us. As we agreed, no attempt will be made to get in touch with you until you request such a meeting by cable, at which time you are to be met at the prearranged place. I urge you to consider the urgency of this matter, and the position of importance in which your skills have placed you. We anxiously await further word from you.

Sincerely,
(signed)
Milton Goodrich
President
General Motors Corporation
August 8, 1977

Arthur gloated. The letter had been delivered to Pascal by hand two days earlier on the dock at St. Tropez. As arranged, the messenger had recognized Pascal by the rose behind his ear.

Yes indeed, this was a little different from the receptions he had received earlier in his career. It certainly gave him cause to bless the memory of his mom, dead these six years. Her generosity had allowed him to escape even the occasional legal problems that arose from what Mom used to call his sophisticated appetites – tastes befitting an unusual intellect. It amused him that Goodrich would attempt to stir him with a call to his patriotism. Arthur had spent the last eight of his forty-two years abroad, where people's attitudes in personal matters were so much more civilized. He sniffed at the air, recognized the smell of burning food and ran rapidly to the kitchen.

*

By nine-thirty Arthur was frantic. 'Where the hell can he be? It's not like him,' he said aloud. Perhaps, he thought, philosophical for a moment, he has decided to leave me. After all he has the Honda. Maybe that's all he had in mind. These pretty boys are like that sometimes. I hate to be alone. Suppose some terrible person comes here late at night and robs me. He could beat me, he thought, and rape me.

He consoled himself by turning on the television set and watching Gary Cooper and Akim Tamiroff in *The General Died at Dawn* on Monte Carlo TV. Then he went to bed.

When Arthur awoke the next morning, the sun was well up. He glanced at his watch, wrapped a towel around his middle and padded outside barefoot to the yard to pick up his copy of *Nice-Matin*, which had been thrown over the wall and into the rosebushes as usual. He went back inside placed the paper on the table in the kitchen and busied himself with his breakfast of coffee and crisp French bread with butter. He dropped four irregular cubes of unrefined sugar into the cup, adjusted the glasses on the bridge of his nose and scanned the front page.

MEURTRE A LA PLAGE
(v. Section St. Tropez)
Jeune Homme Trouvé Mort

Arthur thumbed through the paper to the page with St. Tropez in large letters at the top.

He scanned the story with his usual speed and his eyes bulged. Holding his glasses against his face, he won the race against his loosened bowels. When he came out trembling, he read the story again. Pascal had been found 'indisputably the victim of foul play at a beach in Pampelonne near St. Tropez.' A rigorous investigation of the matter was under way under the able direction of Inspector Riez. It was expected that the case would be referred to a Juge d'Instruction at the sous-préfecture in Brignoles.

Arthur threw the remains of his tartine in the garbage can

and poured the half-finished coffee in the sink. He stood for a moment, dabbing at his eyes with the back of his wrist, then turned, went into the living room, sat down at the desk and turned on the calculator.

Four

Footsore and weary from the heat, and discouraged from the endless series of blank stares they had received from the merchants of St. Tropez, Riez and Tombal had given up the ghost just before the afternoon exodus began. They had piled into their cars and flowed with the traffic, already beginning to crawl, down the road to La Foux and on up the hill to the Hauts de Grimaud where Riez lived.

Their lack of success was largely forgotten among the affectionate and excited greetings of Natalie Riez and the children, and the passing around of an enormous box of candy that Tombal had pulled from the trunk of his car.

When the sun went down, they retired to the house and watched and chatted as Natalie prepared the last details of a sumptuous dinner, redolent of herbs and spices, principally garlic. Tombal's eyes sparkled in anticipation. Natalie laughed at him. 'Pierre, your nose twitches like a rabbit's when you smell food.' They ate for hours.

Tombal stretched his head back to pick out the Big Dipper, took a drag and inhaled deeply. 'I'm afraid that I do have to go back. It's only about an hour at this time of night. I'll just drive up to Le Luc and catch the main road from there. Ugh,' he patted his stomach again, 'those curves are the worst in France. When God created the Massif des Maures he must have wanted St. Tropez to be deserted.' He struggled to his feet. 'I'm going to get the hell out of here, before I fall asleep in my chair. Look, you keep me posted on this business, and I'll see if I can't further improve the information that we get from our friends in Paris.' He paused for a moment and turned back. 'And by the way, old friend, be careful.' He held up his hand.

Riez raised the hand with all of the fingers, 'I promise not to lose any more. I'll keep you informed, mon commandant.'

Tombal said good night to Natalie Riez and the children and got into his car to begin the drive back to Toulon.

'You know, Natalie, I think that I'll have just one more look at town tonight,' Riez said.

'Is there anything special going on? Has the Pègre arrived en masse from Marseilles?'

'No, not that I know of. And in fact,' he said, kissing her soundly on the mouth, 'they are welcome to the whole goddamn mess – tourists and all – if they want it. I won't be late. It's my friend the fag. It's bothering me. I think I'll take a run out to the beach too.'

'Would you like to borrow one of my dresses?' she said.

Riez grinned, 'No. If they don't try to steal my badge, I won't walk behind them in sneakers.'

Tombal had survived the harrowing drive through the mountains to Le Luc and had made it to his house by half past midnight. He contented himself with a nightcap of brandy, reported his whereabouts to the permanent operator at his office and went to sleep.

It was just after four in the morning when his phone rang. Looking sleepily at the clock, he reached for the direct line to his office, which buzzed uninterested in his ear. Finally, he figured that it was his regular phone and picked it up.

It was Du Long at St. Tropez. He was calling from the house of Inspector Riez. His breath rattled with emotion.

'I can't believe that he's dead. Inspector Riez! It doesn't seem right! Of course, I came here first. I felt that it was only right. I've shut off everything – the road, I mean. I've worked for him for twenty years.' His voice cracked again. 'I found him myself. On the road to Tahiti Beach. He told Mme. Riez he just wanted to take one more quick look. His throat was cut from ear to ear.'

Tombal swallowed. 'Was he ... disfigured? Like the other one?'

'No, thank God. But I think he was dead before he was cut. There's a terrible gash on the back of his head.'

'I will be down as fast as I can. You called the doctor for Mme. Riez, of course?'

'Yes, sir. Have you any other instructions?'

'Search who you can. Question who you can. Keep the town as tightly bottled as you can. I want everyone up. Everyone is to be on duty.'

'I have already done so, mon commandant.'

Tombal held the phone away from his ear for a moment and looked at it, tears welling in his eyes. 'Yes, of course, Du Long.'

Donald Hamilton reached for the knob on his office door, convinced that he had avoided his colleagues for the moment.

'Aha,' said a voice behind him, 'I do believe that I see a master spy. Or is it possible that it is just a common garden-variety axe murderer?'

Donald turned, smiled sweetly and said. 'Merde.'

Victor Saulnier threw his arm around Donald's shoulder and accompanied him into the office. 'Had I known, when we began this project together, that you were going to be a source of publicity, as well as a font of architectural knowledge, mon cher, I would have been doubly pleased.'

'Go away, Victor. Va-t'en.'

'But Donald,' he said in a hurt tone, 'I am just voicing my appreciation for the energy with which you have submerged yourself in French culture. Not many Americans have your facility with our language or the ability to join in our everyday life style.'

Donald sat at his desk. 'Victor, I learned to speak French in high school. And I have a French girlfriend. Now go away. We have a meeting on the soil strength tests and foundation engineering in half an hour. If we don't get it over with, we'll never get the goddamn hole dug, and we won't finish the hotel on time.'

Saulnier got up from the edge of the desk. 'Your reticence on the subject of your fame is not like you, Donald. Could it have been your ex-wife? Perhaps she mistook that fellow for you?'

Hamilton sat back in the chair and laughed. 'You could be right. The guy's balls were cut off. Sounds just like home.'

Saulnier paled a bit and said in a serious tone, 'You're kidding, of course.'

'I am like hell. Cut off and stuffed in his mouth. Some sight.'

Saulnier paused and his voice changed tone. 'Listen, are you sure you're all right for this meeting? Maybe you'd like to take a few days off?'

'Thank you, Victor. No, I don't want to do that. I just want to get back to work and forget the whole damn mess. We've spent two years planning this project, and it's going to be the most beautiful hotel on the Côte d'Azur. It's a dream job for me. A year, maybe eighteen months, in one of the most beautiful places in the world, doing the kind of work I love. Let's just consider this an unpleasant accident of fate. But I'd prefer to talk about it as little as possible. It probably didn't make any papers outside of the Riviera. I'd hate like hell to have it get to my kids in America through the firm.'

Saulnier reached out and patted him on the shoulder, 'Don't worry about that. I'll see that the subject is dropped. And I'm sorry I kidded you about it.'

'Forget it, Victor. You didn't mean any harm.'

Saulnier started to leave, then turned back, 'Donald, you don't think that you could be further involved, do you? There's no danger to you personally, I mean.'

'Not very likely. As I told them at the inquest, I never saw the guy before in my life.'

La Brousse looked up from his desk at the stocky figure

before him, then looked down again at the identity card with the picture. 'You have an appointment, Commissaire?' The man nodded and La Brousse showed him to a chair, then walked briskly down the hall of the Middle East Section of the organization known phonetically as SDEC (officially, Service de Documentations Extérieures et de Contre-Espionnage). The chief of this section of the Deuxième Bureau had particularly unimpressive quarters in an old building overlooking the Seine. The walls, more than modestly peeling, were painted the bland institutional beige to which the French government is partial. He stopped outside the door at the end of the corridor and knocked.

'Come.' To La Brousse the voice sounded like crushed glass. He opened the door, and standing just to the side, scratching aimlessly at the jamb with long, rather dirty fingernails was Robert Pineau des Charentes, Général de France.

In the heat of the small room, La Brousse was as usual undecided as to whether he should be overwhelmed by the smell of garlic, to which the General ascribed the robust health of his seventy-seven years, or by the blue cloud of smoke from the ever-burning pipe produced by the worst tobacco the state monopoly could manufacture.

La Brousse was a career Secret Service officer, who at forty was immaculately dressed and professional in the way of modern government officials. His superior sported worn and infrequently cleaned three-piece suits which bore the marks of his most recent meals, and which were reportedly provided by his son-in-law.

He looked suspiciously at La Brousse. 'So? What has the new generation to teach me today?' He scratched a little at his head, which according to unfailing schedule had been shaved clean a week earlier, on the thirteenth of the month.

La Brousse cleared his throat. 'A Commissaire Tombal says that you are expecting him.'

The General frowned and rubbed first at his wild eyebrows, then at the tobacco-stained white walrus mustache. 'Well, then get out of here and bring him in.'

La Brousse was almost halfway down the hall when he realized that the General had spoken his last sentence in Arabic.

When La Brousse opened the door to admit Tombal, the General was walking in a tight circle around his desk with his hands clasped behind his back. He took the pipe from his mouth and pointed at the single hard chair in front of the desk.

'Sit.' Glancing at the black ribbon pinned to Tombal's sleeve, he said, 'You have lost someone?'

Tombal sat stiffly on the edge of the chair, his fat thighs spread a bit apart. 'Yes, General, an old friend.'

The General took the pipe from his mouth and turned to face Tombal.

'I have lost many friends. When one is old – very old – one has fewer and fewer to lose. It is no less difficult. In any case I am sorry. It is harder when one is young like you.'

'I came to ask for your help, General. I believe that the death of Inspector Riez was the result of an investigation that we were making into a murder that took place in his district.'

'What has that to do with this old soldier?' he said.

'I think it was done by an Arab.'

'Ah,' the General said around his pipe, 'that gives you,' he checked a paper on his desk, 'four hundred twenty-seven thousand, six hundred eight to choose from as of this morning.' He closed his eyes. 'That I know of.'

Tombal wiped his mouth with his hand. 'I know that it seems odd that I should end up in your office. But the first murder was odd in many ways. It did not seem to fit any of the various patterns with which we are familiar. Riez, and he was a good cop, felt that there was a significance that was not understood. He pestered me to come down from Toulon to look around.' He paused. 'I am a trifle late perhaps, but his death convinced me.'

The General began to pace again without talking. He stopped for a moment and gestured in the air with his pipe, as though speaking to someone only he could see. Then he scratched himself vigorously and sat heavily, slumping in the chair behind his desk, opposite Tombal.

'Tell me your story, Tombal.' Then he closed his eyes.

Tombal related all of the details about the death of Pascal Lambert and the subsequent investigation that a mind inured to such recall could manage. He faltered after the first few minutes because of the silence of the old man in the chair before him. With the change in pace of his speech, one of Pineau's eyes popped open inquiringly, and Tombal continued. When he had finished he sat silent looking at Pineau. The General sat still and slack in the chair, his bulk cradled between the back and one of the arms. Tombal cleared his throat.

'Shh!'

Tombal started to turn his hat in his hands and noticed that he was perspiring. He averted his eyes and looked out of the dirty window at the quay. A sparrow flew to the sill and ruffled its feathers, then pecked at some invisible nourishment between its tiny feet.

'Wake up, Tombal! How did you find me?'

Tombal looked back. Pineau had not changed his position. 'I called a friend of mine at the Sûreté. With the death of a police inspector, Paris has taken an interest in local affairs. There has been a considerable influx of talent in the Var since the death of Riez. I had talked to my superiors about the possibility of getting an expert in African affairs involved on the basis of Riez's suspicions.'

'Who did you talk to at the Sûreté?' the General interrupted.

'Colonel Brunschwig.'

'And he said ... ?'

'He said I was hallucinating and offered me condolences again. He says that the Ministry is principally concerned that such a professional job was done because Riez was stumbling close to an apparatus of organized crime. The Ministry wishes, he said, to avoid any further embarrassment with the American government and the American press with respect to illegal drug manufacture in the South of France. He said that brutality was not unusual in gangster matters. He further indicated to me that the matter was quietly passing from my hands, that it was a poor idea for a policeman to become involved professionally in a case in which he had a personal interest.'

'Then are you disobeying orders? Why are you here?' Pineau asked brusquely.

'He said that I seemed upset and that I should take a week's leave before I went back to work.'

'That was when?' The General began to stir in his chair, then reached out a hairy mottled white hand to the arm-rest and pulled himself to his feet with some effort.

'Yesterday,' said Tombal. 'Monday.'

The General walked around the desk and stopped directly in front of him, his bulging vest almost touching Tombal's chin.

Tombal lifted his head and looked first at the white-stubbled jowls, then into the eyes in their bed of wrinkles.

'You have been a bad boy, Tombal.' There was an un-mistakable humor in the voice and the eyes. 'But of course, we agree.' He turned and began to walk again, then stopped and said over his shoulder, 'Brunschwig is an asshole. Of course it was an Arab. Brunschwig,' he continued walking, 'is also a eunuch who is afraid to offend. But then of course,' offering his hands in a shrug to God, 'all French are stupid.'

He walked to the wall at the side of the desk and addressed it. 'You were going to tell me how you got here.'

'My friend at the Ministry told me that you were sup-posed to be the last word in all matters related to Arabs, their habits and their culture. That you were the man re-sponsible for ...'

'Oh bullshit! Do you know why the Ministry of the In-terior resurrected me from my grave? Because they have no one else. I am seventy-seven! I quit in 1956. I took my pension and I ran. I had enough of the French government. I have, as a matter of fact, had enough of France and of the French to last a lifetime even longer than the one to which an unjust God has sentenced me. They scream for action from the Left. They go to the barricades. They occupy factories. They install weak governments. Then they begin to argue. They splinter. They fragment. Then,' some spittle began to form at the corners of his mouth, 'then they shit in their pants. They tremble from fear because in the end what they want, what they demand, is strength from the top. It eliminates thinking. Bread, wine and cigarettes is what they really want. Those and an inflated sense of their own importance in world affairs. So, when democracy fails, as it has in its short periods of life here, we have Napoleon, then kings, then Napoleon III, seventy-five years of ruinous wars and stupid governments, and then De Gaulle and his,' he pointed his thumb over his shoulder out of the window toward the Quai d'Orsay, 'followers. They are,' he said in a thunderous voice that could be heard the length of the hall, 'all goddamn stupid.'

His chest heaving with the expenditure, General Robert Pineau des Charentes flopped into his desk chair and stuffed his pipe from a square package of cheap blue-gray paper, then lit it.

'Look over there, Tombal. Well, look!' He pointed the pipe at the wall.

Tombal rose and put his hat carefully on the desk, then walked to the wall. Fixed to a nail was a blue ribbon bordered with red and white stripes from which a small bronze cross, tarnished with age, hung. At the center of the cross was an eagle surrounded by a wreath.

'Do you know what that is, Tombal? That is the Distinguished Service Cross. That is the highest decoration that the United States Army gives to foreigners. Only the Congressional Medal of Honor is more highly prized. It is my only war souvenir. That,' he said tapping his chest, 'and a bullet in my left lung from the famous strategic maneuver of the French Army in 1940. I got it in Italy – at Monte Cassino. General Clark personally,' he emphasized, 'gave it to me. I led the Tirailleurs Marocains up that stupid hill to that pile of crushed rock which was a monument to God and killed the Boche.' He stopped to light his pipe, holding the match until the flame brushed his skin. 'I lost half of my people. I was in Indo-China in the '20s. Then in '33 I was sent to North Africa, Algeria, then Tunisia, then Morocco. I was an economist. Did you know that, Tombal?'

Tombal shook his head to indicate his ignorance.

'After that grand stroll down the Champs Elysées in '45 I went back to Morocco. And after eleven years of hard work trying to make a country out of it, they threw us out, with the government of assholes,' he indicated the Quai d'Orsay again, 'cooperating in every way. They offered me a post at NATO. I said shit to them. I still say shit to them. I retired to my farm and watched on television and the newspapers as the new generation of assholes built and destroyed. Arabists are not made in universities, Tombal. They are made by contact – personal contact – daily contact – with Arabs and Arab problems and personalities.'

'It must be difficult to learn their culture,' Tombal ventured tentatively.

'Horseshit, there's nothing to know,' said the General. 'Their culture died in a pyramid of a million bleached skulls before the gates of Samarkand in the thirteenth century. Their culture died when the religious freaks in Spain threw them and their Jew friends back to the savages in 1492. The Turks reduced what the Mongols and the Church had not been able to efface to the rubble in which I spent my time. Nobody needed me for my cultural insight. Arab culture, the new Arab culture, is spelled oil. And oil means power and it means dealing on the level of the Souk. So after the French government spent twenty years alternating between burning the Arabs' balls with electric shocks and kissing their asses with French tax money, it decided that if it wanted to find someone who could tell it what the Arabs were doing in France, and in the rest of the world, and maybe in enough time to prevent them from doing it to France, it had better get someone who really knew Arabs. So Interior opened my coffin, pulled me erect and gave me as my headquarters for Counter Intelligence,' he waved merrily, 'this palatial office, and all of those,' he held his nose, 'scholars down the hall. In a year and a half, and they are precious at my age, I have learned nothing and accomplished nothing.'

'Why,' Tombal asked with some exasperation, 'did you agree to see me?'

'First, because I was asked to by an old friend who is not stupid. Because, so he said, you are not stupid. Second, because there is something stirring in the Arab intelligence community here in France and, I am told, abroad. Particularly in America. Third, because in France, as everywhere else, the murder of a police official is taken no less lightly by organized crime than by the authorities. They cannot operate in the temperature that such an act creates. Fourth, because it seems to me that the death of a part-time fag should not end in the death of a senior police official. And last, because the technique is certainly Ethiopian or Arab and we are not much beset by aboriginal Ethiopians. Most of the ones I know are much more polished than the average Frenchman.' He paused. 'And on top of that, Colonel Brunschwig said you are wrong and as I have mentioned to you before, Brunschwig is an asshole.'

The General rose again, more gingerly. 'Now let me ask a few questions. Was Lambert a Jew?'

Tombal shook his head no.

'How about Riez? Did Riez have much to do with Jews in general? The official Jews, I mean. The one-eyes.'

'Not that I know of,' Tombal said, 'no more than anyone else. There are a certain number in the population, about seven hundred thousand, I think.'

'Yes,' grumbled Pineau, 'it's the biggest Jewish community in Europe. So, you can investigate Riez's contacts to make sure. Don't shake no at me, policeman. Do it! Checking Arabs one by one in France is like counting straws in a wheat field. No use to that. I'll have La Brousse do some donkey work on known Arab agents in your corner.' He slapped at his naked scalp and smiled broadly. 'What time is it?'

'Ten-fifteen,' Tombal replied.

'Good. It won't be too early then.' He leaned over the desk

and picked up the phone, stuck the pipe in the corner of his mouth and dug a rat-eared address book out of one of his waistcoat pockets. He turned back to Tombal. 'Half of France is waiting for the telephone to be installed, and the other half is waiting for the dial tone. I hate them.' He paused. 'Phones, I mean.'

André Rhabbouz padded down the corridor of his apartment overlooking the harbor in Cannes. His slippers clicked irrhythmically as he picked up speed on the tiled floor. He turned sharply at the door of the water closet and emerged a moment later smiling sleepily. He continued in the direction in which he had been headed and opened the bathroom door. Leaning over the sink, he pulled at the hem of his wrinkled striped cotton pajamas and stuck out his tongue broadly at the mirror. Gingerly, he pulled at the lower lid of each of his eyes, examining the whites and pupils intently. It was a comforting habit, even though it was without purpose.

He yawned, scratched his substantial stomach and fumbled about for the toothbrush and paste. He massaged his scalp with lotion, then combed his long scanty black hair and turned his head to and fro to admire himself in the mirror. His calm was disturbed shortly by his inability to find the electric razor.

'This year, I will divorce.' He thought malevolently of his wife of thirty-seven years who slept peacefully down the hall. At the point of verbalizing his frustration, he discovered the razor in the cabinet.

Shaven, he padded back down the hall to the large bedroom and took off his pajamas, throwing them on the floor. His clothes, including socks and underwear, were laid out neatly on a chair. He put them on and looked at himself in the full-length mirror on the closet door.

'Your choice of shirts was remarkably uninspired this morning.'

'Mmmm,' the sleeping figure replied.

'I prefer the red shirt with the light blue pants,' he said accusingly. 'You put out the dark blue one.'

'Mmmm.'

'I think that you do it because you are jealous that another woman will take me away from you.'

'Mmmm.'

The phone rang. 'Answer the phone,' he said. 'It's probably your sister.'

A hand appeared from beneath the pile of blankets, picked up the receiver and pulled it back into the pile. 'It's for you,' said the muffled voice. The hand reappeared with the receiver.

'Yes. Who? Yes, I am Rhabbouz. Yes, I'll hold.'

'Rhabbouz, sale juif, is that you? Yes, well who did you think it was, you old fool? Do you think that you have that many admirers in Paris? You are having dinner with me tonight. I'm arriving at Nice Airport at four. And drive carefully, I'm warning you. And stay out of sight. I'll take a cab. Get me a hotel room in Cannes. The Majestic will do very nicely. No goddamn excuses. I know that it's the middle of the season. That's your problem. Not mine.'

The phone clicked in his ear and he hung up.

'Do you know who that was?' he asked the inert bundle on the bed.

'Mmmm?'

'General Pineau.'

She sat up and threw the covers down, her brown hair a bird's nest on her head. 'No, no, and again no. Absolutely not. Whatever it is – no! In no way, in no shape, in no form are you going to do anything for that crazy old man. You are sixty-seven years old. You are retired. You are not a spy. You are a fat old grandfather. No, no, no!'

'Oh, shush, do I bother you when you work for Hadassah?' He sat at the edge of the bed, sucking thoughtfully at a tooth. 'And besides,' bristling with masculine indignation, 'is it you who gives orders here now?'

'Bah,' she said, lying down again and pulling the covers up over her head. She lay still for a minute, then pulled

44

the covers slightly aside so that she could see him sitting at the edge of the bed. 'Anyway, you'll be careful, won't you?'

'Yes, yes, I'll be careful. And by the way, maybe you are old,' he said, thumping himself resoundingly on the chest, 'but I am young. And I am not fat! I am going down to have a cup of coffee and to look at the young women on the Croisette. If you want to join me,' he said slapping her where he assumed her backside to be, 'you are welcome.'

It was the last week of the summer tourist frenzy, just before the September lull, after which the Scandinavians and Germans would hurl themselves into the South of France to benefit from the still superb weather and the lower rates.

Rhabbouz left Cannes at three and was parked at the entrance of the Arrival Terminal of Nice-Côte d'Azur Airport at three-thirty.

At ten after four Rhabbouz looked up from his newspaper at a commotion which seemingly involved three or four porters at a door. Robert Pineau des Charentes, Tombal and La Brousse in tow, emerged from the crowd, shouting at a porter and poking him with the end of a walking stick. When he shouted, he pulled his head into his overly snug shirt collar in the fashion of a turtle, creating a substantial bulge of excess flesh which pushed up against his earlobes.

'A cab, you moron! A cab I said!'

The porter put the bag in the back of the cab along with the small one that belonged to Tombal, and the driver shut the door. The General flipped a five-franc piece which the porter rescued just above ground level.

'Merci, monsieur,' he said.

'Merde,' said the General. Then he shouted directions to the driver and they got in and left. 'Do you speak English, driver? How about Arabic?' The General asked each question in the appropriate language. The driver did not move. 'How about you, Tombal?'

'English, sir.'

'Good. Then we can get a head start, because it is clear that this moron speaks neither,' pointing at the front seat.

45

'If you look out of the corner of your eye, you will see an old fool who is losing his hair driving a loud red Italian car meant for a much younger man. That is our friend. He will follow us to the hotel. He will park, and he will meet us in a horrid little bar in which pederasts congregate at night. Jimmy's it's called. He dislikes it intensely. That's why I always meet him there,' he said with satisfaction.

'That unlikely looking man is the agent for the Shin Bet in the South of France. He's from North Africa. I knew him there. Now he checks up on Arabs from time to time for the Israelis. Never gets involved in anything dangerous, though. I must assume that the Israeli Secret Service has fallen on hard times over the years. I myself have known him for almost thirty and I never would have chosen him. But then of course,' he sniffed, 'he thinks that God already has.'

Five

George Hultz stood behind the mahogany desk in his office on the twenty-second floor of New York's General Motors Building. He slipped the drawings and photo-mockups into the sturdy leather briefcase in front of him, then carefully checked over the desk once more to be certain that nothing had been forgotten. He closed the case and pressed both of the locks shut with a firm click. Hultz walked to the door and unlocked it with a key ring from his pocket. He clipped the chain which dangled from the handle of the briefcase to the heavy gold identification bracelet on his wrist and walked smiling past his secretary.

'I'll be with Mr. Goodrich, Jan. Hold all calls.'

'Yes, sir.' She smiled.

He strode down the wide corridor to the other end of the floor to a set of large paneled doors with expensive brass fixtures, knocked and entered. Glistening polished wood walls and plush dark carpet framed an extraordinarily pretty woman behind a desk in the twenty-foot-square room. She looked up at the familiar ruddy thin face with the pocked skin and crooked nose.

'Hi, Mr. Hultz. Mr. Goodrich is expecting you. Go right in.'

Hultz opened the door. The corner office looked on Central Park to the north, and west to New Jersey across the Hudson River. August sun streamed in through partially open floor-to-ceiling blinds, giving life to two medium-sized Seurats on the wall opposite the Park. A massive desk and table stood at the west side of the room.

Goodrich sat in the desk chair, his feet on the edge of the table, talking animatedly into a private phone which sat apart from the call director connecting him with the outside world through the General Motors switchboard. He looked up and waved Hultz toward him.

'Well, frankly, Mr. Fosburgh,' Goodrich said, 'I would be hard-pressed to believe that your views on automobiles operated by non-fossil fuels are not compromised by your position as president of Royal American Oil.' He directed Hultz to sit in the chair next to the desk, then held his finger to his lips in a silencing gesture. He pushed a button on the little box at the side of the phone and made both sides of the conversation audible.

'... intending to show that programs with Mary Poppins's aims are a waste of the stockholders' money. I take a damn dim view of your suggestions that I am suffering from a conflict of interest! I expect that I am even more aware than you that there is always the chance that the Arab states will turn off the tap. But I think that their desire for hard currency, if only to meet their defense budgets, will prevent them from doing it for any length of time. I think that it's also apparent that if this country gave some reasonable regard to the Arab political posture in its foreign policy, the risk of even a temporary shutdown would be de minimus.'

Controlling his exasperation, Goodrich said, 'I don't think that you and I are talking the same language. You are talking geopolitics, and I'm trying to focus on a corporate policy of spreading the risk through diversification.'

There was a pause at the other end of the line, then Fosburgh said, 'Each of us is charged with the responsibility of a chief executive officer of a major company. I suppose we each have our own way of discharging that responsibility. I'm not telling you how to run General Motors, Mr. Goodrich. I do know that the business of the company, other products notwithstanding, is to make cars, and that the investment of billions in productive facilities is in gasoline engines. As a director of the company, I want to make sure that investment is protected, and that further funds aren't wasted in large-scale programs away from the main corporate thrust. And you can be sure that at every meeting of

48

the Board of Directors. I will make myself heard on the subject.'

Goodrich gritted his teeth till the muscles in his jaws bulged visibily. 'I think we understand each other very well, Mr. Fosburgh.'

'Yes, I dare say we do,' Fosburgh replied dryly. 'Oh, by the way, if there are any communications that need to come my way, I'll be on the *Glen Pool*. I'm sure that your girl has the radiophone number. We'll be docked at St. Tropez. Probably into the beginning of September. When is the next meeting?'

'On October 15. You'll get an official notice in the usual manner.'

'No doubt. Well, I'll see you then, Mr. Goodrich, and do try to consider what I've said.'

Goodrich replaced the receiver in its cradle, his face drawn and tired. He smiled wanly at Hultz, who sat across from him, squinting a bit in the light.

'Nice,' Hultz offered.

Goodrich shrugged. 'Just lovely.'

Hultz lifted the briefcase. 'I guess he wouldn't be all that pleased if he knew about this. Do you think that he could make enough of a stink to stop us?'

'I don't know, George, but then I don't want to make a test case, either.' Goodrich pulled a small key ring from his jacket pocket and repeated the same door ritual that Hultz had performed in reverse only a few minutes earlier.

'Put it over here, on the desk, George.' He picked another key from the ring and undid the left latch of the bag. Hultz, with a key from his own chain undid the right, then unclasped his bracelet.

Goodrich pointed his chin at the ceiling and forced his head back to stretch the cramped muscles of his neck. He looked at Hultz with affection, smiled broadly and clapped him on the shoulder.

'Okay, let's see the latest modifications. Christ, it's hot in here. The air conditioning isn't working right.' Goodrich took off his pin-striped blue coat and threw it over the arm

49

of the desk chair, then undid his tie and the first three buttons of his shirt. At forty-seven, even the few curly hairs that straggled from the base of his throat had begun to turn to silver. He reached into the case and withdrew the sheaf of papers. Selecting a photo, he held it up in the light.

'All right. That's more like it.' Goodrich gestured with his free hand. 'The flatter roof line makes it look cleaner, more stylish. Have you got a top view in here too?'

'Yes, Milt. Right on the bottom of the pile.' Hultz pulled out a color rendering of an auto, remarkable only for the series of rectangular plaques affixed to the rear deck on the trunk lid.

Goodrich looked sidelong at Hultz. 'Who did the photography, George?'

'I did the whole damn thing myself. The drawings, the art work and the photographs. If you check these,' he said, selecting two more prints, 'you'll find that I've been able to reduce the width of the forward deck as you suggested, to reflect the probable size of the power plant, and yet maintain maximum interior space. The comparison of weight and size to power makes the Wankel look like a diesel locomotive.'

Looking ruminatively at the drawing, Goodrich said, 'And inside of this chassis, the weight to power ratio is going to translate itself to good performance.'

'I can't be sure of either top speed or acceleration until we get the rest of the information from our strange partner. You haven't heard from him, have you?'

'No. Just from Paul Fosburgh. That pompous self-important son of a bitch.' He bit the words off with uncharacteristic venom and force.

Hultz shook his head. 'What do you expect him to say? Everybody in the oil business still has a hard-on for you for junking the big engines and going for low fuel consumption. I'll bet it's the only time in history a man got made president of a company for recommending a two-billion-dollar write-off.'

'Could be. But I intend to stay here as long as I can.

Fosburgh or no Fosburgh. I just have to keep working around him with the rest of the board until we have something concrete to show them. God Almighty, I hate working in a fog like this. Christ knows,' he said in frustration, 'we've tried to find something in our own divisions, and with independent battery people. But nothing seems comparable to the work of our crazy friend. It still checks out?'

'Step by step. So far no mistakes.' Hultz paused momentarily, as though collecting his thoughts. He looked at Goodrich and asked himself if this was the man he had known so long. First a display of near temper, then a moment of doubt. Hultz suppressed a smile at the idea that Milton Goodrich, the ice-cold automaton, might have some of the characteristics that had held George Hultz back occasionally.

As though reading his mind, Goodrich said, 'Stop looking at me as though I had gone mad.' He laughed softly. 'I have yet to throw a drink in the face of a bank vice president and then stalk off through the midst of his gladiolas.'

Hultz winced at the memory and broke into a grin and doffed an imaginary cap. 'Manners makyth man,' he suggested. 'Anyway, I don't see how this fellow does it. He has no mechanical equipment, no testing facilities. He's operating strictly in the realm of theory, and there should be some error in the translation from paper to test bench. But that hasn't been the case. He's departing entirely from accepted concepts of power storage and the conversion from solar light to power. He's constructed a universe in his head, made his own rules and then applied them to our own world of physics and chemistry – successfully.'

Goodrich stood and stretched. 'So this is how we are going to change the world. A hot-tempered engineer-cum-production chief, that's you,' he pointed. 'Coughtry, a technical wizard who does yoga and is constantly babbling about his high principles, a loony inventor, and me – who doesn't understand what the hell the three of you are talking about.'

*

A threatening night sky gave hope that rain would restore New York's temperature to a bearable level. The thermometer hung at ninety-four though it was 10 P.M.

George Hultz, his low boiling point not improved by the heavy weather and the frustration of working in the dark, turned his head sharply away from the window, and from the city, brilliantly lighted but without movement.

The second key turned in the lock, and the door opened.

Donald Coughtry, tieless and without shoes, stretched a little on the couch, put the sheaf of papers that he had been reading down on his chest, pushed the glasses from the bridge of his nose to his forehead and rubbed his eyes.

'Hi, Milt. Anything happening?'

From halfway across the room, Goodrich threw the flat leather portfolio that he had been carrying. It landed in the chair beside his desk. 'Not a whole lot that would concern you. Just another finance committee meeting. You people come up with anything?'

Hultz, who had turned completely so that he was facing the middle of the room, kicked hard at an imaginary can. 'Not a goddamn thing. The schematic is almost complete, so far as we can tell. There are the solar panels, made up of numbers of contiguous solar cells; thin layers of glass with alternate layers of cadmium sulfide and copper sulfide. Nothing new there: they have been in commercial and experimental use all over the world for years. An electric motor which, at least to us, looks like something out of *Mechanix Illustrated*; no great technical stride there either. So much for the direct power source and the drive train.'

Coughtry, a prototype of an MIT grad, young, lithe, Waspy and crew-cut, save that he stood about five-foot-three, rose from the couch and began to talk. 'The battery system, or auxiliary power and storage assembly, at least what we have of it, doesn't seem new either. Gould National mercury-base or nickel-cadmium cells of about the size of a regular twelve-volt auto battery. The difference, of course, is that he recommends the use of many fewer than in our experimental models, or in the European designs we've seen.

And, of course, these are dry, not wet cells. No acid, that is.'

Goodrich rubbed his jaw and said, 'So why are you so sure that it will go farther and faster than anything that now exists in the electric automotion field?' He didn't wait for an answer. 'When you looked at the original work he sent in six months ago, you agreed that it was worth putting up with all of his unusual working conditions to find out what he had in mind. Since that time we have had exactly four communications from him. All delivered by different messengers to various places in the South of France. All of them recognized,' he said incredulously, 'by a rose behind their ears. I agreed to go along with you first of all because,' he looked at Hultz, then Coughtry and smiled a little, 'I trust you implicitly.'

Hultz nodded in appreciation. Coughtry assumed a pose akin to attention and lifted his chin. Goodrich was unable to tell whether or not he was serious.

'Secondly,' Goodrich continued, 'because my job as president of this company is to remember that thousands of products in dozens of industries aside, it's automobiles that make General Motors run, and we are feeling the pinch in that department. We are feeling the pinch very badly. Chevy will do well to sell eight hundred thousand cars this year, and the industry, maybe five and a half million. That's down fifty percent in less than five years.' He shook his head. 'What the hell am I supposed to do, fire everybody in the sales department because people are not pleased about paying exorbitant prices for gasoline?'

Hultz smiled crookedly, his homely pocked face distorted with amusement. 'Not yet, Milt.'

Goodrich rubbed his nose. 'Okay,' he said, annoyed, 'not this week. Next week, then. In the meantime, between blackmail, economic strangulation, political humiliation and Christ-knows-what-else, the need for sources of power has caused me to go ahead with this project. Not to mention net-after-tax profits, for which, recently, dwindling is not the word. And you tell me that at this point, all we have is a collection of prosaic materials and old-hat systems. We

53

haven't spent any real money on this yet. All we've spent is time. But it's your time. And it's the time that's supposed to be digging us out of the hole. Eventually, even if no one can trace the funds, somebody at a directors' meeting is bound to ask what the hell you are doing and what you are coming up with. When they do, and it's on the calendar for every meeting every month, what am I supposed to do? Tell them that it's a secret? I can dissemble within reason. But, I'm telling you now, you have a very good chance of being thrown out on your behinds.' He paused. 'And so do I. Then there's always the possibility that Fosburgh will dig something up – one way or another – before we're ready. You know he'll try!'

Coughtry sat disconsolately at the edge of the couch. In his clear Midwestern voice, he said, 'If you want me to resign, then I will. If you want me to tell you that we should never have been dealing with a technology under dime-novel conditions, I will agree. If you ask me why we are looking at, what did you call it, a mass of prosaica, I will tell you that I don't know. But if you ask me if we should continue, I will sure as hell say yes.' He looked up directly at Goodrich. 'When you break down the components of this system, those that we have anyway, you get what you said. When you look at the whole system, its rated horsepower, or what translates in laymen's language to rated horsepower, when you discuss Grecian simplicity and economy in the transmission of sunlight, in any, I repeat, any sort of daytime conditions, up to and including fifty-foot visibility in fog, then I tell you you're talking about something extraordinary. Milt, we're dealing with a nut, a nut whose name I don't even know because you won't tell me. He is an unknown quantity. He is also,' his voice rose, 'a miserable son of a bitch and a pervert. He is teasing us. Enough to see that he is right. Enough to see the product of genius. Enough to keep us panting, working. But not enough to understand it all.' He sat, took a breath and said, 'He is a prick, Milt. But he's a genius.'

Goodrich turned slightly in the chair and looked inquiringly at Hultz's pock-marked face, the mouth drawn to a grim white line.

'He's right. He has my complete support. According to the schematic and the estimated operational data, if the sun is above the horizon, this machine will suck all the juice necessary to operate directly and still pull in enough to recharge the batteries for use under night conditions – fair weather or foul.'

'What are you telling me, George? That he's invented a perpetual-motion machine?'

'To the degree that it requires no propellant other than sunlight, yes, that's exactly what I'm saying. But it will require maintenance, and the cells will have to be replaced. Nevertheless, the fact is, so far as I have been able to judge, that with plate replacement every thousand miles, we will be able to reduce the direct ratio of propellant cost from ten cents per mile to about four cents per mile, maybe even less. And what's more, we will be using a non-depletable source of power. A combination of copper and cadmium in traces, sand and lime for glass, and sunlight. If you want my opinion, it's worth every bit of the gamble. If you're asking me to gamble my job or my career on it, I will. Yes, we lack understanding of certain components of the system. We lack details about the quality and exact nature of the formulas for his solar cells, also of the makeup of the panels. For all I know, he has nothing more than the guts of a process patent. Using existing materials and technology in a heretofore unused combination to produce an entirely new or different effect. They aren't worth much in a lawsuit, but that doesn't mean that they don't work. And if we can get off of the ground with this kind of machine, get a head start, it won't matter all that much if we are caught up with. We still will have reduced the cost of making, selling, buying and maintaining automobiles, and people will buy the hell out of them. And that's what we want.'

Goodrich rubbed his nose again and looked at the ceiling. 'All right. What's the next step?'

*

A fly buzzed past Arthur Edelman's head. He waved at it in annoyance. When he looked down at the calculator again, he had lost track of the number set, and was forced to clear the machine and start from scratch.

He entered a few digits, then shook his head, turned the machine off and got up from the desk. He gnawed at his knuckle as he paced. What kind of person kills, he wondered. He had known petty jealousy, great anger even, in the course of his affairs. But to kill?

Increasingly, in the aftermath of Pascal's death, he found himself too depressed to think clearly, to immerse himself in his work as was his habit.

Given the size of the technical problem, the absence of absolute concentration was a guarantee of failure. Loneliness aside, the death of Pascal required that another messenger be found. Either that, or to expose himself personally.

He stood still momentarily, aware of the emptiness of the room, conscious that he was afraid. Perhaps he should give up the project entirely. He shuddered and shook his head negatively, then sat down again to confront the calculator.

Six

William McCandless Smith sat upright in the tub of the late William Howard Taft, the last President of the United States who had approached three hundred pounds, and fumbled on the stool for his eyeglasses. Ten years before, when he had stopped being a quarterback and started being a Congressman, he had had neither the spare tire around his middle nor the glasses. He dried his hands on the towel on the floor before reaching for the leather folder and its daily 'Eyes Only' report on the energy crisis in the Mideast.

The report gave a statistical array of the American petroleum stocks and energy position, as well as the most recent demands made by the Arabs and their friends in the Third World in exchange for an improvement of those statistics. In smaller type were the howls of indignation from the United States' only ally in the Middle East. He glanced over the marginal changes and, with some disgust, he banged the folder down on the stool and hauled himself to his feet. He took a big terry-cloth bath sheet off the hook over the antique tub and stepped out gingerly onto the mat.

He ran his fingers through the damp and thinning blond hair on his head, then dried himself and put on a pair of jockey shorts. He reached for the door handle, then stopped as he heard a noise outside.

'Janet, that you?'

'No, Mr. President.'

He smiled, opened the door and threw the towel across the room in the general direction of the voice.

'Morning, Jack. How's your ass?'

'Fine. And yours?'

'I suppose you prepared that mess on the stool? Is it your idea always to start the day with the same gloomy message?'

'I know nothing. I'm just following orders.'

All of the chairs in the private Presidential dressing room and study were oversized, but Jack Kugel overflowed his. He matched the President in size – they were both over six and a half feet tall – but where Smith was classically handsome and still fit though thick about the middle, Kugel had the proportions of a Sumo wrestler. As Roosevelt had had his brain trust, so it was said that Smith had his beef trust.

As Smith started to reach for his clothes, he said, 'Gasoline stocks were down another three million barrels in the past week, Jack. That's more than one and a half percent, no?'

Kugel beetled the heavy black brows that almost met above his nose. Quite formally, he replied, 'Mr. President, that's an accurate estimate, though somewhat affected by peak seasonal demand. Still, petroleum stocks have been dwindling marginally every week since you took office. During the same period, the price extracted from American oil companies by OPEC is up twenty-three percent and the mid-continent price for gasoline has risen twenty-one percent.'

'So. Do we let Israel go down the drain, pull out the Sixth Fleet, and so forth, Mr. Kugel, to comply with Arab requests?'

Wearily, for he had not slept well, Kugel looked up from the sheaf of papers in his stubby gnarled fingers and smiled a crooked smile around his even white dentures. 'No. Fuck 'em.'

'Jesus, Jack, suddenly I feel a hundred. What's on the calendar today? You seen Carson?'

'The appointments secretary tells me,' Kugel said with a wry smile, 'that you have an appointment at three with His Excellency Mohammed El Kaffar.'

'With a message direct from Colonel Ben Kelb, no doubt.'

Kugel ushered the President out of the door before him, and smiling, said, 'No doubt at all.'

Smith sat in the Oval Office with his back to the desk, looking at a copy of the St. Louis paper. The cartoon on the editorial page showed his substantial form in caricature with a rope tied to each of his powerful arms. At the end of the rope to his right was a sad-looking average citizen labeled 'America's Needs.' On the left were a group of rather wicked-looking fat men with rolls of excess blubber and Semitic faces seething with greed, labeled 'Special Interest Groups.' They were pulling Smith in the direction of figures of equal height with huge obscene hooked noses, one with an eye patch, one with a burnoose. The caption at the bottom read 'Between the Horns of a Dilemma.'

He hardly stirred when he heard the knock at the door, and the firm click as it closed.

'He's here, Mr. President.'

'Let him wait a few minutes, Jack. Do you have any idea what his proposal is?'

'Not the slightest. I think that we are going to be talking price again. He wants you to use the Energy Resources Emergency Act, centralize all imports of oil through the government and cede all American oil properties in the Middle East to their respective landlords and hosts.'

Smith turned sharply in the swivel seat. 'Yes, and wouldn't he also like me to nationalize all our private oil companies? So that he would deal with a President and a Congress subject to tremendous political pressures rather than a diverse group of companies whose self-interest is the only protection we have? Have him come in, Jack.'

The President adjusted his tie and buttoned his jacket, then stood to gain the substantial personal advantage of his full height. 'Please come in,' he responded to the knock at the door.

The Foreign Minister of Quahrein found himself sandwiched between Smith and the mountainous Kugel.

'Good morning, Mr. President,' he said.

Smith held his hand out at the level of his own waist, forcing Mohammed El Kaffar to reach upward.

'Good morning, Your Excellency. Please be seated.'

El Kaffar moved smoothly to the chair at the side of the desk as Smith walked behind it. He was supple and of light complexion for an Arab. His people, the Berbers, had been moved back from the edge of the Mediterranean by fiercer tribes in an unrecorded history, so that hidden in the Atlas Mountains they retained a fairer skin and, as he had, unwavering clear blue eyes. He was dressed in the ascetic fashion of his revolutionary government. His suntan uniform of cotton twill was bereft of insignia or medals. He carried an unadorned black peaked military cap.

He and Smith appraised each other for a moment without speaking. He was about thirty-five, Smith judged. His smooth skin and even features made him look younger. The muscles of his jaws gave an air of underlying stubbornness.

The silence stretched overlong. 'Mr. President,' El Kaffar began, 'I have come to you this morning to explain the irrevocable position of my government with respect to its commercial affairs with the United States of America. Though I would prefer if the conversation were held in private, since I am acting as spokesman for our Revolutionary Council and for its Chairman, Colonel Ben Kelb, I have no objection if you wish Mr. Kugel to remain.'

'Thank you, Your Excellency,' the President said dryly. 'Mr. Kugel, please be seated.'

'I would like to make it clear that I am not here to posture with you. The release of our discussion to the press, whether in the United States or elsewhere, will be a matter I leave entirely in your hands. It is on the authority of Colonel Ben Kelb that I make this commitment.' Smith noted again how El Kaffar's otherwise unaccented and flawless English gave way to stilted structure when he intended unpleasantness.

'As the years have passed since the movement for the liberation of our people replaced the antediluvian autocracy which preceded it, we have hoped that the government of

60

the United States would see fit to recognize our legitimate aspirations. In the same sense that our capitalist neighbors in the world community seek an increasing standard of living, so do we in the Arab world. The tool for achieving this deserved equality for our people, a modern socialist state equipped,' he underlined, 'to deal with the future and its hazards, is our natural resource base.' The President nodded somewhat wearily at the oft-repeated phrases. 'At the same time, sir, intruding into the meticulously organized pattern which has been developed for the prosperity of our people, is the ever present and imminent danger presented by the European usurper in our midst.'

Neither Kugel nor Smith moved perceptibly. They reckoned the first part of any discussion with El Kaffar to be the dues to be paid for the real purpose of his visit.

'Unfortunately, your position has been one of relentless opposition and frustration of our position.'

Smith closed his eyes for a moment and pictured the photo of El Kaffar and Ben Kelb sitting together on top of an old British Centurion tank in the street in front of the Royal Palace in Quahrein City. El Kaffar's right arm was thrown about Ben Kelb's shoulder. Both were grinning. Held aloft was the head of the aged King Yaoud, the white beard stained by the blood which dripped from the severed neck.

El Kaffar placed a meticulously manicured hand on the polished desk and leaned slightly forward in the chair. The President sat upright and waited, expressionless.

'The Western press is often given to hysteria,' El Kaffar began. 'If we desire that the wealth of our countries be returned to us in the form of reasonably distributed profits, it is blackmail. If you threaten us with a parasite which daily, through the need it creates for armed might with which to protect ourselves, saps the fruits of our countries, that is in aid of the self-determination of nations.'

'I assume you mean Israel, Your Excellency?' Smith inquired blandly.

Ignoring the jibe, El Kaffar continued. 'This is the moment that we have chosen to determine our own fate. At this time we provide approximately three point seven percent of your annual demand for petroleum and oil-derived products. While we recognize that our small voice cannot be expected to sway the conscience of a . . . superpower, we feel that we are unable to continue the charade in which we succor the mainstay of our enemies.'

'A price increase perhaps,' the President offered.

'We are not businessmen in burnooses, Mr. President. We in Quahrein are not medieval pashas with Cadillacs and air-conditioned harems. While economics interest us insofar as they pertain to the growth of our citizens, morality and pride in our manhood is more important to us than bread. Scraps from the tables of Western bankers cannot buy dignity in the eyes of Allah.'

'We are all too familiar with Colonel Ben Kelb's philosophies, Your Excellency.'

El Kaffar went on. 'We repudiate unilaterally' – Kugel took a pad and began to take notes – 'our participation in the agreement signed by the Organization of Petroleum Exporting Countries. If in the next sixty days the Sixth Fleet is not withdrawn in all of its elements from the Mediterranean Sea, we will seize as public domain the properties of the Royal American Oil Company which are located within our borders. Whether or not the seizure takes place, as of January 1, 1978, the price for a barrel of Quahrein crude oil will be increased by one hundred percent. If during this period there is not also a public repudiation of your flagrant pro-Zionist policy, we shall instruct our agents to debarrass us of the approximately four billion dollars in American currency which we accepted in modest payment for the rape of our resources – despite its questionable value as a medium of exchange – and require further payments to be made in gold!'

He sat back slightly in the chair and removed his hand from the desk.

Smith asked casually, 'You haven't brought up the subject of direct government purchases of oil for the improvement of our national welfare. Why?'

'That is an old horse, sir. It is handy for the old syphilitic in Saudi Arabia. It is useful when dealing with many companies, or consortia. But we only have to deal with one. If, in fact, you do see the rectitude of our position, we feel that Royal American Oil, in exchange for keeping half of what it likes to call its crude reserves intact, together with its refinery and drilling investment of nearly two billion dollars, will be quite pleased to suffer a reduction in its bloated margin of profit. We are happy to deal with the capitalist system on its own terms.'

'Royal American doesn't have enough shareholders to make a coup d'état here, Your Excellency.'

'Quite so, Mr. President. But there are enough to make the rumblings of change felt deeply. Deeply enough to revise your Middle Eastern policy and to secure our future.'

'And if that does not prove to be true, Your Excellency? If these pressures do not suffice to change our national will?'

'Mr. President,' El Kaffar said, leaning forward again, grim-faced, 'Colonel Ben Kelb has asked me to remind you that though small in number we are a people of great conviction. If by the first of October, thirty-two days from today, you have not agreed to our terms in writing, we are prepared to return to the purity of the desert whence we sprang. If you will not free us, we will free ourselves. We will blow up the Royal American installations. We will set fires in the fields that will not be extinguished for a generation. Our country is crossed by the pipeline from Homs in Syria to Gibraltar – we will destroy it. The trans-Arabian pipeline from the Gulf States to Oneitra on the Mediterranean coast will be destroyed – every pumping station, every foot of pipe. Colonel Ben Kelb is prepared to lead all Arabs to the freedom of the desert, if the West denies us freedom in the world of machines. You will grind to a halt and flounder. And we will rebuild on your ashes.'

Unemotionally, Smith asked, 'You do not intend to make these demands public?'

'Under no circumstances. We know that to trumpet like children in a schoolyard will serve only to create agitation in your unruly press that will prevent you from acting in a sensible manner, and portray us to the world as mad dogs. It has not been lost upon us, Mr. President, that most important negotiations in America take place behind closed doors. Our frustrated public displays are at an end, Mr. President. We shall act. If, in fact, you do not comply, we shall make no public statement. There will be no formal note. No cries of blackmail. Only action. This conversation contains our entire message. And I am sure,' he smiled thinly, 'that if it has been taped, you would not want to relive your predecessor's most uncomfortable moments.'

William McCandless Smith rose to his feet. 'Thank you, Your Excellency, for coming in.' He did not bother to extend his hand.

Seven

It was no great surprise to Du Pont, the SDEC agent assigned to dog his steps in America, that El Kaffar met at the Sans Souci Restaurant with the American stockbroker Edward Nicholson and the Swiss banker Bernard Bauermann. As a matter of routine he would ship that information together with everything else he had picked up during the week concerning El Kaffar to La Brousse in Paris.

Nicholson was the host. A senior partner of Bates and Company, one of the larger American brokerage houses to survive the death of Wall Street, he was red-faced and bluff, veiny in the cheeks from too much drinking, strained eyes surrounded by wrinkles as the result of too much worry. El Kaffar avoided his every attempt to bring up business at lunch. As a result, his pleasure was as great as his surprise when he was invited to join the Minister at the Embassy.

Du Pont disengaged himself from the bar stool as they went out, watching El Kaffar pass a few words to his driver and climb with the others into the Cadillac limousine that belonged to Nicholson. He left them at the Embassy door, to be watched by another agent across the street, and went to his own office to prepare his message to headquarters.

El Kaffar led them up the stairs and into the office of Ambassador Dhaib. Two crossed Quahrein flags hung draped from the stand behind the desk. At the back of the room a life-sized portrait of Colonel Ben Kelb hung from the wall. On the desk was a photograph of El Kaffar in uniform, signed in Arabic.

'Please, gentlemen, sit down and make yourselves comfortable,' El Kaffar said, seating himself behind the desk and indicating the sofa opposite him.

'Mr. Nicholson, I am given to the most direct possible path in the solution of all problems. Mr. Bauermann, would you acquaint Mr. Nicholson with the figures I gave you last evening?'

Bauermann, a fat man in his forties, even more flushed than Nicholson, rose to his feet, taking some papers from a bag at his side. His voice was too loud.

'Edward, His Excellency informs me that as of this morning, his nominees own about twenty-eight percent of the outstanding stock of Bates and Company.' He paced another step or two and seemed ready to continue.

'Thank you, Mr. Bauermann, you may sit down now. Yes, indeed, Mr. Nicholson. We have been quietly acquiring the stock of your company for some time. In little bits and pieces, of course.' He smiled. 'We wouldn't want to upset the market or tip our hand.'

Nicholson fidgeted, confused.

'We have been very sure not to violate any of the regulations of the Securities and Exchange Commission. But we could amass sufficient votes to exert some control. We also, through various means, primarily our interest in banks, hold substantial amounts of your debt. We note that you have been a little hesitant to meet your obligations on that score. By the way, Mr. Nicholson, you are also a fairly heavy borrower personally, are you not?'

Nicholson nodded, wordless.

'Well, then, it seems that under the circumstances we can be of substantial mutual benefit to each other. With the substantial funds at our disposal, we are in a position to aid you by directing various large sums at our disposal through your firm at comfortably negotiated rates. How much of Bates and Company do you own, Mr. Nicholson?'

He cleared his throat. 'May I have a drink?'

'Why, of course, Mr. Nicholson. Though we Muslims do not drink spirits, we always keep a supply in stock for our Western friends. Bauermann, get Mr. Nicholson a drink.

Now then, Mr. Nicholson, your ownership in Bates and Company?'

'I own eleven percent of the common stock. My wife, she was Jack Bates's niece, owns another six percent.'

Bauermann placed a Scotch and soda on the table in front of the shaken man.

'Are there any other large stockholders in your company, Mr. Nicholson?' El Kaffar asked politely.

'The next largest one, besides you, I guess, owns about seven percent.'

'Who would that be, Mr. Nicholson?'

'Paul Fosburgh, the president of Royal American Oil.' A half light came into Nicholson's eyes and died. He drained the glass.

'Mr. Bauermann, please give Mr. Nicholson the papers. You can't imagine how many interests we have in common with Royal American, Mr. Nicholson. I am sure that we can agree, Mr. Fosburgh and myself, who should be the next president of Bates and Company, once we have working control. What's the price of Bates and Company stock today?'

'Eighteen, about.'

'Fine. The papers in front of you have already been signed by the various buyers. You are selling your interest and your wife's, I understand that you have power of attorney, for thirty dollars a share. That will enable you to liquidate most of your debts, Mr. Nicholson. I'm sure that will give you considerable peace of mind. And we have arranged for you to keep a one percent interest in Bates and Company.' His smile gleamed. 'Fifty-one percent will quite suffice for our purposes. Name a salary that would interest you while you are signing, Mr. Nicholson.'

A look of greed crept over Nicholson's face. 'Shall we say two hundred thousand.' Then he paused. 'Above the table. Then I can take the other three hundred thousand abroad. In various currencies at various banks.'

'Ah, you understand, Mr. Nicholson. We shall hang together. But we shall hang high. Congratulations, Bauermann.' Then he turned back to Nicholson. 'You are every bit as weak and unprincipled as he said you were. And as greedy. Sign, please.'

When Nicholson had affixed his signature to each of the papers, for his own account and that of his wife, El Kaffar rose and brought him an assortment of certified bank drafts, eleven in all, made out for various odd amounts.

'Please endorse these. You will note that you are left, after payment of principal and interest, with about eighty-six thousand dollars in cash, above and beyond the payments of all of your major bank loans, with interest computed as of the close of business today. Here, by the way, is a list of your sales of securities on the form required for insider trading by the SEC. It's all quite correct. You can read it if you like. Also there is a contract of employment. You may read that at your leisure. Just fill in the numbers, as per our agreement. Of course, only the first sum will be mentioned.'

Nicholson signed, then asked for another drink.

'Not quite what one has come to expect from a camel driver, Mr. Nicholson? It seems that civilization has come to the sheik, does it not?'

'What do you want me to do?'

'Good, good, you are as direct as I am. I know that I have caught you at something of a disadvantage, Mr. Nicholson. We looked very hard to find someone at such a disadvantage, someone sufficiently aware of the importance of our relationship with him that we need not fear his wiles and skills will be turned against us. We know you are an embezzler, Mr. Nicholson. Does that surprise you?'

'I'm surprised the subject has not come up before.'

'You have participated in many corporate raids, have you not, Mr. Nicholson? You are skilled at the massing of stock without the knowledge of the public and the authorities?'

Nicholson smiled wryly. 'Clearly, I have much to learn from you, Your Excellency. Who do you want to take over, and why, if I might ask?'

'Why is the easiest part. Oil is very important now. We have not had anything but oil to give or to take for centuries. While there will probably always be a use for oil, and

68

in large quantities, the present stranglehold that we have on the West will not last forever. The greatest efforts of Europe and America are directed, scientifically speaking, at undoing the fate which has placed you in our hands. Oil substitutes, controversial methods of propulsion, substitute bases for all petroleum-derived products, new sources of industrial heat and power are primary in the efforts of Western research and technology. When they are found, you in the West will be able to despoil without consequence what humble petroleum resources your greed has left you. And what then will become of us, Mr. Nicholson? We will return to the posture which has been so familiar to you over the centuries. We will be supine.

'We have not had the time, nor until recently the money, to educate our people to the level of modern technocracy. Laborers, yes, by the thousands. Some even skilled. But engineers, scientists, marketing experts able to build multi-faceted economies that will endure? No, Mr. Nicholson, that we do not have. We have currency. Currency buys goods, and it buys time. My problem, Mr. Nicholson, is to make sure that it buys enough time. The cry of Jihad is to still the empty bellies. The puerile flag-waving is to take the intensity of the Arab mind from the emptiness of the Arab pocket. Thank God for Israel, Mr. Nicholson, and thank Him as well for America, or our people would recognize how long it is taking us to climb out of the Middle Ages.

'While we wait, while we train our young people, we must take advantage of our resources, Mr. Nicholson. We cannot create an industrial state overnight. So we shall buy one. And we shall do it in such a way that we will forestall, to the last possible moment, the interruption of the power of our petroleum resources.'

Nicholson sat at the edge of the couch staring, his half-finished second drink, the ice melted to nothing, on the table. 'Who are you going to start with, Your Excellency?'

El Kaffar rose from the chair and leaned forward on the desk, staring at Nicholson. 'We are going to start with General Motors.'

Eight

'Tell him to go shit in his hat,' Pineau said, pulling up his tie.

'The Minister of the Interior, General?' La Brousse inquired politely.

'Whoever is on the phone. I will call him back after I have had my breakfast and gone through the endless nonsense that your scholars send down every morning. I am on vacation. Tell him that. I want to be left alone.' He turned away and continued with his toilet.

La Brousse turned and went through the doors of their adjoining rooms at the Majestic in Cannes. 'He is indisposed at the moment, Minister,' he said to the telephone. 'He says that he is most anxious to speak to you and will call you back at the earliest possible moment. Yes, sir, I shall make sure that he receives your best regards, and I am sure that he returns them.' He stared at the dead receiver, then hung it up.

La Brousse winced when the General walked through the door, his walking stick held aggressively before him. His blue tie did not go well with the brown jacket taken from one suit and the gray pants taken from another. A button on his shirt was undone. He wore his snap-brim natural straw hat.

'So, did you tell him?'

'Approximately.'

'Weakling! I want breakfast. Let's go down. Where are we to meet the heir of Isaac, Abraham and Jacob?'

'At the pétanque court in Cabasse.'

'Good. I need the exercise. And besides, I like to take his money. It hurts them, the Jews, when you take their money.'

70

La Brousse took the weather-beaten leather attaché case from the chair next to the door as the General pushed past him into the hall and locked up behind him.

'This morning,' the General said, as they waited for the elevator, 'we will drink breakfast at the Carlton.'

They walked out of the lobby of the hotel and began a leisurely stroll down the inland side of the Croisette. It took about fifteen minutes to reach the Carlton, for the General walked slowly. He sat heavily in a white wrought-iron chair in the cafe and rapped his stick on the floor. A uniformed waiter appeared and took their order. By the time he had arrived with a bottle of white wine for the old man and coffee and rolls for La Brousse, Pineau had read through a fairly thick pile of correspondence.

Juggling the tray in one hand, the waiter attempted to move the papers which lay face down on the table. 'Hands off, bungler,' the General snapped. He pointed his thumb at La Brousse, who replaced them in the case.

'La Brousse, write.'

La Brousse produced a narrow lined pad and a mechanical pencil.

'To Section Four, remove Belmont and Douarnez from Beirut. Off to Tripoli. Tell them to sell lots of fruit.' He smiled. 'To Magloire, why is the Middle East Airlines Office in Rome up in staff from eleven to sixteen in two weeks? To Du Pont, why, if he hears there has been a private confrontation with Smith and El Kaffar, does he not know any of the details? I want whatever he finds out delivered in person. He is to use the usual private system. Nothing in writing from now on.

'Who is Edward Nicholson? I want everything I can get. Background. Affiliations. Political persuasions. More information on Bauermann and Bankhaus Reitz, Zurich.' He stopped, turning his head slightly at a sound behind him. A hefty grandmotherly-looking American, dressed in a loud silk dress, clinked by on overly high clogs, dragging a miniature poodle in her wake. She disappeared down the steps and he turned back to La Brousse.

'Can we trust Durand at the Embassy in Washington? How clumsy is he? Is he being paid by someone? Who is his direct allegiance to?'

'He reports to the Ambassador, General. That is in fact, as well as on paper. I served with him in Algiers for two years. Nice fellow. Bright. A good young career Foreign Service officer. He is ready for an important consulate. I trust him.'

The General arched an eyebrow. 'Is he your friend?'

La Brousse repeated the litany. 'I have no friends. He is competent and can be trusted. He knows how to keep his mouth shut.'

'My God, La Brousse, don't tell me that at the age of forty you are finally learning something? All right, I want a dossier on the president of Royal American Oil. Everything gettable. Not the usual nickel profile. His name is Fosburgh. He makes political noises. He reminds me unpleasantly of the French industrial clique in the late '30s. Very patriotic, but not too sure of which system the flag should represent. The bulk of his oil and his profits come from Ben Kelb. For a country with three million people, we hear a lot from Quahrein.'

'Luck of the draw, General. Allah gave them the oil.'

'Then I may assume that Holy Mother Church gave us Ben Kelb and El Kaffar.'

By ten they were in the gray Mercedes which they had rented for their stay, with La Brousse driving. They climbed the hill behind Cannes to the Autoroute Côte d'Estourel.

They left the Autoroute at Le Luc and drove the few remaining miles into the small town, its streets old and winding around a small plaza, the buildings, no more than two or three stories high, joined like Siamese twins, gray stone with red tile roofs. The General slept quietly, with his pipe stem clenched between his teeth. La Brousse crossed the small bridge and parked in the shade of a large chestnut tree to avoid the strong sun. In a rutted dirt rectangle perhaps one hundred yards in length, shaded by more gnarled old trees, groups of men were throwing scored iron balls through the air in the direction of smaller wooden balls on the ground. From time to time an argument broke out as the distance from the larger to the smaller was measured with millimetric accuracy by strings, sticks and rulers.

'General?'

'I am still breathing, La Brousse, if you are concerned.'

The General and La Brousse carefully skirted two groups of men busily engaged in the arguments that make pétanque so appealing to the Frenchmen of the South. A small man, with a face as gnarled as the tree by which he stood, doffed his soft peaked cap to the General. Pineau looked intently at the man, then deciding that it was no more than respect for his age and imposing bearing, continued on.

Near the end of the court, Rhabbouz, splendid in tailored sport shirt and slacks, with white patent leather shoes, practiced the peculiar underhanded delivery which gives the ball its spin on the uneven ground, enabling the best players to rest the iron ball against the smaller wooden one.

General Pineau and La Brousse sat quietly on a green wooden bench to one side and watched. After a few minutes the General rose, undid his tie and took off his jacket and hat.

He walked quietly to Rhabbouz's side and said, 'So, Jew,' ruining his aim, 'cheating by practicing.'

Rhabbouz smiled disarmingly. 'Certainly, you would not want to take advantage of my lack of skill, when compared with your own vast experience.'

'Are you calling me an old man, Jew?'

'The thought had occurred to me. But not in those terms, of course.'

They played and talked. Rhabbouz picked up the General's balls, but only after they had been carefully checked. La Brousse was not invited to play. He sat languidly on the bench, enjoying the late summer afternoon. From an angle he could see the small man who had doffed his cap edging toward the two players. He rose unobtrusively.

The man worked his way around a tree about twenty feet from the General, who continued immersed in his game

73

and conversation. La Brousse undid the buttons on his jacket and stepped slowly forward toward the tree.

'Well, La Brousse, you moron,' the General said conversationally in English, 'are you going to go and get him or are you going to let the little bastard shoot both of us and steal the money from our corpses?'

Without hurrying, La Brousse walked past the General, shielding him from the view of the tree with his body. Then, in two quick steps he dodged behind it and gently but firmly wrapped strong fingers around the bony arms of the little man.

'Watching the game, old friend? You can sit on the bench next to me if you like.'

'That's my general,' the man said indignantly. 'Let go of my arms. I can damn well watch him if I want to. I'm from Cabasse, you know. I'm secretary of the Concours des Boules. This is my responsibility. This pétanque court. If you don't let go, I will call the Municipal Guard.' He indicated a tall rustic in his early thirties who was playing several dozen yards away.

'What do you mean, he's your general?'

'I walked behind him over three thousand miles for four years.'

'Then come and say hello.'

'What the hell is this, La Brousse,' the General said, 'a side show? First you let him crawl up my behind. Then you put me on exhibition like a trained seal. What can I do for you?' He turned squinting, his eyes boring into the little brown man.

In one motion he swept off his cap with one hand and grabbed the General's hand with the other, kissing it.

'Salaam. It is Inch' Allah that I see you again.'

'So it may be,' said the General, taking his hand back, but gently.

The man's face lit up in a toothless grin. He stood as close to attention as his years and arthritis would permit and gave the facsimile of a salute. 'Tirailleurs Cous Cous. You remember?'

74

The General's face softened. 'You are one of my children?'

'Yes. From Oran to the big mountain in Italy with the church which you said your God had damned.' He reached over, pulling up a trouser leg to show a prosthetic foot.

General Pineau made a small bow. 'Business can wait. Will you join us?'

Without a word the man hobbled with surprising speed to a distant bench and returned, carrying three scarred and rusted balls.

Before he arrived the General turned to La Brousse. 'Go stop Tombal before he gets in here. He was probably one of mine. But who knows, so are you, La Brousse, and he may not be on my side this time and less incompetent than you are.'

La Brousse was hesitant to leave Pineau and Rhabbouz in what might be a dangerous position, but a year and a half with the General had taught him not to contest or temporize. He went to the car and drove up the road to cut off Tombal, who would come via the Autoroute on his way up from Toulon.

La Brousse returned in about twenty minutes, having parked the Commissaire in a cafe on the road, to find the three men embroiled in a bitter argument over the placement of a ball. The man from Cabasse, who turned out to be an old Moroccan named Kareeb, drew a folding pointer from the pocket of his grubby jacket and measured with precision.

'In all fairness, Kareeb, you are the closest, and you have won,' the General said. 'But I shall never forgive you.'

His smile was so wide that La Brousse saw several black teeth.

'Come, La Brousse, we are going to take these Semites to buy them a beer.'

They left Kareeb smiling and laughing in the cafe, already telling war stories to friends in the game of belote he had entered.

'Note La Brousse, that it is a tribute to the French men-

75

tality that the favourite game of cards is played with a deck of thirty-two. It is all that they can manage at the same time.

'Rhabbouz, this is all your fault. You picked this godforsaken hole. You said that no one ever comes here, that no one would recognize us. That poor soul will have recounted every step of his wartime journey fifty times before he sleeps tonight. And he will have described me, testified that I came to the South of France from heaven, where he believes retired generals live, especially to see him, and that I am embroiled in something very important.'

La Brousse interjected, 'But why would he say that? The subject never came up.'

'You see what I mean, Rhabbouz, you can't teach Arabs in a university. You have to learn them in person. Well, there's no helping it now. Where did you put Tombal?'

They found the Commissaire in the roadside cafe, staring morosely into the shards of a third piece of tarte aux pommes, the ashtray beside him filled to overflowing.

He looked up when the substantial shadow of the General crossed his plate. The General looked at the armband. 'It is healthy and respectful to mourn. What have you done to help your friend Riez?'

'I have followed your instructions to the letter. I have gone over every document pertaining to the case. In addition, I have read all the newspaper accounts as you suggested, and the transcriptions of all testimony.'

'Is there anything there?'

'Nothing.'

'Good. We will start all over again. Rhabbouz, where is your safe house here?'

'I'll take you, but do you think that it's necessary?'

'Tombal,' the General turned back to the seated policeman, 'when did Colonel Brunschwig of the Sûreté arrive?'

The Commissaire took the cigarette out of his mouth and stubbed it out in the ashtray. 'This morning – unannounced. I don't think that he knows that you have a tail on him.'

'I don't. I just know the slimy little bastard. He must stick his crooked pointy nose into everything. That, of course, with all due respect, is the job of a policeman. On the other hand, his efforts generally result only in the interruption of the valued work of others. He does very well at internal matters. His mother must have been in the Pègre, he knows them so well. But as far as anything to do with our external security, he knows only how to make excuses.'

Rhabbouz clapped the policeman on the shoulder. 'I see that you have eaten a piece of pie. Do you think that despite that you can manage a little light lunch? My friend in the area is in the food business.'

Tombal beamed and pushed back his chair. 'I can manage.'

It was past four when they pulled up to the door of an old château which had been redone into a restaurant and inn. It overlooked a small valley and hills which ran to the sea beyond their view. Three or four dark young men with the tinge of the desert to them stepped forward to shake Rhabbouz's hand. One of them departed, returning shortly with a rotund elderly man in white shirt and slacks and dark glasses.

'Shalom, Rhabbouz.'

'Shalom, Emil. Got a private room?'

'Always for you. How shall I feed your friends?'

'Tajine. Tajine with almonds. No interruptions after the food.'

They were led upstairs to a room with old oriental carpets on a polished wood floor. Large comfortable cushions were spread about the floor, interspersed with round brass tables on ornate wooden legs.

Only Tombal had problems in placing himself. The others were accustomed to sitting on the floor.

'The dark ones, Rhabbouz, they don't look like yours,' said the General.

'Iraqis. Baghdadians. There are almost none left. Most of them ended up hanging from lamp posts. It takes the people's minds off their empty bellies to see a Jew hang.'

They finished the steaming dishes heaped with lamb and

77

almonds. Then the honey-sweetened Middle Eastern pastry and hot mint tea.

'The matter must now be joined directly. I want to see witnesses personally. I don't intend to interfere in police business, Tombal. I want you to understand that. On the other hand, there are things that I will be looking for that a policeman will not. I want a list of all of the witnesses. Especially, I want to see the man who runs the queer club in St. Tropez, the barman at the beach club, and the American, what's his name. Yes, Donald Hamilton. Who is also missing is the Portuguese boy. In order to find more about Pascal, we have to find out more about where he came from. Then we will find his suspected friend. Oh, by the way, Tombal, you have gotten a list of the yachts in port at St. Tropez since the day before Pascal was killed?'

'Yes, and a running count since then. Are you sure you don't want them searched?'

'Yes, there are only a few that interest me. I don't want to scare away anything that will in the end determine the greater game. This is, in fact, more than just a murder or two, you know. I want to know what the hell is going on here.'

The door opened slightly, and Rhabbouz, who sat facing it, answered the call of a beckoning hand. When he came back his face was hard. 'I must call Nana to tell her that I will probably not be home until later.' As he felt him brush by on his way to the phone, La Brousse recognized that he had been frisked, quickly, professionally.

Pineau continued to speak. 'Then tomorrow, we shall meet with Hamilton, and the other two. There is no longer any need to play it too quietly. Without question, if there are ears listening, they will have found us out by the end of today. Shame, Rhabbouz, shame. If I never see Cabasse again, it will be too soon.'

They rose to leave, thanking their host, who seemed very quiet when compared to his enthusiastic greeting earlier. Only the youngest of the waiters were in evidence.

'General, if I may?'

78

'It's your safe house, Rhabbouz. Run it as you like.'

'Thank you. Tombal, you leave first. The General and La Brousse will leave in twenty minutes, then I will follow. Where shall we meet in the morning?'

'Breakfast at the Carlton, Rhabbouz? You should feel very much at home there.'

'Bless you, General. Do they have a kosher kitchen?'

The policeman left as scheduled. The others waited and chatted aimlessly, then the two left.

As soon as he heard the engine start, Rhabbouz threw himself down a flight of stairs at the back of the second floor and jumped into his car, which had already been started. It was dark, but the moon shed sufficient light to enable him to drive surely across a dirt road cutting through the grape fields. At the top of the hill, he could see the headlights of Pineau's car winding slowly down the macadam toward him.

As the General's car moved between two hedges which were the last cover from the public road beyond, a figure rose silhouetted, then three more. They were about forty feet from where he stood.

The first to rise turned slightly and in a stage whisper said, 'Now!'

When the first shot rang through the still air, La Brousse jammed on the brakes and turned out the light in the same motion. He drew the gun in his waistband and threw himself across the General. He heard shots but did not fire because he saw nothing but an occasional flash of light. After a minute that seemed like an hour there was silence. He heard Rhabbouz, 'General, La Brousse, are you all right?'

'Yes, I am fine, Rhabbouz. But from the smell and the heat, I think that a goat has fallen on me.'

La Brousse, still keeping his head down, opened the door and dropped to the road beside the car. He moved quickly to the hedge, listening.

'It's all right, La Brousse,' he heard a voice directly above his head, 'you can come out now.'

He stood and turned. Rhabbouz was standing on the

79

hedgerow with a smoking Uzi machine gun in his right hand. 'Look what I found.' He reached down and grabbed a form-less bundle by the hair and with some effort threw it down on the road.

The General reached over and turned the light back on. The crumpled corpse of the little Arab from Cabasse leaked life in slow rivulets on the country road. Pineau turned on the high beams, catching the three Iraqi waiters walking down the road towards them, in black pants and sweaters, heavily armed.

'Go, La Brousse. See you in the morning, General.'

La Brousse got in and started the motor. The General leaned out and said, 'Good night, Jew. Not bad.' Then they pulled away.

Rhabbouz threw the Uzi to one of the boys. 'Clean up this mess. Bury that treacherous little bastard and his friends deep. I have to go home. My wife will kill me.' He hurried off to his car.

La Brousse and Pineau drove in silence almost all of the way to Cannes. At the red light in Super Cannes, La Brousse turned and said, 'I thought you said Rhabbouz never gets involved in anything dangerous.'

The General shrugged and waved his pipe. 'That didn't look dangerous to me. He wasn't the one who got killed. Let's go home. I feel seventy-seven.'

Nine

Donald Hamilton did not even bother to curse when the phone rang. He opened his eyes and slid his hand between his mouth and Marie Jo's, then rolled over and took the receiver from its cradle.

'Hamilton,' he said crankily.

'Good morning, Mr. Hamilton. This is Tombal. I didn't wake you, did I?'

'Should you have? What time is it anyway?'

'It's eight-fifteen.'

'Frankly, you cut into the middle of my working day. What can I do for you, Commissaire?'

'Do you have a really full day, today? I should like to take up some of your time in the early afternoon. Possibly the whole afternoon. There is someone who would like to meet you.'

'It's Saturday, isn't it?'

'Yes, it is. Does it discommode your plans? I shouldn't like to be insistent, but it is quite important.'

'Now, look, Commissaire,' Donald bridled. 'I think that I've been more than cooperative. I've made myself available for inquests and postponed meetings in an effort to be helpful. I know that it's not your fault that I found that stiff, but by the same grace, I don't want to spend the next three years making plans around my obligations in this matter. I would just as soon not come. I have a life to live. And besides, I have a guest.'

'Often, in my line of work, Mr. Hamilton, one sees that the luxury of choice can be diminished.'

Donald sat bolt upright in the bed and said in a loud voice, 'Well, I sure as hell don't see myself in that light.'

Trying another tack, Tombal said, 'I was certainly not trying to indicate that you had no choice in the matter. I cannot demand that you meet with us, Mr. Hamilton, It is simply a matter of my asking your cooperation one additional time, fully aware that it is an imposition.'

Somewhat mollified, Donald said, 'Who is this person you want me to meet?'

'He is a government official. He is interested in a possible connection between the death of the man you found and Inspector Riez. Perhaps you remember, he was the policeman you first met. He had several young children . . .'

Donald began to feel uncomfortable. 'Would this . . . meeting . . . take a long time?'

Marie Jo sat up and shook her head violently in disagreement. Donald held up his free hand to quiet her.

'Not really. Perhaps we could speed it up. Maybe an hour or two.'

Beginning to get annoyed again, Donald, said, 'Fine, right in the middle of the afternoon, I suppose? We were planning to go to the beach. Commissaire . . .?'

There was a pause at the other end of the line, as though Tombal had covered the phone with his hand. 'Actually, Mr. Hamilton, it would suit us best if we could meet at Moorea Beach. Perhaps you could bring your guest. In that way, we would accomplish our ends and interrupt your day as little as possible.'

'That sounds a little better. What time do you want to meet?'

'Shall we say one o'clock at the bar. By the way, Mr. Hamilton, is your guest pretty?'

'Absolutely smashing. See you at one.'

Marie Jo Du Fresne sat fully upright in the bed, cross-legged, her tousled black hair not quite covering firm medium-sized breasts. Her wide mouth, which kept her at the outer edge of real beauty, was turned down at the corners. Slightly oriental green eyes above a smallish upturned nose were narrowed to slits. 'God damn it, Donald. You promised me the whole weekend. I wangled for two weeks to get a girl to change routes with me. I have to put in about four extra hours next week. And on top of it, I had to tell my parents that I couldn't go to a party they have been planning for a month. Can't this wait till Monday?'

Hamilton lay back on the pillow and looked up at her, smiling, 'You speak very good English for a foreigner.'

'Damn it, Donald, I'm serious. Can't you call whoever that was back and tell him to go away? This was supposed to be our weekend.'

Hamilton reached out and patted her cheek. 'Don't pout, pretty girl. That was the police. It's about that guy I found. There was a policeman killed there shortly thereafter. I guess they think the two may be connected. They asked me to help.'

Her eyes widened in alarm. She took his hand between her own and said, 'You aren't getting into anything dangerous, are you?'

'No, not at all. You know the whole story, Marie Jo. They probably want to go over it one more time to see if they overlooked anything in my testimony. And besides, the cop that was killed had a bunch of kids. I couldn't very well say no. But it's nothing more than you read in the papers, plus the gory details I filled in.'

She kissed his hand, then pushed it away. 'Well, anyway, it's going to spoil the whole day. I'm going to end up sitting on my behind waiting for you. When do you have to go?'

He pulled himself up and sat on the bed facing Marie Jo. He leaned his elbows on his knees, resting his chin on closed fists.

'What would you say if I told you that the meeting was to take place at Moorea Beach in St. Tropez? We can have lunch, and you can show your tits,' he reached out and patted her, 'to all the nice policemen. Then when they leave, we can walk around to the cove under the Parc de St. Tropez and make love in the sunshine. That is,' he leaned over and pulled her into his arms, 'if you have any energy left by then.'

*

They pulled into the parking lot at quarter to one. Donald paid his two francs and drove around behind the first row of cars to find a place in the shade under the bamboo covers. He had to drive around a second time because of the crowd of parked Rolls and other expensive machines.

'Where do they all come from?'

'The trouble with you Americans is that you can never realize that there is a lot of money in Europe too. Look at those license plates. Italy, France, England, everywhere.' She patted the little red Alfa Romeo on the hood after she got out. 'You're just a man from an underprivileged country in a cheap car. I am the only touch of class that you have.' She stripped off her shirt and slacks, standing topless in orange panties. 'What would you do without me?'

'I don't even want to guess. Come on, harem.'

The beach boy approached them as they walked onto the sand from the board runway. 'Can I help you? There are two mattresses left by the water. Right in the center.'

'Thank you,' Donald said, handing him ten francs, 'and an umbrella and a little table if you please.'

They lay down on their stomachs on the mattresses and surveyed the crowd. 'Don, look at that.' She pushed at his shoulder and directed his eyes toward the entrance to the beach.

'Good grief. Maybe things in Europe haven't changed as much as you think. He looks like an illustration from a history book.'

The old man walked forward ploddingly on the sand toward the bar, his walking stick extended before him like a lance. He squinted in the bright light, and his lower lip protruded aggressively beneath a stiff white mustache. He wore white shoes and socks and a loud Hawaiian shirt. His head was covered by a ragged straw hat. A step or two behind him was a younger man in dark swim trunks, a strained expression on his face.

'It is obvious that I have wasted my life,' said the General. 'Look at those tits. Marvelous. Just marvelous. Hey you, bartender, give me a bottle of white wine. Yes, a whole bottle.' He thumbed at La Brousse. 'He drinks peppermint and mineral water. Says it cuts his thirst.' He laughed grossly and struggled to the top of the wooden stool which had just been vacated. 'It was nice of her to keep the seat warm for me, no? Where is that policeman? What time is it?'

'It's just one, sir. I'm sure he'll be here any minute.'

'Here I don't mind being kept waiting. I just mind being seventy-seven.' He downed the first glass of wine at a gulp, then poured himself another.

In a moment, Tombal padded out onto the sand, wearing longish boxer trunks in dark stripes and a terry-cloth beach shirt.

'Ah, Tombal, I almost didn't recognize you. You know,' General Pineau said in a low conspiratorial tone, 'I think we older men look better in street clothes. Sit. Drink. I know you eat, but do you drink?'

'Yes, yes indeed I do. Hello, Claudie. Could you make me a Kir please?' He mopped his head with a handkerchief from the breast pocket of his shirt. 'Unusually fine weather for this time of year. Quite a crowd too. Listen, has our friend the architect showed up?'

'Now how would I know, Tombal. I've never seen him, and the picture you gave me stank. But all I see here is tits. I don't mind if he doesn't come at all.'

Tombal picked up his glass and walked away from the bar toward the water. Hamilton was just coming out after a short dip, pulling a laughing Marie Jo after him.

'Hello, Mr. Hamilton,' Tombal shouted. 'It's me, up here.'

'Well, hello there. We'll be right up.'

They dried quickly and walked to the bar, where the Commissaire had found another stool. Avoiding an introduction, Tombal said, 'Shall we just go over to our table? I have reserved for lunch.' He led them past the rows of tables covered with red and white checked cloths and protected by parasols to a little patio set apart next to the cabana which served as an office.

'Please be seated. Let me make a few introductions,' the Commissaire said. To Donald's surprise, the ratty-looking old man had come with them, as well as his pained friend. 'This is General Pineau and this is Mr. La Brousse. Mr. Hamilton and Mademoiselle . . .'

'Du Fresne, Marie Jo Du Fresne,' she said, extending her hand.

The General swept the hat from his head, leaned the stick against the table and took her hand in his own. 'I am charmed, my dear, to have the opportunity of such lovely company.'

'Why, thank you, General. Are you a policeman too?'

'Good heavens no, my dear. I am just an old retired soldier. A pensioner, you might say. I just came down to have a pleasant chat with Tombal. He was kind enough to invite me and my associate along for lunch. I expect that the business which he might want to transact can wait till after we have eaten and had a chance to get acquainted.'

Taking the cue Tombal said, 'Oh yes. I wouldn't want to bore either you or the General, Mlle. Du Fresne. The few details that I want to go over with Mr. Hamilton will certainly wait until later. Then you can swim or sit in the sun without being involved in our ball of red tape.'

When the introductions were at an end, Tombal signaled to a waiter, who in turn called to the patron. 'Good afternoon, Inspector, I want to take your orders myself. When we have important company, we always like to make sure that they see our best side. May I suggest the crevettes? Fresh and excellently cooked. A touch of oil and garlic and some salt. Or the grilled sardines to start? The plat du jour is leg of lamb. I would cut it for you myself. It is very good.'

Everyone nodded agreement, and after a few minutes of idle conversation, the waiter returned with the first course. 'The patron has suggested this Estandon Blanc de Blanc with the fish. It is with his compliments.'

The General leaned across the table. 'Let me ask you, Miss Du Fresne, why do you speak such good English? You are French, no?'

'Learned at home and at school, General. How about you?'

86

'It took me a war. I'm glad I learned, but the tuition was rather high. Do you spend a lot of time on the Côte d'Azur?'

'As much as I can. I just have the weekend off. I'm a stewardess with Air Inter.'

He turned to the other side of the table. 'Listen, Hamilton, you don't happen to have her phone number? Perhaps she is impressed by mature men.'

'You have my permission to ask her, General. But you are no grayer than I.'

The lunch went cheerfully enough, with no mention of the main purpose. After dessert was finished, Marie Jo stood, turning to give the General the benefit of her figure. 'Well, I'm sure that I'm in the way. I'm going to take a dip and then try to catch up on my tan. Thank you very much for lunch, Inspector. It was very nice to meet you all. Donald, you know where to find me when you're through.'

'Well, Hamilton,' the General said, watching her retreat down the beach, 'you are certainly a man of taste. She is lovely.'

'I gathered that you thought so, sir.'

'How long have you known her?'

'About three months. I picked her up on a flight from Paris to Toulon and took her out for a drink.'

'Thank you.'

'General, can we get to the point? Commissaire Tombal asked me to come down here to talk to him. I assume it's again about my finding that fellow Pascal Lambert. But I told everything I know – at the time and again at the inquest. And what have you got to do with it?'

Without taking his eyes from Hamilton's face, Pineau snapped his fingers and stuck his hand in the direction of La Brousse. La Brousse stuck several sheets of paper in his hand. With the other hand he drew a pair of gold-rimmed glasses from his shirt pocket, shook them open, put them on and began to read aloud.

'Donald Hamilton. Born April 8, 1940, in Locust Valley, New York. Father Arthur Hamilton, investment banker, deceased May 1971. Mother Louise Pritchard, born St. Paul,

Minnesota, resides Locust Valley, New York. No brothers or sisters. Attended Locust Valley Friends School 1946–1958, University of Virginia 1958–1962. Graduated with honors, Bachelor of Science, Engineering. United States Army, active service December 1962–January 1965. Entered as Second Lieutenant. Served in Indo-China December 1963–December 1964. Military advisor to Seventh Montagnard Brigade. Decorated twice for gallantry on the field of battle,' he looked up and hesitated, 'Bronze Star and Silver Star. Twice wounded, two Purple Hearts. Honorably discharged as a Captain. Subsequently promoted to Major in the Army Reserve. Attended Yale Graduate School of Architecture 1966–1969. Married June 15, 1962, to Thelma Carpenter, born Flint, Michigan. Two sons, Michael, fourteen, Christopher, twelve. Divorced September 1974. Currently . . .'

'What the hell is this all about?'

'Calmly, Major, calmly.'

'I am not a major. I am a private citizen. And I would like to know what you are doing with a dossier on me. If I don't find out, and soon, I am going to go join that girl over there, and the next time you want to see me, you can bloody well have me arrested.'

'All right, Hamilton,' the General said, with authority in his voice, 'we didn't ask you to come down here to play games with you. I haven't any more time to waste than you do. I wanted to talk to you myself. I have read your testimony over and over again. I wanted your record because I wanted to know if you could, frankly, be of any further use to us. You met Inspector Riez shortly before he was killed. We feel sure the deaths are connected. If there is something more you can tell us to help establish that connection, we are going to get it from you. Do we understand each other, Mr. Hamilton?'

Hamilton was still annoyed and very confused. 'Not yet. Just who are you?'

'Let us say that I am a government employee. A fonctionnaire, we would say here. La Brousse works in the same department that I do. Tombal is a policeman. He works in a different department, but for the moment, he is working with me.'

'I have told you, and I told him,' Hamilton indicated Tombal, 'that I have given all that I can. I found that guy in the cabin with his balls stuffed in his mouth. I went to the man who owns this place and told him to call the cops. I didn't see anything else, and I don't know anything else.'

'That is what you believe, Mr. Hamilton. But because of things that we know now that we didn't know before, we can ask you questions to which you did not know you had the answers. For instance, have you been coming here regularly?'

'That was the fourth or fifth time I was here. I live in Toulon for the moment; my firm is building a hotel in Ste. Maxime across the bay. I spend three days a week down here while they are digging the foundations. I'll probably be here five days a week once the structural work is begun. I am supposed to be coordinating the entire project. I just come down here in my spare time. I was told by some friends that this was the best of the beaches. They say that Tahiti is too crowded and the Club 55 is too quiet. I tried them all and I think that they're right.'

'Do you ever look at anything but the girls here?' Tombal asked. 'There are quite a number of young men for sale too.'

'It's not my style. I'm strictly heterosexual, Commissaire. But sure, I saw a lot of fags at the beach. They're all over the place.'

'Did you know that Pascal Lambert was a fag?'

'I didn't know Pascal Lambert at all. Maybe I saw him once or twice.'

The General hunched forward, with his head tucked between his shoulders, turtle style. 'Do you remember seeing him with anybody? A boy. We are looking for a young Portuguese boy.'

Hamilton shaded his eyes with his hands and tried to remember. 'A good-looking kid. Maybe fifteen or sixteen. Tall and very thin. Dark enough to be maybe half colored. Long hair.'

'Yes,' the General said, 'like that. Do you remember anything about him? Why,' leaning still further forward, 'did he stick in your mind? That's very important too.'

'When I see a boy walking up and down the beach like a model in a fashion show, and he is wearing a bathing suit skimpier than anything I've ever seen in a strip show, I tend to take a second look. Long uncombed hair is not new to me. My oldest son wears it like that. But, fortunately, for me at least, he doesn't wear eye shadow, rouge or lipstick. This kid did. So to me he looked like a cartoon queer.'

'Did you notice anything else about him? Do you remember who he ended up with?'

'I only remember seeing him the one time, General. He played cards at that big wooden table over there with some older fellows. All good-looking, in their twenties, I'd guess.' He scratched his head. 'It seems to me that I saw another freak. He was an old guy. Sixty, maybe. With a head of really bright white hair. He was big, well over six feet and at least two-twenty, maybe more. But what struck me is that he was wearing a Japanese karate suit.'

General Pineau sat upright. 'That, Mr. Hamilton, is what I was looking for. Or part of it anyway. Listen, Mr. Hamilton, I may have further need of you. Are you now reasonably convinced that I need you? That this is something special? There is a limit to what I can tell you, but if you are willing to waste a little more time occasionally to humor an old man, perhaps you will learn more.'

'I have a suspicion that my choices are limited. Clearly, I don't want to obstruct justice. On the other hand, I have my work to do, and I don't want to get involved more than absolutely necessary.'

'To be sure, Mr. Hamilton,' the General replied, waving the pipe, 'but on the other hand, you have spare time. Even taking your athletic preferences into account. By the way, I would be pleased if you would keep your information and anything regarding our conversations very much to yourself.' He nodded suggestively in the direction of the beach. 'One reason I wanted your record is to be sure in my own mind that you could keep things to yourself. It seems that you are a very private person.'

'In the world I grew up in, General, talking too much is considered a sign of weakness.'

'You may expect to hear from me. But I have held you long enough. Please go now to join your attractive friend. Will you be at the beach for a while?'

'Yes. If not, we'll just go for a walk. But we have to come back later anyway. Our car is parked in the lot.'

'Good. And we know where to reach you, either in your office or home in Toulon, or at the building site.' The General closed his eyes for a moment. 'Now we are going to talk to the bartender. Perhaps he will be able to identify the elderly karate expert. Thank you, Mr. Hamilton. Tombal, would you ask Claudie if he could take a few minutes off to speak to us?'

Donald rose and shook hands around the table, then walked down to the edge of the water and looked out at the boats. A small tender, in vivid colours, plied the water between the beach and the moored pleasure craft. He walked a step or two into the water, cooling his feet from the searing sand, then turned to walk down the shoreline to the mattress where Marie Jo lay sleeping in the sun.

He sat down quietly to avoid disturbing her, watching her bare back and shoulders move gently with each breath, then looked over his shoulder toward the restaurant. He couldn't see the table from the beach.

'Donald,' she said, without opening her eyes, 'what did they want?'

He hesitated a moment, 'Just to clear up some points of interest about my testimony. Just as simple as that.'

'Don't you think it's strange that they asked you to come all the way down here? I thought that Tombal had his office in Toulon. Who were those two other men, really, I mean the General and that quiet man with him, the one who never says anything?'

'Oh, they are friends of Tombal. I don't think that they have a whole lot to do with the matter.'

She turned on her side and leaned against her hand, balancing on her elbow. 'That doesn't make sense, Donald. Then what were they doing there?'

'Got me, toots.' He slapped her lightly on the backside. 'Let's go for a walk.'

'Is that all the information I'm going to get?' she pouted.

He looked at her carefully, then jumped to his feet. 'Yup, let's go.'

When Tombal got up to get Claudie the General turned to La Brousse. 'Is he as solid as he seems?'

La Brousse considered carefully. It was not the General's habit to ask his opinion. 'Yes. He is one of those rare birds who is completely visible in his dossier. His personal appearance, his frankness match neatly with his printed outline.'

'Quite so. Except for the children, he seems to be unattached. He won't say anything to that girl, I'm sure.'

'Are you setting him up?'

'Yes. We are altogether blown. Rhabbouz has done what he can, I think. He will continue to look around, of course. But after the recent unpleasantness, he is exposed for what he is, rather than for what he seemed. We are, of course, watched. If they begin to watch Hamilton, it is possible that they will use someone who is unknown to us. Perhaps we will be able to find out who picks up Hamilton. Then we may be able to get at the base of this mess.'

La Brousse looked down at his hands. 'I have no friends.'

'Yes, there is a risk to him, certainly. But justified. Here comes Tombal with our bartender.'

Claudie looked nervously at the two impassive faces, standing until he was offered a chair.

'Claudie, you mentioned a Portuguese boy once. Do you know anything more than you told us?'

'No, just what I said.'

'How about a big fat man who wears karate costumes to the beach?'

Claudie brightened. 'Signor Carelli. Very important. A big cheese from Torino. He comes every year. A big tipper.'

The General patted his hand. 'Thank you, Claudie. That's

all. Oh, Claudie, just a minute. Is he a fag?'

The barman shrugged expressively. 'A voile et à vapeur. He goes both ways. Lots of people do,' he added cheerfully.

'Are you going to set Claudie up too?' La Brousse asked.

'No. Nobody will bother. He is the local fountain of information. He will talk to anybody about anything. That is his function. He is a combination bartender and gossip center. La Brousse, make a phone call and see that Hamilton is shadowed from the time that he leaves this beach. Professionally.'

Ten

In the two weeks since Pascal Lambert had been killed, Arthur Edelman continued to find it difficult to concentrate on his work. He took to leaving the house for lunch and dinner. Though he enjoyed cooking for others, he did not enjoy dining alone. He sat in a little cafe in the Massif des Maures above Grimaud, stirring his coffee absently and contemplating his fate.

His mother had raised him on Dad's insurance money after the war had claimed his father's life. He was her tie to existence, and she guarded him from the dangerous world which had robbed her of her husband with all the ferocity that a great capacity to love can focus on its only subject. He was to be studious. He was to be sedentary. He was not to engage in the dangerous physical games which risked the well-being of his peers in the schoolyard every day. He grew as she had intended him, introverted, overintellectual, narrow and alone. Alone save for her. No one was to stand in the path of his genius. No woman was to take him from his mother.

When he had reached his fourteenth birthday, she had seen him from a window, walking a girl home from school. She had been beside herself with fright and jealousy, and the preview of loneliness.

Arthur had never shown any interest in girls, or in sex for that matter. He had never asked any questions of her, nor had she volunteered any information on the subject. Because she had forced him, and then because he had adopted the habit, he came home directly after classes, to read and to study and to improve his mind. In reward for obedience to her wishes, she filled his slack obese body with sweets and elaborate cooking, first developing and then pandering to his taste for both.

When he had dropped the girl off at her house, across the street on Avenue J, and come upstairs, she had been waiting for him, determined that it should never happen again.

She waited patiently until the programs that he watched on television after he finished his afternoon session with his homework were over. She had planned a special dinner in celebration of the report card he was to bring home. It was, as expected, all As. As was his habit, he took his bath at six. She walked in and out of the room, which was unlocked, as was natural with any mother and her baby. From time to time she scrubbed his back.

Arthur was late in his physical development. He was a rather sickly child and had only just entered the rude process of puberty. He had had an occasional erection, she had noticed, but neither of them had ever mentioned the fact. To save him from the separation from mother love that she knew would be destructive to them both, she determined to provide him with an outlet for his energies.

'Hi, Mother. What's for dinner?' he asked, taking off his shirt.

'Something special for my baby. I saw that report card. Dad, God rest his soul, would have been very proud of his little Arthur if he could see that. I made home-made gefilte fish, with horseradish, just the way you like it. And chicken in the pot with matzoh balls. And the most beautiful chocolate cake that you ever saw.' She sat on the bed as he neatly folded the shirt, which was still clean, and hung his trousers in the closet after brushing off and putting his shoes in the rack on the door. He took off his socks and underpants and held them in one hand. He turned to face her and said, 'Okay, Mom dear, I'm going to take my bath now.'

She glanced downward to see a few curly black hairs clustered around the base of his still small penis, which protruded below his soft white paunch.

'I'll help you wash, dear.'

He got into the tubful of warm water which she had run

for him, and leaned forward, sitting. She took the rough fiber glove and soaped it thoroughly, then sat on the closed toilet next to the tub and rubbed his back in gentle circular motions. He hummed tunelessly in time with her hand. After a moment or two she stopped and he leaned back to rinse himself. He reached for the soap to finish, but she said, 'Don't bother, dear, Mother will do it for you.'

He lay back in the bath with his eyes closed and relaxed in the warm water as she knelt beside him on the bathroom floor. There was a small inflated plastic pillow under his head. She worked the soap into a lather over his chest and under his thin flabby arms, then inched her way along the floor on her knees to his legs, skipping his midsection.

'Hey, Mom, that tickles,' he said, as she did his feet. Then he relaxed again, half asleep as she finished his legs. He arched himself a bit as she reached under him to clean his behind, about which she had always been very particular. She rubbed gently against his rectum with the soapy water. At the same time, with the soap in her other hand she began to wash his private parts in a motion almost lost to her memory. In a moment, the wrinkled organ began to fill and harden under her touch. She rubbed gently but persistently until with a sigh Arthur Edelman experienced his first orgasm.

'There. Now you dry up like a good boy, and Mother will get the table ready. Then we can have a nice dinner together before you finish your homework.'

Arthur opened his eyes and stopped stirring his coffee when the proprietor of the cafe stood over him, clearing his throat suggestively. He looked up, and then down at the table where the check rested on a small plate. He pulled the purse from his pocket and threw a note on the plate. The man took the money, gave the change and said thank you.

Arthur left and walked for a few minutes up and down the road. Then he stopped and turned more purposefully in the direction of his car. He got in and headed toward St.

Tropez, its lights beckoning across the hills in the distance.

At ten o'clock the second round of incoming traffic slowed but did not block the single road to the presqu'île. Arthur drove past the red light at the entrance to the town and then turned left into the gigantic parking lot. It was full and he had to park at the farthest end, leaving him a long walk to the port. He traversed the lot and walked past the small boats and then toward the center of the docks where the great yachts were parked motionless in their splendor. As he passed the *Glen Pool* he noted with pleasure the classic musculature of the mustachioed sailor who sat, dark and brooding, at the foot of the gangway.

At the end of the center of the dock he walked into Le Gorille, full of young of both sexes. 'Est-ce que je peux me servir du petit coin?' he asked. Directed to the bathroom, he took the rouge and mascara from his pocket and applied it. He looked in the mirror one last time, then snapped his fingers and reached deep into his pants pocket. He turned and affixed the thin gold earring, pirouetted before the mirror again and left.

At the far end of the port he climbed the short hill to the little plaza, with its few old stunted trees and its fountain, then turned down the little alley till he came opposite the Stereo Club. The bouncer stood, young and bristling with muscles, protecting the door. When two young men went in, Arthur glanced from across the street to see that the club was packed even at this relatively early hour. He crossed the road and stood before the man at the door. The bouncer looked down from his considerable height at the made-up face and the earring, and the grotesque little body, smiled and opened the door.

'S'il vous plaît, monsieur, vous pouvez entrer,' he said.

Arthur slid forward through the door, patting the bouncer's hard flat stomach as he passed, and into the red-velvet-lined room, dark and warm with smoke and bodies, and edged his way toward the bar.

*

The boy leaned forward and turned his ear closer to Arthur's lips. Dozens of hushed conversations blended into a white noise that made hearing difficult. An occasional voice rose momentarily above the throng, in laughter or in anger.

'So you see,' said Arthur, moving his hand casually up the lanky thigh, 'I have been largely alone almost all of my life. If it hadn't been for Mother, I don't know what would have become of me.'

The boy ran his hand through waxen blond hair above his drawn face. 'Well, no one gives a shit about me either, Arthur. All this year at school, they made fun of me. My father, my own father, called me a filthy pervert. I don't see why people like you and me can't be left alone.'

'You're so right, Stanley. Who can say where someone will find happiness?' He moved closer on the red velvet bench. 'Even a chance meeting is better than solitude. I have only these few moments to escape from the pressure of my work.'

'What do you do?'

'I'm in technical research. Just a statistician, you might say. When do you have to go home again?'

'I was suspended for the first term, so I don't really have to be back until after Christmas. My grandmother was kind enough to give me a decent allowance after my father insisted that I get a job delivering things, or something like that. It's all my stepmother's fault. All she ever thinks about is his money, or her dirty old pussy.'

'Do you have enough to live on comfortably? I'd hate to think that someone as sensitive as you would have to live from hand to mouth. It's so unreasonable that people don't seem to be able to accept other people's preferences.'

'Oh, I have enough to get by on, if I don't eat too much.' He smiled a girl's smile and looked deprecatingly at his narrow chest and hollow stomach.

'Well,' said Arthur, running his fingers tentatively up and down the zipper, 'I think that we can probably change that. I'm not the kind of person to let others suffer while I have plenty. I envy your youth. It must be wonderful to be sixteen, and free of all the prejudices of the adult world. People trying to make you do things you don't want to do all the time. And trying to keep you from the things that give you the greatest pleasure.'

Stanley indicated by his posture that Arthur's hand was not bothering him. He looked from the corner of his eye and said conspiratorially, 'Once I found out what I really like, nobody could stop me. An old man blew me in the movies once when I was twelve. After that, I knew I had found something that would give me pleasure. When did you fall in love for the first time, Arthur?'

'Oh it took me a long time. I didn't even jack off till I was fourteen. I was very busy at school. My work has always been important to me. My mother was a real stickler when it came to my work. She made me understand that I should never let anything get in the way of my making something of myself. There was a girl across the street, I would give her half of my allowance and she would let me stick my fingers in her and she would show me her tits, but I wasn't really interested. She would touch me sometimes,' he closed his fingers, 'but she never let me come or anything. She was the one that got me in trouble in the beginning. We were in her bathroom and I got hard and she said that she wouldn't help me.' His voice took on a whine. 'And I pushed her down because I wanted to do something to her, but she yelled. Her brother, he was sixteen, must have just come home. He came into the bathroom and found us wrestling on the floor. He threw his sister out of the room. My pants were down and he threw me across the bathtub and hit me across the backside with his hand. He must have hit me fifty times. Then he stopped. It sounded like he was out of breath, and I was crying that he should let me go. Then he took something out of the medicine cabinet. It must have been Vaseline.' He giggled. 'After that, I used to give money to him every week.'

La Mar adjusted the black belt which held his white silk

kimono closed, slipped his feet into his clogs and rose to answer the knock at the door. The small office at the back of the Stereo opened onto a street opposite the main entrance of the club, and was insulated against the noise on the other side of an adjoining door.

Pineau sniffed suspiciously as he preceded Tombal and La Brousse into the room. 'This place smells like a whorehouse. Don't you ever wash?'

La Mar held a handkerchief to his nose. 'I might ask you the same question. Who is this man, Commissaire Tombal?'

Tombal shut the door behind him and sat down in a small chair next to the door. 'Shut up, La Mar. That's General Pineau. This is M. La Brousse. Now if you don't want me to find two ounces of heroin in your desk drawer, you'll answer their questions politely.' Tombal lifted his nose. 'And besides, it does smell like a whorehouse. Why does a man who has three children play at this game?'

La Mar flopped down in the desk chair, threw up his feet and lit the long black cigar he had pulled from the desk drawer. He threw the handkerchief on the floor and grinned broadly, 'It impresses my clients. What can I do for you, gentlemen? Would you like a drink?'

The General cut in on Tombal. 'You wouldn't happen to have a bottle of white wine sitting around?'

'Champagne if you like.'

'No. In my youth, yes. But now it gives me gas. How did you get into the business of pimping for fags?'

La Mar choked slightly on the cigar. 'You are certainly direct, General. Well, I was running a rather unimpressive little bar on this very site about six years ago. I had bought it with the remains of what was going to be the largest motorboat dealership in Marseilles. My wife and I took turns poisoning the tourists and serving watered drinks. We managed to hold on that first summer. But we were so broke, we stayed here in a little rented house all winter. Kids and all. The locals were rather slow to accept us. They tried to get the man who rented us this place to close us down, so there would be less competition in the off-season. Fortunately, he was too stingy to give it a second thought. The next May, I guess it was, a couple of fags walked in around dinner time. They had the place virtually to themselves. It was sheer luck that I still had a couple of bottles of cassis and some white wine. If they had ordered much else I wouldn't have been able to serve them. They were playing around and dancing to the radio. My wife said I should throw them out. They were my only customers, so I told her to go home instead. They thanked me when they went home, and came back the next day with three more. My wife hasn't been back since. We have a big house in the heights of Grimaud, and the kids are away at school in the winter at Marseilles. And now I have red velvet on the walls and anything you can think of at the bar. But no more food. Just sandwiches.'

General Pineau wiped the wine from his mustache and put the pipe back in the corner of his mouth. 'I'll bet you won't still be working at my age. But then, of course, you may not still be here at my age.'

La Mar nodded in agreement and took a sip from his glass. 'Very likely, General. Very likely.'

'You knew the policeman who got killed?'

'Riez. Yes, I guess you could say we were friends. He never bothered the customers or the club. And I made sure that nothing unpleasant happened here. Nothing illegal in a large sense, you understand. I also occasionally provided a useful bit of information. He was a nice man, I felt sorry.'

'I know you were questioned,' the General continued, 'but I want to ask a little more. I read your statement. Did you ever see a Portuguese kid here, about sixteen? Thin? Pretty?'

'Possibly. They come and go. If you read what I had to say, you know that I was aware of Lambert. He was what we call a heavy cruiser.'

'So? He was here often, then. He was the one I wondered about, as far as the Portuguese kid goes.'

'A heavy cruiser is one who picks them up and puts them down just as fast. He changed faces with the ticking of the clock. I never got to know him. I never even talked to him.

But he had a substantial source of funds. He was very good-looking. One would have thought that he was a seller rather than a buyer. But on the contrary. He was forever buying drinks for that trash out there. He liked them young. That's why I was aware of him. That was one of my deals with Riez. No funny stuff on the premises, and no juveniles. It's hard to police, sometimes, but when they show up straight out of grade school, as they sometimes do, we catch them on the doorstep and throw them out. If they want to peddle themselves, they can do it elsewhere. The tough ones are the ones that grow big or fast. Sometimes you get a kid fifteen the size of a grown man, six feet plus. But we've always done the best we can to cooperate on that score.'

'Do you ever turn any of them in to the police?'

'There have been rare occasions. When the president of such-and-such large company's son has decided to run away, et cetera. We've had a couple of those. Riez would give me a missing persons bulletin from time to time. We would try to cooperate without giving the customers the idea that their privacy was being invaded.' Continuing with enthusiasm, as he poured more wine, La Mar said. 'We had one special case here two summers ago. A kid was getting a reputation around town in the early part of the summer. Except for an occasional stroll through the club in my uniform,' he indicated the robe and the lace handkerchief on the floor, 'to add a little personal touch, I keep away from the place. I am interested in the cash register and the inventory. But there was considerable talk about this kid who for fifteen francs would provide a blow job, or get fucked without ever taking off his clothes. Just slipped his pants down over his hips and bent over. After a while one of the flics picked him up doing a number for some old guy on the rocks beyond the end of the port. He grabbed the old man, and the kid tried to run, but his pants slipped. When the flic caught up with him and turned him over, it turned out that he was a girl.'

The General roared with laughter, the tears streaming

down his face. 'My God, what a farce. She must have ruined the reputation of half of the fags on the Côte d'Azur.'

'She was the weirdest I have ever run across. She was thirteen. Flat as a board. But tall, maybe five-six or five-seven. No hips. Short hair. She looked like just the kind of soft boy these types like the best.'

'Listen, La Mar,' Pineau said, wiping at his mustache again, 'these heavy cruisers you were talking about, are there many of them? Is it a distinct type, like the ones who are the girls and the ones who are the boys?'

'No, not really. It's an economic, rather than a sexual, classification. Many of these fellows have money. We cheat them blind out there. A whisky and soda is forty francs. You are obliged to have at least one drink. We sell tickets at the door. But rarely, even among the dirty old men, do you find one who takes a "drinks are on me" attitude. It's not the style. They come to meet. They try each other on for size, as it were. If the relationship takes, for two days or two months, the one with the money keeps the one who has none. Sometimes they form very real relationships. It's not my bag, but I've been around them long enough to begin to understand.'

'So then you were, as you said, aware of the existence of Pascal because he took this unusual posture. He tried out lots of people.'

'Yes, but he was a phony. Not altogether, but certainly in part. I think he was a switch hitter. Dominic, he's the door-man, told me that he saw Lambert pinching some girl's ass in a car one night. I think that maybe he was hustling on behalf of some other interested party.'

General Pineau forced himself to his feet. 'That is very helpful, La Mar. Two questions. Do you have any idea who his patron might have been? Or where he might live?'

La Mar shook the hand that was thrust at him. 'No, I don't on either score. But Dominic might know. Could you see him in the morning? I don't want to take him off the door, and it would look like hell if you talked to him in front of the club.'

'Let him know that we'll be back in the morning. Is eleven all right?'

As La Brousse, Pineau and Tombal walked out of the office and strolled toward their car, Stanley Harris put his head against Arthur Edelman's shoulder. 'You really are a swell guy, Arthur. That room I'm staying in is pretty crummy. I think it would be great if we could stay together at your house. Do you go to the beach during the day?'

'Oh no. I work from early on in the morning. But you can certainly go if you like. I live behind the beach, but it's a long walk. Do you have a bike?'

'No, I don't.' Stanley sat up. 'I sure wouldn't want to be trapped out there with nothing to do. Especially if you spend the whole day busy with your job.'

Arthur paid and they walked down the quay and through the little alley across the street from the Auberge des Maures where Stanley had his room. Arthur walked up to the Place des Lices while Stanley gathered his clothes, and pulled his Peugeot out of the lot.

'Arthur, where were you? I've been standing out here for ten minutes. I thought you were going to walk out on me.'

Arthur got out of the car. 'Here, let me have that bag. I have a little surprise for you.' He opened the trunk lid, then stood back to watch Stanley's eyes light up as he saw the shiny new Vespa motorbike. 'I bought it at the shop across from the parking lot. Now you'll be able to get around.'

Tombal cursed and slammed on the brakes as Arthur's Peugeot darted out into the alley in front of him. The General, shaken from his reverie, said, 'What's the matter with you, Tombal? If I were a flic, I would give you a ticket for reckless driving. Get us back to our car. Even La Brousse is more competent than you.'

104

Eleven

'I believe that in the end there is a basic misunderstanding in the United States of the needs of the Arab people. They must identify with their history. They must be as large as they see themselves.'

Madeleine stretched herself like a lioness in the sun. 'Yes, Paul. I dare say that they do want that. But in the end what will happen if they do grow to be so large? Won't our Russian friends, in control of all the oil of Araby, be able to pluck Western Europe like a ripe fruit? To turn on the faucet, and turn it off as they see fit.'

'Bah. Jew chatter. The Russians are enough occupied with their Asiatic flank without making trouble for the rest of the world. Their system is a failure. They borrow money from the West to realize the potential of their own resources. They fall behind in marketing and industrial technology No, we have nothing to fear from that quarter. Our risk is from within as always. If we could forget the illusory debt that we owe to the State of Israel, and allow the Arabs their own proper aspirations, then the Arabs would be our friends. It makes good common sense. In any case, my darling, as I have told you before, it's only good business sense. The Israelis have nothing to give us. The Arabs have half the oil reserves of the world. That's the food of industry and earnings. And productive power is what makes the world go round.'

'Paul, touch me, there.'

'You have no morals,' he said, reaching out to her. 'There, that will do. What if one of the crew should show up?'

She moved her hips up and down rhythmically against his outstretched hand. 'It won't matter to them. They are used to using women. Push harder.'

He took his hand away and smiled down at the writhing naked figure. Then smoothed his gray neat hair. 'I think that fifty is a fine age for a man to enjoy a mistress like you. Have you always been a nymphomaniac?'

'No, Paul. It's really that you bring out the worst in me.' She giggled and looked up at him, sitting relaxed with his long legs crossed in the deck chair at her side. 'I think it's your money.'

He raised a slender arm and slapped her viciously across the stomach, leaving the print of his hand in vivid red on the tanned skin. 'Don't be rude, my darling.'

She pulled the hand between her legs and ground herself against it. 'No, Paul. I won't be. I promise.'

He pulled the hand away with a jerk when he heard footsteps. 'Can't you knock, Aboussara? You walk like a cat.'

'I knock when there are doors, Mr. Fosburgh. There is a radio telephone call for you. Please excuse my clumsiness, madame.'

Madeleine's eyes bored into his back as he crossed the deck to walk down the gangway to the main cabin. Paul rose to his feet, the gold buttons on his blazer glinting in the light, and followed.

Madeleine got to her feet and walked naked to the rail to look across the water from their mooring to Moorea Beach, two hundred yards in the distance. She fumbled at the rail and detached the binoculars from their hook, then picked out a particularly plush young girl lying on her back on the beach. As she watched through the glasses, she began to rub herself slowly against the stanchion.

Below, in the tastefully decorated, paneled salon, Paul Fosburgh lifted the telephone from its cradle. 'Fosburgh, Your Excellency. It's very good to hear from you. I see. You had your meeting and everything is going according to schedule? You found Nicholson to be a satisfactory agent? No, oh no, Your Excellency, we are most happy to co-operate with you in this matter. We are cognizant of the partnership with you that has enabled us to do so well.

When we are given the opportunity to be of service, we are pleased. I look forward to seeing you. I can fly over to Quahrein whenever you need me there. My plane is at Nice. If you should speak to him, please don't forget to give my warmest regards to Colonel Ben Kelb.' He turned the phone over to Aboussara, who began to speak rapidly in Arabic. Waiting, Fosburgh adjusted his patterned silk cravat at a mirror on the door. After a moment, Aboussara replaced the receiver.

Fosburgh said, 'Get New York, Aboussara.' Fosburgh paced while the dark stocky figure hovered over the electronic gear. Aboussara turned and handed him the phone, then moved toward the door. Fosburgh shook his head negatively and motioned him back.

'Hello, yes. Yes, it's Paul. Has there been any further movement? Can you give me any information?' He listened briefly, then replied in an icy voice, 'Even your excuses are stale. I have heard each of them before. I am well aware that you are not privy to this kind of information, but nonetheless it is your job to obtain it.' He paused again, then said with exasperation, 'Let me spell it out for you. There is little question that the type of technical information you are looking for will represent a departure from internal combustion engines. I think that that has been established. What you must find out is what kind of testing program is being carried out. Also very important, is there a working model? Next question, which European plant is being used as a test headquarters? It is clear that no one department has all of the component pieces.' He listened again. 'Well, that indicates that the traverse of information may not be from Detroit or New York to the test facility here.' He frowned and chewed at a fingernail. 'If I were Goodrich, I would insist on having my project origination close at hand, so that I could keep on top of the assembly of information. Then spread out the testing into hard-to-recognize components. Still, it's unrealistic to ignore the possibility that it's being done the other way round. Another thing, the level of progress can be checked through the amount of money spent.

See what you can get out of research budgeting. Look for a special fund. No, no, nothing need have been expended yet, not on a grand scale anyway. What you'll want to see is an unticketed authorization for research marked "Need To Know Only," signed by Goodrich, or possibly by – what's his name – yes, Hultz. The amount will not be the key. It will be the absence of a specific project outline. If I have definitive information that the project exists, that can be backed up through documentation, I can create a confrontation, and insist that Goodrich is exceeding his authority. Have you seen any signs of disruption or confusion in the past couple of weeks?'

He paused again, then said, with rising anger, 'You are unable to tell me even if the elimination of the messenger has slowed their progress. All you really know is that they are at work on a secret project. That is always true in a company the size of General Motors. It is not necessary to support your extravagant tastes in exchange for generalities. Do you know when they are to deliver more information?' He nodded dully. 'Hah, you don't know that either.' His tone changed to ice again, 'If I were you, I would make every effort to improve my performance. My patience is at an end.' He hung up abruptly.

Aboussara stood, emotionless, near the cabin door. Fosburgh drummed his fingers on the table top, then looked up and said, 'It seems that elimination of the messengers creates no visible disruption. Perhaps,' he pondered, 'the flow of information *is* from Europe to America. In which case, if we are to disrupt the chain we must strike at the source here.' He stood. 'Aboussara, when we are informed that another message will be passed, you will not kill the messenger, you will follow him.'

Aboussara nodded slightly.

Fosburgh scratched at his chin, then said, 'Get Anderson for me at the office, then you may leave.' Aboussara moved back to the radio equipment, made the connection, then left without further words.

Fosburgh sat at the edge of a straight-backed chair.

'Andy? Good, how are you. What's going on? That's fine. Yes, I just spoke to El Kaffar. He was his charming self. No. I think they'll keep their agreement, for the time being at least. No further increase in the Quahrein tax bite on Royal American until they get a substantial overall price rise out of their crude. If they get what they're looking for, we should end up, including the projected tax increase, with a realization of about eight to ten percent more per barrel.' He chuckled in reply to Anderson's remark, then listened a moment more. 'You're hearing that too? I have a source that says GM has something hot cooking in non-fossil fuels. Well, I'm trying to keep tabs on it, Andy. But as an outside director, I'm fairly limited in my access to information, especially in consideration of my obvious self-interest. All right, Andy. Just one more thing, you remind those area sales managers that we want the stations to be on the dole for gas. Make them want every gallon they get. Sure, Andy, I know. But, find a way to hold back. Leak it to the independents if you have a storage problem. You know where to find me. Talk to you soon.' Fosburgh hung up, rose, adjusted his jacket, then climbed through the hatchway onto the upper deck. Madeleine sat naked, Indian style, with her face to the sun.

'Please, Paul, can we go to the cabin for a while?'

'Certainly not. It's midafternoon. Perhaps after tea.' He looked at her speculatively. 'You're going to have to be punished for your rudeness, you know, Madeleine.'

She shivered with pleasure and threw herself face down on the divan.

'Scratch my foot.'

'My God, old woman. You have become so demanding as the calendar has passed you by that I may have to get a divorce.' Rhabbouz turned on his side, muttering as the green golf cap fell forward into his eyes, and reached down to attend to the waiting foot.

'Say, Rhabbouz, do you know who that is?'

'Do you mean that old fool over there holding hands with the little Italian?'

'Yes, he's the assistant director of the Opera. Can you imagine?'

'This is the only place where I am a virgin. Why do you like to come here? It's the most expensive beach in Cannes. Fifty francs a day, it costs me. Even if we don't eat. The mattresses, the umbrella. A charge for changing clothes, even when I don't change them. You are quite mad. As I said ... you have become demanding in your old age.'

'Why were you so late getting home the other day?'

'Why do you always ask me the same stupid questions? I told you, I got stuck in a game of pétanque. Then they offered to buy me dinner. Do you expect me to turn down a full plate of Tajine on the house?'

'It must have something to do with that Pineau.'

He stopped scratching. 'My God, Nana, can't you ever shut up? You are the one who is always telling me that I am a retired civil servant and that I should stay out of things. Why are you always looking for trouble? Let me enjoy my declining years. There, I scratched your foot. Now read me the letter from the children.'

When she was halfway through the affectionate banalities from their youngest daughter and her husband, the beach boy came up to them. 'M. Rhabbouz, there is a telephone call for you.'

'Oh merde. Who the hell is that? It's Saturday afternoon. I want to enjoy the sun. Maybe it's one of the kids.'

He walked awkwardly over the burning sand to the cabana at the back of the beach and took the phone. Hearing the voice at the other end, he turned his face to the wall. 'What's the matter, Emil? What? That old son of a bitch. He's set him up. He must be using him for bait. Where did you get this from? François? Should be the real thing then. He's trying to flush out the problem. He must be in a hell of a hurry. Did we make a report to him? No? No contact since that charming dinner at your place? No repercussions on that? Fine. Inch' Allah. They must not have reported where they were going. How's business? Ah, good, glad to hear it. Shalom, Emil.'

He bit at his fingernail for a moment, then hung up the phone. He lifted it again and started to dial, then changed his mind and hung up. He quietly edged his way toward the stairs which led to the level of the street. He crossed quickly, wincing as a pebble ground into the sole of his bare foot, and dodged into the telephone kiosk on the sidewalk of the Croisette in front of the Grand Hôtel.

'Kalman, go to the parking lot of Moorea Beach. Hamilton is there. Yes, that's the American who found the fag. Follow him. Watch out. He will be followed by someone from SDEC. He's been set up. It's all very good to exchange information but I want mine too. And keep your eyes on your work. I am told that he's with a girl with long black hair and great tits. You have his picture, right? Fine. Stay well, friend. No, I don't think that he's your responsibility. I am sure that the General will try to keep him alive. Keep your nose down.'

When he returned to the beach, Nana was sitting up, reading a magazine. 'You know, you are going to have to do something about your kidneys. Or perhaps your liver. I saw you go to the phone, and then you disappeared. The bathroom again. You are not regular. You should see a doctor.'

He patted her head. 'Bah. You worry too much. I just overindulged myself. It will pass.'

Avoiding the algae and the rocks in the little cove, Hamilton threw himself naked into the tepid water and came up blowing like a whale. Marie Jo lay exhausted on the little patch of sand between the rocks under the cliff. Streaks of red spread in the western sky as the sun began to set, and the wind picked up.

He returned to the beach and struggled into his bathing suit.

'Come on. Let's go. It's a long walk back to Moorea.'

'I'm coming,' she said, without moving. 'I'll be with you

in a second.' He pulled her to her feet and kissed her firmly on the mouth. 'You can't go like that.' He knelt in front of her and slipped the suit around her feet as she leaned for balance on his shoulders.

When she leaned over to pull up the suit, he kissed her breast.

'That's nice. You made up to me for leaving me on my own all that time.'

'Oh, I didn't mind. I guess I'm just good-natured that way.'

They wound their way around the rocks, then walked the crescent of beach to the middle of the Bay of Pampelonne and Moorea. The beach was almost empty. They hurried to their mattress and pulled on their clothes.

'Let's have one last drink. I love to stand here while the sun goes down.'

'L'heure douce, we call it,' she said.

'I'll tell you what. We'll have our drink, then see how the traffic is, leading out of town. If it isn't too bad, I'll take you to La Bouillabaisse at St. Raphael. Then we can come back here and dance at Papagayo till we feel like going home.'

'We could really stay overnight.'

'What the hell. It's not a long drive, especially late at night without anybody on the road. And besides, there's no guarantee that we could find anything here anyway.'

At about seven they finished their drinks and walked arm in arm to the lot. As they pulled out onto the dirt road, they heard the sound of a motorcycle engine starting. If Hamilton had looked in his rear-view mirror as he sped down the Tahiti Beach Road toward St. Tropez, he would have noticed that he was followed at regular intervals by two cars and the motorcycle.

Twelve

It was unusual that an accredited Ambassador of a sovereign state arrived at the White House in a plain black Chevrolet sedan with GAO plates. But Samuel Zvi Aharon was inured to what he called the 'Jew's Gate' of 1600 Pennsylvania Avenue. A quick check of his false identity papers, and those of his driver, an officer in the Presidential Secret Service contingent, and he was whisked past the trade entrance and through the kitchen to the elevator whose sole egress was seventy feet below ground.

Unaccompanied, he walked down the corridor to the shining steel alloy door and pushed at the red button beside it. A small panel beneath the button opened, exposing a plastic plate. He put his right hand between the indicated graven lines and waited as the mechanism whirred, and the door slid soundlessly open. He stepped inside through the metal-detecting portal and knocked at the wooden door before him.

'Come in, Mr. Ambassador.'

He turned the handle and entered into a softly lit paneled room with comfortable furniture and a complicated-looking telephone console, manned by a braided and bemedaled officer with two gold stars on his shoulder boards. The President of the United States stood in another portal in baggy slacks and a tee shirt.

Jack Kugel appeared at his side, waved and said, 'Come in, Sam.'

The President smiled and shook hands with Aharon, then ushered him into the office, guiding him to a chair.

As Aharon sat down he smiled. 'I can't make up my mind whether you have invited me to a traditional Sunday breakfast of bagels and lox or to ask me to surrender Dizengoff Street as a final solution to your energy problems.'

'Shall we say,' said the President, 'a combination of both.'

Sharp black eyes glittered through round thick lenses above the jowly cherubic face. 'It is fortunate for both of us that I have already satisfied my famed appetite. Is there something happening in our little corner of the world about which you wish to inform me?'

Smith rose and stretched. 'Quite the contrary. I was rather wondering if there was something that you knew that you wanted to tell me.'

'I am not famed for my reticence. You asked me to come here, Mr. President, on the Sunday morning of Labor Day weekend, with the precautions usually reserved for more unusual occasions – wars, and such.'

'Let's not fence, Mr. Aharon. You are aware that Mohammed El Kaffar has been in to see me recently. He made an unusual proposition to me. Or rather, an unusual set of demands.'

'Unusual even for him?'

'Shall we say, unusual even for Colonel Ben Kelb.'

'I would not pretend that I am not curious.'

'The demands were in keeping with the usual public bombast, but they have not been accompanied by such bombast. Both Mr. Kugel and I have spent the last several days, in conjunction with certain members of the Cabinet, trying to discover what the source of his desire for a new confrontation might be. So far as we can tell, nothing has changed. Further, our sources in and near Quahrein tell us that they know nothing. I thought that you and I might have a chat to see if the Shin Bet has come up with something.'

Aharon took off his glasses and began an elaborate cleaning ritual. He put the glasses back on his nose and studied his fingernails.

The President sat down again and waited. Kugel, silent, sipped at a cup of coffee.

'I checked with home on the scrambler,' the Ambassador said conversationally, 'before I came. There has been no military movement of any moment by any of our neighbors in any meaningful period of time. There is nothing that I can tell you about the opening and closing of the oil faucet. You know more than we do. And besides, that's always done on the front page of *The New York Times*.' He leaned forward a bit in the chair. 'Naturally, we would like to know what he said. But I certainly don't want you to think that we are prying. After all, in the end we only have one ally. We don't want to seem presumptuous.'

President Smith bit at his lower lip, feeling the frustration that generally accompanied his meetings with Aharon. An ex-Oxford don, he combined Talmudic logic with an oriental turn of mind, and an exquisite command of the English language.

Kugel, watching the now-tapping foot, intervened. 'Sam, I think that the President would like to know if there is any information available from the Shin Bet as to why we would suddenly be confronted with a hardening of the position of Quahrein with respect to our oil supplies. What can they do militarily? They have three million citizens and an army of twenty thousand. The literacy rate is among the lowest in the world. The hundred and something Mirage IIIs are ...'

'One hundred and seventeen,' Aharon interrupted.

'Okay, one hundred seventeen. They are about five hundred miles away from you. You tell me that there are no movements either on the Syrian or Egyptian sides. A simple answer to a simple question, Sam – do you know anything?'

There was another pause. 'Gentlemen, I will give you a personal opinion. Of all of our neighbors, I underestimate Mohammed El Kaffar the least. In a book I read once, in the office of a banker friend in Zurich, there was a history of Russia. In the twelfth century, I think, there was a Czar named Vladimir Monomakh. He had various internal problems which prevented him from taking power as he wished. He had what you like to call a lack of consensus. He agreed, it is said, to accept the throne and its responsibilities, only after a "general mobbing of the Jews." El Kaffar understands that principle. We are necessary to them in terms of time. We are at least necessary to El Kaffar in his time frame. He is the intellectual. He has played the beast. He has played the jingo, the revolutionary, the warmonger. But of all of our neighbors, he is the one who understands the principle of cashing in your chips while you are ahead of the game. How much do you expend each year in government funds to produce alternatives to fossil fuels? An alternative, let us be realistic – to oil. Ten billions is it now, or is it fifteen? Nuclear power for electrical energy, hydrogen as a supplement or replacement for gasoline, solar power, battery-powered and steam-powered cars, extraction of liquid fuel from shale in Colorado or the three-hundred-year supply of coal with which you have been invested. El Kaffar understands that there is a short fuse on the oil bomb. That is my personal judgment. You want to know what the Shin Bet knows? You may have it. You have paid. The Jews of America have paid, in terms of gold, for that which we lose and have lost in terms of blood and youth. Shin Bet, as of ten minutes before I left the Embassy, knows nothing of importance. Had they known, you would have been informed as a matter of course. Either through me, or CIA or Foggy Bottom, or any of the channels that we have developed over the years.'

He stood and began to pace. 'I don't know what El Kaffar hung over your heads. I don't know what threat, empty or otherwise, he laid at your door. But I can tell you that of all of our neighbors he is the one to be feared the most. If he were not burdened with that raving lunatic Ben Kelb, he would be the first man of Araby. Because in the end, he is not willing to build a bank account in Switzerland. Mohammed El Kaffar is a patriot and an idealist. If I were you, gentlemen, I would not look to the Shin Bet. We are preoccupied with being Jews, with being hounded, chased, with wandering and dying, and spending eternity as lampshades for German sadists. El Kaffar is less interested in killing us than in using us. Look to your own backyard, Mr. President. Look to those who would profit from the last vestiges of an energy crisis created by a failure to foresee the future. Or possibly,' he stood gazing candidly at the President, 'those who understand as well as El Kaffar that hay must be made while the sun shines. To whom is conscience subordinated to profit? Who has placed the largest bet on Middle Eastern oil?

'You support us because you have understood that if the Middle East were controlled by the client states of your adversary, a Europe without your resources would fall. We harbor no illusions. We have had two thousand years to become inured to being dirty Jews. You must recognize that Mohammed El Kaffar has had nearly the same period of history to grow distasteful of being a camel driver. What he will seek this time is not military. He is feinting, Mr. President. There is no new Masada in the offing. I would say that he fears his friends to the East as much as he fears you, and certainly more than he fears us. But his greatest fear is that the time for action will pass him by. He does not want to be another anomalous ink blot in the confused history of the Arab peoples. As I said before, I hold no mysterious secrets. There is nothing in the Cabala to assuage your concern. I fear that this time the devious Jews have nothing to hide from their allies.'

The Ambassador left, with the thanks of Smith and Kugel, to spend the rest of the day with his family. Neither Smith nor Kugel, sitting in their leather chairs, said a word for several minutes after he left.

'Jack, I don't like having to ask him for something. And I don't like him *not* asking me. I don't want there to be another Masada. I won't let there be another Masada while I hold office. But he doesn't act like a client.' He rubbed his hands on his knees. 'Get me everything that you can find on Paul Fosburgh, and anyone else you think may have a vested interest in Quahrein.'

Thirteen

In a country with standstill traffic and good weather, a motorcycle is a great advantage. There are many of them on the French Riviera. They range from the smallest Velosolex bikes, with 49-cc motors that fit on the front wheel, costing about one hundred twenty-five dollars, to the great Japanese and German racing machines and street bikes that come equipped with 750-cc to 1100-cc engines capable of going up to one hundred forty miles per hour, and cost three thousand dollars or more.

Abdul Aboussara was mounted on a Honda 750. While Hamilton, followed by both a French agent and an Israeli one, struggled ten feet at a time down the road, Aboussara zipped between the lanes of stranded automobiles to a cafe at the crossroads of La Foux, and waited.

Though by preference an active man, Aboussara had learned the lessons of patience, first growing up in the agonizingly poor Palestinian village of his birth, then in the trenchant filth of a refugee camp in Jordan after 1948. He had learned a mechanic's trade in the camp during the same period that he became a silent soldier in the cause of his people. When King Yaoud fell and Ben Kelb took power, he walked a thousand miles on the Mediterranean coastline to join the revolution in Quahrein.

About six months before, Colonel Ben Kelb had placed him aboard the yacht of the American oil man Fosburgh. 'Watch him,' the Colonel had said, 'and await my instructions.' He had suffered patiently with the stoicism of his race and of all good soldiers the indignities that had been heaped upon him as second mate of the *Glen Pool*. Though Fosburgh knew that he was an agent of Ben Kelb, he treated him as a servant nonetheless.

Then his orders came. A message was to be delivered by a foreigner to a man on the dock at St. Tropez. The man would be recognizable by a rose behind his ear. He must not live to pass the message on.

Abdul Aboussara stretched his shoulders, then relaxed and leaned against the bike, watching the oncoming traffic. He felt a certain pride in having performed his duty well. The man with the rose was no more. He kicked in annoyance at the powdery dust beneath his feet. Then, he thought, things began to go wrong. Things beyond his control. First that damn fool had gone into the cabin. Perhaps he had seen something. He pictured Hamilton in his mind's eye. Perhaps he had been another link in the chain. Hamilton had been on the beach, he could have talked to Lambert before Aboussara had had his chance. Then that damn cop, poking around, could have exposed him, or prevented him from further serving Ben Kelb. The cop had had to be eliminated. He had phoned Ben Kelb. Get rid of the other man at the beach, Ben Kelb had told him. Take no chances. If he is a part of the system to transmit these messages, he must be eliminated. If he is not, nothing will be lost by his death.

Aboussara raised his head, then mounted and started his motor. Hamilton passed in his car talking comfortably to his girlfriend, followed by the car that had passed him on the Tahiti Road. They turned toward Ste. Maxime at the crossroads. Aboussara waited a moment or two more, then followed after them. Impatient with the crawling traffic which seemed to cover the coastal road as far as he could see, Hamilton turned left at the Casino in Ste. Maxime and sped off on the nearly empty road to Le Muy and the Autoroute. Aboussara hung back to confirm his suspicion that Hamilton was being followed by the second car. When he was sure, he sped past both of them to the toll booth at Fréjus and parked in the gas station beyond it, feigning a minor motor adjustment. He watched as Hamilton, and then the second car, a black Peugeot 404, exited from the Autoroute and turned down the hill toward St. Raphael.

Kalman Jacobs, the Shin Bet agent, armed with a bit of conversation that the assistant bartender at Moorea had passed along, struggled down the coast road through St. Aygulf and into St. Raphael. He parked on the side of the railroad overpass that crosses the Place du Marché and waited. First Hamilton and his girl, and then their shadow, arrived at the little hotel and restaurant, Donald and Marie Jo choosing a table on the sidewalk outside.

The French shadow the General had provided, an Action Force tough, took a table inside, near the door. A grim man, tall and forbidding, with crew-cut blond hair and a wicked scar over his right eye.

'Bah,' Kalman said to himself, 'you would think that they typecast them for the role. If Hamilton had any sense, he would spot that oaf a mile away.' He stretched his legs across the front seat of his car and began to read his paper.

'Jesus, if I eat another bit, I'm going to drop dead. Look,' said Donald, pushing his chair away from the table, 'look at that, will you? It looks like I swallowed an inflated balloon.'

Marie Jo sucked elegantly at the claw of her last langoustine, wiped her fingers on the cloth tied around her neck and began a new attack on the soup.

'Where the hell do you put it? It doesn't show in a dress. It doesn't even show when you're naked. I hate people who eat without showing it.'

Marie Jo tidied up the plate, eyed the platter on the service table to the side, still heaped with fish, took a sip at her wine and said, 'All right. I give up too. My God, I wonder if anybody ever finishes what they serve here.'

'Hell, look at that poor guy in there by the door. The one with that awful scar. He has hardly touched his.'

After they left the table, they took a walk on the waterfront, busy with laughing people and running children. Half an hour later, they returned to the car and headed for home.

When the Israeli agent saw them climb into the little sports car, he put down his paper and waited. They drove off and he hummed to himself patiently, expecting to see the shadow appear momentarily. After two or three minutes had passed, Kalman Jacobs began to get nervous. He started the engine of his car and pulled off in the same direction that Hamilton had taken, toward the highway.

Robert, the General's shadow, had paid when he saw Hamilton pull his chair out. The SDEC man had walked across the street to a row of shops and begun examining the merchandise in their windows, at the same time watching Hamilton and the girl through their reflections in the glass. When they left he followed them for a short distance. Convinced that they were simply going for a walk, he returned to his own car, which was parked around the corner, to wait for the exaggerated sound of Hamilton's supercharged engine a block behind him, and to his rear.

He stood for a moment beside the car, taking a cigarette, its coarse black tobacco wrapped in yellow paper, from the pack in his pocket. He took out the key and let himself in, then closed the door, put his hands on the steering wheel and stared out into the darkness through the windshield.

Soundlessly, in one fluid motion, Aboussara moved from the floor in the back seat of the car. Before Robert could react, Aboussara had pulled the six-inch strand of piano wire attached to two hardwood sticks against his throat. Exerting very little of his own strength, he crossed the sticks behind Robert's neck, crushing the agent's larynx and severing his spinal cord. Aboussara quickly removed the sticks. The dead man's eyes stared blankly at his lap, the unsupported head lolled, chin against the chest. His hands still clutched the steering wheel. Aboussara pushed the button on the long knife he had taken from his pocket. He reached out with both hands and with a practiced motion cut Robert's throat from ear to ear. He ducked down again and wiped the knife and the blood-stained wire with a cloth from his back pocket, then checking first to make sure that the street was empty, opened the door, got out of the car and walked unhurriedly to his motorcycle. He stopped for a moment at a trash barrel, pulled the sticks apart from the wire and dropped one of them in. He stuffed the wire in his pocket and threw the other stick into an empty lot. Operating with the same conviction and instinct as Kalman Jacobs, he drove his bike to the top of the hill near the entrance to the Autoroute and pulled to the side of the road, shutting off his motor to wait in the dark.

'Have I ever tried to teach you dirty songs?'

'Not that I remember. Do you want to? How would you like it if you sang the dirty songs while I did a belly dance?'

Donald paid the toll. 'That would suit me fine. As a matter of fact, almost anything would suit me fine. I had a splendid day at the beach, met interesting people, ate too well and . . .'

'Yes?'

'Got laid. None of which,' he squeezed her hand, 'is bad. Hey, let's find out how fast this thing will go.' The road ahead, though unlighted, was broad and well banked. Though it was still relatively early in the evening, there was no traffic. He tromped on the accelerator and the needle on the speed indicator spun past the hundred mile an hour mark. The air from her open window snapped Marie Jo's hair into a flowing stream behind her.

Aboussara, who had started only half a minute behind them, was hard pressed to catch up. He leaned forward over the handlebars to reduce the resistance of the wind straining against his body, and thus huddled watched the dial, with its faint green light, as he hurtled along through the darkness in pursuit.

It had taken Kalman Jacobs a short time to realize that he had made a serious mistake in judgment. While it was not important that he keep track of the SDEC tail that General Pineau had put on Hamilton, he had counted too much on Robert's professionalism to do the work assigned to him. He was sure that Hamilton had headed home. He waited impatiently as the guard at the toll booth fumbled at some papers before handing him his change. He hoped that the Renault 17, which had been bought with a little help from Shin Bet special funds, would prove sufficient to catch up with Hamilton's superior machine.

'Have you had enough fun, Donald? Come on, please slow down. If you bump into something this car will disintegrate and take us with it. Besides, I'm freezing. This wind is blowing me to pieces. Please, Donald.'

'Spoilsport.' He took his foot from the accelerator and smiled with satisfaction as the engine began to wind down and the speed dropped. At ninety, he exerted a steady pressure on the pedal to hold it at speed. 'That okay?'

'Yes, how fast were we going?'

'It's hard to tell with a factory-installed speedometer, but give or take five miles, one hundred and thirty. Were you scared?'

'I may have wet my pants. Christ, look at that nut.'

Aboussara passed them without slowing down. He continued at a shattering pace for about ten minutes, well past the exit at Le Muy. He pulled the bike off the side of the road and shut it off, sitting beneath a tree at the blind side of a curve on top of the hill. He figured that he had gained about three minutes.

The tire blew and Marie Jo screamed as Donald fought to regain control of the careening automobile. Her eyes wide with fright, she watched the beams cut first to one side and then to the other of the black pavement. Her voice mingled with the sound of peeling rubber as the three remaining tires gripped uncertainly at the road's surface. The smell of burning brakes filled the car. Turning desperately in the direction of the last skid, Hamilton threw his right arm across her chest to protect her from the expected impact. Then, with the sound of gravel splashing on the shoulder, the car spun to an abrupt halt, one wheel in the air against the embankment.

Kalman Jacobs clung grimly to the wheel of his car and strained to bring the last ounce of pressure to bear on the accelerator, his foot pressed against the floorboards. The needle would not move past one hundred seventy kilometers, and he still heard nothing of Hamilton's car in front of him. He came around a huge curve, tires squealing, on to a straightway with a slight downhill pitch, gaining a little extra speed. Rounding the curve at the bottom, he smiled and reduced his speed a little. Fixed in the bright lights a half a mile down the road, Hamilton rolled his spare tire along the ground toward the front wheel, while Marie Jo sat, disconsolate and shaking, on the grass of the roadside bank.

Kalman sped by to wait for them at the exit at Le Luc, where Route 98 descends to the sea and Toulon.

Aboussara listened intently, as he waited in the dark. Either his sense of time was misleading him, or Hamilton had slowed down further still. He pulled the cork from the one-liter wine bottle he had taken from the saddlebag at the back of his motorcycle and spilled some of the gasoline on the blood-stained rag from his pocket. He replaced the cork so that it held part of the rag firmly in the neck of the bottle, well submerged in the gasoline. He took a sulfur match from his pocket and held it between his teeth. Then he took another which he held in his hand. He cocked his head slightly when he heard the racing engine. Staying well within the shadow cast by the great tree, he edged his way toward the road. When he judged from the sound of the motor that the car was at the bottom of the turn, he struck the match in his hand against the zipper of his pants. It broke without light, and he cursed silently, took the other from his mouth and struck it against a stone at his feet. He held the flame to the rag just as the lights streamed past the curve, and cocked his arm. With practiced judgment, he waited until the headlights were level on the road, giving him the broadest angle, then threw the bottle above and between the lights.

Kalman Jacobs saw only a brief flash of light and then his windshield spider-cracked and splintered with the impact of the flying bottle, showering him with glass and flaming gasoline. He screamed, slapping futilely at his burning face before he lost control of the car. It pitched violently into the restraining barrier in the centre of the road, flipped into the air and crashed on its roof, exploding as the burning fluid from the bottle mingled with the gas from the ruptured tank.

Aboussara started his machine and pulled onto the road. He sped off without looking back.

Moments later, his tire repaired, his speed tempered by his recent close call, Hamilton approached the wreck of Kalman Jacob's car. 'Oh Holy Jesus. Look at that.' Hamilton pulled to the side of the road. The flickering light of the still-burning car cast shadows on Marie Jo's ashen wide-eyed face.

He got out of the car and ran across the road. He swallowed against the sour taste rising in his mouth as he looked down at the mangled and disfigured corpse. He knelt by the terribly burned body, seeking without hope a remaining trace of life. The clothes and hair had been burned off, and the features were unrecognizable. On one twisted forearm not entirely blackened by heat and smoke, he could make out faint blue numbers tattooed on the death-white skin.

Fourteen

Secretary of the Interior Walton Carver moved uncomfortably on the rustic bench and clenched his hands while he listened. When the President had finished he began to speak again, following the same line of reasoning that he had used during the entire evening. 'But, Mr. President, we are not just talking about a fundamental flaw in an energy policy or the exhaustion of resources. No, sir, we are talking about an underlying characteristic of the American way of life. Mobility is, at least as I see it, the most universal of all American characteristics.'

Smith leaned on the window sill and looked out into the still air of the low Maryland mountains. 'The concern of the moment is to comprehend how best we may use the resources at our disposal. What I am disputing with you is the possibility that the national characteristic of mobility is the great national flaw. If it is, then we should seek measures to change the pattern permanently rather than find new ways to pander to an old bad habit.

'Mr. Secretary,' continued the President, turning back to face him, 'we represent six percent of the world's population, but use about one-third of the world's energy resources. A large part of those currently irreplaceable resources are expended in what our neighbors and some of our best and most serious thinkers feel is unnecessary waste. We have developed a life style in which we have become inured to use energy as we see fit. We cannot gorge ourselves on our own resources and then reach out for those needed desperately by others and expect to be cordially welcomed. Do more, bigger and faster cars represent progress to you, Mr. Secretary?'

'Isolated, out of context, Mr. President, certainly not. But as a part of the ability to interchange ideas, to broaden the availability of education and material goods, to the degree that a twelve-million-car year means those things, yes. People should never be hungry or cold or unclothed. But more important, they should not be deprived of ambition and personal initiative that stems from the desire for personal gain. The tools of equality, and the educational tools to excel, must be provided by the government to everyone. But the variation in the abilities to use such benefits to excel cannot be legislated out of existence.'

Oscar Johansson cleared his throat, and the others in the room turned to look at him. The Secretary of State stood, gaunt and imposing, a perpendicular element against the great stone which formed the mantel of the fireplace. A gold chain glinted from the pockets of his waistcoat.

In a low-pitched but pervasive bass voice, Johansson intoned, 'We are faced with a circumstance in which a purveyor of a much-needed product to this country is, in fact, going beyond the bounds of ordinary blackmail to which we have become so inured. I have at least intellectually understood the position of the Arab governments with respect to the sale of their most important, in reality, their sole, resource. They are no less anxious to protect the future of their inhabitants than we are. We have been saturated with statistics illustrating that in the absense of a manifest change in our own resources at our current rate of growth, we will be dependent for about twenty-five percent of our energy supplies on the Middle East in five years. In one sense, we have been well served by Mr. El Kaffar. Well before the point of no return, we have been officially notified that if we do not change our foreign policy to the detriment of our allies, and to the detriment of world security, the severest strictures will be applied against us. There were times in the history of the world, gentlemen, when that has been considered cause for war.'

The silence in the room became palpable. The President looked at the man he had chosen to formulate the country's foreign policy. 'Do I understand you correctly, Mr. Secretary? Are you suggesting that we take a preemptive military action against the Republic of Quahrein?'

'I am suggesting that the possibility exists that if we wish to maintain our economic interest in the Middle East, or rather to preserve a non-aligned balance in this part of the world, to save Europe from following the Soviet Union unwillingly in the Balkan manner, it may be necessary to encourage a political change in Quahrein. Possibly a popular revolution by parties whose views are more like our own. It may be necessary to point out to our allies in the area that there are indications that Quahrein is financing an imminent attack on them by their neighbors. It is possible that in the face of a massive move by their government to preempt or destroy the assets of the eight thousand American citizens there, it will be necessary for us to protect them with military force.'

George Gaines, the Secretary of Defense, said, 'You know, sir, that we have such a contingency plan. It could be implemented in three stages. Each of them would take forty-eight hours. Six days in all.'

President Smith turned, staring wide-eyed at the Cabinet officers before him. He began to speak, then chewed nervously at his finger. To fill the gap, Gaines continued. 'I don't think that it will be necessary to bring the maneuver to its conclusion. I believe that El Kaffar is bluffing. If, however, it is required that we intervene, I am sure that it can be made clear to our Soviet counterparts that we are acting in the interest of world safety and not purely for the purpose of expanding our own hegemony. They are well aware that we cannot permit an unreasonable reduction of the international security balance.'

'I've had a tiring day, gentlemen. I think it would be better for all of us if we could continue this discussion in the morning. May I ask you not to go back to town tonight? It's already ten. I don't like to keep you from your families, but under the circumstances, it would be in our mutual interest to meet at, shall we say, nine, for breakfast.'

They glanced at each other, and without further discussion, shook hands and bid the President good night, then filed out to make their phone calls, and to retire to their rooms and their thoughts.

The President fell heavily into the leather chair and looked blankly at the ceiling. 'Are they serious?'

Kugel pulled himself upright, went to the bar and busied himself with the making of drinks. He rattled the cubes of ice against the glass and Smith reached out to take it from him. 'They're not all mad, are they, Jack? They are contemplating the beginning of the Third World War.'

'They are considerate men, Mr. President. I think that they have come to the conclusion that we cannot be pushed any further without serious physical damage to the country. I'm not talking in terms of posture. They clearly feel that the strategic position of the United States of America would be so impinged by what El Kaffar demands, that we would eventually succumb, either by being nibbled to death or in the course of war.'

'Do you agree with them, then?'

Kugel's shoulders bent, as if under a mammoth weight. 'Quahrein crude represents about four percent of our imports. If you add to that the refined products imported from other industrial nations which are derived from Quahrein crude, it adds up to seven percent of our consumption. In my opinion, the elimination of that source, or even of the use of that source as a bargaining token in international politics, represents an intolerable threat to our security. Add to that the threatened destruction of so much more ...'

Smith shook his head in disbelief. 'I'm not sure that any one man is prepared for the physical or intellectual weight of the Presidency. Is there a reasonable reading on the likelihood of real reprisal by the Soviet Union if we act according to this plan?'

'I don't know, but I'm sure that Gaines has it documented. Those are statistics. The question is really what your sense of the Chairman's probable reaction is. Will he fight if we act in Quahrein?'

Smith stood up abruptly. 'It's a question that I don't want to consider just yet. My God. I have a pain in my intellect. I know, instinctively, that this is wrong. Wrong as hell! But what are the real alternatives? Get a piece of paper. I want the following: a digest of all alternative sources of crude oil, domestic and foreign, together with delivery dates; an outline of domestic refining capacity and planning with completions; a précis on the availability and consumption of coal, nuclear energy, hydroelectric and hydrothermal power projects; and the cost and possibility of conversion of all conceivable present uses of oil to an alternative source of power, including natural gas, and where we stand on that. Further, I want to meet with, and you work this out with Walton, a group of five or six oil people. The biggest, the most trustworthy, and particularly, the most reasonable. Monday is Labor Day. Make it Wednesday. In my office. Throw up a screen for the press.' He stopped to ponder for a moment. 'Get hold of Milton Goodrich, Jack.'

'You're fishing in troubled waters. He's not a Smith supporter.'

'He has talent and courage. I want to see him on Tuesday. Give us the whole morning. Make it here. No reporters if possible. It seems to me that I can use an outside opinion. Then there's Congress.'

Kugel's face brightened for the first time in several hours. 'Yes indeed, sir. As you say, there is then Congress. To which group of lions would you like to be thrown first?'

'I think that we'll hold the lions at bay for the moment, Jack. I want to find out what I think we should do first on the basis of information. We'll get done with the Cabinet tomorrow. Then I'll get the data from you. Then Goodrich. Then the oil people. Then we'll try out the leaders of the House and Senate. Strictly person to person. And Jack, bipartisan.'

'Yes, sir.' He frowned.

'What's on your mind, Jack?'

'Milt Goodrich. There are lots of other people that you could choose.'

'I don't have time, Jack. He is responsible for the largest corporate entity in this country, in its most important industry. I want a feel for the cutback in oil from an industrial point of view, and I want an inside view of the probabilities of a change in the source of automotive power. That much he will know. He has made his position clear on William McCandless Smith. But I'm sure I'll get honest answers. Good night, Jack. See you at breakfast.'

'Good night, Mr. President. Get some sleep.'

'Very funny.'

As he double-timed through the heavy gray sand, perspiration running from under the fatigue cap tickling the back of his neck, Sergeant Connolly thought, 'All fucking U.S. military installations are the same. By the time they're through, there won't be no sand on the fucking beaches.'

A foot to his right was a flat asphalt road that stretched across the plain to distant trees. He passed a sign. 'Carry Your Load – But Not On The Road!'

Turning a bend, the Sergeant saw Brigadier General Elmo White taking his afternoon's exercise. He sat atop an M-113 armored personnel carrier, a gleaming gold star on his helmet liner. As the Sergeant drew within speaking distance, a voice from the amplifier in the control tower behind him sounded, 'Ready on the firing line.'

With a fixed smile on his sweat-streaked black face, General White pulled the cocking lever of the .50-caliber machine gun twice toward the rear and with practiced facility began to stitch the targets five hundred yards to his front. Adjusting the elevation and traverse with each burst, he placed five or six shells in the center of each target until the belt had been expended. The General raised his arm and the voice in the tower shrilled, 'Fire at will.' With a cacophonous roar, the gunners on the sixty APCs stretched on either side of the range began to shred the man-shaped silhouettes before them. When they had finished, the tower ordered, 'Secure all weapons. Next firing order.' The General put down his binoculars with a look of satisfaction.

'General White?'

The General jumped lightly to the ground, returning the Sergeant's salute.

'Sergeant Connolly reports to the General as ordered, sir. There is a priority-one communication at Company A field headquarters. By hand only.'

Without hesitation the General turned and waved to another non-com leaning against a jeep with a red flag bearing a single white star on its front fender. The driver scrambled into the vehicle and drove by, barely stopping to pick them up.

The jeep sped down the highway for several miles, then turned off onto a dirt track road leading to a large cluster of tents hidden in the trees. In front of the tree stood a tethered helicopter. The General entered the command tent to find a full colonel in dress uniform waiting alone. They exchanged salutes wordlessly. General White took the proffered envelope and wrenched the DOD wax seal from the flap. The single piece of paper inside bore the signature of the Secretary of Defense in red ink with an identifying counter signature. Above the signature were five words in capital letters:

PALM BEACH TANGO
IMPLEMENT IMMEDIATELY

The Colonel watched impassively as General White tore the letter and the envelope into small pieces, put them in an ashtray on the map table and set them afire. When they had been completely reduced to gray ash, and the ashes scattered on the sand floor, the General signed two copies of a sheet bearing the words 'Message received.' He put one in his dispatch case and gave the other to the Colonel, who saluted and without a word left to board the helicopter.

Admiral Harold Thurston sat relaxed in the battle chair

on the deck of the *John F. Kennedy* as it drove steadily through the calm waters of the eastern Mediterranean. Unconcerned, he watched as the Russian 'Bear' reconnaissance plane, its trim silhouette disfigured by the irregular bumps of its electronic gear, circled lazily above the vessel's gigantic flight deck. The flag assistant, a full commander, asked permission to come onto the bridge, saluted and handed the Admiral a small black book and a teletyped message. The Admiral returned the salute, and with a questioning look at the younger officer took the book from his hands. At the top of the message, which was a jumble of letters and numbers, were the words 'Eyes Only.'

The Admiral pulled the reading glasses from the pocket of his suntan shirt and with a pencil began to decode the message:

PALM BEACH UMBRELLA
IMPLEMENT IMMEDIATELY

He carefully tore and burned both the coded and decoded messages. 'Make to DOD. Message received.'

Arlow Hunsacker had sworn once annually for twenty-eight years that someday he would become a commercial pilot and benefit financially from the training that he had received from the United States government. He was, after all, forty-nine years old. He had survived the Korean and Indo-Chinese wars, and had flown everything with wings and more than one engine. How much was it that 747 pilots get now? About seventy thousand. Free travel. Stewardesses.

He looked out of the window of his office. A gigantic C5A, capable of carrying seven hundred fifty passengers or staggering cargo loads, lumbered down the runway, straining its engines against the bonds of the earth. Once off the ground, its cumbersome bulk was lost in the infinity of the sky.

Hunsacker said, 'Come in,' when he heard the knock at the door. The Colonel, in Air Force blue, entered, saluted, then handed him the envelope addressed to General Arlow Hunsacker, Commanding Officer, Military Air Transport Service. When the Colonel left, carrying the signed receipt, Hunsacker reached for the phone on his desk. He could still see the message in his mind's eye:

PALM BEACH HANG TEN
IMPLEMENT IMMEDIATELY

Fifteen

It was already ten by the time Rhabbouz had roused himself sufficiently to complete his morning toilet and descend to the Croisette for coffee. Nana preferred to remain behind to deal with the laundry, her unfinished correspondence and her Saturday shopping list. He stretched his legs under the table and rested comfortably, taking a sip of coffee and a bite of his croissant, pushed his glasses up his nose and opened *Nice-Matin*. The stories of Kalman Jacobs's death and the murder of Robert struck him like a blow. After a moment or so, he beckoned to the waiter, asked for his check and paid. He rose, carefully folding the paper, and walked down the street to the Majestic.

He went straight to the room and knocked at the door.

'Yes?'

'Rhabbouz.'

La Brousse opened the door. His face was weary, dark circles under the eyes. He was coatless, and the holster with its blue-black automatic flapped unbuckled against his wilted shirt.

'I have been expecting you.' The General sat, looking very old, in an armchair in the corner. His legs stuck out from the hem of his crumpled terry-cloth robe, ankles swollen with the edema of age. White stubble covered mottled cheeks. The pipe in his mouth was cold.

'I am sorry, Rhabbouz. Was he an old boy?'

'Auschwitz. DP camps. Yours?'

'Please. Sit down. Robert was a professional. Hard man. He was careless. That is the normal obituary in this trade.'

'Who found Kalman?'

'The American. It was meant for him, I think.'

'We are so wise, General. You set him up so Robert could catch the subject. I had Kalman follow Robert so my information would be as current as yours. The bait escaped and the shark ate both fishermen.'

'Yes. Now we shall pay the price. I am told that I am to expect a visit from Brunschwig. The Minister called. I shall tell him that we acted independently. You are not popular at the Ministry of the Interior.'

'Nor at the Elysée Palace. Can you keep me covered?'

'Probably not. He is no doubt having me watched. You had better get out of here.'

'I cannot let go now. You know that.'

'Sentiment?'

'No. It's not Kalman. I have to do my job.'

With visible effort the General struggled to his feet, shuffled across the room and took Rhabbouz's hand. 'Take care, Jew. We are old for these hard times.'

Colonel Brunschwig of the Sûreté gave notice of his intentions by telephone. By the time he arrived, the General had bathed and changed. La Brousse answered the knock at the door.

'Good morning, mon général.' He extended a manicured hand. 'You are well, I trust.'

The General eyed the tailored suit and carefully combed hair, then briefly shook the proffered hand. 'Well enough.'

Brunschwig cleared his throat and toyed absently with the diamond stickpin in his gray tie.

The General gestured toward a chair. 'Sit.'

'I see you lost Robert. Too bad.'

'Yes.'

'You know who the perpetrator is, of course?'

'No. Do you?'

'I could hardly know, mon général. There has been ... a certain lack of coordination in this operation, one might say. It seems that you have shared your information more readily with the Israeli Shin Bet than with our colleagues in the Ministry of the Interior.'

The General opened his mouth slightly, then closed it again on the stem of the pipe.

'It has been suggested that perhaps our two departments should cooperate more closely in the future. Subject, of course, to your approval.' Brunschwig brushed at the ends of his gray pencil mustache like a cat.

'What is it you want, Brunschwig?'

'Just a spirit of closer . . .'

'What do you want to know? I appreciate the niceties of your diplomacy. But I have work to do.'

'I want to know what you're looking for. What is happening here? Is this a matter for something beyond the military police?'

'In the first place, I am not a policeman. I am a soldier. I will thank you to keep that in mind. Secondly, it seems that your policemen have been pitifully ineffective in handling whatever it is that is going on. The ability of Paris to help the provincial force seems to be non-existent. You lost a man down here, you know?'

'Most unfortunate. But it is rather unusual for you to become interested in the death of a single officer, is it not? How did you become involved? Was it one of our people?' he asked casually.

The General smiled. 'We all have our sources, don't we, Colonel?'

'Then I can assume that you are investigating the death of a police officer for personal reasons.'

'Brunschwig, let's not fence. I am investigating the death of the officer because it seemed to be connected to the death of a meaningless pederast. And now, in the process of following the trail, a valuable and skilled military undercover agent has been brutally eliminated.'

'Along with certain others.'

'Yes, along with certain others. Thus confirming that the matter of the first death was more than it seemed. And that there was and is a connection between that death and the loss of the officer. Before you bring the subject up again, let's have done with it. It is not a matter of organized crime. It is an international matter. It is a matter of Arabs.'

'Then may I suggest that though it certainly lies within your sphere of professional competence, my dear General, the overall implications may lie outside the scope of Counter Intelligence.'

'You may suggest what you please, Brunschwig. You are in it now, and there will be no getting rid of you. But keep your people out from under my feet. I am old and lack both the time and the patience for your interference.'

Brunschwig rose from his chair and retreated with dignity toward the door. 'Naturally, we will make every effort not to complicate your operations. So long as we are kept completely informed. By the way, we are holding a Mr. Hamilton – as a material witness, you understand. He was at the scene of a particularly hideous auto accident. I'm sure that you read about it in the papers. He has mentioned your name several times. And the name of a certain Commissaire Tombal. As I recall, he had something to do with the death of the policeman.'

The General walked slowly across the room and thrust his chin forward so that it was almost touching Brunschwig's. 'Let him go. Now. And the girl. Now. Do you understand?'

Brunschwig swallowed. 'Naturally, General. If it would be of use to you.'

The General backed up a step to let Brunschwig have access to the door. 'Thank you.'

The General stood without moving for a few minutes, then lit his pipe. He turned to La Brousse. 'Make sure that someone picks Hamilton up as soon as he is released. And make sure that he and Brunschwig's man don't fall all over each other, guaranteeing a repetition of last night.'

'Bank failure is always unpleasant.'

'Yes, Your Excellency.' Bauermann dried his palms on his pants.

'But, as I understand it,' El Kaffar said, 'it is regarded as more than a general misfortune in Switzerland. Rather as a heinous crime.'

'At best,' Bauermann admitted.

'But your establishment will be free of any such problems as long as it has strong backing from its principal depositor. Don't you agree, Bauermann?'

'Yes, certainly.'

'Well,' said El Kaffar, 'you can count on the continuation of that support as long as my instructions are carried out to the letter. Just remember: no word is to be mentioned about this affair to anyone. If it is necessary, you will carry your instructions to,' he paused, 'your grave.'

Bauermann nodded.

El Kaffar continued. 'Under no circumstances are you to reveal anything of my plans to anyone. Is that clear to Mr. Nicholson?'

'Yes, Your Excellency. The combination of his satisfaction with his new prospects for advancement, and his concern about your ... information will serve to keep him quiet. As for me ...'

El Kaffar reached out to pat the back of Bauermann's hand. 'Yes, my friend. I am sure of your unswerving loyalty. In my judgment, it will take until the third week of this month to accumulate sufficient stock to ask for representation on the Board of Directors of General Motors. Do you agree? And do you feel that the buying has been spread widely enough to avoid suspicion?'

'As per your instructions, Excellency, the program has been carried out with the utmost care. Other than Bates and Company, no broker handles more than five percent of the orders on any given day, and no broker receives orders two days in a row. And even at Bates the buying apparently comes from a variety of their branch offices – they have over a hundred.'

'Well, that should suffice very nicely. I am going away, Bauermann. I will be in touch with you within ten days.'

'If I need to contact you ...'

'You will not need to contact me if you follow orders.'

'Will you be at home? I can always reach you through the Presidential Palace?'

'I must believe that you have a hearing problem, Bauermann,' El Kaffar said softly. 'If I wished you to know my whereabouts, I would make them known to you. Listen carefully, Bauermann. So far as the government of Quahrein is concerned, I am taking a brief holiday. Any attempt by you to contact me will result in a sudden and permanent reversal of your fortunes. What we are attempting here cannot take place in a department store window. It would be unfortunate if, in your obituary, you were described as a man who had interfered with the progress of mankind, Bauermann.'

Bauermann's eyes bulged. 'I only wish to be of service, Excellency. To be at your beck and call.'

El Kaffar smiled. 'I know, Bauermann. I know. Then serve me and my cause as I see fit, not as you imagine my needs. I will help you, Bauermann. You will meet me on the fifteenth of September to report your progress. Do you know Aix-en-Provence?'

'Yes, Excellency.'

'There is a hotel, the Roy René, about a block from the university. You will ask for M. Meyer. Then you will wait in the lobby. You will be contacted. That should help ease your mind. In the meantime, old man,' he said jovially, 'just follow my instructions and everything will be just fine.'

After Bauermann left the large office, El Kaffar walked to a narrow panel at the side of the desk and pushed a hidden button. The panel slid aside and he entered a small lighted cubicle whose walls were of dully finished metal. On a table in the rear of the room was a set of sophisticated radio telephone equipment from which two cables led: one, the power source, the other an antenna relay into the steel skeleton of the building. The door slid silently shut behind him. He glanced at his watch and sat down at a chair in front of the set, turned on the power, keyed the frequency and waited.

In a moment a complex series of beeping sounds was emitted by the speaker. He listened carefully, then broadcast a corresponding pattern with the Morse key before him. The process was repeated twice more, each time with a varied initial pattern and response. In the end, he reached out and turned to voice transmission.

'Yussuf,' he said.

'Yes, my brother.' A harsh guttural quality was discernible in the voice.

'Your message has been delivered. It was as I said. There was no response. They were not emotional. I have given them until the first of October to respond.'

'Have you convinced them, my brother, of the serious nature of our position? There is no doubt in their minds that Ben Kelb will do what Ben Kelb says he will do.'

'They believe you, Yussuf. I have made them understand. In the end, I think it was the fact that we are not making our demands or our threats public. It was unexpected.'

The voice became more strident. 'We do not threaten, my brother. We instruct. We proclaim that the charade is at an end. The world will recognize that. We will deal with our industrialized clients in a way that will let our Arab brothers know that we mean to unify the cause of the people. That we intend to lead the way. We have nothing which can be taken from us. The desert and the mountains are forever ours. Spirit and strength are forever ours. Our anger is without limit. And our ability to destroy. What we can do in our oil fields, we can do in others. Once this is understood and accepted, we will lead and the others will follow.' He paused, then said more calmly, 'Are you there, my brother?'

El Kaffar shook his head, staring as though transfixed at the radio, then came to himself and replied, 'Yes, Yussuf. I am here.'

'They will follow, Mohammed. It will be as I said. Every sheik, every king, every Arab. Or we shall tear them from their thrones, or from their tents. We will force unity down their throats, and it will nourish them and make them strong. Then we will be first among equals in the community of nations. If it were not meant to be, my brother, why else would Allah have placed the life's blood of the industrial world in Arab hands? You have done well to make this clear to them, my brother. You are my eyes and my tongue.' The pitch of the voice became conspiratorial. 'In the matter of the money, is that proceeding as you wished? You have taken much upon yourself, brother, it is the dowry of a whole nation.'

'It is proceeding exactly as planned, Yussuf. I have been able to find proper agents. Men who are competent, but easily controlled. We are making ourselves felt in more than one way.'

Again sharply, the voice replied, 'Do not forget that it is the fear of action which moves the mind of the clerk, no matter how high. In the end, it is physical fear and not the taste for gold which dominates. Better to share wealth and power than to be buried mutilated in a golden coffin.'

'I shall pursue the affair. There should be some concrete developments in the next two weeks. I shall not contact the Americans again. The matter is now in their hands. It is for them to respond to us. I will go to Europe now, to direct the financial operation. I have left it with Smith that they are to contact the Embassy here in Washington if they wish to confer with me.'

'Do you believe that they will attempt military intervention?'

'I do not doubt that they have a plan to deal militarily with such a contingency.'

'Perhaps they will send the Jew dogs.'

'Across five hundred miles of desert? No. Not likely. If they wish to interfere, they will attempt it directly. There has been no sign thus far.'

'If they do, they will inherit ashes and corpses. By the time I have finished, Europeans will use the blood of their children to fuel their machines, for there will be no more oil. You will call me again, in the same way, on the fifteenth. The next day I go to the desert to seek Allah. I will need his strength and my own good judgment if we are forced to act. I return on the twenty-sixth to lead our forces.'

'What if they attack while you are on your pilgrimage?' El Kaffar asked carefully.

'It will make no difference. Instructions have been given. All will be destroyed. All killed.'

'What will have been gained?'

'Not gained, brother, but lost. For them it will represent the loss of time. The loss of time will upset the careful balance of the great machine which is their world. The schedule by which they operate grows less tolerant of error or delay with each passing day. The desert that yields the oil to lubricate the machine can also yield the sand to bring it to a grinding halt.'

'And what of the other producers?'

'The politicians and the despots? They are not Arabs in the true sense, my brother. They vacillate. They temporize. They sell themselves and the birthright of the Arabs. When we give sand, they shall also give sand. For that is all we shall leave them to give.'

'Will that make a united Arabia strong, Yussuf? Will we not condemn another generation or two to ignorance and poverty? Will we not present to them the gift of sand as well?'

'The desert contains everything for us, Mohammed. The sand, which is eternal, is the symbol of our unyielding strength, which is also eternal. Believe, Mohammed. Believe in me, and in the strength and character of the people.'

'I believe in what you have said, as I believe in the Prophet, Yussuf.'

'Allah be with you, brother. Till the end of this month then.'

'And with you, Yussuf.'

El Kaffar turned the power switch to the off position, drew a deep breath, then rose and left the room as he had come.

Sixteen

Donald and Marie Jo had spoken very little as he guided the car carefully on the winding road from Brignoles to Puget-Ville toward Toulon. When they passed through the town she turned and said, 'After all, Donald, they are policemen. We were witnesses to a tragic accident. I don't think you should have talked to him that way.'

Donald scratched at the stubbly beard, ground his teeth in irritation and replied. 'I still think that he was a prick, and that's what I told him. We weren't material witnesses to a robbery. Some poor bastard ran himself off the road, and we were unlucky enough to be there to find him. I'm sick to death of being in French funeral processions. First that faggot, then that poor Jew. I am sick to death of the French police – that crazy old man – then that headwaiter type, asking all of those irrelevant questions. I want to be left the hell alone. I came here to build a hotel, not to participate in a bad movie script.'

'I will be glad to get some sleep. I don't know how you can even drive. At least they left us some of the weekend.'

He reached out to pat her thigh without turning his head. When they came down out of the hills, the noon sun was sparkling on the water. He pulled into the lot behind his building, led Marie Jo through the door and went upstairs.

Donald beamed as he retrieved the envelope from the floor and kicked the door shut behind him. 'Well, how about that. They're about a week ahead of schedule.'

'Who is?' Marie Jo asked, slumping loosely into a chair.

'My sons.' He tore open the envelope and removed two sheets of lined paper. Sanskrit, maybe, he wondered. 'Ah. Now I feel better.'

'Good. But why?'

'They're good for one page each a month. They stagger them so that I get a letter every two weeks. Now this one,' he held it out, 'is one week early and has two pages, one from each of them, At first I was concerned.'

'And now . . .'

'And now I understand. They have explained, each in his own way, but with a common Aristotelian logic, why they need new bicycles.'

'What are you going to do?'

'I have a responsibility to see that they are brought up properly. Even though I'm in Europe for the time being and they're in Locust Valley. I am going to ponder the pros and the cons and then . . .'

'And then . . .'

'And then I am going to send them the check.'

'Uh huh. That's what I thought. You miss them a lot?'

Donald nodded. 'One of the fortunes of divorce. Like a war, it isn't good for children and other living things.' He shrugged. 'Oh well, they'll be over for three weeks at Christmas time. We can go skiing. You want something to eat?'

'I want to sleep.' She got up and headed toward the bedroom. 'Do you think that we'll get our names in the papers?'

'We'd better not,' Donald bristled, 'that little bastard with the mustache promised. I don't want to hear anything further from my friends at the office about my adventurous life. Actually, they've been pretty good. Not a squeak to the office in New York. At least it wasn't mentioned when I talked to my senior partner on the phone last week. Also, he seemed pretty satisfied with our progress here.'

'That can't be all bad.'

'True,' he said, sitting on the edge of the bed and pulling off his shoes. 'But think how much better things would be if we'd never heard the name Pascal Lambert.'

Previn stretched, put the paper down on the bench and

rose to walk across the street to the cafe next to Hamilton's building.

'May I use the phone?'

'Of course, monsieur. Where would you like to call?'

'To Cannes. The Majestic Hôtel.'

The woman dialed, and when the hotel operator answered, she pushed the button on a timer on the counter, handing the phone to Previn. He gave the room number and waited.

'Hello.'

'Is he there?'

La Brousse passed the phone to the General, who said, 'So?'

'He's home. With his friend.'

'Any other company there?'

Previn craned his neck and looked out of the window down the block. A black Citröen with two men in the front seat was parked opposite Hamilton's door. 'Yes, very obviously. Two. Official plates and all.'

'Brunschwig's idea of subtlety, no doubt. Just as well. It will keep people out of the way. Try not to be as clever and guarded as they are, Previn. You'll give my staff a bad name. Is there someone on the back door?'

'Yes, and the roof.'

'It sounds fine, Previn. Leave him alone, but keep him safe, or you will not live to get your pension.'

Previn smiled and hung up. The woman checked the clock and looked up the tariff in a book. Previn paid, thanked her and left, casually sauntered down the street to his bench, passing the police car without a glance, and sat down again to read the paper.

Madeleine gasped in pain as Fosburgh pinched her nipples. She rested on her knees, straddling him as he thrust up against her from the floor of the cabin. He relaxed his hands for a moment, then strengthened his grip to the maximum, bringing tears to her eyes as he arched his back high in the air in a final spasm of pleasure.

'Harder, harder, once more,' she rasped. He thrust again and twisted with his thumbs and forefingers. She screamed again, pushing against him, then collapsed panting on his chest. They lay still for a moment, then he threw her roughly from his body and walked into the bathroom. When he returned she stood in front of the dressing table mirror in her bikini briefs brushing her hair. She appraised herself in the glass and asked, 'It doesn't show, does it, Paul?'

He walked behind her, now dressed in white slacks and shirt, put his arms around her and pinched her again sharply. 'They were already pink, my dear. Hurry and join me for breakfast.'

He went topside and walked out onto the afterdeck, surveyed the jetty, then sat down at the awning-shaded table. He glanced over the front page of the morning paper, first the *International Herald Tribune*, then *Nice-Matin*. A large picture of a demolished car took up one corner of the French paper. He read the accompanying story, first idly, then with growing interest. One man alone, burned beyond recognition, the only identifying mark a concentration camp tattoo. The police were searching for relatives. Fosburgh's eyes narrowed and a vein throbbed in his neck. He looked up toward the bridge. 'Aboussara,' he called, 'come here for a moment.'

Aboussara trotted down the gangway and stood impassive before the table. Fosburgh pointed at the picture. 'That's your work, isn't it?' Aboussara's expression did not change. 'A Jew. An Israeli agent no doubt. I forbid you to do your political hatchet work in a way that will end with my involvement. Is that clear?'

'Yes. It was my work,' Aboussara said calmly. 'And I killed a French agent in St. Raphael as well. Has that made the papers too?'

'You what?'

'Let us clarify matters, Mr. Fosburgh, I am on loan to you from the Republic of Quahrein. I have my work to do, and I am doing it in the way that I see fit. I am following the instructions of Colonel Ben Kelb.'

Fosburgh rose to his feet slowly and looked down into Aboussara's face. 'You were instructed to help me in the disruption and discovery of an industrial messenger system which might lead to a substantial diminution of the assets of your country. It is altogether possible that by getting yourself caught, or by involving me, you will have accomplished the very end that Colonel Ben Kelb and I,' he emphasized, 'are trying to prevent. You are not here because of your ability to think, but because of your ability to maim and kill. Need I clarify your subordinate position with Colonel Ben Kelb, or will you do as I tell you?'

Aboussara's mouth opened slightly, his eyes shone with hate. Fosburgh was simply a tool of his government, a lackey of the man to whom he reported directly, Colonel Ben Kelb. But his information from many quarters was still needed. And for the moment his money was needed. Quahrein would never have known about this thing which might lessen the value of its oil if it had not been for Fosburgh's connection with General Motors, or his inside source of information. Their day would come, though; the Colonel had said so himself. And then Aboussara would personally cut Fosburgh's throat and fill his mouth. He closed his mouth and nodded his head almost imperceptibly, as though it caused him pain. 'As you wish, Mr. Fosburgh,' he said, then turned on his heel and walked away.

Fosburgh watched him retreat toward the bridge, then sat down, buzzed for the steward and began reading the paper again.

Arthur Edelman turned his head to look at the white pimply rump of the boy before he closed the door behind him. He walked to the shutters and opened them, blinking in the strong light.

Humming, he opened the drawer of the desk with a key, taking out a sheaf of papers, sat down and switched on the calculator. He thumbed through the papers till he came to a graph labeled 'Charge Curve,' then a statistical sheet similarly named. Working steadily at the calculator for a few moments, he completed the numerical array, then turned off the machine and filled in the rest of the dots on the graph paper. When he had finished, he held the graph up to the light and smiled. He unscrewed the cap from a bottle of India ink, picked up a stylo pen and connected the dots.

'A bell,' he said aloud, 'a perfect bell.' He briefly considered the possibility that in actual testing, the materials would produce results different from those on his chart. He immediately rejected the idea. The vertical index of the chart was marked 'Energy Absorption Potential,' the horizontal index 'Average Available Daylight Hours 12 Months New York City.'

He pursed his lips. If he had the use of a computer, he could cut the required time to fit material requirements to the curve in an hour with the proper programming – two days in all, at the most. General Motors had many computers. Or time could be hired at computer service centers even in the South of France. But that would risk exposure – an unacceptable idea. So the final triumph would have to wait at least two weeks, probably three, as by trial and error and algebraic formula he sorted out the permutations that would lead to the physical and chemical mix of the light-sensitive plates, and so to the completion of the project.

He had determined that he would proclaim the existence of the last link in the chain and then make them come to him. A delightful idea. To bring those captains of industry who were at the top of the General Motors tree halfway across the world to pay homage to the intellect, nay the genius, of Arthur Edelman, who, unarmed with the tools at their disposal, had conquered the problem of energy, and freed mankind for another great thrust forward. I must begin, he thought, to consider the selection of appropriate counsel. They must pay, not only in homage, but in cash. Not for him the fate of Steinmetz, his hunchbacked shadow forever cast over the empire that is General Electric. Honored in memory but never in his lifetime. Honored in the word but never in the deed. Not for Arthur Edelman, he thought again, rising abruptly from the chair. He pulled closed the flowered dressing gown, knotting the belt at its waist with determination. Then he sat down again to compose a cable on a sheet of yellow foolscap.

Seventeen

Kugel led Milton Goodrich into the Oval Office, where Smith stood before the desk, framed by the flags behind it. The significance of his pose did not escape Goodrich.

'Good morning, Mr. President.'

'Thank you for coming, Mr. Goodrich. Please sit down. Would you like some coffee?'

'No, thank you, sir, I had breakfast on the plane on the way down. Did you have a pleasant weekend?'

Smith grinned. 'I made a speech yesterday. Other than that, I saw my wife and children, and that's an improvement from the norm. How about you?'

'I made a rare attempt at a normal weekend. A remarkable lack of success. I heard your speech, though.'

The President waited, then said, 'The silence is deafening.'

It was Goodrich's turn to smile. 'We have never been aligned politically, Mr. President.'

'I have noted that, Mr. Goodrich. I take it that you again found cause to disagree.'

Goodrich glanced at Kugel, who was standing quietly at the still open door.

Smith looked up. 'Jack, please tell Mary that I don't want to be bothered – for any reason. If it is important, tell her to give it to you.'

'Right.'

When the door closed behind him, President Smith said, 'Mr. Goodrich, it was in some respects our differences of opinion that led me to ask you here today. I need an opinion from someone who will not too readily agree with my point of view, nor be swayed by it. But at the same time, it has to be an educated point of view, one with a real feel for the business climate. And I have great respect for what you have accomplished.'

Somewhat taken aback, Goodrich smiled again and said, 'You could always have invited Dr. Friedman, Mr. President, he never agrees with you.'

Smith shook his head in amused agreement. 'True enough.' He leaned forward with his elbows on the desk. 'But I don't need or want a theoretical approach. My problem this morning has a broader spectrum than economic theory, or its applications, even. We are not closely acquainted, Mr. Goodrich, as men. But I know your reputation, and I feel that I know you. I believe that I can trust you.'

'I am complimented, sir. How can I be of use?'

Smith walked to a window and looked over the White House lawn, then turned back, looking intently at the seated man. 'I need to make some decisions. I need to make them quickly. They have to do with the immediate and long-term welfare of the people and the country. I need all of the input that I can get, from as objective a source as I can find. I am going to share some information with you, Mr. Goodrich, classified information which must not leave this room. Then I want to pick your brain. I want your opinion on several questions. Before we begin, I must ask that you give me your word that no portion of this conversation will be divulged by you to anyone.'

'Of course, Mr. President,' Goodrich said, even more intrigued at why he had been asked to come.

'Don't think that it's going to be all that easy. We are going to have to think of something polite to say to the press. The whole White House corps will descend on both of us the moment that you leave. I have planned to spend the entire morning and luncheon with you, if that suits your schedule.'

'I am not expected to return to New York until tonight.'

'Thank you, Mr. Goodrich.' He sat again, and told Goodrich about Operation Palm Beach. When he finished, he said, 'I have two questions. Will I have the support of industry if this course of action becomes necessary? And can industry, or more specifically General Motors, contend with the results if I do nothing and the Middle Eastern oil fields are crippled – possibly for years – or if I attempt to handle the situation by military intervention with a substantial probability of the same result, and the added risk of triggering the Third World War?'

'I take it, then, that you have discarded entirely the other alternative?'

'You mean compliance?' He looked at Goodrich intensely. 'I was not elected to office to dilute the sovereignty of the United States of America, nor to place its foreign policy in the hands of another government. Are you of a contrary opinion, Mr. Goodrich?'

Goodrich stood. 'I assume you asked me here to speak my mind.'

'I did.'

'I recall a campaign speech that you made. You said that your predecessor had turned over the foreign policy of the United States to a group of independent entities – the oil companies. As I recall, you said that they had no allegiance to this or any other country. And that the foreign policy that they had concocted – your word, I believe – was not to the benefit of this country. Are you still of that opinion, Mr. President?'

'I am no less convinced now than then that multinational corporations in general serve only themselves. They go toward profit.'

'That is not an ignoble aim, Mr. President. High profits generally are indications of high efficiency, not of monopoly as is so often stated. Monopolies stale quickly. It shows in their income statements. Their profits grow more slowly than their sales – and then begin to decline. That should be quite apparent from the success of the Soviet state monopoly. Inbreeding produces idiots.'

'Then I must assume that lack of competition in the oil industry produced the foreign ventures that got us where we are now?'

'I think you are dead wrong. From the mid-1950s to the early part of this decade, while the price of everything else was skyrocketing, the prices of petroleum products remained largely the same. The major part of the increases in gasoline prices, for example, during the period came from additional taxes, federal, state and local.'

'True enough, but the prices of petroleum products, when they did go up, did so largely at the behest of those few companies who control the overall supply.'

'There is competition among countries as well as companies, Mr. President. Our country fell behind. When it cost a dollar forty to lift a barrel of oil in Saudi Arabia, it cost three fifty in the U.S. When it cost fifty dollars per square foot to build a refinery in the U.S. it cost thirty dollars in Italy. When American refinery workers cost nine dollars per hour including fringes, the same labor in Southern Europe cost four dollars. It was the dislocation of extraction and refinery capacity that kept the pre-tax price of oil stable for twenty years. Then no one complained. When the producing countries finally woke up to the fact that they had us by the balls, Mr. President, everybody started to yell, "Break up the Yankees." What did we save in the interim by benefiting from Arab oil and overseas refineries?'

'Tell me, Mr. Goodrich, when you made the decisions to shift the locus of production and refining of something as important as petroleum outside of the country, wasn't that making foreign policy?'

'No, sir, that was the absence of a reasonable domestic policy. Let me restate that. It was the absence of any policy at all. We wanted to give the rest of the world a chance to catch up after the Second World War. So we maintained the level of the dollar while everybody else devalued the hell out of their currencies. Then, as our costs rose, particularly labor costs, we reduced our tariff barriers to nothing, and the rest of the world maintained theirs. So we started to run huge balance-of-payment deficits, and the rest of the world bellyached about our exporting our inflation. I'm sorry, Mr. President, but no administration after the war ever looked realistically at global competition. The Japs, and who should know better than I, sold cars at half the price in America that they could be bought in Japan, and nobody said a word. When Detroit yelled "dumping," nobody felt the slightest pang of regret. That was more than a case of self-pity and self-interest on the part of the motor industry, it was a case of feeling sorry for America. If we are supposed to be operating under equitable conditions, then let the American government lend Detroit money at three percent when the world market is twelve percent, and hundreds of millions for fifty years at that. Why not? The Japanese government does it. It's in the national interest. That's government subsidy, Mr. President. It lowers the cost of capital and the cost of production. Selling cars that are financed with that kind of capital is dumping. It's against international law. Why didn't anybody yell about that? Where was Ralph Nader?'

'Okay, Mr. Goodrich. Now, I'll tell you my side. It has to do with what I call the modern triangle trade. As much of a triangle as the molasses to rum to slaves of the eighteenth century. I believe that there was a conspiracy in this country. I'm not sure that it was formal. I'm not even sure that the conspirators recognized it as such. But it did exist. Your switch to high-mileage engines was a step in destroying it. The triangle trade, Mr. Goodrich. I won't make low-fuel-consumption engines if you in the oil and construction industries and the cement industry will support road building programs to expand the market for automobiles, and withhold your support and influence from public transportation. Conversely, we in the oil industry will support road building programs and will keep out of the engine development business if you will support tax benefits for the oil industry, particularly the depletion allowance. Likewise, we in the cement industry will back the hell out of depletion allowances, and fight environmental standards for automobiles, if you in the oil and auto industries will push the hell out of federal road building and aid-to-the-states road building. And so it went. From oil, to autos, to cement. For thirty years.'

'I saw smaller engines as the only way out. My motives were no more noble than that.'

'The effect was the same, regardless of your motives. Now what happens, in your opinion, if in one fell swoop there is no more Mideast oil? Not for a considerable time. I think that is the likely outcome, whatever the road we take.'

'Dislocation. Massive worldwide dislocation and the collapse of the industrial West.'

'You are aware of the progress that has been made in new technology. Shale extraction, surfactant recovery from existing wells. Expensive yes, but no more expensive than extortionate Mideast prices.'

'Dandy for us, Mr. President, but what happens to Japan? What happens to Western Europe? They depend in large measure on that source of oil. We don't live in a vacuum.'

Smith nodded in agreement and stood to look out of the window. He stayed silent for a considerable time, then said, 'We have the resources to serve the world in the interim, Mr. Goodrich. There is as much oil under the ground in capped wells as has been taken from them since Colonel Drake drilled the first hole in 1859. We can release that oil with detergents and surfactants. It is not economically attractive, but it is possible. We can massively increase recovery from the Colorado shales. Again, possible, if expensive, but a longer-term solution. I'm afraid we need to share now, Mr. Goodrich – right now. We need to share that which we do not have.' He paused. 'And we need to find a way to soften the blow of sharing to our own economy. We need to find a way to do that practically in one month.'

Goodrich looked at the President strangely. 'How are we to do that, Mr. President?'

'I thought I would ask you the question. Everyone has heard the story of the pill you add to water to make gas. Most people believe that Detroit could make a car that would go sixty miles on a gallon of gas, that there is a carburetor that would double the mileage of any car. Many people believe that things like that have been on the drawing board for years—and kept there. Do such things exist,

Mr. Goodrich?'

'No, sir. There is no genie stored in the bottle.'

'Can we find a genie in six to eight months? That is the time span we need. We can maintain an eighty percent level of operations in the United States and Europe for about six months at present consumption levels. But we need a way to drastically reduce consumption of fuel. We need to be able to provide the rest of the world with petroleum products in some reasonable measure to prevent other economies from toppling. The best way to do that is to find another source for our own supply. It is clear that the answer is not a research program. We haven't the time. Let's assume that money is absolutely unlimited. Let's assume that I can force a program through the Congress that would give you an unlimited source of government support. Would that make a difference?'

'You are serious?'

'I am. We are about to embark upon a course of action that will risk the stability of the world to maintain our own integrity. If we make the decision to protect our citizens in Quahrein, we must face the fact that Ben Kelb may be as good as his word.'

'And the Russians?'

'I have reason to believe that they will not move against us. But that will not resurrect the Mideast oil fields if Ben Kelb blows them up. And even if they were so disposed, the Russians haven't the resources to bail Europe out in terms of oil. We have to do it ourselves. As I said, we can manage for about six months. After that, we require something more. A miracle will do.'

'A strict rationing program would help. Ban pleasure driving altogether. Ban new car sales. Change the mix of refineries entirely to industrial fuels, heating fuels and sources of petrochemicals.'

The President grinned. 'Why Mr. Goodrich, I'm surprised at you. The thought had occurred to me. But you know as well as I do that if we dislocate the automobile industry and its related industries, and we don't replace its product line with something else immediately, we will have destroyed the economy in any case.'

Goodrich studied his nails. 'Mr. President, are you prepared to ask for emergency powers – as in time of war?'

'I don't think that we are in a situation any less grave. But, at the same time, I don't believe that I can do it now. I cannot request war powers without calling Ben Kelb's bluff and perhaps pushing him to action. I can't consult with our allies for the same reason. Yet, unless I reveal the problem and the time limit, there will be no seeming reason for the Congress to grant such powers.'

'The possibility exists that we could change the energy balance. It depends on the development of a process which we at GM have been considering for some months. The initial stages are near their end. To put it into production in the time frame you suggest would mean a massive shift in the industry. It would require absolute authority to commandeer materials, plants, work forces. It would involve enormous waste at the outset. Junking billions in investment.'

'If the power existed to create the necessary manpower and the budget had no limit, could it be accomplished?'

'I don't know. It's conceivable. An inventor – an independent – has developed a solar power conversion system that applies to automobiles. We don't have all of the details. He is a very peculiar man. We don't even know where he is. He is about to provide us with the last piece in the puzzle. He is enjoying the mystery. It is the only practical hope that I can hold out along those lines, Mr. President. It isn't much, but it's all that I have to offer. And assuming that he comes across with the final elements of his creation, it would require all the unusual powers you could be granted to effect the conversion for new vehicles. There is no way the power system could be applied to existing machines.'

'That doesn't matter. We can stop or slow the use of existing automobiles as long as we don't stop production in the industry and cause a general economic collapse. We need time. What can I do to help you?'

'Nothing. Not now. Our inventor has an axe to grind with us. He takes an obvious delight in twisting our tails. But we are at the end of the line. He is about to arrange for a meeting in which we will negotiate his financial contract and our rights to the product.'

'I can do this much,' said the President, 'I will back any financial deal that is required of you. Further, when the time comes, I will get those special powers and use them to the extent necessary to make early production of the vehicle possible. The government will underwrite the cost with loans or grants. Whatever is required of me I will do.'

'We really haven't much to go on, Mr. President.'

'Mr. Goodrich, it's better than the alternatives that I had when you walked in the door. Let's hope that between now and the first week of October the Good Lord sees fit to take care of your inventor, or to take Colonel Ben Kelb to His bosom – or both.'

Eighteen

The brief mistral of the first week in September had temporarily driven the tourists away, and Cannes seemed empty under a gray sky. Tombal scurried from his car to the front door of the Majestic to escape the few drops of rain and the blustering wind. When La Brousse admitted him, he saw that the General sat with his feet up on suitcases.

'I asked you to come because I am leaving, Tombal. I am going back to Paris. We have come to a dead end. There is little else to be done here. Since the death of Robert and the other man, nothing has happened. It seems that the violent party has gone to earth, leaving us to guess at his purpose. I am sorry, Tombal, that we could not do more to help in the matter of your friend's death.'

'What of Hamilton, General?'

'He has been under continuous surveillance since the evening Robert was killed. Both by us and by the Sûreté. Colonel Brunschwig. Probably by the Shin Bet, as well.'

'Will he continue to be watched? Perhaps our party is waiting.'

'He will be watched at least for the present. I have asked him to meet me here this afternoon. That is one reason that I called you. I want him to know that if he has any problems he can go to you.'

'Is he aware that the Molotov cocktail was meant for him?'

'No. I had considered telling him, but he seems quite hostile to French authority at the moment.'

'Wouldn't it be better for him if he left?'

'Probably, but it would not be better for us. He is the only link that we have left with this matter. And besides, he has a certain stubbornness. I am not sure that he would leave even if we told him that he had been set up. It is even possible that he would run to his Consulate to complain. That would be awkward at best.'

'General,' La Brousse interrupted, 'may I remind you that we shall have to leave soon, whether Mr. Hamilton arrives or not. We have our plane.'

The General glared at him and shrugged. 'Fucking nurse-maid. That's what you are. Have you any vacation coming? I would be glad to get rid of you.'

La Brousse was spared further comment by a knock on the door. Hamilton entered and greeted them stiffly.

The General said, 'I assume you thought that you were rid of me, Hamilton. Well, hopefully, this will be our last meeting. I wanted to thank you for your cooperation and to apologize for the difficulties which you have experienced. I trust that you will be able to complete your hotel without further untoward events.'

'Yes. Well, I hope so too.'

'If you have any difficulties, Commissaire Tombal will be glad to help you. He is stationed in Toulon, as you know.'

'I trust, General Pineau, that the kinds of problems that I would take to Commissaire Tombal are behind me. Do you know something that I don't know?'

The old man grinned toothlessly. 'I know many things that you do not know, my friend. Come downstairs to the bar. We will have one last drink together – on La Brousse.'

The sky over Cannes remained gray, but the last of the rain had disappeared and the wind had died down. General Pineau led Hamilton and Tombal out to the terrace while La Brousse took care of the bill and instructed a porter to go for their bags. Only a few boats plied the bay between the old port and the Palm Beach Casino, bouncing on the white-caps. A waiter took their order, returning shortly since they were his only clients. He muttered under his breath about people who drink on terraces on nasty days. The General eyed the Pernod in his glass speculatively, then reached for the carafe of water. It exploded in a hail of glass fragments.

The three of them sat for a moment, looking stupidly at the mess on the table. A pinging sound rang out as another shot ricocheted off the bronze window frame behind them. Hamilton dove to the floor as Tombal scurried from his chair. The General sat calmly waiting. La Brousse, who was on his way out the door, rushed forward to place himself between the General and the beach. He reached out and took the old man by the arms and lifted him bodily to his feet, then shielding him as best as he could, helped him back to the lobby.

Seeing the commotion, the manager got up from his desk chair and came forward. 'What has happened?' He looked at the table. 'How did that glass break? Goodness, General Pineau, it seems that your friend has been badly cut.' He stared oddly at La Brousse, whose leg was bleeding profusely from a last unheard shot.

The General took La Brousse by the arm. 'You are looking rather gray, La Brousse. Shall we go upstairs? Monsieur,' he addressed the manager, 'we shall certainly stay the night.'

'Of course, General. I will have your bags brought upstairs. Would you like me to call a doctor?'

'No,' said La Brousse. 'It is just a simple cut. I must have done it when I passed the table.'

Tombal and Hamilton followed them into the elevator. With a bellboy hurrying on before them, the foursome made their way slowly down the hall to the room. The boy opened the door and waited, took a tip from Tombal and left. When the door closed, La Brousse collapsed on the floor.

The General took a switchblade knife from his pocket and clicked it open, handing it to Tombal. 'Cut his pants leg.'

An ugly blue-lipped hole trickled blood in the meat part of his thigh; there was an exit wound, ragged and bleeding profusely on the opposite side.

'Nothing broken, I think. Is there a police doctor who can be trusted in this town?'

'I don't know, General.'

'Get Rhabbouz on the phone. Tell him to hurry. He'll

know someone. Explain to him. Hamilton, don't just stand there like an idiot. Get a towel and wrap that wound. Get a pillow under his head. Merde. He's gray. Must be shock. Loosen the tie, the belt. Elevate the feet. A blanket. God damn you, hurry.'

Galvanized by the General's instructions, Hamilton obeyed. He moved quickly and mechanically.

In less than five minutes there was a knock at the door. Rhabbouz appeared with a suntanned man carrying a medical bag. He glanced quickly at the wound. 'I can fix it. Nothing broken. Some loss of blood. Must everything be done here?'

'Yes,' the General replied.

'All right. When I finish with the bandage, I'll go out and get an IV kit and some plasma. Give me a suitcase.'

The old man pointed to his bag. 'Take that. Just dump it. Have you some morphia?'

'I can't, he's out. Shock, I suppose.'

'You suppose. Tell him, Rhabbouz, what I shall do to him if anything happens to that man.'

'He can guess. Fix him as best you can, Henri. Is there anything we can do to help?'

'No. I'll give him a stimulant. Then it's the plasma and rest.' He probed a bit at the wound. La Brousse groaned and stirred. 'No major vessels hit. He'll be all right. I was afraid that he might exsanguinate.' They lifted him to the bed, where the doctor finished his patching, then covered him and left with a promise to return as soon as possible.

'Exsanguinate. Bleed to death.' Hamilton offered dully. Then with a little more spirit, 'I should stay the hell away from you, General. Somebody wants you dead. Where do you suppose those shots came from?'

'They came from a boat. Very good marksman too. He must have been way out. Thank God for the choppy water.'

'I'm going to get the hell out of this lunatic asylum before someone else takes a crack at you. You are a very interesting man, General, but your company is unhealthy.'

The General dropped in a chair, pointed at another with

his walking stick and said, 'Sit down, Mr. Hamilton.'

'I am sorry, General Pineau, but I am going home.'

'Mr. Hamilton. They were shooting at you.' He paused to let his statement sink in. 'Rhabbouz, Tombal, we might as well all have a drink. I think perhaps Mr. Hamilton would like to know what is going on. As a matter of fact, Tombal, call the room service people and have them bring up a big bottle – make it two – I think they will be needed.'

'All that questioning the other night ... about the accident,' Hamilton mused, only half aloud.

'Not an accident, mon vieux. Not at all an accident. The man you found was murdered. There were fragments of a glass bottle two hundred meters behind the wreck with traces of burned gasoline. The crash was caused by a Molotov cocktail. It was a dark night. I may suppose that the bastard who threw it thought it was you. He threw at the lights.'

Hamilton shook his head as though to clear it. 'Who the hell are all these people, General? The man who was killed ... an innocent stranger. Commissaire Tombal, I know. This man,' he pointed at Rhabbouz. 'Is the doctor somebody special too? And La Brousse, you say that was meant for me too?' He turned to look at the heavily breathing form on the bed.

The General closed his eyes and rubbed them with his hand, then began to speak. He was interrupted by a soft knock at the door. Rhabbouz put his hand into the pocket of his blue blazer and walked to the door. He stood against the wall next to the door and asked, 'Who is it?'

'It's Henri.'

Rhabbouz opened the door a crack, then stepped to the side. The doctor entered quickly and kicked the door shut behind him. He opened the medical bag which he had left at the side of the bed and removed the stethoscope. He turned back the covers to pull aside the dress shirt which they had left on La Brousse. He checked his heart. Then, seemingly satisfied, examined the dressing. The others watched intently in silence as he opened the suitcase he had brought, and set its contents out on the second bed.

He selected a small instrument which resembled a calculator, attached a plastic tip to the end of a cord which led from it, and placed the tip into La Brousse's slack mouth. He held it there with one hand and turned the switch on the appliance with the other. Digits flashed on a small screen. He withdrew the tube and turned to the wondering audience. 'Digital thermometer. Instant reading. His temperature is about normal, just in case, though . . .' He took two vials and two disposable syringes from the bed and laid them on the night table. He injected one and then the other into La Brousse's arm. 'Tetanus antitoxin and penicillin. Standard procedure.' He checked the dressing. 'This seems all right. The pressure seems to have controlled the bleeding.' He discarded the syringes, vials and the old dressing in a brown paper bag, then bound the wound again, smearing a drop of blood on a glass slide as he closed. Silently, he turned to a kit and applied liquid to the slide from several glass bottles. He waited a moment, nodding in agreement with himself and tore open an insulated package. 'André, be a good fellow and set up this stand.' He indicated a group of aluminum tubes with a thrust of his chin. Rhabbouz complied. When the stand was completed, a single silver pole thrust upright from three legs, the doctor hung the plastic envelope which had been in the package from the hook at its top and positioned it next to the bed at La Brousse's right side. He fixed La Brousse's arm to a board with several pieces of tape so that it was rigid at the elbow, tied it off with a strand of fine rubber hose and palpated for the vein. 'Aha,' he said with satisfaction. He took a plastic cap from the needle at the end of the hollow tube dangling from the bag and inserted it with practiced ease into the vein. He reached and turned a valve. The blood coursed down the tube with a small smacking noise to replenish La Brousse's dwindled strength. La Brousse moved restlessly, then was still again.

Hamilton rose and walked to the bathroom. The General raised his eyebrows and scratched at his naked scalp, whose itching served as a reminder that his monthly shave was less than a week away. There was another knock at the door. 'Stay in there,' the General said sharply to Hamilton, then nodded at Rhabbouz. The doctor rose and walked casually into a corner. Rhabbouz put his hand back into his pocket and assumed his position at the side of the door. Before he could speak, a key fitted into the lock. The General leaned forward in his chair, as though to rise. The door opened a few inches, then stopped when it hit the foot Rhabbouz had put in its path.

'Room service.'

Rhabbouz glanced quickly through the crack in the door, then withdrew his foot, remaining with his back against the wall. The door swung open to admit a mousy waiter balancing a tray with two bottles of Scotch and a siphon in one hand, dangling a key from the other. Rhabbouz let him enter the room, then shut the door behind him. Startled at the sound and by the scene before him, the man almost dropped the tray.

'Nitwit,' the General remarked, 'idiot, imbecile. Put that down. You are going to crack my skull with that thing – and waste my good whisky besides.' The man put down the tray and handed the check to the General. He signed it and dug a ten-franc note out of his pocket. 'Take this and get out.'

Rhabbouz turned to the General as he left, closing the door behind him. 'Toujours, noblesse oblige, mon général.'

'Incompetents irritate me. There is no shame in being a waiter, but to be an incompetent waiter ... All right, Hamilton, you can come out of the toilet now.'

'What the hell is going on here? What am I into? And most important, how can I get out?'

'Slowly, Hamilton. One step at a time. All will be explained.' He hesitated a moment as he mixed Hamilton a drink, then handed it to him. 'First, say hello to André Rhabbouz.'

Hamilton nodded in acknowledgment.

'Rhabbouz, as you can see, is an old Jew. He is a retired civil servant. It was my misfortune to have him in my employ when France was still a world power – and a colonial power at that. Since then he has drifted into retirement and melodrama. Have you ever heard of the Shin Bet, Mr. Hamilton? The Israeli secret police. An organization of blackguards whose aim it is to make the world unsafe for anti-Semitism. They are so hard-up, Mr. Hamilton, that this washed-up old rug merchant runs their operations in the South of France. That,' he indicated the doctor with a thumb, 'is the local Jew witch doctor, I suppose.'

'Henri Levy, at your disposal.' The doctor made a small bow.

'Tell me, Rhabbouz,' said the General, 'where did he develop his skill with gunshot wounds? I thought all his type ever did was an occasional prostatectomy.'

'He spent four months in Israel after the Yom Kippur War, treating burn cases and other wounded. I suppose the experience stuck with him. Not so, Henri?'

'Yes,' Levy said somberly. 'And the faces, and the fingerless hands, and the eyeless sockets, and the young without arms and legs. I am not likely to forget.'

'So you see,' Rhabbouz continued, 'he has the skills to provide specialized medical help on the rare occasions when it is needed, and the motivation to make his contribution to this unusual cause.'

'I am more confused, not less,' said Hamilton, squinting a little into the few rays of sun which had begun to seep through the window before him. He rose to close the curtains.

'Stay away from the window, Hamilton. If you want to close the drapes, do it from the sides.'

'Thank you, General,' he said wryly. 'I am sure you don't want to have both the beds in this room littered with your dead and wounded.'

'You are in the midst of something quite beyond your imagination, Hamilton.'

'So I can see.'

'You remember meeting a man at the station at Brignoles the other night? He would have questioned you.'

'A prissy-looking guy with a pencil mustache? Oily and unpleasant? Overpolite?'

'That's the one.'

'I called him a prick. He was the one who wouldn't let us go.'

The General nodded sagely. 'I usually call him an asshole. That is Colonel Brunschwig. He is my opposite number in our Ministry of the Interior. His organization, Défense et Sécurité du Territoire, is the equivalent of your FBI.'

'And yours the equivalent of our CIA?'

'Let us get to the heart of the matter. The day of the accident, the day we met at the beach, I set you up.'

Hamilton half rose from the chair, gripping its arms with whitened knuckles, and said in a rising voice, 'You did what?'

'Be calm, Hamilton. Sit down. You survived.'

'No thanks to you.'

'True enough. We tried to use you while we protected you. The man who died in the automobile accident was an agent of the Shin Bet. He was following you. He was not the only one lost that night. There was an agent of my department as well. He was found in St. Raphael with his neck broken and his throat cut.'

'You make a hell of an acquaintance, General. Your company doesn't seem to have done much good to La Brousse either.'

'It is all a matter of circumstance, Mr. Hamilton. You had the misfortune to find Pascal Lambert. If he had been only a dead pederast, it would have been nothing but a horrid memory. But clearly, Mr. Hamilton, that was not all. Then the policeman Riez was murdered. He came to Tombal,' he pointed at the Commissaire who sat in a corner staring at the floor, 'because he believed that there was something unusual about the case. Instinct, perhaps. Professional judgment more likely. In any case he was dead, and it seemed to us that it was the Pascal matter that cost him his life. The pattern of brutality and mutilation was not typical of professional criminal acts, and psychopaths don't trap and murder experienced policemen. Therefore, we had to be dealing with something more complex and more sinister. It occurred to Tombal that the taking of Lambert's genitals was an act of someone from an Arab or African country, so he came to me. It is certainly possible that it could have been an individual act in the case of Pascal, but then again, why the Inspector? An individual could have run. There was nothing to connect him. He need not even have run. He needed only to remain quiet and circumspect. Heaven knows we had no clue. There are stirrings in the Mideast, in Washington. We don't know what or why. But the signs of activity are there. We have learned to recognize them. To attempt to decipher the signs, and perhaps to get at the cause of the deaths of Lambert and Riez, I called upon my my old friend over there,' pointing to Rhabbouz. 'Subsequently, an attempt was made on our lives. I am no master spy, Mr. Hamilton, dealing with international intrigue on a daily basis. I am a civil servant involved in a variety of security matters. But I am principally involved in the drudgery of daily paperwork, and am no more accustomed than you are to have my right to live taken in vain. You were the last link between the known and the unknown. We asked you to come to visit us to learn what you knew firsthand. But we made the meeting public, so that those who were involved would imagine some connection between the SDEC and yourself. Then we set Robert, the agent who was killed, on your tail. This old Jew did not trust me to pass on the information, so he sent a man of his own – Jacobs. It was he that you found in the car wreck. Fortunately, our assassin or assassins missed you.'

'I had a blowout,' Hamilton said. 'I almost did the job for him. I lost control of my car. That other man, Jacobs, must have passed me to wait further down the road so that I wouldn't suspect anything. So that gasoline bomb was meant for me. Jesus Christ.'

'Yes, indeed. As was the bullet that passed through La Brousse, and the one that smashed the decanter, and the others. Mr. Hamilton, what has been done cannot be undone. I am truly sorry that you were forced into this mess. As I see it, you have a variety of choices. Most practical, of course, is to go home. You can simply leave France. We could provide you with protection until you are safely on the plane. Or you could take a vacation for a while. Go any-where until this matter blows over.'

Hamilton shook his head negatively. 'Listen, General Pineau, if this plot and the nonsense that goes with it has the global implications that you've hinted at, I can't go any-where. What am I supposed to do, go home to visit my kids and get them killed too? You almost managed to have my girlfriend done in with me the other night. Should we go away on a vacation somewhere? Perhaps someplace secluded to make it easy for them? Would you suggest the Club Méditerranée in North Africa? If I did go home and these people went after me, could I ask for protection from the police in America or the CIA? You'd have to tell them what I was doing in this mess. And what you were doing. And you wouldn't do that, would you?'

'I'm afraid, Mr. Hamilton,' the General shook his head, 'that that would be impossible.'

'What if I went to the American Consul here in Cannes?'

'What if you did, Mr. Hamilton? Official telegrams and telephone calls. Conversations between the Quai d'Orsay and Foggy Bottom. Some embarrassment for me possibly. But no help for you.'

Warming to the subject, Hamilton said, 'You could find a safe place to keep me for a while, until this thing blows over, but then what would happen to my project and to my life? And besides, that sort of thing has a built-in time limit. It seems to me that I am out of options.'

The General rubbed his nose pensively, then said, 'Of course, there is one possibility which would likely bring the entire matter to a speedy conclusion. We can find out who has been creating all of these inconveniences. We can catch him and stop him. Or get to the bottom of the matter altogether, and eliminate the need for your ... disposal.'

'How do you propose to do that, General Pineau? You've

been remarkably unsuccessful up to now. All you have to show for your efforts are two dead spies and one damaged one.'

'We can always continue to use you as bait.'

Hamilton fixed him with an unbelieving stare. 'You led me right into that. You are a miserable bastard. Has anyone ever told you that?' he said in a rising tone.

'Many times. But what are your options? You have yourself described your very limited opportunities for continued good health. If you work with us, we can afford to give you the kind of protection that may keep you alive. In addition, it will give us an opportunity to bring the whole matter to a head. You are still the only link with the death of Pascal. You know nothing, but there are those who don't understand that, or rather do not want to take the risk of your interfering with their plans. Therefore, you will continue to be a target, Mr. Hamilton, whatever you decide to do. It seems more practical to me that we should at least benefit.'

Hamilton poured himself another drink and sat back in his chair, musing. 'I am surprised that you didn't appeal to my patriotism, or my sense of responsibility to the families of those who have already been killed.'

'You underestimate me, Mr. Hamilton. I think that all flags should be cut up for use as toilet paper. As for the rest, whenever I have seen men die at my side, and as a soldier I have seen many, my sole emotion was to thank God that he took them and not me. You agree, then? You will be the clay pigeon?'

Hamilton turned the glass in his hand and said evenly, 'You have some fucking nerve.'

'Hmm?'.

'I said,' he leaned forward, raising his voice, 'you have some fucking nerve. What makes you think that I have any desire, for whatever reason, to place my life in your chubby hands? I have no intention of playing Trilby, General. The part doesn't suit me.' He rose and put the glass down on the table. 'I don't see myself as being without choice. I may well be just where you put me – in a corner. But that doesn't mean that I have to acquiesce to any scheme your devious mind dreams up.'

'No,' the General snapped, 'you can go out and get killed.'

'That's right! On my terms. If I decide to run, then I'll run. If I decide to stay and take my chances, that's my decision too. Maybe I'll go out and hire myself a French goon to watch over me. There seems to be plenty of unemployment around here. Then I'll be able to do my job and lead my life without the lunatic fringe of the French government watching me take my morning crap!'

The General thumped his stick on the floor. 'Nonsense. We have every intention of continuing to watch you. And besides,' he continued with a sly smile, 'you can't tell me that you don't find your involvement a little intriguing. Come now, Hamilton, wouldn't you like to find out how the chess match ends?'

'Not as a pawn, thank you.'

The General cocked his head and looked up at Hamilton. 'Well, what would you say to playing a more active role? As a co-conspirator, shall we say?'

Hamilton suppressed a quick answer.

'A less passive role? Sit down, Mr. Hamilton.'

Hamilton remained stubbornly erect. His eyes locked with the General's. 'No one hanging around my office?'

'Agreed.'

'No eaves-peeping in my bedroom?'

'Exhaust yourself in peace.'

'How much do I get to know in advance? I don't want any more surprises.'

'I will see that you are informed in advance of any planned operation.'

Hamilton sat. 'It's still no good. You talk. I jump. I expected to die of old age in my bed. If I don't, I want to pick the way out myself.'

The General leaned forward and put a hand on his knee. 'All right, Mr. Hamilton. Then shall we say that we shall consult first on any planned operations? Do you want a veto?'

Hamilton laughed. 'Let's not get carried away, mon général. You're not going to give me any veto.'

'You are a realist, Mr. Hamilton. I am not going to give you a veto.'

'How do I know that you're to keep your word about the rest?'

'How do I know that you're not going to shake hands, agree with me, then get into your car, drive to the airport and go home?'

Hamilton picked up his glass. 'I suppose in a sense that makes us equal.'

The General shrugged expressively.

Hamilton looked at the floor, then drained his glass and said, 'All right. Where do we go from here?'

Nineteen

'It can't be done,' said Coughtry, stubbing out the last of a chain of cigarettes. 'It just isn't physically possible.'

Hultz, pacing, kicked at some imaginary object on the rug. 'Don's right. You'll be thrown out on your ass if you suggest the idea. There isn't one man on the board who wouldn't think that you're certifiably insane. To say nothing of how Fosburgh would react. You'll lose all of your supporters if you make an issue of this. They'll can you.'

'I didn't ask for a political analysis of the Board of Directors,' Goodrich said wearily. 'I asked whether you think we could be in mass production with the solar car in six to nine months, assuming that money was no object.'

'Look, Milt,' Hultz said with some sympathy, 'I'm not a production man. Neither is Don. We're basically research and operations people. But you're in a corner. The people who could probably give you a reasonable guesstimate haven't got the information necessary to come to a conclusion. We don't dare invite them in for fear of a leak. After all, we stand the chance of our prima donna holding out the last link in the chain. Even if we had the last link, we'd still have to deal with him. We'd need him here.'

'Would you back me, if despite all you've said, I decided that it was in the best interests of the company to go ahead?'

Hultz chewed at his lip momentarily. 'Intellectually, I am unable to understand why you want to throw the energies of this company into what must still be considered a fringe concept in the early development stages. But our relationship has been more than intellectual. Yes, I would back you.'

Coughtry had sat down and was running the center piece

of his slide rule back and forth with his fingers. As the seconds ticked by, his silence became more pointed. Finally, Goodrich asked, 'And you, Don?'

He looked up. 'I would say nothing. I couldn't go along on the basis of what I know. I'd hate to say that I have no opinion. Maybe I didn't understand you correctly. You said you want to halt production of the bulk of our internal combustion engines and convert the plants to manufacture of the solar car. This on the assumption that you could get all of the suppliers to go along, and again,' he underlined with his voice, 'assuming that money is unimportant. And all of that to be done within six to nine months.'

'That's the hypothesis,' Goodrich agreed.

Coughtry put the slide rule down on the table in front of him. 'I think that it would destroy the company. To bank on the car is certainly premature. Even assuming that it were technically feasible from a design point of view, it would create havoc in every industry in America. No sir. I think that it's a destructive idea. I would never fight you, Milt. But I couldn't back you.'

'When will they be here, Jack?'

'Twelve sharp, Mr. President,' Kugel replied. He looks old, Kugel thought, as old as I looked to myself in the mirror this morning. The Presidency devours the vestiges of youth. It carves lines in faces. Even Kennedy aged ten years in less than three.

Smith glanced at the mantel clock. 'Ten minutes.' He began to pace up and down in the windowless room.

'They're going to think it's strange, meeting down here.'

Smith laughed without humor. 'A mausoleum is a fit place to do this kind of business.'

'You still don't think that we should hint to Aharon? Perhaps ask the Prime Minister?'

'No. We can't. I'll do what I can to protect them. Doesn't Palm Beach foresee the possibility of immediate reprisal by Egypt and Syria?'

'Not really. Its purpose is to secure immediate tactical superiority, blanket air cover and land strike capability in the shortest possible time at a given point.'

'I'll ask Gaines if there is room for modification.'

'If they are totally unprepared, they'll take a terrible shellacking.'

'Jack, they're never totally unprepared.'

Kugel frowned. 'The Syrians have been waiting for the opportunity. They'll hit the cities.'

'Not when they realize what has happened. Not when they see what triggered the invasion. Not when the Arabian oil fields start to blow up.'

'The Egyptians ... I agree. The Syrians will never even stop to think about it.'

A red light over the door began to blink steadily with a small clicking sound, as the relay which operated it opened and closed.

'They're in the elevator,' Kugel said, then licked his lips.

After a silent moment the door opened to admit the Secretaries of Defense, State and the Interior.

The President showed them to the table in the center of the room. A green-shaded lamp hung over its green baize cover.

'Mr. Gaines ...'

'Mr. President?'

'Palm Beach Phase One is complete?'

'Yes, sir. The Sixth Fleet is split into two task forces patrolling about eighty miles off the African coast, short maneuvers back and forth, stopping at the imaginary line extending from the borders of Quahrein.'

'Not an obvious move?'

'No, sir. We've done it before. It is one of the normal steaming patterns that we've adopted; it's indistinguishable from routine. In fact, only Joint Chiefs and Admiral Thurston are aware that Palm Beach is effective. And General Smith is running an exercise in air base defense from ground attack, again a seemingly routine maneuver, so that his people will be in field gear ready to go within half an hour of the designated runways.'

'And General Hunsacker?'

'He is running an unscheduled inspection of the wing. There has been the usual grousing about canceled passes and alert status. We've even gone to the trouble of alerting Air Force IG that there is to be a readiness alert inspection at the base. Naturally, the word leaked back out of channels.'

Smith rubbed his chin. 'George, what happens if some of the more hysterical Arab governments take this as a general attempt to overthrow? Won't they throw everything they have at Tel Aviv and Haifa?'

'Possibly, Mr. President.'

'If we don't alert Israel, won't they be caught flatfooted?'

'I rather think so,' Gaines replied a bit smugly. 'But I wouldn't worry about them too much, Mr. President. They can generally take care of themselves.'

Boring in, uncharacteristically, Smith said, 'You're telling me to let the devil take the hindmost. I'm asking you if given an attack by American forces on the soil of an Arab nation, there will be immediate reprisal against population centers in Israel?'

'I shouldn't be a bit surprised.'

'Or sorry,' Smith said explosively.

The men at the table turned to look at each other questioningly.

'I rather think that that is a harsh appraisal, Mr. President,' Oscar Johansson interposed. 'I think that George means that we cannot very well inform the Israelis because they will certainly mobilize, or begin an evacuation from the cities, thus neatly tipping our hand. And possibly, I might add, provoking the Arabs, who are equally uninvolved in the Quahrein matter, to make a preemptive strike at what they believe to be preparations for hostile action. That's the sense of what you meant, isn't it, George?'

The red-faced Secretary of Defense nodded gratefully.

Still unsatisfied, the President pressed on. 'All right. Let's make the assumption that a warning is not feasible. Is there a contingency plan to give them air cover until they can get their air force off the ground?'

'Not at present,' Gaines answered, recovering some of his composure. 'But that could be arranged. There is a general plan for air cover of Israel in the case of massive air attack.'

'Does it concern itself with population centers?'

'Yes, sir. It does.'

'Okay,' Smith replied, somewhat mollified, 'do it. I want it to be fitted in to Palm Beach.'

'It may detract from our total strike capability,' Gaines said defensively.

'Enough to hamper the operation?'

There was a pause. Again Johansson filled the void. 'I feel it incumbent upon me, Mr. President, to point out that any reduction of air support for our troops and transport planes, especially when they are unloading and most vulnerable, may trigger a response from the Russians who would otherwise be restrained by our force of arms.'

'I appreciate the point, Mr. Secretary. We are taking a calculated risk at best. As I recall, sir, mobilizing for Palm Beach was an idea you promoted. If the Chairman is going to call it cause for World War III, the absence or appearance of air support in one corner of the Mediterranean or another isn't going to change his mind. Are you still of the opinion that he will not choose war?'

Johansson measured his words carefully. 'I am still of the opinion that there will be sufficient time to inform him of the facts. And that the certainty that at least some of Ben Kelb's plans for destruction will be carried out should provide sufficient proof. Then more positively, 'He won't fight.'

'All right. Then give the Israelis anti-missile cover. As much as you can without endangering the operation.' He turned back to Gaines. 'Understood?'

'Yes, sir.'

The air in the room was heavy. Kugel ran his finger between his collar and his thick bulging neck. Smith toyed with his pencil. The others waited silently.

Abruptly, the President asked, 'Mr. Johansson, what will be the reaction of Europe to our action?'

'Abject horror, Mr. President. The entire world will think that we have gone mad. We can explain from now until the knell of doom. The French will proclaim that to salve our egos we have sacrificed the economy of the world. The Japanese will commit hara-kiri en masse.'

'The result will be roughly the same if we don't act, isn't that so?'

'If we do not concede to Ben Kelb's demands, yes, the results will be exactly the same. A large degree of destruction in the Mideast fields disrupting the supply of oil, hurting America to some degree, and most especially Europe and Japan. As for the underdeveloped nations ... a quick trip back to the Dark Ages.'

'Yet you have never indicated that we should make the concessions.'

Johansson drew himself up in the chair, his silver hair almost touching the shade of the lamp, the light casting strange shadows on the austere hollow-cheeked face. 'Mr. President, you appointed me to serve in the field of foreign policy as Secretary of State. I am sure that you feel as I do that my responsibility is to this state. The thought of submitting to coercion has, truthfully, never entered my mind.'

The President covered his mouth with his hand to conceal his amusement. He closed his eyes and thought, You are trapped, Oscar.

'If we take the responsibility for precipitating economic disaster on our sister nations, and the chance of total, exterminating war, then should we not be prepared to salvage something for the rest of the world other than our untarnished sovereignty?'

Johansson raised his eyebrow a trifle and leaned forward on his elbows. I have been had, he thought.

Gaines and Carver turned their heads from Smith to Johansson and back again, as though watching a tennis match. Kugel tugged at his collar again.

Well, Smith thought, here goes nothing. 'I want to propose something to you, gentlemen. I believe there is a way to expiate the sin of wanting to maintain our sovereignty.'

Kugel took a deep breath and looked at the ceiling.

'We are, by our actions, depriving the world of its principal supply of petroleum. I suggest that we apply the strictest controls over domestic consumption, and announce simultaneously with our actions in the Mideast that we intend to make up that deficit out of our own production to the degree that will allow our allies in both Europe and Asia to operate their economies at the same level of capacity as we do our own.'

Walton Carver exploded, 'Mr. President, you can't be serious.'

'I am indeed.'

'But, Mr. President,' Carver continued, 'the dislocation will be staggering. In the first place, in order to manage any reasonable level of productivity under such circumstances, you'd have to increase production by perhaps one hundred percent. Probably more.'

'I am aware.'

'Think of our defense posture,' Gaines interjected. 'We would run through our proven reserves of petroleum in a few short years at that level. And assuming that it could be done equitably, you would reduce our level of industrial output to perhaps seventy-five percent or less of capacity. You are talking about throwing millions out of work. You'd have twenty percent of America standing on breadlines. A complete economic collapse.'

Johansson said, 'Drastic reductions in industrial output, transportation, utility services. Massive unemployment. The complete disruption of society. What will it profit us to try to maintain an independent foreign policy if we are to bankrupt ourselves attempting to save the world?'

'What shall it profiteth a man if he shall gain the whole world and lose his soul?'

The three Cabinet members stared at Smith in surprise.

'How long shall we survive if we emerge standing proudly erect on top of a heap of ashes? We don't live alone in the world. If we want to set the example of strength, then we must set the example of sacrifice.'

'And when we have sacrificed all of our assets?' Johansson interjected.

The President relaxed in his chair and put his hands on the table. 'We shall innovate, Mr. Secretary, and we shall take a risk. I have made my decision on the basis of a technical discovery made by General Motors. They are on the verge of producing a solar-powered car. I propose to finance the changeover with government funds. I propose to go on a wartime footing and to request war powers from the Congress. I want the power to dislocate industries, move work forces, shift capital. I want to take the half of the economy that lives on automobiles and transform it by main force so that we can maintain an operative economy, and at the same time free our petroleum resources for sharing with the rest of the world.

'We have sufficient petroleum reserves and production to maintain a reasonable semblance of economic activity in the United States while taking up the slack from the Middle East for six, or perhaps nine, months. By the end of that time, the availability of the new car should reduce the need for gasoline sufficiently to permit a change in refinery runs and increase the production of heating oils, industrial fuels and the base for petrochemicals.

'If need be, the government will go into the used-car business and the finance business. How many cars are there on the road now? A hundred million. Times a retail value of, on average, two thousand dollars. That's two hundred billion dollars. If we salvage fifty percent, that's one hundred billion. In reality, of course, it would be somewhat less than that. The savings that result from the modernization of plant and equipment plus the influx of funds from abroad to pay for our oil should defray much of that cost. By the time that we're through with that program, and heavy research on other fuel sources and other energy media, we ought to come out somewhere near even. And with a completely rebuilt industrial power. It will be just like losing a war.' Smith leaned back and appraised his advisors. 'Well, Mr. Johansson, Mr. Carver, and Mr. Gaines, will I have your support?'

After an eternity had passed, Oscar Johansson pushed his chair away from the table and stood. 'Mr. President, if you will excuse us, we have much to consider. There is much planning to be done. I must face the problems of explaining our course of action to others. Possibly a speech, by you of course, before the United Nations. It will have to be done quickly. We won't be able to get help without tipping our hand. And of course, Walton ... Walton will have to consider the incredible problem of mobilization ... and George. Palm Beach must be altered ... the defense implications. Who can deal with the Congress? We have so little time ...'

'Yes, Oscar,' said the President, 'we are very pressed for time. Please come back ... shall we say, in two days. Does that suit you?'

Carver and Gaines rose and shook the President's hand wordlessly. Johansson hung back a moment, then offered his hand to the President, the muscles in his jaws twitching, emotions struggling beneath the parchment skin. Smith thought that his hand was curiously warm; he sensed a slight tremor.

Kugel showed them out, then returned to the room. 'Do you know what he said as the elevator door closed?'

'Who?' Smith asked wearily.

'Oscar. He said that he knew how Roscoe Conklin felt the day Chester Arthur threw him out of the White House. He said that he has discovered the President.'

Goodrich looked at the cable that he had removed from the sealed envelope, folded it through its center, then opened it to read it again, as though in disbelief.

Suddenly conscious that he was not alone, he looked up at his secretary, who had brought him the message. 'That's all, Jean. Thank you.'

She hesitated, as though reluctant to leave. 'Mr. Goodrich ...'

'Yes. Is there something that I can do for you?'

'Yes, sir. You know I'm starting my vacation now? I've been planning it for some time.'

He smiled. 'I'm sorry.' He glanced at his calendar. 'I'd forgotten. Let's see. You're supposed to go at the end of the week and be back the first week in October. You reminded me two weeks ago.' He shook his head ruefully. 'Just make sure that I'm covered by someone competent from the pool. And tell her about my idosyncrasies. What is the date today?'

'The fifteenth of September. Thursday.'

'That'll be just fine, Jean. Would you ask Mr. Hultz and Mr. Coughtry to come in now. And hold all calls. I don't want to be disturbed once they arrive.'

Goodrich sat silently behind his desk, folding and unfolding the cable. In short order there was a knock at the door. First Hultz entered, then a moment later Coughtry.

Goodrich motioned them toward his desk, then stood, stretched and held out the now worn piece of paper. 'Gentlemen, the game begins in earnest.'

Hultz fairly ripped the paper from his hand, holding it so that the anxious Coughtry could read over his shoulder. 'So the little bastard is finally finished. I can't make up my mind whether or not I am relieved. I'm torn between anxiety over the possibility that it will turn out to be a bomb, and the feeling that I am participating in a kind of Genesis.'

Goodrich said, 'At least for the moment, I want to enjoy the elation. Note if you will the continuing posture of self-effacement.'

Coughtry read aloud, ' "Goodrich" . . . nice friendly beginning . . . "only minor details remain. Prepare legal matters as you see fit. Have competent, repeat, competent scientific and technical man available to me simultaneously. Prior to delivery of last item, will require certified check made out to Swiss Bank Corporation for one hundred thousand dollars. Delivery to be made to my representative in usual place by hand. He will provide further instructions to your messenger about delivery. Messenger should be authorized to agree to time and place of closing. Having him here at

11 :00 A.M. Saturday, September 17." Signed A.E. It was sent from St. Raphael. That's on the Mediterranean coast.'

Goodrich nodded and said, 'I get the impression that we are actually about to meet our genius face to face. Who should we send, I wonder? I am sorely tempted to go myself.'

'Didn't he say that he wanted a scientific type?' Coughtry asked.

'I think that was for the closing, wherever he wants to have it. This is just the preliminary. Still and all, if he wants that money, I suppose that it would be best to have somebody who can talk the language. Which one of you wants to go?'

Hultz and Coughtry looked at one another tentatively. Hultz spoke first. 'I think that Don is certainly more qualified than I am on technical grounds.'

'I am,' Coughtry agreed, 'but insofar as negotiating, or handling people is concerned, I am sure George would do a better job, if our friend is anything in person like he is in print.'

Goodrich thought for a moment, then clapped his hands once sharply. 'George, you're elected. Got your passport handy?'

'I'm all set.'

'Fine. I think you ought to leave tonight.' He reached for the intercom. 'Jean, would you bring me a check request please? Made out for one hundred thousand dollars to the order of the Swiss Bank Corporation. Tell them downstairs that I want it certified.' He paused, listening. 'Tell them to charge it to research and development.' He hung up. 'Let's skip the dining room today. I think we deserve a special lunch.'

When Goodrich came back from lunch, Jean was already instructing an attractive dark-haired girl in the intricacies of serving as his temporary secretary for the two weeks or so that she would be gone. He passed on into his office,

184

signed the check request and ordered it sent down to Hultz, then took a plasticized card from his wallet. Using his private phone, he dialed the number and waited. Presently, the buzzing stopped, a voice at the other end answered, 'Yes?'

'Milton Goodrich,' he replied.

There was a pause of half a minute.

'Good afternoon, Mr. Goodrich,' said the voice of the President.

'Good afternoon, sir. The message has arrived. The project is complete. We are sending someone over to talk to him now.'

'Someone reliable?'

'Our Senior Executive Vice President, sir. George Hultz. He has been with me for many years. He's been involved in this matter from the beginning.'

'Do you think that he should be accompanied by security people? In consideration of the new importance of this matter.'

'I don't think that I'm competent to judge that, sir. However, our friend is a very peculiar customer. He said just the messenger. I would hate to have him scared away.'

'So would I, Mr. Goodrich, but just the same, I think we ought to have some kind of coverage. Just one highly efficient man, dressed in a pair of slacks and a summer jacket. Another tourist. All I need to know is the plane Hultz is going to take.'

Goodrich read him the details from the slip on his desk.

'Thank you, Mr. Goodrich. I am sure that we can get all of the information that we require on Mr. Hultz from State Department passport files. If this project turns out to be as you have suggested, then I want you down here to discuss the practicalities of proceeding with the program.'

Twenty

'Hah. Cripple. I heard your third leg.' The General pulled open the door of his office to admit La Brousse, who was about to knock. He entered sheepishly, leaning some of his weight on a malacca cane.

The General went behind the desk and pointed at the side chair. 'By the way, La Brousse, I have inquired at the Invalides to see if they have room for another useless pensioner. Would you prefer something with a view or the quiet of the inner court?'

La Brousse looked at the old man speculatively. Since they had returned to Paris, two days after he was shot, the General had not missed an opportunity to jibe him about his impairment. But he had visited him at the hospital every day during the ten days he was there. And La Brousse overheard him threaten bodily harm to the doctors if they failed to provide for the healing and comfort of his – what was it? – ah, yes, prize moron. A strange man, the General, La Brousse thought.

'So, Cripple, no answer. Well, then I shall have to choose your accommodations myself. Unless perhaps you regain your usual form and make it possible for me to retain your dubious services. Well, you came. Have you something to say, or is this a social call?'

'I had a call from Colonel Brunschwig. He wants to know why we are still keeping a cover on Hamilton. He would also like to know why, since we are keeping him under wraps, we let him wander about as he pleases, at all hours of the day and night.'

The General snorted. 'Well, call him back and tell him it's none of his fucking business.' He paused and looked suspiciously at La Brousse. 'Why the hell didn't he talk to me?'

'I told him you were out. I said I was just following your instructions.'

'Ever the diplomat. You would have done well in the dock at Nuremberg. You would have been hanged. What is happening with Hamilton? Not so much as a half-hearted attempt to maim or disfigure him?'

'No, sir. I was wondering if perhaps they had decided that he wasn't really a danger to them. Perhaps we should leave him be?'

'We have only been at this for two weeks. It took God one week to make the earth. Leave the security on him. They will try again. Have you heard anything from Rhabbouz today?'

'Not a word. You know, he sent me flowers at the hospital.'

The General harrumphed and dug at the papers on his desk. 'He must have thought you were dead.'

Donald stretched his arms toward the ceiling and yawned. He sat balanced on the stool with one foot touching the floor. He looked at the pile of blueprints on his drafting table and the list of numbers beside them, most of them showing tiny checks to one side. He gnawed at his pencil. He was right. He had ordered one hundred twenty thousand foundation bricks. And one hundred twenty thousand bricks had been delivered and set in place. The bill showed delivery of one hundred forty thousand. Was it the brick company? Maybe? More likely it was somebody on the payroll building a house for free. The construction industry is no place to look for saints, he thought. He looked with pride at his design and then at the shambles across the road which told his practiced eye that it was beginning to take shape.

He checked his watch. It was nearly half past five. He could hear his young French assistant grumbling from the cubicle across the hall that he was ready to leave for the day.

The great machines that were digging the hotel foundation across the road were stilled. Despite the fresh breeze blowing across the Gulf from St. Tropez and the relatively late hour, the tin quonset hut that served as Hamilton's office retained the heat of the day. He wiped at the perspiration on his forehead with the back of his hand. Tomorrow, he thought, is Friday. Then, cheered, the day after tomorrow is Saturday. And on Saturday Marie Jo will arrive at Nice Airport promptly at noon. She has three days off. I will, he thought, take Monday off. He lit a cigarette, looked down again and said, 'The hell with it. I can't finish it in one day. Hey, François. Let's knock off. I'll bet you want to go home.'

He put his packed briefcase into the tiny trunk of the car, stopped for a moment to appreciate the twilight, then got in and began the drive back to Toulon. From force of habit, he checked his rear-view mirror to see if his permanent shadow was there. As reliable as the sunset itself, he thought. The black Peugeot pulled out of a driveway some meters down the road from the construction site and followed him at a comfortable distance.

He fiddled with the radio until he found some pleasing music and considered the past two weeks. Two days after La Brousse had been shot, Levy, the doctor-cum-spy, had permitted his return to a hospital in Paris. He had heard no word from the General, but had become quite aware of his shadow. On occasion he had been tempted to try to lose him. He would definitely do something about it for the coming weekend. He liked to make love on the beach and did not relish the thought of being inhibited by a permanent audience. He recalled La Brousse, collapsing on the floor, and the remains of the late Kalman Jacobs. Big deal, he thought. We've all got to go sometime. At least I'll go happy. He whistled with the music and considered some techniques for evasion.

*

George Hultz allowed the rubber conveyor to carry him through the sepulchral corridor that led from Satellite Three to the central terminal building. He stepped off and onto the line which led through passport control. When he had been cleared he walked forward onto another conveyor, then leaned forward against the pull of gravity as it bore him upward through the clear plastic tubing that led to the upper level in the open center of the surrealistic structure that is Charles de Gaulle Airport. He found his bag, rented a car and drove the thirty minutes to Paris.

At the office of the law firm which represents General Motors' interests in France, he was ushered into a sumptuous, if creaky, board room, where he was greeted by the partner in charge. Following Goodrich's instructions, he arranged for the partner to be available during the succeeding ten days wherever his presence would be required. He left the building less than half an hour after he had entered.

Hultz crossed the broad expanse of Avenue Foch to his parked car, then drove to the Alma and across to the Left Bank and Boulevard St. Germain. By luck he found a parking space quickly, and stuffed himself with bœuf à la mode at Brasserie Lipp. Content, he drove himself back to the airport to catch the four o'clock flight to Nice. As he boarded the plane, he looked past a man about his own age and height in a sport jacket and slacks who had sat calmly waiting at the airport since they had arrived from New York together.

As Hultz slept soundly in his room at the Byblos in St. Tropez, recovering from the effects of the previous night's flight, another plane arrived at Charles de Gaulle Airport from New York. Ten minutes later, the radio telephone on the bridge of the *Glen Pool* rang. The steward answered, pushed the intercom button that signalled the crews quarters and said, 'Aboussara, there is a call for you on the RT.'

There was a pause, then a sleepy voice replied, 'Tell them to hold on. I'll be right up.' In less than a minute, he arrived, dressed only in a pair of skin-tight black slacks, his splayed bare feet slapping the deck as he hurried. He picked up the receiver from the table, then turned and glared at the steward, who still stood in the room, aimlessly dusting. The boy stopped dusting and left the bridge.

'Aboussara. Yes. Welcome.' He listened attentively. 'Yes, I understand. Forty-two or three. About six feet-two. Graying. Yes, I understand. On the jetty. Where the other one was. You are coming here. Fine. Yes, I'm sure you will be rewarded in just the fashion that you wish.'

He hung up and walked down the gangway to the stateroom section. He listened for a moment at the door. It was a curious advantage to deal with people who are noisy when they rut, he thought. It saved many embarrassments. He knocked softly.

'Yes, who is it?' Fosburgh replied.

'Aboussara. May I speak to you for a moment please?'

'I'll be right out.'

He emerged in a couple of minutes, his eyes still dull with sleep. 'What is it?'

'I think that perhaps we should go up on the bridge where it is quiet.'

'All right, what's the matter?' Fosburgh said, settling himself in the helmsman's chair behind the wheel.

Aboussara remained standing. 'It's our friend from New York. They have sent someone here from the company. A man named Hultz.'

'They must be near the end,' Fosburgh said, rubbing his chin. 'He is one of the most important men in the company. Any word as to whom he is to meet, or where or when?'

'Yes, this morning, on the jetty, at eleven. No mention of who.'

'Well, I know what Hultz looks like. He's quite tall, mid-forties, craggy face.'

'Yes, I was told. There was also mention of some kind of special reward.'

Fosburgh grinned nastily. 'That will come later. Just make sure that you make contact with the people that are supposed to be met by this man. The Colonel and I are very interested in what they are up to.'

'And the man Hultz, what am I to do with him?'

'Just find out whom he is to meet – not a messenger this time: the man behind the messenger.' He turned his palms up and smiled again, 'Then kill him and do as you did with the first one – cut off his balls.'

Fosburgh spun himself gently to and fro in the chair and thought how much he wanted to see the look on Goodrich's face. His little mystery permanently disorganized. His triumph shattered and still-born. His right-hand man dead, his balls bulging in his mouth. Fosburgh slapped his thigh, rose, and, laughing, made his way to the stateroom and the waiting Madeleine.

Arthur wet the tips of his fingers with his tongue and dabbed at the cowlick that stood up in the middle of Stanley's freshly combed hair. 'Now repeat it to me once more.'

'But Arthur,' he whined, 'I understand. We've already been over it six times.'

Arthur tapped his foot on the floor and crossed his arms. His face set in stubborn lines. Defeated, Stanley started again.

'I put this rose,' he held it up, 'behind my right ear and just keep walking up and down the jetty until a man accosts me.' He giggled. 'He will be wearing a suit and tie. He will give me an envelope without markings, except that it will have M.G., 767 Fifth Avenue, New York, New York, on the back flap. I will tell him that a note,' he held it up, 'will be waiting for him at Le Senequier after six under the name of Mr. Weeks. In the note he will find instructions as to where he is to go for the next instructions. Then I am to take the envelope that he gives me, write Post Office Box 818 on it and take it directly to the St. Tropez Post Office. Then I am to go to the beach and to meet you at the Stereo at seven sharp.'

Arthur took Stanley's face between his hands and kissed him convincingly on the mouth. 'You are a good boy. Now remember what else I said. You just think of something you want from Arthur and it's yours. But you say nothing about this, Stanley. Not to anyone – or no present.'

Arthur watched Stanley hop on his motorbike and buzz down the little road in the direction of St. Tropez. Thoroughly satisfied with himself, Arthur went inside to the desk and sat down. Before him were several neat piles of papers and some heavy simulated-leather cardboard covers. He punched holes in the sets of papers, then lined them up and inserted them into the binders, each one imprinted *Edelman Solar Propulsion System*. Finished, he rose and went to the kitchen. Once there, he kneeled before the stove, reached under it and pulled several tiles away. With some effort he drew a heavy steel box from the hole, dialed the combination, opened it and replaced the papers. Then he replaced the box and the tiles and rose to his feet, brushing his hands together.

'That,' he said aloud, 'they will get when I have a completed contract.'

Arthur felt strangely sad. Triumph was at hand, but the game was over. He would, of course, demand complete scientific control over the development of his discoveries. But that meant dealing with the realities of offices and ties and suits and reasonably regular hours. Well, at least he would see to it that he had the nicest possible surroundings. Perhaps he should make them build him a laboratory. Once his fame was established, he had to take care to comport himself in a manner that would force history to recognize Arthur Edelman the man, as well as the scholar, inventor and genius. Dignity goes well, he straightened himself, with the Nobel Prize. There will have to be sacrifices, he felt regretfully, thinking of Stanley.

He wandered to his clothes closet to select something appropriate for the meeting. Then went to the bathroom to shave. As he looked in the mirror, a chill came over him, and he thought for the first time in weeks of Pascal Lambert.

*

Bauermann glanced at his watch for the hundredth time in the half hour that he had been pacing up and down the sidewalk in front of the Hôtel Roy René. His tongue clove to the roof of his mouth as it always did when the specter of El Kaffar arose in his mind's eye. So precise, so exquisitely polite and well spoken, so frighteningly cold and threatening.

He had done well for El Kaffar, Bauermann thought. He had followed instructions to the letter, and it had not been easy. Nonetheless, El Kaffar now held the biggest private block of General Motors in the world, and was well on the way to being able to demand board representation – ten or twelve percent should do – and a substantial voice in the company's affairs. And even now, certain persons in Paris were trying to buy the block that was owned by Bloch – he corrected himself – he meant Dassault, the old Jew. Dassault was the largest individual holder in the world. He didn't want to sell. Perhaps if he was told it was for the Arabs, who were after all the best customers for his Mirage fighter planes, he would be more favorably inclined.

His musings were interrupted by a horn honking just behind him. He turned and looked through the windscreen of a red sports car into the smiling face of Mohammed El Kaffar. He started to walk toward the car, but El Kaffar motioned him away toward the hotel.

He went inside and sat at a table in the corner of the little bar. He ordered a glass of white wine, and presently El Kaffar arrived, dressed in a business suit – well cut, dark and conservative.

He stood to shake hands. 'Good evening, Excellency.'

They sat. El Kaffar ordered citron pressé.

'I was not aware that you spoke French so well, Excellency.'

'Yes, I know, Bauermann, you didn't realize that camels understand French.' He smiled with the other man's discomfort. 'Well, dear Bauermann, how are we faring? Are we a success in our little venture? I have been rather out of touch.'

Bauermann handed El Kaffar a three-by-five-inch card that had been in his inside pocket. It was slightly damp with his nervous perspiration.

El Kaffar took no notice. 'Ah, well done, Bauermann. You are to continue as before. Up to the limits which I have given you. We are well on the way to our little victory.'

Bauermann hesitated, then exposed the idea he had had about Marcel Dassault.

The smile faded from El Kaffar's face. 'That would be quite stupid, you know. After the considerable pains to which I have gone to mask my transactions, you intend to approach the third-richest man in France and ask him to give up a possession of which he is inordinately proud, and convince him, in fact, by revealing the approximate identity of your client. You are an incredible fool, Bauermann. It is definitely the will of Allah that I have been sent to you to prevent you from further despoiling your wife's birthright.'

'I never thought of it that way, Excellency.'

'That is quite clear. I must go to my room to wash. Are you staying here?'

'No, Excellency. As per your instructions.'

'Well done. You can wait for me here in the bar. I shan't be long.'

El Kaffar took the key from the desk and mounted the stairs to his room. As he had requested, they had put him on the top floor overlooking the street. He opened the door and turned on the lights, saw that his bags had already been brought up, then sat in a straight-backed chair by the window. By craning his neck, he could see the impressive spire of the Church of St. John of Malta down the boulevard, grafted in the middle of the fourteenth century to the church built a hundred years earlier.

There was a calm air to Aix-en-Provence as evening fell. He looked down on the ancient plantain shade trees which lined the Cour Mirabeau, the heart of the city. He rested for a moment, then took a deep breath and stood to reach for his briefcase. He removed the small white card and looked at it again : at the 20/9, and at the curious diagram in ink, the sixpointed Star of David pierced through by a crescent moon. Then he tore the card into small pieces and carefully burned them in an ashtray.

Tuesday would be the twentieth. That left six days exactly. By next Monday it must all be complete. The effort, the years of planning, the posturing. Or it might all end on the gibbet.

He removed a sheaf of papers from his suitcase, checked his appearance in the antiqued mirror above the highboy on the wall and went downstairs to join Bauermann.

'The restaurant here has a great reputation, Excellency. Four stars in the *Guide Bleu*.'

'Yes, I know. That is good, Bauermann. People who do not enjoy food are robbed of one of the pleasures of life.'

They strolled into the comfortably illuminated dining room, all crystal and linen and starched waiters, requested a table for four in a corner and sat down.

After ordering, El Kaffar asked, 'Do you have the rest of the information that I requested?'

'Certainly, Excellency,' Bauermann replied. 'It is very easy to come by. They are required to print such things in their annual financial reports, and in publicly available submissions to the government as well. Here is a list of all of the foreign subsidiaries and affiliates of General Motors, together with the location of their factories. This next page, which was assembled by the research department of my bank, indicates the approximate product mix of each plant, the number of employees, a rough approximation of the sales in dollars and in local currency, and the year in which operations started.'

El Kaffar studied the papers carefully as the two men worked their way through appetizer and soup. He drank only Evian water. Bauermann had all but finished a full bottle of Meursault and was beginning to nod a little from its effects.

Wiping his lips fastidiously, El Kaffar turned to him. 'You

see, Bauermann, it can be done. They can build manufacturing facilities anywhere, even on sand. They are not so particular as a negative press would have you believe. They have a need for labor, in the capitalist fashion, as cheap as possible. But they need and want willing hands. Though they are the flagship of American commerce, they are completely international in scope.' Warming to his subject, he continued, 'What they need, Bauermann, is a new Japan. A land with the resource of effort and perspiration. Amplify that if you will with petroleum, the staff of industrial life, and you can see what potential there exists in Araby.'

Bauermann leaned forward and said confidentially, 'Bah, the damn Jews would only blow it up.'

El Kaffar winced, as though in pain; then his eyes clouded over. He finished his meal in silence.

Bauermann staggered slightly, brushing against El Kaffar as they walked out of the door onto Boulevard du Roi René and turned down to the Avenue du Parc toward the University City. A slight mist had settled, giving an uncharacteristic chill to the air. They walked in silence for several minutes, El Kaffar striding purposefully, Bauermann struggling to keep pace with him, breathing heavily.

El Kaffar turned his head without stopping. 'Bauermann, are you still there?'

'Yes, Excellency,' he panted.

'I am hopeful that this little walk has dulled some of the effects of your wine and sharpened your senses. I have further instructions for you.' He stopped before the darkened entrance of an hôtel particulier.

'Yes, Excellency.'

'You have until Friday the twenty-third to complete your program. You are to be a little less cautious in your buying. The number of shares which was agreed upon is to be assembled by Friday.'

'But, Excellency, the price. If we attempt to buy that many shares the price will go up perhaps ten, or even fifteen, percent.'

'Is there sufficient money even at that rate?'

'Yes, Excellency. More than enough.'

'Can it be done with reasonable anonymity?'

'I don't know, Excellency. It is a very large quantity.'

'Well, then, can anonymity be preserved at least until,' he paused and considered, 'shall we say the following Tuesday? That is, the twenty-seventh.'

'There will be considerable coverage by the press if the price of the stock rises rapidly, especially if the volume is extremely high. But, if our brokers dodge the questions, we should be able to stay hidden for at least that long.'

'And the government, will they not inquire?'

'It is possible. But certainly not likely. It only becomes their affair if some irregularity is suspected. There is no law against buying large quantities of shares – even in General Motors.'

'Not even by a foreign interest.'

'Correct.'

'All right then. Do as I have said. Instruct Nicholson. He is probably in the best position to attract institutions into selling some or all of their positions. Buy, Bauermann. Buy all that you can until Friday. Then stop, you will receive further instructions. Go home.'

'Where may I reach you?'

'We have trod this road before, Bauermann,' an unpleasant edge to his voice, 'I will not go over it again. You have your instructions. Do not attempt to contact me at the hotel. I am leaving now.'

He turned on his heel and walked swiftly down the street in the direction from which they had come, leaving Bauermann shaking his head in the doorway.

Twenty-one

On the clear comfortable Saturday afternoon, with the flags hanging limply before the myriad government buildings, Jack Kugel pondered the logistical problem of getting the Secretaries of State, Defense and the Interior into the White House and then out again, unnoticed by the occupants of the Press Room.

Walton Carver stood in the line of visitors waiting to tour the Executive Mansion. He was dressed in a sport coat and slacks and wore dark glasses. By prearrangement, he left the tour when it passed the state dining room, and whisked into the special elevator to the vault. Gaines came in a delivery truck. Johansson arrived at noon with his wife, ostensibly for luncheon with the First Family in their private quarters.

One by one they reached the sterile silence of the presidential bunker.

The President sat, stern-faced, across from Kugel at the poker table. 'Please, gentlemen, sit down.' He did not rise. Dark circles were visible under his eyes. 'Mr. Gaines,' he began without preliminaries, 'have our decisions of the last meeting been implemented?'

Gaines regarded a stack of papers before him. 'Yes, sir. The state of alert still exists. White is still at war games near the SAC base, the MATS wing is still on alert, and Admiral Thurston, with minor variations, is continuing his patrol pattern.'

'What variations?'

'As you ordered, sir. The missile cruiser *Long Beach* has been shifted to the extreme eastern wing of the maneuver fleet and is now patrolling about forty miles from the Israeli coast, well within range of her anti-missile radar and missiles. The second and third carrier flight wings of the *Ticonderoga* have been assigned to anti-aircraft and cover support for the Israeli Army over Golan and Sinai.'

'Mr. Johansson?'

'As you instructed, Mr. President, I have personally written by hand, no copies, a speech which will announce our actions to the world, together with an explanation of our petroleum support program as you outlined it.' He handed a yellow pad to the President. 'I hope that it will meet with your approval.'

Without being asked, Walton Carver began, 'I have a complete prospective on the maximum capability of this country to produce crude oil and refined products during the next eight months. I have estimated,' he said with self-deprecation, 'the approximate cost of the dislocation that would be necessary to proceed with the development of the solar automobile, and have outlined a plan of execution.'

Johansson interrupted, 'I have attempted to prepare a legislative program which would provide the required enabling acts, so that Walton's measures will have a legal basis. I cannot attest to the degree they will find Congressional acceptance. There is no way to know until we have tried.'

The President rose and stood for a moment facing away from the table. His shoulders were stooped. Then he turned to face them and said, 'Gentlemen, two days ago I was informed by Mr. Goodrich that the inventor has completed his project. I may say I have not slept since. A senior officer of General Motors has been dispatched to arrange preliminary negotiations. The entire matter is to be settled by the middle, or at the very least the end, of this week. I have secured the promise of Mr. Goodrich, who intends to go to Europe to close the matter himself, that there will be no announcement until I have given him the word.

'In a sense, of course, I am relieved. The possibility which we have discussed is becoming a reality. The technical capability required to execute this plan is now in our hands.'

He wiped his forehead and sighed. 'On the other hand, it is now our responsibility to take the drastic military steps which make our dependence on this slender thread of hope so necessary. Ben Kelb is away from the capital and has not responded to an urgent request for another meeting. El Kaffar cannot be reached.'

The men at the table leaned forward in anticipation.

'We have a meeting with Congressional leadership Monday night. I am directing, by Executive Order, that the final stage of operation Palm Beach be commenced immediately, that the alert be transformed to a state of military action, and that at 0500 hours on the morning of Tuesday, September 27th, Quahrein time, the armed forces of the United States launch combined air, naval, and airborne infantry action against the People's Republic of Quahrein for the purpose of preempting to whatever degree possible the destruction of lives and property in that country and its neighbors.' He turned away again, choked with emotion, then said, muffled, into the corner, 'The entire defense establishment is to be put on war alert simultaneously, all anti-aircraft and missile defense systems are to go on a war footing at 0400 Quahrein time of the same day. I will speak to the Chairman at 0500. I hope to God he will understand.'

A gray cast came over the patrician face of the Secretary of State. He removed the cigarette from the gold and onyx holder and stubbed it out. Then, just audibly, said, 'Amen.'

Twenty-two

Donald Hamilton had been foggily surprised when the phone rang at a little after seven on Saturday morning. Friday, like Thursday, had seemed endless. Though he liked his work, he disliked his petty French assistant with his constant whining. He had had to let him off early in the afternoon on the premise that his mother was sick. As a result, in order to keep up with the day's schedule, he had been forced to do the work of both, and was stuck in the cheerless quonset hut until nearly seven. It was nine o'clock by the time he had gotten back to Toulon. He had treated himself to dinner at the Grand Hôtel, then gone to the little bar down the street from his house and gotten liberally soused.

His head buzzed as he took the receiver from the hook and mumbled a faint hello.

'Donald, darling. It's Marie Jo. Wake up.'

'What the hell time is it?' he asked, pulling the covers over his head to keep out the offending light.

'Ten past seven. Donald, are you there?'

'Yeah, I'm here. What's up?'

'I got shifted around ...'

'Oh shit,' he said, 'you're not coming.' He sat up and fumbled for a cigarette and matches.

'No, darling, quite the contrary. I wanted to tell you that I'm coming earlier than I had expected. I'm calling from the airport. Donald, say something. If it's too early, or if you don't want me, I can always ...'

'I want you. What's the new schedule?'

'I'll be on the eight twenty-five from Paris. It arrives at Nice at nine thirty-five. Can you pick me up, or is it too early?'

'Are you wearing a bra?'

She paused for a moment, puzzled. 'Yes. Why do you ask?'

'Can you take it off – now?'

'Yes, I suppose. I'll flop a bit in my uniform, but I can.'

'Okay, I'll make you a deal. You manage to take off the bra, and I'll manage to be on time to pick you up at the airport.'

'Pervert.'

'Love you. Goodbye.' He hung up laughing, swung his feet over the side of the bed, dropped the unlit cigarette on the table and went whistling to the bathroom, his hangover suddenly gone.

After he had shaved and showered, he pirouetted, still stripped, before the mirror. His pot seemed to have diminished. Not bad at all, he thought. Considering the age of the article.

He threw on a pair of white slacks and a silky red knit shirt, picked a pair of socks out of the drawer and stuffed them in the pocket of his blazer, then put on his shoes. Just in case we want to go someplace fancy, he thought. With a gleam in his eye he chose an almost invisible nylon bathing suit he had bought a couple of days before.

It was twenty to eight when Donald skipped out of the door of the apartment house and headed toward his car. He got in and revved the motor till it turned over properly, then pulled out into the street in the direction of RN 98. His bleary-eyed shadow, just finishing his shift, cursed loudly, started his car and chased after him, missing his replacement who was a minute behind.

Donald horned impatiently, stuck in the morning traffic heading down the Boulevard des Anglais. He dodged through the slowly moving cars till he finally reached the entrance of the airport. Tires squealing, he pulled into the parking lot, jumped out of the car and ran toward the terminal. He rushed over to the gate and then, laughing at his own impatience, saw from the digital clock above the portal that it was only nine-twenty. He bought himself a paper and a cup of coffee and sat down to wait. Promptly at nine-thirty-five, the audio system announced the arrival of the Air Inter flight from Paris.

Within three minutes of the announcement, Marie Jo appeared, flushed and smiling, carrying a small suitcase. As advertised, she flopped a bit. They met in the middle of the hall and exchanged a lingering series of kisses.

Marie Jo opened one eye. 'Donald, we're drawing a crowd.'

He laughed, took her suitcase in one hand and her waist in the other, and led her out to the car. He started to pull out, then stopped at the curb. In the side mirror he could see his shadow running along the sidewalk toward his car, a cardboard container of coffee spilling in every direction. He got in and started the engine. Donald waved casually and rolled forward.

'What was that all about?'

'Oh, just a man I know.'

'Donald, would you pull over up there?' Marie Jo pointed to the parking space that overlooks the Baie des Anges at the top of the hill where the Autoroute begins. He did, parking the car parallel to the side of the road to get the best view of the bay and the sinuous mountainous curves of the Marina Residence.

'Did you mean what you said? On the phone, I mean.'

'What was that?'

'You said you loved me.'

'I thought that I said that I would pick you up on time if you took off your bra. I kept my word.' He reached out to cup her breasts in his hands. 'And I see that you kept your half of the bargain.'

'You did say it,' she pouted. 'You said, "Love you, good-bye." I heard you. I felt that that deserves something extra.'

She took his hand between her own and slipped it up her skirt. He felt the soft mass of curly hair and the moist warmth beneath. 'I took off my pants too. Did you mean it, Donald?'

He looked at her face, fresh and young, and moved his

fingers, caressing her gently, then reached out his hand behind her neck and pulled her face forward to kiss her. After a moment, he released her. 'Yes. Yes, I dare say that I do.' She threw her arms around his neck and crushed his lips against her mouth. A horn tooted as a car full of youthful voyeurs rode by. They separated.

'Another time and another place perhaps, mademoiselle,' he suggested. When he straightened around, he blushed to find his policeman shadow sitting on the front fender of a car parked twenty feet away. The policeman was eating a sandwich from the airport cafeteria. Donald banged on the side of the car and motioned him to get out of the way. The policeman threw away the remains of the sandwich with a sour look and left in his machine.

'Are we going to the beach?'

'Unless you'd rather find a quiet corner to fuck in.'

'You are vulgar ... but a man of inspiration. Can we stop in town first? I don't have any suntan oil.'

The Place des Lices was crowded with Saturday morning market, forcing them to park up the hill next to the Byblos and walk down to the jetty. She had shed her uniform in the car and thrown it in the tiny space behind the seats, putting on the bottom of a bathing suit and a tube top from the little suitcase. Donald kicked off his shoes and they walked barefoot down the centuries-old cobblestones to the shining harbor.

Donald turned to look at a gangly teen-age boy sitting disconsolately on a mooring stanchion by the side of the pier. He frowned. A memory flitted about just out of reach.

Marie Jo said, 'Oh, let's go in here. They have the kind that I like. See in the window. Piz Buin. It's Swiss, I think. They don't carry it at the shop on the beach.'

Aboussara watched Hamilton as he walked down the jetty and glanced furtively at the boy with the rose, confirming his belief that the American had more to do with this whole matter than anyone suspected. He still smarted from the remarks that Fosburgh had made after the business with the Jew in the car.

Aboussara watched Donald and Marie Jo walk into the pharmacy, then turned to watch the boy with the rose again.

Hultz threw back the shutters and inhaled deeply of the fresh air. He had laid out the suit and tie prescribed the previous evening. But it seemed to him that he would look very odd in such a costume, and so he changed into a pair of slacks and a blue blazer over a sport shirt. He slipped the envelope containing the check into the inside pocket of the jacket, checked his watch and walked down to the harbor. He strolled slowly until his eye fell upon Stanley, sitting next to his motorbike. He wanted to make sure he wasn't mistaken about the boy, so he sat down in a chair outside of Le Gorille and ordered a cup of coffee.

At the same time, Murchison, his Secret Service tail, also dressed in blazer and slacks, walked down the quay to preserve his anonymity, at the same time looking for a place where he could observe Hultz. Inadvertently, he brushed into Stanley, who said in his squeaky voice, 'You looking for me, Mister?' turning his head to expose the rose fully.

'Not hardly, young fella,' Murchison replied, walking quickly by.

After watching the performance, seeing that the boy had stopped a man who was dressed and had an appearance not unlike his own, Hultz was convinced that the boy with the rose was his target. He paid and walked over to him.

'Are you looking for an envelope?' he asked softly.

'Yeah. You got one? I got one for you too.'

'Well, let's not make a spectacle out of it. Meet me in the parking lot in back of the Byblos. Will that toy of yours make it?' He pointed at the bike.

'Aw, shit,' Stanley replied, hopped on, pedaled a few paces to kick off the motor, then shot into a side street and disappeared. Hultz, feeling self-conscious, ambled back to Le

Gorille and sat for five more minutes through a cup of the strong black coffe, then walked back up the hill. Giving him an adequate head start, Murchison followed.

Aboussara, leaning on the rail outside of the bridge, was beside himself. First Hamilton had appeared, confirming Aboussara's long-standing belief in his implication. Then the little fag with the rose had been approached by a middle-aged man too formally dressed for St. Tropez on a Saturday morning. Minutes later, another man, answering virtually the same description as this Hultz he had been told of, and dressed almost identically, had passed more words with the boy, then gone to the cafe. Now he had gone back toward the hill, and so had the boy. Aboussara made a snap decision, turned and clapped his hands sharply in the direction of the little Quahreinian steward who was polishing a brass hand-rail.

'Come here,' he said in Arabic. The steward sauntered over. 'I said come here, next to me on the rail.' The steward leaned on the rail facing Aboussara, who edged forward until they were almost touching. 'Do you know who I am, brother?'

'A member of the crew.'

'Other than that?'

'That doesn't concern me.'

Aboussara had carefully slipped his hand between them. He closed it now on the steward's testicles and exerted considerable pressure. The man turned red and gasped.

'You will make no sound, or I will tear them off and stuff them in your mouth. You do know who I am. You will do as I ask you. You will do anything that I ask you. Failure to obey will mean the loss of these poor things.' He closed his fingers savagely. The steward's eyes began to roll upward in their sockets. Aboussara released him.

'Do we understand each other?'

The steward, bent slightly forward, nodded yes.

'That's fine. When do you get off duty?'

'The afternoon steward comes on in five minutes. I am through at noon.'

'Until what time?'

'Until tomorrow at noon.'

'Good. You can be of use. Go and change your clothes now. I want you here in five minutes. Do you understand? And you are to say nothing. You have no plans?'

'No, no, nothing at all.'

Aboussara looked at him and patted his fly. 'Good. Hurry.'

The steward came back dressed in old white ducks and a plain tee shirt. 'Come with me,' Aboussara said, walking him by the arm down the gangplank. 'There is a couple in the drug store, I will point them out. You will follow them. The man drives a red roadster. Can you ride a motorcycle?' The man nodded yes. 'Good, take the little Suzuki that is used as a tender. If they go to the beach, you will tell me which one. If they go too far, or do not look as though they will stop, you will call me on the phone, understand? There, look through the window, the man with the graying hair next to the woman with the tits.'

Aboussara went to tell Fosburgh he had an errand to run on behalf of the Colonel.

'Well, Aboussara, I hope that the next errand you go on will result in some advantage to us, rather than more sensational headlines about your mechanical efficiency.'

Aboussara ignored him and made his way down the gangway, watching over his shoulder as the steward unslung the bike from its davits on the stern and lowered it to the jetty. He crossed into a side street where his own powerful machine was parked and started it. He eased forward through the Place des Lices, where the market was beginning to break up, and up the hill behind the Byblos. He arrived just in time to see Stanley start his motorbike and head down the hill. He saw one and then the other of the two men in blazers walk down the steps from the street to the lobby level. He cursed under his breath and followed the boy. He continued behind him as he rode across the jetty, where no vehicles are allowed during the day in season. When Stanley stopped at the post office and entered, he hopped off his machine and ran after him. He halted at the door and saw Stanley hand an envelope to the woman behind the counter. She dropped it into a mail bag and the boy walked out. Aboussara followed him on the road out to the beach, saw him turn at the Tahiti Road and move into Moorea.

Well, Aboussara thought, that's that. The little fag has performed his mission. He'll be here all day. I can come get him any time I want. I must deal with the others now. He threw his leg over the bike and rolled it around in the direction of town. As he cruised slowly down the road, he heard a horn signaling an oncoming car. He pulled to the side and watched Hamilton and Marie Jo run past him. About fifty yards further behind was the steward. He hailed him down. 'Well, now things are starting to go a bit in my direction. Listen, you need not watch them anymore. I have a new job for you. Have you any money?' The steward shook his head negatively. Aboussara reached into his pocket and gave him a one-hundred-franc note. 'Consider this a bonus. You will find a boy on Moorea Beach. He will not be hard to recognize. He is blond and pale and very frail-looking, as though he needs badly to be fed. He is a fag. He is about sixteen. Don't talk to him, but watch him. Follow him wherever he goes. If he leaves, you will have no trouble keeping up with him. He has a pale green Vespa Ciao. Call me if he goes somewhere and stops. If I am not at the boat, just stay with him. Is that clear?'

Aboussara ran the big Honda around the corner to the Tahiti Road and parked on the shoulder. He fumbled in the kit bag at the back and came up with two bottles. He walked casually across fields picked bare of their grapes. He stepped behind a clump of reeds some twenty feet high and emptied the bottle of motor oil onto the ground. He leaned over the edge of a culvert that ran by the reeds and washed the bottle out, filled it with the murky water and replaced the cork stopper. As an afterthought, he uncorked the other bottle, filled with clear fluid, and spilled a drop into the culvert. There was a flash of heat and light, and then nothing. He continued his walk across the fields until he came to the reeds that bordered the back of the Moorea Beach parking lot. He peered through to locate the attendant and Hamilton's car. The attendant was sitting on a small stool at the entrance opposite him, in conversation with a little boy. Hamilton's car, by good fortune, was in the row nearest him, about fifty feet further toward the beach.

Aboussara slipped into the lot and walked to the car. He tied a piece of string to the cork stoppers and opened the trunk. Measuring with his eye, he slipped both bottles under an edge of the spare tire which lay flat, and jammed them in firmly. He lowered the trunk lid until he could barely get his hand out. He removed the cork from the water bottle and held his thumb over the opening and slid the string and the cork carefully through the space between the frame and the top of the trunk lid, then replaced the cork in the water bottle as quickly as possible to minimize the spillage. He turned his hands over palm down and loosened both corks as much as possible without letting them fall out, then slipped out his hands and closed the lid quietly.

The man and the boy were still talking. He slipped back through the reeds to his bike and headed toward the Byblos. There were many things that the West had taught the Arabs over the centuries. For instance, that naphtha burns on contact with water. That was a Byzantine gift – Greek fire.

As angry as Aboussara had been with his fate earlier, when it seemed that he alone would have to follow the paths of at least four people, he was equally grateful to Allah for having had the foresight to force them all into his path again. The boy and Hamilton were safe in his grasp, spending the day – Inch' Allah – at the same beach. Now if he could find the two Americans, and could get a positive identification as to which was Hultz, his problem would be solved.

Providence was firmly on the side of Aboussara. George Hultz, told by Stanley to pick up a note from the cashier at Le Senequier after six that evening, lunched at the Byblos and went upstairs, determined to do something that he had always wanted to do, go to a nudist beach. When Aboussara arrived, Hultz was in his room changing into a pair of faded chino pants and a tee shirt. He took a bathing suit with him as an extra precaution. He slipped on his sandals and went to the desk to ask the directions to the beach at Pampelonne. The clerk raised a polite eyebrow, then explained. Murchison sat waiting for Hultz in a chair near the stairway. To Aboussara's delight, they emerged almost at the same time and drove off in the same direction, toward Ste. Maxime. At the red light at the crossroads, both turned left with Aboussara in unheeded pursuit. They parked at Pampelonne.

Aboussara watched as the first of the two men left his car, taking a towel with him, and walked toward the water. When he arrived near the edge, among the tawny naked men, women and children, he hesitantly began to disrobe. When he stood, white and naked in the sun, he sought, as many first-time nudists do, the safety of the sea. The other man stayed in the car. Then Aboussara knew that he was the shadow.

'But he's sure to recognize me. He sees me all the time. I can't be of any use to you if I can't go back anymore,' the dark-haired woman said.

'I'm sure it can be arranged so that you can see him without his seeing you,' Fosburgh said. 'You worry too much. Haven't you always been taken care of? By the way,' he said, thrusting an envelope out on the table, 'I think that you will find this a recompense for your troubles. There will be more later – when the job is finished. You won't need to go back.'

'But won't I get into trouble? Aren't there legal complications?'

'Certainly not. There is no connection. You have been with General Motors for three years. You have done yeoman service. A perfect record, in fact. Is it not possible that you have simply tired of working? Or even found something more to your liking? See – you agree.' He looked through the porthole and saw Aboussara mounting the gangway.

'And your special reward. I think that you will have it now. Excuse me, won't you?'

Fosburgh walked out onto the deck and greeted Aboussara.

'Well, have you run our subject down?'

'No. But everything is well in hand. I know where all of the parties are. Hamilton, I have fixed once and for all. If he tries to open his trunk or goes over even the smallest bump, he will fry – or at the very least die of fright.' He smiled.

'Another technical triumph,' Fosburgh said with irony. 'Now about Hultz, have you found him?'

'Almost certainly. He has a shadow, though. Very professional, but getting sloppy due to the dullness of his quarry. Hultz is currently exposing his manhood to the air at Pampelonne.'

Fosburgh furrowed his brow. 'The man following him may be U.S. government. In which case, either his removal or Hultz's could lead to problems for me. They will no doubt check the yacht register and see that I am a director of General Motors. No, dear Aboussara. I fear that we must allow Mr. Hultz to keep his balls. We must satisfy ourselves with resolving the problem of finding our inventor and disconnecting him.'

'As you wish. His death is of no importance to me, this Hultz.'

'Do you still need positive identification, or are you sure enough?'

'They both go together, of course. But I would prefer to be sure. It can be done this evening when he comes back from the beach. There is no hurry.'

'You must be careful, Aboussara, to avoid letting him see our guest.'

He grunted.

'I would like you to meet our guest, Aboussara. You will have a couple of hours at least to get acquainted. You remember the mention of a special reward this morning. Well, I think that you can play a part in it. Come in.' He led the way to the bridge. Madeleine was there, curled up catlike in a chair, wearing the bottom of a bikini. With her was the dark-haired woman.

'Oh, Paul,' she said, 'I'm glad you've come back, but we were having a nice chat.'

Fosburgh turned and said formally, 'Abdul Aboussara, may I present you to Jean Chandler. Come, let's go down to the salon where we can be more comfortable.'

'Aboussara, being a Moslem, doesn't drink,' Fosburgh said, having made one for himself and the two women. 'He is a very stern man. A valuable member of my crew. Though – if you will excuse me, Aboussara – I find that at times he tends to have a rather cruel nature. But, then, of course, that would interest you, Jean, wouldn't it?' He walked over to the chair in which she was seated and patted her dark head. 'Jean was one of the first young ladies with whom I shared my more perverse physical interests, Aboussara,' he continued in a conversational tone. 'In the end, I think that she was more addicted to certain fetishes than I. We met about ten years ago when I hired her for a small private company in which I have an interest. We became very close. Soon I learned that I could trust her judgment, as well as enjoy her company. So I sent her off to another company in which I had more of a competitive interest. She was very helpful in providing much needed information. Then through careful planning, I was able to have her installed as Milton Goodrich's secretary at General Motors.'

He patted her again, then went to the bar to pour himself another drink. 'We still see each other occasionally, but I'm afraid that our relationship has been sullied by money. Jean has quite a bit put by toward her eventual retirement. But I'm afraid she has rather a problem in finding a man like myself to meet her needs.' He walked back to her chair and stroked her head softly, then unexpectedly pulled savagely at her long dark hair. 'Isn't that right, Jean?'

She gasped, and he pulled again. 'Yes,' she said.

'So I wondered, Aboussara, if you could not find relief for

your tensions, and at the same time provide Jean with the reward she so richly deserves for her good works.' He grasped the flesh of her cheek between his thumb and fore-finger and squeezed. 'Would you like to go with Aboussara, my dear?'

Stifling a cry, she nodded her head yes.

'And you, Aboussara. You would not object?'

He twirled the ends of his mustache as he appraised her. 'Why not?'

'Good. Take her to cabin number two.' He turned to Jean. 'It's very well insulated. You should have a marvelous time.'

After Aboussara and Jean had left down the companion-way, Fosburgh finished his drink, then led Madeleine to cabin number one. He sat cross-legged, Indian style, at the head of the bed while Madeleine stretched out full length on her stomach in front of him. He reached out and turned a switch. The mirror on the wall, which ran the length of the bed, became transparent, showing the next cabin.

Aboussara walked across the room to where Jean sat at the edge of the bed, and with no apparent effort ripped the top of her dress to her waist, exposing her heavy breasts. He kicked aside his sandals, removed his shirt and then dropped his pants.

Aboussara stood in front of Jean with his hands on his hips hiding her from their view. He reached forward and did something with his hands, something that required strength, for they could see his powerful arm muscles bulge.

'Paul, turn up the sound. Can't we hear too?'

He twirled a dial as the sound of Jean's voice broke through, sobbing softly. 'Ow. Ow. That hurts.'

Aboussara lifted her to her feet and tore the rest of the clothes from her body as she stood trembling. He turned broadside to the mirror.

'Truly incredible,' Fosburgh said.

Aboussara lifted her kneeling to the bed and approached her from behind. He spread her buttocks with his fingers

213

and thrust himself forward.

'Please, wet me, wet me, it hurts.'

Fosburgh shook his head wonderingly as he turned off the sound, and said to Madeleine, who was already otherwise occupied, 'You know, that's the first time I've ever heard her scream, or him laugh.'

Twenty-three

As Pedro Cibao lurched into the front seat of his father's Rolls Royce, he cursed the name of the man who had invented Ricard. And then he cursed the father of that man. His head swam. Playing backgammon in the sun for six hours was bad. Losing seven thousand new cruzeiros was also bad. But to become sick to one's stomach from drinking too much of that licorice-tasting sweet drink was unthinkable. He lurched backwards without looking just as Hamilton and Marie Jo walked down the wooden pathway from the beach to the parking lot. They had a spectacular view of him ramming into the rear end of Hamilton's car.

Donald ran after him yelling, 'Hey, you little son of a bitch. You dented my car.' Then it blew up.

The watchdog, who was not far behind them, ran down the walk at full tilt, clutching his automatic beneath the towel wrapped over his arms. He breathed a sigh of relief when he saw Hamilton and the girl standing awed in the lot.

Pedro Cibao lurched to a halt in front of Hamilton. 'My God. I only gave it the merest of – how you say – bangs. A little dent maybe. But to blow up. What can I say? To make amends. I am perhaps not well, somewhat. Let us not make trouble with insurance and police. I will give you a check. No – better money. Right now. Will that do? It was how much?'

Hamilton said, 'Huh?'

'No, do not misunderstand. I wish to make amends. You speak English? No. French, then? Portuguese?' he asked in a pleading tone.

'English, English,' Donald said dumbly, still surveying the now-smouldering wreck. A crowd had begun to gather.

The watchdog stepped to Hamilton's side. 'You will come with me please. And Mlle. Du Fresne also. We must phone.' He turned to Cibao. 'You too will come. I am a policeman.'

Cibao put his hands to his temples. 'My God, my father, he will kill me.'

The pompiers pulled into the lot with their peculiar ululating siren at full pitch. They sprayed the car with chemicals from a fire extinguisher, producing a peculiar acrid stench.

'Whose car is this?' the captain of pompiers asked.

'Mine,' Hamilton replied.

'Were you carrying an explosive or something flammable other than gasoline? The smell is very peculiar.'

'Not that I was aware of,' he answered in total honesty.

The watchdog intervened. 'I am taking care of this matter.' He showed his identity card.

The pompier smiled weakly and backed away. 'Yes, of course.' Then he mounted his truck. 'Shall we have the fourrier municipal come to pick up this wreck?'

The watchdog thought a moment, then said, 'Yes. As soon as possible.' Then he led Hamilton, Marie Jo and the miserable Cibao back toward the office. The crowd dispersed and went on its way.

When the watchdog entered the office with Hamilton and the others and showed his badge, the patron slumped in his chair. 'Not again, Mr. Hamilton. Please. I implore you.'

'You implore *me*? I'm beginning to think that this beach brings me bad luck.'

'May I phone?' the watchdog asked.

The patron waved at the phone on his desk. 'You would like me to leave, I suppose?' He left.

The watchdog dialed a number and waited. When no one answered, he hung up and tried another. After a moment he began to speak in rapid French. When he stopped, Hamilton and Marie Jo heard clearly across the room a single exclamation. 'Imbecile!' They turned to each other smiling. Hamilton said, loudly enough to be heard, 'Give the General our regards.'

Somewhat uncertain, and somewhat shaken, the watch-dog hung up the phone. He smiled weakly at Hamilton. 'He said that he,' he indicated Cibao, 'is an asshole. To take the cash from him now and to let him go would be an enormous generosity on your part. Otherwise, bang into the dungeon.'

Cibao cringed and fished out his wallet. 'Name the price. It would be a generosity.'

Hamilton thought briefly. 'The car was eighty-seven hundred dollars new, including tax. The camera was three hundred, and then there was the lady's suitcase.'

Cibao smiled brightly. 'Let's call it ten thousand even. Will dollars do?'

'Cash?' Hamilton queried.

'Why not?' Cibao said. He removed an envelope from the leather wallet hung from a strap over his shoulder, spent five minutes counting and put back the envelope. 'Would you like to check?'

'No,' said Donald, 'thank you anyway. I'm sure that this will be fine.'

'I can go then,' Cibao asked.

The watchdog agreed. Cibao shook Hamilton's hand furiously, kissed Marie Jo on the cheek and ran out of the door.

'The General said,' the watchdog began, 'that we should stay here. That he would fly down in a plane to the little airport at St. Raphael. He said that he would be here in no more than an hour and a half. He told me to tell you that you should watch me to see that I don't hurt myself.'

Her face white as chalk, Jean Chandler clutched Aboussara's midriff as she sat behind him on the speeding bike, leaning forward awkwardly to alleviate the raging pain in her backside.

He came to a smooth halt and parked on a flat sandy space across from the entrance to the beach at Pampelonne. 'Sit down here, next to the bike. You can see without being seen.'

'I prefer to lie on my stomach, thank you.' She wore a scarf over her head and large dark glasses.

They sat silently for about a half hour. Then a figure wearing slacks appeared at the top of a dune before them, whistling and skipping along in the sand. He went to his car, got in and pulled away, followed shortly by another car.

'That was him. That's George Hultz.'

They mounted again and drove back to the boat.

'You'd better stay out of the way. He might see you somewhere in town. Do you intend to stay here?' Aboussara asked.

She rubbed her buttocks gingerly. 'I don't think that I'm up to it.'

'Too bad.'

The General shuffled along as fast as his aging legs would permit, puffing with the exertion. When he had crossed the sand of the parking lot and arrived at the end of the board-walk, he turned, gasping, 'Well, Cripple, hurry up. I can't wait here forever.'

La Brousse limped along after him, muttering under his breath. It was his first day without the cane. When he reached the office, the old man was sitting slumped in a chair, mopping his brow with a dirty handkerchief.

'You see,' he said, 'I told you that he would come, how-ever long it took. Faithful La Brousse.'

'Good evening, Mr. Hamilton, Mlle. Du Fresne. I am sorry to have kept you.'

'Not at all, M. La Brousse,' said Donald. 'We had no plans.'

Marie Jo pouted.

'It is possible,' the General began, 'that we can have the driver take Mlle. Du Fresne somewhere if you think it ad-visable, Mr. Hamilton.'

'Aucune chance! I am not going anywhere. Ever since I met you my life has been disorganized. I am not going any-where. Donald . . .' She turned, pleading.

Donald turned up his hands in futility. 'You heard the lady, General.'

'Very well, then. You will promise to keep your mouth shut about what you hear, and you can stay.'

'Agreed.'

'Well, it appears that we have flushed them. We have been waiting. More than two weeks, it has been. Can you think of a reason that they have reappeared, or that your life has again become important to them?'

'No. I didn't do anything or see anything that aroused my suspicions. It was crazy. That Brazilian backed into the car, and whoosh, no more car. I've been going over what I've done in the past several days. Nothing really. I've been working my ass off to keep on schedule with the hotel and leading a perfectly normal, if monkish, existence. But you know all that.' He pointed at the watchdog who sat at attention on the windowsill.

'Ah, yes, him,' the General remarked. 'How, I wonder, has he managed to keep you alive.' He turned on the man. 'You realize, naturally, that it must have been some kind of pressure- or shock-sensitive device. You also know that had that accident not occurred, Mr. Hamilton would have gotten into his car, gone over a bump and been fried. And there would have been no place for you to hide.'

The watchdog paled, 'Oui, mon général.'

'La Brousse and I are quartered at the Byblos. What were your plans?'

Marie Jo blushed. Hamilton hesitated.

'Yes,' said the General, 'all well and good, but where did you intend to perform this monumental act? Are you staying here, or were you planning to go back to Toulon to-night?'

'We were going to play it by ear. We had enough clothes to go somewhere nice for dinner if we felt like it. Or to go to a hotel.'

'I think that you should stay in St. Tropez this evening. It will give you greater exposure. You will be a better target, and we will have a better chance to trap our quarry. Unless you feel uncomfortable about Mlle. Du Fresne. How do you want to handle it?'

'The question is who is the hunter and who is the game. I think you're right. Let's get it over with.'

The General looked ruminatively at Hamilton. 'Would you feel better with a gun?'

Hamilton nodded. The General turned to the watchdog. 'Have you a spare, clown?'

The man rummaged in his bag and turned over a gleaming blue Lebel service automatic. Hamilton slipped it into his beach bag after checking the clip.

Marie Jo thought for a moment, her brow wrinkled. 'Donald ... Donald! Do you mean that they are going to make us bait? You are trying to make somebody kill you?'

'Now you see why the General suggested that you go back to town with an escort. I am afraid that I have been bait for several weeks. That's how La Brousse acquired that dignified limp. Somebody was shooting at me and shot him instead.'

She got to her feet, bristling. 'You are mad. You are all mad.' She turned accusingly to General Pineau. 'But especially you are mad. Maddest of all.'

'Now then, my dear. If Mr. Hamilton has seen fit to co-operate with us in our efforts to keep the peace, I don't think that constitutes madness. Especially since he did so of his own free will. Not so, Mr. Hamilton?'

'In a manner of speaking.' He turned to Marie Jo. 'Now listen, young lady. I had the time of my life convincing this gentleman over here that I was the kind who likes to call the shots in his own life. I don't want to start having any problems with you. I didn't like the idea of being in a shooting gallery any more than you. But my choices were limited. When the General invited me in, I accepted. You can go home any time you want to. Nobody's stopping you. Is that clear?'

She nodded agreement, her eyes filling with tears.

'As a matter of fact, maybe you ought to get the hell out of here.'

She crossed to him and took his hand. 'If you want, I'll go.

But I'd rather be near you. I'll stay out of the way.'

'That's better.'

'Bravo, Hamilton. That's the way I used to do it. La Brousse, call someone and have them make a reservation for Mr. Hamilton at the Byblos. Make it a double room. I hate to inconvenience you, Mr. Hamilton, but I'm afraid that to-night you are going to have to share your accommodations. As our guests, of course.'

Twenty-four

Hultz pulled into a parking space just in front of the entrance and trotted down the steps into the lobby, grabbed the key at the desk and went up to his room. He stripped off his clothes and jumped into the shower, soaping vigorously to get the salt off his body. He washed his hair thoroughly, laughing at his own behavior. If only the Board of Directors could have seen him on the beach, mother-naked with the other nature enthusiasts. After a while he had felt quite comfortable and uninhibited. A great story to tell at home.

He dressed quickly and descended to the lobby. He asked the desk clerk about a place to eat, mentioning that he had to drop by Le Senequier to pick someone up. The clerk suggested L'Escale and recommended that he try the bourride. Hultz thanked him and left, going down the stairs that cut into the hill leading directly to the Place des Lices rather than out the front door.

In so doing, he avoided the steward, who sat disconsolately on the Suzuki outside of the front door, but ran into Abdul Aboussara, who was leaning against a tree near the hill steps, ostensibly watching a game of pétanque.

To see a little more of the town, Hultz continued halfway down Rue Gambetta, past the little food shops and notions stores, and then down the sharply pitched street, through dark and closed stalls in the fish market and out onto the jetty.

He emerged fifty paces from Le Senequier and asked to see the cashier. Providentially, she spoke some English, and with that and some gestures, he managed to acquire the envelope that had been left for him.

Hultz backed up against the wall to see if anyone was watching him, then opened the envelope. His untrained eye missed Aboussara, who hung around, looking bored at the edge of the jetty just opposite.

Messenger: I am prepared to meet you to arrange details for the closing of our deal. I assume, perhaps unwisely, that you understand something of what I am doing. If by now you have arranged the transfer of the check which I requested, you will find me in a nightclub called the Stereo Club after 10 P.M. You will not be able to get in unless you give the name Weeks to the bully at the door. I will be sitting with the same young man to whom you gave the check. Walk over to the table, tap on it three times, then sit at another table. I will come to join you. We will talk and then you will leave alone. I will stay. Make no further effort to contact me, save what we arrange between us. Destroy this note as soon as you have read it. Destroy it thoroughly. A.E.

Hultz shook his head, halfway between amusement and disgust. He started to walk out, then stopped and asked the cashier for the location of the lavatory. It was small and it stank. He tore the letter and the envelope into little pieces, threw them into the bowl, and then as an afterthought, pissed on them and flushed the toilet.

At seven-thirty, about an hour after Hultz had left Le Senequier and sat down to eat at L'Escale, Stanley emerged from the front door of the Hôtel Byblos to pick up his motorbike. He stuffed his hand into the pocket of his jeans and was reassured by the crinkling of the thousand-franc note nestled within. The older gentleman from South America had been very generous to him, albeit demanding. He had a son just a bit older than Stanley, who was a scandalous playboy, and who spent money as though there were no tomorrow. But after all, he said, patting Stanley's thigh, what are fathers for?

The steward, falling asleep from boredom, almost missed Stanley and indeed would have, had it not been for the proximity of Stanley's Vespa, and the fact that it backfired when he pedaled it to a coughing start.

The Stereo Club was around the corner from the Town Hall and the little square its unattractive bulk dominated, and across from a plaque which commemorated the birth of the Baillif de Suffren, St. Tropez's leading historical figure, who distinguished himself in the service of the King of France by losing India to Lord Clive.

Stanley parked his bike against the wall of the Town Hall and strolled around the corner, squeezing his pocket one more time for good luck. Ordinarily, he would have been refused admission as underage, but since he was the property of a good customer the bouncer smiled as he passed through. He spotted Arthur sitting at a table in the rear of the room, tapping nervously with a swizzle stick on the glass in front of him.

'You are a bad boy. Where have you been? I was beginning to worry.'

'I did what you told me, Arthur. I spent the day at the beach,' he lied, fingering his pocket, 'then I just fooled around a little on the bike and came straight here.'

'Well, you can't have eaten, and they don't serve food in here, so I was thoughtful enough to bring us both a sandwich.' He fished out a brown paper bag and withdrew two round breads stuffed with salad and tuna. 'See, pain bagna.'

Around a large bit, Arthur said, 'You did very well, Stanley.'

'How do you know that?'

'Because I have the check. Or rather I had it. I picked it up at the post office on my way into town, put it in another envelope and mailed it.'

When the steward saw that Stanley went into the Stereo Club, he ran his bike down to the quay and headed toward the boat. Then, about fifty yards from the gangway, he stopped and backed up to where Aboussara stood, opposite L'Escale, idly picking his teeth with his finger.

'Aboussara,' he hissed, 'the boy has gone into the Stereo Club.'

'Stop acting like an idiot. Talk softly but normally. Where has he been all afternoon?'

'First he went to the beach. He stayed there until about four or four-thirty, I don't have a watch. Then he went to the Byblos. He must have met someone there. He didn't come out until a little while ago. Perhaps ten minutes.'

'Well, he couldn't have been with our American, we know where he has been. He probably found a buyer for his wares. Go back to the Stereo and see when he comes out.'

'Should I follow him?'

'Just see what direction he is going in. If it is out of town by the road to La Foux, we can catch him anyway. When he leaves, stop by and see me for further instructions. If I am not here, then you will have to follow him.'

'Aboussara, I am getting sleepy.'

'You will sleep for eternity.'

Hultz burped. He had finished the last of the filleted fish and the heavy creamy soup, redolent of garlic, which had been suggested to him. The waitress, clearing his plate, asked him if he wanted cheese or dessert or both. He shook his head wearily. 'Coffee . . . café, please.'

Now I am a stuffed nudist. He looked at the time, nine-thirty. I'd better go meet our friend. I am really looking forward to this. I wonder what he's like.

He drank only half of the coffee, it was much too strong for his American tastes, paid the check and left. Then he turned back and asked the waitress the location of the Stereo Club. She looked at him, somewhat taken aback, then with an expression of distaste pointed toward the end of the jetty. 'Up the hill to the square. The first street on your right. Enjoy yourself.'

Murchison, who had been nursing a beer at Le Senequier while keeping an eye on Hultz, got up and followed.

Still puzzling over the woman's attitude, Hultz got to the door of the Stereo, its electric sign in shades of iridescent blue and violet, and found his way blocked by the bouncer.

'My name is Weeks. I am expected.'

'Weeks,' the bouncer repeated. 'Weeks. Oui. Oui. Entrez dans.'

Hultz blinked several times after the door shut behind him, to accustom his eyes to the dim red light. He turned his head slowly to take in the scene. Small groups of men, many of them couples, stood at the bar talking softly and sat at tables which ringed the walls. Rock music played in the background.

A goddamn fag joint, he told himself. Then he spotted Stanley at a table. It was hard to make out the features of the man with him, but no doubt he was the screwball inventor. And undoubtedly a fag too. I'd better make sure we're never in the lab alone.

He walked to the table, checked his identification of Stanley, then knocked three times with his knuckles. The man looked up, squinting through thick glasses. A face to remember, Hultz thought. Then casually, Hultz walked away and sat at a free table on the other side of the room.

Murchison debated the practicality of going into the Stereo. On the one hand, he knew where his man was. The likelihood of his ducking out the back way was very small. He didn't know he was being tailed, and even if he had known, had no reason to avoid Murchison. On the other hand, the information which he had received from the President himself, the fourth such he had guarded in twenty years of Secret Service employment, indicated that the person Hultz was coming to meet was at best peculiar, and might be expected to do something irrational. The man that Hultz was going to meet was also more important than Hultz. He was to report in if he found him. His job was to protect Hultz as best he could, but his contact took precedence.

So he had to go in. But he had witnessed the scene with the bouncer and wanted to avoid any fuss. He didn't know whatever code word Hultz had used. He decided on the universal language.

He strode to the door. The big man barred his way. Murchison stuck out his hand palm down. The bouncer took it, glanced down briefly at the two hundred-dollar bills now in his palm, opened the door and ushered Murchison in with a sweeping bow.

To avoid notice he went directly to the bar, as though he were familiar with the place, and ordered a beer. He turned over the ticket that had been foisted on him when he entered. Then he slowly turned to scan the room.

Hultz was sitting in the corner with a small man with thinning hair. It was hard to make him out in the dark. They were deep in conversation. The longer I stall, Murchison thought, the greater the chance that I'll blow it. He asked if he could use a phone.

'Where do you want to call?'

'Cannes.'

'Okay. The phone's down at the end of the bar. When you get the number, wave your hand, and I'll start the timer.' The bartender reached under the counter and pulled out a clock-like device.

Murchison walked to the end of the bar and dialed the number which was on automatique. The third vice consul in Cannes picked up the phone on the first ring.

'Yes.'

'This is Murchison, 28-A.'

'We were told you might call.'

Murchison cupped the phone between his hands to muffle his voice, looking over his shoulder at Hultz and Edelman. 'Ask home if I should watch the original or the copy.'

'How fast do you need an answer?'

'Instant. Fifteen minutes the most, I would judge.'

'Okay, call back in ten.'

'Well, Mr. Hultz, it certainly is nice to meet you,' Arthur said.

Hultz did not disappoint him. 'The privilege, sir, is entirely mine. I have been involved in the project from its beginnings, with Mr. Goodrich and Mr. Coughtry. You are a great scientist.'

Arthur beamed. 'I appreciate your promptness in following my instructions,' then still more cordially, 'especially the check.'

'That will be pittance, Mr. Edelman. Mere pittance.'

'I have assumed so. Naturally, before we proceed, we must sort those matters out. But that is for another time and another place. I trust that you have made arrangements for lawyers and such.'

'Oh yes indeed, we have. Our entire European legal staff awaits your pleasure.'

'I am sure that you will like to see the rest of the project information.'

'I certainly would. As a matter of fact, we felt that a man of your stature would insist on my seeing it as a precondition of going forward with the negotiations.'

Arthur, a little confused, said, 'Hmm. Oh yes. Of course.'

'When and where would you like me to look at this material?'

'I'm not quite finished. Perhaps if you could wait until Monday, or Tuesday shall we say? Then we could meet again, and I could show it to you.'

'But then when would you like to hold the negotiating sessions, Mr. Edelman?'

'I want to hold them next week. There is no sense in wasting time. Will Mr. Goodrich be coming?'

'Wild horses couldn't keep him away.'

'Fine,' Arthur chortled. 'That's just fine. I'll want to hold the meetings somewhere in this area. I shall, naturally, be represented by competent counsel.'

'Naturally.'

'When next we meet, I will tell you whom I have selected. You will call them, give them a retainer of, shall we say fifty thousand dollars, and tell them that I will contact them, and that they are to follow my instructions in every particular.'

Hultz choked a bit, covered his mouth, then answered, 'Yes. Certainly. That will be fine.'

'I am curious, Mr. Hultz,' Arthur said in a conspiratorial tone, lowering his voice, 'how will it be possible for Mr. Goodrich and you to commit yourselves legally to this matter without the approval of the Board of Directors?'

'Mr. Goodrich has a certain latitude in these matters.'

Murchison alerted the bartender and went back to the phone. He dialed the number in Cannes again and waited. The phone rang five or six times before it was answered.

'Yes.'

'Murchison, 28-A.'

'Sorry. I just got off the horn. Leave the original. Watch the copy.'

They hung up.

Twenty-five

'Get out,' the General said.

The agent who had picked him up with La Brousse at the airport stepped out of the car.

'Go home with him,' the General pointed at the watch-dog, then continued, 'and get some sleep. I want you bright and cheerful tomorrow morning. Nine o'clock in front of the Byblos. We will take over your duties for the evening.'

'But where should I stay?' the watchdog said.

'That's your problem. La Brousse, are you able to drive or shall we be chauffeured by Mr. Hamilton?'

'Thank you, I can drive.'

'Get in then and stop dawdling. Mr. Hamilton, Mlle. Du Fresne, are you coming?'

Donald and Marie Jo got into the back of the car. She bundled against him in the slight chill and rested her head against his chest. The General struggled in, pushed away the helping hand of his recent chauffeur, who shut the door after him.

'Have you French money, Hamilton?'

Donald looked through his wallet. 'Yes, about a thousand francs.'

'Fine, then we will drop you off in the Place des Lices and you can buy some clothes for yourself and for Mlle Du Fresne. You look quite ridiculous, you know. It's chilly and late in the season to wander around at night half naked. La Brousse and I will be parked in the Place des Lices. Do your shopping there. Then walk straight across the Place to the stairs to the Byblos. Go up and sit in the lobby. I think we will all eat there tonight. At separate tables, of course.'

'General,' Marie Jo said, 'do you mind if we eat at Le

Yaca instead. I've been looking forward to it.'

'Not at all, my dear. I love lamb. Just the same, wait for us in the lobby of the Byblos. La Brousse is impaired, you know.'

The three miles into town were silent and uneventful. La Brousse parked the car on the corner of the square, and Hamilton and Marie Jo descended and began to check the shops across the green.

'Is it not clear, La Brousse, that these attempts on Hamilton will continue?'

'Yes, sir. This afternoon's incident is a result of something that happened without Hamilton even realizing it.'

'He must have been recognized by the assassin. But even that should not have triggered such a response. He has been following his normal pattern for a couple of weeks. It is logical, then, to assume that the arrival of Hamilton in St. Tropez today was coincidental with another circumstance of which we are ignorant. It then follows that the assassin continues to follow Hamilton, and that he has been provoked in some way. Ergo – attempted murder.'

La Brousse glanced across the square to make sure of Hamilton's location, then turned back to the General. 'Do you think that it is time to begin a full-scale investigation? Check hotel rosters, the inhabitants of rented houses in the area, the people on the yachts in the harbor? Try to roust him out?'

The General tamped his pipe, shaking his head. 'No, La Brousse. He has been here for a long time. We can search all that we want to. He cannot be flushed from hiding. He has stayed here through a variety of critical moments, when anyone less practiced and self-confident would have run. If we try to use main force, and it would require a cordon around the entire peninsula, road blocks and so forth, boat patrols, it will cause him to sit absolutely still, like a hare between a hunter's feet. Then we shall never know what brings on these spurts in his activities. We shall wait and watch.' He looked up. 'By the way, have you checked with Rhabbouz today?'

'No, sir.' He started the car. 'There they go, toward the stairs.'

'All right. Go up to the Byblos. You can call Rhabbouz while they are checking in. I will go to their room first to see if they have company.'

La Brousse was about to say something when he heard a reassuring meshing of metal parts, then saw the dull gleam of the weapon in the General's hand.

Donald walked up to the desk and inquired if there was a reservation in his name. 'Mr. and Mrs. Hamilton? Yes. Passports please,' the clerk said nastily, looking at Marie Jo.

Donald replied coolly in a normal tone of voice, 'No, that will be a double room for Mr. Hamilton and Mlle. Du Fresne.' He dropped the passports on the desk. He put his hand into his wallet and fished out the wad of bills that had been given to him by Cibao. 'And while you're at it, please put this in the safe. I'd like a receipt.'

The clerk counted them twice. 'That's ten thousand, two hundred dollars.' He took the money, put it in an envelope and gave Donald the key to his room. 'Have you any luggage? I'll have a boy take it to your room.'

'Just a paper bag,' Donald smiled.

'Well, I'll have the boy show you up anyway.'

The General lumbered down the stairs from the parking lot with La Brousse following behind.

The clerk motioned to the bellboy. 'Take them to 307. It's just down the hall overlooking the swimming pool,' he said in an aside to Donald.

The General walked down the hall just in front of them, ignoring their existence, but in such a way that neither they nor the bellboy could pass by him. He passed 307, waited until he heard the boy turn the key in the lock, then dropped a five-franc piece on the tile floor.

'Crotte de bique. Merde!' He struggled to bend over.

'Get that for him,' Donald said to the boy. 'We can let ourselves in.'

The boy retrieved the coin and handed it to the General.

'Merci, jeune homme. Vous êtes très gentil.'

'Il n'y a pas de quoi, monsieur.' The boy turned back to Donald, who still stood at the door with Marie Jo. Donald gave him a couple of francs, he tipped his hand to his head and left.

The General motioned them out of the way. He opened his coat, exposing the beltless top of his pants, slightly rolled under the weight of his stomach. He withdrew an antique-looking 1898 Mauser pistol, waved it and said, 'War souvenir from an Italian officer – dropped only three times, and never fired in anger.' He motioned them back with the barrel and presented himself at the door. He turned on the light switch and walked in, stuck his nose into the bath-room, pushed the drapes with the barrel of the gun and opened the closet.

'No visitors. Welcome to your chamber of love.'

'Why, General,' Marie Jo said, 'I didn't know you cared about young love.'

'Bah. You are young, but he is old. I have pity for other old men. At his age one does what one can, not to despoil his good luck, and to conserve what remaining juices still flow.' He put the gun back in his waistband and closed his coat. 'If I were still young, I would give you a real exhibition of masculinity.' He closed the wooden shutters, then the drapes. 'Leave them that way. It not only discourages voyeurs, but eliminates sniping. I will wait for you in the lobby.'

Donald and Marie Jo showered together, dried, and dressed in the clothes they had bought. Slacks and a new knit shirt for him, a loosely clinging low-cut cotton dress for her.

She pirouetted in the middle of the room. 'Not bad,' Donald said. 'If we ever see young Mr. Cibao again, we must thank him.'

Once out into the night air, they strolled slowly down the hill toward Le Yaca, measuring their steps to avoid outdistancing the General and the limping La Brousse behind them.

They passed an open fountain where a woman sat washing clothes, oblivious to the children playing ball around her, then walked up the three steps into the lobby of the tiny hotel and through the garden. A hostess met them and seated them at a table under the huge tree which shaded the entire flagstone court. They could see the legs of lamb hanging over a lighted charcoal brazier.

'May we offer you an apéritif? A glass of champagne and cassis?'

'Kir royale,' said Marie Jo, 'that would be lovely.'

As the waiter brought them their drinks, the General and La Brousse appeared, and were seated at a table not far from their own.

'Look at that, La Brousse. Gigot à la ficelle. That is what I must have.'

'May I help you, messieurs?' a waiter asked. 'You will, of course, enjoy our complimentary cocktail. May I suggest that you try the table of hors d'oeuvre. And then . . .'

'And then, young man,' the General said, 'you will bring a plate of that beautiful leg of lamb, dangling there over the fire. It is studded with garlic no doubt.'

'Ah, yes, indeed.'

'Good. Garlic promotes health and maintains sanity. You will see that I have several whole cloves of garlic on my plate, so that I may also maintain my bon mien.'

When Aboussara saw Hultz get up from his table at L'Escale after dinner, he was tempted to follow after him. He was fully aware, however, that Murchison was not far away, and that he would certainly be noticed by the professional if he was impatient. In any case, he knew that it would not be long before Murchison himself moved on.

Thanks to the crowd of tourists, he was able to walk almost on their heels to the square where the Stereo is located. He loitered nonchalantly when Hultz went in, then, amazed, watched Murchison follow.

This is too good to be true, he thought. They have led me directly to him. They are all there. The man from New York, his tail, the little faggot, and the man I want, the inventor. I need only to follow him. I can forget about the man from New York – this Hultz. And the tail is of no importance. So even if they don't go out together, I should be able to pick out the inventor. And if I can't do that, I can follow the boy. I can always get the boy and make him talk. He would certainly tell me everything, that boy. An idea came to him. He milled through the people crowding the square and stopped with his back to the steward, who sat, eyes half closed, leaning on the saddle of his motorcycle.

'Are you awake?' he asked softly.

'Hmm? Awake. Yes. Yes, awake.'

'Go into the Stereo Club and see who the missing person is.' He slipped him five hundred francs. 'One of them, either the boy or the American, will be talking to a man. Go inside, see who it is, have a drink, wait for a few minutes, then come out. I will be sitting on the steps of the Town Hall. Drive up to me. I will stand. You will describe him quickly and accurately. Then you can go back to the *Glen Pool*.'

'That is the place where they use men as you would use a woman.'

'If you do not do as I say, without further question, I will use you as a fisherman uses squid – as bait for a hook.'

Mellowed by the wine from dinner and the drinks at the Stereo, Hultz leaned across the table and looked directly into Arthur Edelman's eyes. 'Listen, Mr. Edelman, answer me a question. Why all this secrecy? Why all these odd meeting places, and the nonsense with the roses and the notes? You're a brilliant scientist, a brilliant man. And you are not ignorant of business practice. This wasn't necessary. You could have come directly to us.'

'What about Steinmetz?'

'What about him?'

'General Electric robbed him blind. He worked his whole life, changed the substance of science and got nothing for his pains.'

'That was a long time ago. What about Wankel? General Motors alone paid an initial royalty of fifty million for the right to work on the engine on a non-exclusive basis.'

Arthur regarded Hultz with cold eyes. 'Wankel isn't a Jewish homosexual. He wasn't driven out of his own country by archaic laws that have since been recognized as, among other things, barbaric and unconstitutional. I agree that this childish nonsense has been my way of extracting a pound of flesh from you, but tell me what kind of a reception I would have gotten if I had come to you with a police record for deviant sexual behavior. Even now, now that you've met me, don't you have a little doubt in the back of your mind about working with me, some small antagonism or distaste? Yes, it would have been simpler for me to complete this project with the test facilities and the laboratories and computers at your disposal. But would I have ever gotten close enough to use them? I think not. I would have been rejected. And very probably, given the basic technological data which would have been required for your – judgment – in the matter, you would have eventually gone on without me and claimed, even in the case of a suit, that the idea was sui generis. And I would have had the pleasure of reading about it in some sleazy gay bar on the West Side, or hearing about it in the New York municipal jail while I was trying to avoid forcible rape by a bunch of drunken hoodlums or to recover from a beating by sadistic guards! No thank you, Mr. Hultz. I am a less ridiculous figure here than I would be there.'

Hultz squirmed uncomfortably in his chair. 'I think you will see, once we get started, and you are installed in the proper facilities, that you've been quite wrong.'

'We certainly shall see, Mr. Hultz.' He looked at his wristwatch. 'I am tired, Mr. Hultz. In a way, this has been the most important day of my life. In another sense, it has been quite anticlimactic. I am afraid that in my desire to make you come to me, to do things as I wished them done, I have rather lost sight of what my end goal is. I will need another two days to get everything in order, as I mentioned before. Perhaps in that time, I will be better oriented to the reality which you represent. I have a little house out in the fields not too far from the beach. It's not in St. Tropez. It's quite secluded. I have a beautiful view of both the rising and the setting sun. I would prefer to finish the matter in this area if that would not discommode you. I will meet you for breakfast in the main dining room of the Byblos – that is where you are staying? – at nine on Wednesday morning. I would appreciate it if you could have the lawyers I have selected – Les Maîtres Bayeu, 25 Quai du Rhône, Geneva – I have it written on this card – available the same day. If it is possible, I would like to meet with your attorneys and with Mr. Goodrich on Thursday. Ask them to draw sample agreements,' he smiled archly, 'but have them leave the numbers blank. We ought to be able to come to terms, have the contracts retyped and executed by Friday. Then I will need a few days to tidy up my affairs. I will be ready to start work in earnest on the first of October. Does that schedule suit you?'

'Eminently, Mr. Edelman.'

'Excellent, Mr. Hultz. You may go now – if you please. I prefer to leave alone.'

Hultz pushed back his chair and turned to leave, then turned back. 'You are wrong, Mr. Edelman. You will be proven wrong.' Then he walked out into the fresh night air, glad to be quit of the close smoky club. As he hiked up the hill toward the hotel he said under his breath, 'And I will see to it myself that you are proven wrong, Mr. Edelman.'

Shortly after Hultz left for the hotel, the steward emerged from the Stereo. He walked over to Aboussara and said, without looking at him, 'He is a small man. Quite homely. With a stomach. He is blond and baldish. He wears thick glasses.'

237

'Good, go home,' Aboussara said.

Aboussara watched the steward roll his bike into the center of the square and head off in the direction of the harbor. Only a patience born of practice and self-discipline allowed him to remain silent and unmoving as he watched the people in the cafes bantering, drinking and eating the night away. Inside he seethed with a sense of injustice.

A few minutes before, Aboussara had heard one flic tell another as they mounted the steps of the Town Hall, 'God-damnest thing I ever heard. This little guy, young as he was, South American, had had a few too many to drink. So he gets into this big Rolls Royce and backs into this red sports car. The sports car bursts into flame, the tank blows up and it burns to a cinder. All this while the guy who owns it is chasing the Rolls. How the hell do you like that?'

'He's lucky he wasn't in it.'

'That's what Boileau said. He said they had to use four fire extinguishers to put it out.'

Aboussara had lost the rest of the conversation as the two men had passed into the entrance of the Town Hall. But he had heard enough to know that Hamilton had escaped him once again. He pulled at the ends of his mustache in frustration.

The clock in his head told him that Hultz had been gone for ten or fifteen minutes. He began to wonder what had happened to his tail. It seemed odd to Aboussara that he would give him such a head start, even if he was sure of where he was going. Aboussara was suddenly uneasy. But there was little that he could do but wait, at least now that his main target was within his grasp.

In the Stereo, Arthur Edelman was still sitting alone at the table he had recently shared with Hultz. His glasses were pushed up onto his forehead. His eyes were closed, and his head rested on the wall behind him. He had ordered a second drink, unusual for him, and was swirling its dregs in the glass. He was fully cognizant of what he had accomplished, and of the difficulties he had imposed upon himself. He was now contemplating the perspective of his future. The occasion to show his brilliance was at an end. From the signing of the license agreement, it would be a matter of hard work. Proving. Testing. Translating innovative theory to profitable production techniques. Working with other people. Organizing. Administrating. Conforming. A concession to black humor.

He pulled down his glasses and squinted, looking around for Stanley, who was deep in conversation with a scruffy type of about twenty with eyes ringed with green mascara.

Arthur motioned to him. At first he talked on, oblivious. Then he lifted his head and saw Arthur beckon. He patted his companion on the cheek and walked over.

'Sit down, Stanley. Here. Next to me.'

'What's up, Arthur? Did you get your business done?'

'Yes. Yes, I did. Stanley, I'm going to have to leave the Côte d'Azur soon – in about ten days or two weeks. I am probably going to have to work all of this coming week as well.'

Stanley looked at him expectantly.

'There is a very good chance that I will have to move back to the States.'

Stanley's eyes narrowed covetously, then opened wide as he whined, 'But Arthur, what's going to happen to me?'

'I'm going to see that you have a little extra to tide you over. With what I give you, and what you get from your granny, you should be able to live quite comfortably.'

'You want me to move out?' Stanley asked tremulously.

'Yes, Stanley. I'm afraid so. There are going to be a lot of strange people around in the next week or so. I have many things to do. Then I'm going to have to go to Switzerland, and then clean up the house. You see, I must be in America by the first of October.'

Stanley sneered. 'What you're afraid of is that all those straights won't understand about you and me, isn't that it, Arthur? You're afraid that they won't understand that you like my cock, right? Or my ass?'

'Stanley, don't talk that way.'

'Oh, don't feel bad, Arthur. It's always this way when an

239

old guy like you picks me up. You play around for a while, then bang, back out in the street for little Stanley.'

'That's not the way it is at all! I wasn't planning on throwing you out in the street. I was going to give you some money. That way you could stay out of sight and have a good time for the next couple of days. Then you could come back on Tuesday to pick up your things at the house – and we could say goodbye.'

'Sure, Arthur, we could say goodbye,' he mimicked.

Arthur fished out his wallet and opened the billfold compartment. He removed three thousand-franc notes, then looking at Stanley, whose face was screwed up in preparation for tears, took out two more. 'There, that's over a thousand dollars. You should be able to get along very well with that.'

Stanley, seeing that he had extracted the maximum from the situation, and noting that his new friend with the green eye shadow was moving across the room, took the bills from Arthur's hand, saying, 'Okay, Arthur. Thanks a lot. Look, I'll drop around Tuesday and pick up my stuff. Listen,' he said, suddenly suspicious, 'you don't want the bike back, do you?'

'Oh, no, Stanley. You enjoy it. It's all yours. Just think of me once in a while when you ride it.'

'Yeah. Sure, Arthur.' He slid quickly out of his chair, and without a backward glance, went back to Green Eyes.

Arthur took the last few drops from his glass, swishing it around in his mouth before swallowing, as though to dispel a bad taste, threw five francs on the table as a tip, then walked out of the door.

Aboussara's eyes glinted in the street lamps. He squatted, bulky in his tee shirt, the night air forming goose pimples on his folded arms. He watched Arthur's timid figure turn uncertainly, first in one direction and then the other, then begin to walk toward the harbor, squirming through the mass of people to avoid contact.

Aboussara thrust himself upright in one motion and watched the bobbing pink scalp recede from view. He took a single step forward, then froze. Murchison walked comfortably, with long strides, in the same direction that Arthur had taken. Aboussara hung back till he was gone from sight, then ran around the corner into the Rue Gambetta and down the steps through the fish market, occasionally banging into a startled tourist. Aboussara hung back in the archway and watched as Arthur and Murchison formed a procession that only he could see through the milling throng. He edged along the side of the jetty by the shops, mingling with the sightseers and shoppers, keeping them in sight.

Arthur turned to the right in front of the Papagayo, past the artists and craftsmen hawking their wares at the end of the pier, and disappeared. Murchison followed.

Aboussara walked straight down the street and came out at the edge of the parking lot in time to watch them choose their respective cars. He considered the possibility of going back for his motorcycle, and of following, then recalling Fosburgh's caution with respect to the American agent, muttered a curse, backed out of the light, and watched helpless, as they drove one behind the other to the gate behind the parking lot.

'It is your duty,' Colonel Ben Kelb had told him. 'It is your responsibility to the Revolution and to our people, Aboussara. You must not fail them, nor me. He must be killed. He must die. It is said that in his mind is a knowledge which will rob us of our hold on the infidel. We must not be implicated. No one must know. But you shall prevail, Aboussara. I know that you shall, as you always have. Among our strong people, you are a tower of strength. Allah wills that a thousand Arabs shall sing your praises.'

Aboussara slapped his thigh. The boy. Perhaps he knows where he lives. The boy must tell me. I will wait. The little man will appear at the window, with his shining head and his fat stomach, his glasses will glint in the sun. I will find a place to sit, and I will wait. I will make a nice neat hole in him. Then I will throw the rifle with the silencer in the water in another place, and we will be rid of him. Then, when the Colonel returns next Monday, praise Allah, from his communion with the desert, I will tell him that I have done his will.

Donald leaned across the table and said confidentially, 'Have you been watching him eat?'

'I have,' Marie Jo whispered, 'and I may never be able to eat again. Where does it all go? I counted three or four helpings from the hors d'oevre and two of lamb.'

'And heavy on the garlic, as we say at home. He eats almost as much as that other cop, what's his name?'

'Tombal, I think. It's odd that he hasn't showed up.'

'Oh, I'm sure he will, if something interesting happens.'

'I would prefer it to remain dull. What are we going to do about a car?'

'I asked the clerk at the hotel to arrange something with Hertz. He promised that it would be waiting for us in the morning. Say, how would you like to go car shopping with me on Monday or maybe Tuesday?'

'I'm a working girl – remember?'

'Shit,' he said succinctly.

'Well, maybe Monday.'

Donald waved wearily at the waiter and asked for the check. La Brousse nudged the General under the table, and he did the same, remarking, 'A very fine table you set here, my good man, though the service could use improvement.'

Once on the street, Donald said, 'Shall we give them a scare and go for a quick walk on the quay?'

Marie Jo shrugged her shoulders eloquently, 'No, you go, Donald, I'll stay with La Brousse and the General. I can read about you tomorrow in the papers.'

'Defeatist!'

'Yes. Now we'll just have to go back to the hotel and go to bed.'

'Dreadful. But I suppose you're right. Oh, well,' he continued brightly, 'we can always go for a walk tomorrow.'

*

An hour later, in the darkened room, Donald and Marie Jo lay a little apart on the bed.

'Marie Jo . . .'

'Yes, Donald.'

'Michael and Christopher . . .'

She lay quite still, waiting.

'They like to fish and to go camping. I miss them. You'd like them.' He inhaled deeply, then blew the smoke toward the ceiling. 'It really hasn't been very pleasant for them. The divorce, I mean. I don't suppose it ever is for kids. Even when they sense that things aren't going well. It's pretty tough to swallow. Especially when it was really a pretty good marriage for a long time. We used to do a lot of things together, the four of us. Thelma and I came from the same kind of families, same kind of upbringing. I guess it started to deteriorate when I began to make some money. It was fun while I was in the Army. We grew up together. In the end, I guess that we just grew apart. It's a shame really. Apart from the kids, there's so little to show for all of those years, twelve or thirteen it was, except for the scars.' He put the cigarette out in the ashtray on the night table. 'They'd like you too . . . the kids, I mean.'

She smiled secretly and moved toward him, her head cradled in the proffered crook of his arm.

Long after La Brousse had fallen asleep, the General sat sleepless at the window, watching the moon. He pulled his old robe closer around him and chewed at the stem of his pipe. He was deep in thought.

Something is going to happen, he thought. Perhaps they have seen that there is no connection between Hamilton and whatever they seek. Either that or there is a better target in view. Rhabbouz confirms what I heard yesterday. El Kaffar has dropped out of sight. Is his fine hand behind this? And Ben Kelb, that baboon, is out in the desert communing with nature. It is quiet in Cairo, business as usual. Damascus is her usual gay self – the tomb of Arab socialism. Rhabbouz says there is nothing stirring in Eretz Israel. God is in His heaven and the Sixth Fleet patrols like a shark in sight of Arab Africa, with a school of Russian reconnaissance planes for pilot fish, nourishing themselves on stray bits of useless information. He scratched his pate. Perhaps it is just senility. But I sense, I smell action. There is smoke and I wish to be gone from the barn. He moved stiffly. God damn you, old useless legs.

Stanley emerged from Green Eyes's room in the Ferme d'Augustin and walked to his bike. Something in his pocket scratched his leg. He reached in among the wad of bank notes and took out a twisted, almost empty tube of Vaseline and threw it into the bushes over his shoulder, then started out on the bike.

He would go into town and stay at one of the little hotels on the harbor. Cheap, comfortable and central to all activities. Tomorrow he would sleep late. There would be no action at the beaches till afternoon.

He pedaled the bike a few feet to get the motor started, then turned on the dim flickering headlamp. The road was unlighted all the way to the first big crossing, a mile after the dirt turnoff to Moorea Beach.

As he approached the Moorea sign his bike stopped abruptly. He spilled heavily over the handlebars and lay stunned on the macadam. Aboussara jumped out of the reeds at the side of the road and pulled the stout stick from where he had jammed it, between the spokes of the rear wheel. He picked the bike up by its frame and threw it into the reeds. He turned to Stanley, who had begun to groan and move a little, stuffed a gas-smelling rag into his mouth and pulled him by the belt into the culvert behind the reeds. He took two lengths of cord which he had run through his belt and tied the boy's wrists and ankles. He waited a moment or two, and when Stanley did not come fully to his senses, he slapped him twice across the face.

Stanley's eyes bulged with fear, and he mumbled futilely

into the gag.

'You have something to say? I am sure. I want to hear all that you have to say. First, we will start with the nodding of the head. Do you understand me?'

Stanley hesitated. Aboussara took out a hammer and slammed him on the kneecap, shattering the bone and tearing the tendons. Stanley vomited around the gag, began to choke and fainted. Aboussara took out the gag, turned Stanley's head, slapped his back and rolled him over again. When he began to breathe normally, he stuffed the rag back into his mouth. He shook him. Eyes welling with pain, Stanley came to.

'Ah, now we understand each other. You will nod?'

Stanley wagged his head energetically and made a sound through the gag.

'I will take the gag out for the moment. You will answer quietly what I ask. Nod.' Stanley nodded.

'The little fat man who fucks you – he does fuck you – where is he?'

'At his ... his ... house.'

'Where is his house?'

'Please help me. My leg ... it hurts so much ...'

Aboussara lifted the hammer menacingly.

'On the road,' Stanley blurted, 'on the road toward Ste. Maxime. Then you turn toward Cavalaire. It's the second road ... it's dirt. It's the only house. It's in the reeds behind the beach. You can't miss it. Please ... my leg.'

'You are sure that that's where he is?'

'Yes, oh please, yes I am.'

'What does he do?'

Stanley's eyes began to roll as shock took control of his body. Aboussara stuffed the rag in his mouth and gently tapped the heel of the foot on his bad leg. Stanley uttered a muffled shriek. Aboussara took out the gag.

'Numbers ... he makes numbers on a calculator. He writes on papers, and drawings and charts. All day.'

'And he fucks you.'

'Yes.' Stanley reached for a glimmer of hope. 'Do you

want me? I can do good things. Let me . . . please.' He groaned and tried to turn toward Aboussara.

Aboussara stuffed the rag back into his mouth. 'That won't be necessary. That rag is very ugly. It should be done away with, don't you think?'

Stanley nodded.

'I do too.' Aboussara took out a match and lit the exposed end of the rag. Stanley made a horrible noise and tried to struggle, but he was held immobile by his bonds and his crushed leg.

'You mustn't move around. Someone might see my little barbecue.' He smashed Stanley's other kneecap with the rounded peen. Stanley gagged again, then lay still. The gasoline in the rag, which had been smouldering, began to burn in earnest, singeing Stanley's nose and catching at the thatch of hair at his forehead. He turned his head weakly, from side to side, trying to evade the pain and the acrid stench. Aboussara watched, smiling, for a moment, then raised the hammer above his head and crushed Stanley's head with a single blow, driving the shattered fragments of his skull through the pulp that had been his brain. He stuffed the rag all the way into his mouth and closed it, quelling the smoke. He took out his knife and severed the bonds, putting the cut cords in his pocket. Then as an afterthought, he undid Stanley's pants, cut off his genitals with a single stroke and dropped them on his chest.

Putting the hammer in his belt, he walked a couple of hundred yards down the culvert, peered up over the side, and seeing no one, hoisted himself up to the shoulder of the road. He crossed over to a clump of trees, rolled the motorcycle down the embankment over the stones on which he had come, started it, took off his white gloves, spotted here and there, put them, the hammer and the cord in the carry bag, and drove off to the *Glen Pool*.

'You did what, you moron,' Fosburgh screamed. 'You animal! You repulsive sadistical idiot! Wasting time indulging yourself instead of doing your job!' Fosburgh slapped him across the face. 'Don't you understand anything but death and pain? Is there no way for you to order your existence? And again you failed! You failed! Ben Kelb will hear of this!'

'It is not a failure. I know where his house is. I will take the rifle with the silencer and I will finish him.'

'With the FBI or the CIA or God knows what sitting there watching? I told you that you were not to interfere with the Americans in any way. If you are caught and connected with *Glen Pool* I will be exposed. Perhaps,' he began pacing, rubbing his chin, 'perhaps we should just give it up as a bad job and get the hell out of here. Oh you great boob!' He sat heavily in a chair.

Aboussara remained standing, impassive.

Fosburgh stood again. 'You will have another chance. They are to meet with lawyers, I am told. It is possible that they will not meet here. If they go out of town, you can kill him on the road. If it's not here, they won't connect it with me. Especially if I'm on the high seas headed home or to Greece when it happens. You will watch. Sleep in the dirt if you must.' He wrinkled his nose. 'God knows you have had enough practice. But watch him. When he gets ready to go – make sure that he packs, or looks like he is going away – follow him. As soon as you are sure that he is genuinely headed away from here, as far from the presqu'île as possible, stop and call me. Then I will weigh anchor and get out.' He paused. 'When you have finished, call the Embassy in Paris. They will see that you are taken care of properly. Don't do anything but kill him. Without him they lose a year, maybe more. Do you understand?'

Aboussara said, 'It is clear.'

'Then get out. And even Allah will not be able to help you if you bungle this. Ben Kelb will see to that.'

Twenty-six

The twenty-first day of September dawned gray in Washington. A threatening overcast lay like a pall on the city. The air was warm, still and humid.

The weather matched the mood of the President, who sat in an overstuffed leather chair, bare feet propped on an ottoman, slogging through the turgid prose and endless figures of Walton Carver's proposed plan for the temporary centralization of economic planning authority.

It had, in the end, been necessary to bring Gordon Aufritz, the Secretary of the Treasury, into the inner circle. Aufritz had been reached by the Secretary of State and informed in a brief meeting of what was planned. It was plain that he considered the President to be mad, and Carver a half step worse, and was clearly peeved at being presented with a fait accompli. Nonetheless, in keeping with the need for speed and absolute secrecy, he had compiled data and prepared numbers like a junior accountant, and worked ceaselessly to produce his portion of the document, now in Smith's hands.

The speeches to Congress and to the public, the details of printed materials were to be ready for distribution on Monday morning immediately following the planned invasion of Quahrein. In order to see that the schedule was met, it was necessary to arrange for typing and making Xeroxes, it having been decided that printing of the documents in the usual fashion created too great an opportunity for a lapse in security.

The job of preparation was to fall to the President's private secretary and an FBI agent named Glastonbury, who, in addition to being a lawyer, was a crack speed typist and shorthand expert. The big Xerox machine with the automatic collator, which sat in the bomb shelter and basement seventy feet beneath the White House, was to serve as the printing press.

Aufritz had commented, 'This is the best-kept secret in American history since Pearl Harbor – and it should have about the same effect.'

Smith wiggled his toes and dropped his glasses on the rug beside the chair. He yawned and stretched and said 'Shit' a couple of times. He put his hand on the coffee pot on the table next to him. It was cold. He shrugged and decided to have some anyway. When he picked it up and shook it, it was empty. As he got to his feet, there was a knock on the door.

'Jack,' he said, 'that you?'

'Yes, sir.'

'Come on in.'

'Morning, sir.'

'Yeah. It is morning.' He stretched again, his arms over his head, almost touching the ceiling. 'God, what a lot of bullshit.' He indicated the papers on the table.

'That's Walton's life's blood you are talking about, Mr. President.'

'Yeah, well,' he sniffed, 'he can keep his frigging blood. He ain't no Hemingway.'

'So what do you think?'

'I don't know. I really don't know. On paper it is feasible. But then, of course, I wanted it to be feasible. In fact, since we have already committed ourselves, it better fucking well be feasible. Walton and Aufritz are coming back at ten-thirty, heaven help me.'

Kugel clasped his hands in attitude of prayer and bowed slightly, showing his bald spot. 'Speaking of heaven, today, from noon on, you will have the greatest cover in the world. Your entire day is replete with Rotarians, visiting Senators – all small matters, and as the pièce de résistance, the Papal Nuncio.'

'Oh, God – you should excuse the pun.' He slapped Kugel

249

hard on the shoulder. 'Come on in and sit with me while I shave and take a bath. You can tell me all about it.'

Smith sat still and listened to Carver and Aufritz hack away at each other for as long as he could. Finally he said, 'Gentlemen. Excuse me. In the fifteen minutes since you have arrived you have belabored both your points to complete exhaustion. It sounds like an argument between psychiatrists, one yelling heredity and the other environment. When you make up your mind that you need to have a positive balance of payments, and so you sell your surplus commodities on the world market, you have a resulting domestic inflation in the price of those goods. If you need raw materials for domestic production to maintain price stability, you must sacrifice export opportunities. What we want to do is to balance the two as best we can, keeping our main political objective in mind.

'And ours is a political objective. To prevent by drastic means a global dislocation of prime energy sources. The need for such measures has been foisted on us by means beyond our control. We must nonetheless deal with them, and your philosophical argument will not accomplish that end.'

Carver looked across at Aufritz and said, 'If I may . . .'

Aufritz nodded politely and listened.

'Mr. President, the political and the economic problem are one and the same, and as you have suggested, there may be no way to skin both cats at once. Despite increasing controls on the operations of American oil companies, existing contracts dating from the late '60s required the exportation of over five hundred million dollars in crude oil and petroleum products last year. The rationale in permitting such exports is the necessity of maintaining the sanctity of our contractual obligations, and the historical commitment of all administrations since the 1930s to a free trade world. To deal with the question at hand, there is no doubt that even with the rationing plan before us, the price of petroleum will rise dramatically if it is necessary to institute the kind of export program envisioned.'

'Neither,' added Aufritz, 'will the attempt to convert the transportation industry to this solar-powered car alleviate the shortage of petroleum, nor the rise in prices. Not over the short or even the intermediate term. Assuming – if you must – that it will work.'

The President shook his head impatiently. 'All right, I understand your doubts in the matter. What I want to know is, given a reasonable prospect of success with this product, or indeed with any of the dozens of other projects for supplemental sources of energy now under way, can we sensibly approach a major program for exporting existing petroleum resources to the rest of the free world?'

Aufritz pulled his neck in like a turtle and stared across the desk. 'That depends on the degree of cooperation you can expect from those concerned. Have you discussed this matter with the Secretary of Labor?'

'You are aware, I think, that I have not,' Smith replied.

'Well, frankly, big labor could screw the whole thing up.'

'To each his prejudices, Mr. Secretary. Let's assume that they don't.'

'You want a hard and fast answer, Mr. President,' he hesitated a moment, licked his lips, then continued, 'it is essentially here.' He pointed at the papers. 'You have made the decision. The circumstances surrounding it are certainly unique, but the problem is, on a much smaller scale of course, fairly common. What we are, in fact, seeking to do, if you will accept the analogy, is to broaden our product line to avoid obsolescence. Accepting your premise that our major object is to supply the entire Western world with energy while maintaining full employment at home involves two commitments. The first is the enormous expense and the second the risk that our conventional energy sources will be dissipated before we have a means to replace them. You are like a corporate president who has decided to go deeply into debt to fund a major research project to completely revamp his production. If you win the gamble –

calculated risk, if you prefer – the return on your investment will dwarf your debt. If you lose ... you lose the
company.'

'Walton, do you concur?'

'Perhaps, I would have used other words ... Yes. I concur.'

The President put his hands down on the desk. 'Would
you take the gamble, Mr. Aufritz? And if you did, what
would you do to minimize your risk?'

Gordon Aufritz allowed himself a small smile. 'No, Mr.
President, I wouldn't take the risk. But I'd be willing to
make the wager on the solar-powered car, especially since
General Motors is sticking its corporate neck out this far. I
would insist, though, that the license be non-exclusive. That
way, you will force other manufacturers into spreading the
cost and amount of research, increasing the possibility that
someone may actually make the damn thing work, and
thereby motivating them through the possibility of their
being obsoleted out of business.

'Then I would back my play. I would gasify the hell out of
coal, Mr. President. There's a real alternative. I grant you
that it's not enough in the context of the political problem,
as it exists. The solar-powered car will have a much more
immediate impact. But we know that we can gasify and
liquefy coal, and we have three hundred years' worth. The
economy won't look the same by the time you get through
tinkering with it, not if that damn car falls on its ass. But
if you back it up with a coal gasification push, you'll still
have an economy left, and energy to run it with.'

'I've never heard you quite so ... involved, Mr. Secretary.'

'Well, frankly, Mr. President, it's a little bit like playing
Monopoly. It's easy to enthuse about a fantasy.'

'What will happen to the dollar?' the President asked.

'Let's answer that together, Mr. Carver. I say it'll go to
hell because of the gigantic increase in national debt, and
the debasement of the currency that that implies.'

Carver smiled, 'I think it will be the strongest currency in
the world, because we will be expanding our economy, forg-
ing scientific and economic progress, and we will be the

major supplier of petroleum to the world, giving us a huge balance-of-payments surplus.'

'That's what I like,' the President said, 'consensus among my advisors. I asume you have the detail of how this coal project will work? And the car project too?'

Aufritz nodded agreement. 'Mr. President, it has been my life-long belief that every time government is involved in industry, failure is guaranteed.'

Carver interrupted, 'While it has been my conviction that where tax dollars and public borrowing form a substantial part of corporate assets or volume, the public should benefit as well as the stockholders.'

'Therefore,' Aufritz began again, 'we compromised. If you approve, all corporate loans will be repaid over a fifty-year period. However, during that period, a special class of stock shall be outstanding, the dividends of which shall represent a specified portion of corporate earnings – we have decided upon twenty-five percent – and that stock shall be owned by the Treasury Department of the United States. Dividends equal to those earnings shall be paid directly to the General Fund annually, a concession to Mr. Carver's point of view.'

Carver cleared his throat. 'However, the government shall not have representation on either the Board of Directors or in management – my concession to Mr. Aufritz.'

'And on that compromise, you agree?'

'Yes, Mr. President,' Aufritz and Carver replied simultaneously.

'Good, then that is how we shall approach the Congress. Do you have the manpower mobilization plans outlined?'

'I do, Mr. President,' Walton Carver answered.

'Then let's get to them. I'm afraid that after tomorrow, I will belong largely to the Secretaries of State and Defense.'

Twenty-seven

Arthur, further chastened by several days of lonely reflection, looked from his porch at the patchwork of waving reeds, bare fields and plucked vineyards, and beyond into the red-rimmed newly risen sun. With a pensive sigh, he turned back to the room. He had packed all of his things and straightened up. In the new neatness and sterility of the spacious salon, his possessions seemed meager. The bound books, rescued from their hiding place under the stove, were perched atop the two suitcases which were the sum and total of his personal effects, one filled with his clothes, the other with his notes and his few experimental samples. A paper bag nestled forlorn between them. Arthur ruefully observed that Stanley had not even bothered to return for his things.

Arthur walked to the mirror near the entrance, straightened the knot in his tie and patted his few strands of hair. There was a small spot on the left lapel of the tan gabardine suit.

With a shrug, he turned from the mirror, gathered his things and walked to the car. He loaded the trunk, keeping the books with him, got in, started the car and pulled out onto the road. After a hundred yards, he stopped again and looked over his shoulder with indecision, then continued on his way.

Hultz was waiting for him at the breakfast table in the dining room of the Byblos.

Hultz pushed back his chair and stood to greet him. Arthur put the books down and put out his hand.

'Good morning, Mr. Hultz.'

'Good morning, sir. And please call me George.'

Arthur sat, smiling shyly, and said, 'That would be nice ... George. My name is Arthur.' He pushed the books in Hultz's direction. 'Here.'

Hultz put his hand on top of the books and rubbed a cover. The waiter appeared at his side. 'May I help you, messieurs?'

'Arthur, what would please you? I have suddenly developed a hell of an appetite.'

'Yes, so have I,' he said enthusiastically. 'Eggs, two eggs – fried. And ham. And orange juice and coffee. And a brioche.'

'What's a brioche?' Hultz asked.

'A kind of semi-sweet roll,' Arthur replied.

'That sounds good to me. Waiter, make that two of everything.' The waiter walked away, and Hultz continued, 'Listen, Arthur, you won't be offended if I start at the back of the book. I've got a lot of the material up front. And, well, I suppose I'd just like to see how it comes out.'

Arthur chuckled, 'Be my guest ... but the butler did it.'

Aboussara was pallid under his tan. His blood raced, and he felt his age. Wednesday morning. He did not know how many hours he had slept since Saturday, but they had been few. He had not eaten properly and he felt logy.

When he saw Arthur and Murchison pull into the Byblos, he went back to the *Glen Pool* and directly to his quarters. He stripped off his clothes, which had begun to stink of perspiration, showered and shaved the stubble of three days from his wan face.

In twenty minutes he was back at the Byblos, trying to avoid being noticed by the American agent who sat, fresh and relaxed, in his car. Murchison had had a night's rest at St. Tropez while a phoned relief took over surveillance of Arthur's house.

Aboussara did not have the advantage of a worldwide intelligence network to support his efforts. He had to provide continuous surveillance.

He opened a thermos of coffee that he had brought with him from the *Glen Pool* and took a sip, grateful for the burning sensation.

Aboussara put his thermos down on a rock across the road and eyed Arthur's car speculatively. It was in full view of the American agent, offering no opportunity from that point of view. Even if the man were not sitting there, it would be impossible to do anything in broad daylight on a public street. Perhaps, he thought, he will stay until dark.

'So you see, George, the essence of the matter is the sensitization of the plates. The formula doesn't change, copper sulfate, silica and so on. It is a matter of treatment and processing. I am not a lawyer, but it seems to me the basis of the whole matter is a process patent. The degree of protection is, of course, moot. It is conceivable that someone will be able to repeat my work. But I think that you have to start with my assumption: ambient sunlight under all but the worst of cloud cover conditions should be enough to produce an electrical reaction.'

'Arthur,' Hultz said, 'I would be a liar if I said I understood how you came to the initial conclusion. This,' he patted the book, 'is a masterwork of scientific deduction and imagination.'

Arthur blushed, 'Thank you. Thank you very much. Now we shall see what happens when we try to translate it to mass production. I assume that every effort will be made to change as little as possible.'

'Don't worry about that. If we change a fifty-cent bolt and washer assembly on five million cars, we piss two and one half million dollars down the drain. That's the stuff pink slips are made of. But I'm sorry about the change of plans for tomorrow's meeting.'

'It doesn't make any real difference, I suppose. I've got to go over to the real estate office and let them know I'm giving the place up. But I can do that this morning.'

'I'll go over with you if you like.'

'That's very thoughtful of you, George. I'd like that a lot.' He paused. 'George, do you have any idea *why* they picked Toulon?'

'I suppose because that's the nearest office of our lawyers.' Hultz leaned across the table. 'Arthur, I want to tell you something. I made myself a promise. Your personal life, at least to the degree that I can arrange it, is going to be very much your own. You aren't going to put up with a lot of bullshit about it. The way I figure it, the personal choices are yours. I can't say that I share your instinct, or your tastes, but they are, God damn it, yours. I think it's a privilege to have the chance to work with you on your project. And I think anyone else ought to think so too.'

Arthur stared down at the table silently, then said, 'I have made a promise too. I am not going to let my personal life interfere with my work. Fortune doesn't give many men the opportunity to affect the world in which they live. I will not miss my chance.'

'Okay. Come on, Arthur. Let's get that real estate thing finished. Then I'll drop my car off at Hertz, and we can drive down to Toulon together to get this started. Milt, Mr. Goodrich, that is, ought to be in some time tonight.'

Twenty-eight

Donald Hamilton kissed Marie Jo firmly on the mouth, then watched her climb the steps of the high-winged propeller plane. He stood in the breeze till the plane took off on its way to Paris.

He hummed to himself as he opened the car door. She was to return on Saturday. He spent the twenty-kilometer drive from Hyères to Toulon considering what to do with her. He was still reasonably gun-shy from his divorce; it was hard to admit to himself that he wanted something more permanent than odd weekends or stolen days with Marie Jo.

He had told the General that he was going to spend the rest of the week in the office at Toulon, trying to straighten out the communications gap that existed between his firm and their French partners, and to try to get them to give him another assistant on the job.

The General had agreed, and told him that he and La Brousse would follow him shortly. They arranged to have rooms in the tiny La Tour Blanche in Super Toulon, high on the hill overlooking the city.

Lest he feel too lonely, Donald noticed, the watchdog remained at a fixed distance, whether he speeded up or slowed, as though pasted to his rear-view mirror.

He parked the car in the lot behind the office, waved to the watchdog, who had stationed himself across the street, and went up in the elevator.

A car was waiting at the airport entrance at Hyères to drive Milton Goodrich and the three lawyers from the Paris office to the Grand Hôtel in the Place de la Libération where they were all supposed to stay.

There was no reason for Goodrich to notice the short, scholarly looking man who had been sitting in the economy section of the plane. He brushed past him in the confusion of the baggage claim area, searched out the dark leather case with M.G. stamped on its side, and left.

The man's bag was a little late in coming and he waited patiently by the side of the conveyor until it appeared. It was an ordinary suitcase and unmarked. He pulled it off onto the floor, and as an afterthought, patted his jacket pocket. He withdrew the passport and glanced at it briefly. American. Alvin Greenberg. Age 57. Owlish eyes peering through heavy dark-rimmed glasses. He replaced it and walked out the door.

The man called Greenberg looked up and down the curb in front of the terminal, then spotted a man of about sixty leaning on an Italian sports car. He walked over to him. The man looked up, then smiling took his bag, put it in the trunk and opened the door for him. When they were seated and had pulled away into the road, the traveler said, 'Shalom, Rhabbouz.'

'Shalom, Samuel Zvi Aharon.'

The Israeli Ambassador to the United States loosened his tie and asked, 'Where are you taking me?'

'To a little hotel above the city. It's charming. Only twenty rooms. A nice swimming pool.' He wriggled a little in his seat as he drove. 'I only wish that we could deliver you better weather. It is a little cool and breezy for my tastes.'

'The hotel is out of the way?'

'Yes. There is only a narrow road, and the cable car to Mont Faron.' He pointed at the stark rock across the haze.

'Du Pont, you are a moron.' The General spat into the phone, cursing his agent in Washington. 'The entire intelligence community must be peopled with idiots. When you find out that Aharon has left Washington, you have the consummate gall to ask your opposite number at the Israeli Embassy where he has gone.' He sneered. 'Then that idiot, overcome by a stroke of genius, tells you that he does not know where he went, but that he was traveling incognito. Both of you should be shot for breach of security; the only question is which of you should go first. And then,' his voice rising to a crescendo, 'to call me on an unscrambled line transatlantic ... unbelievable.' Calming, the General continued, 'Now, if it is possible, shut up, sit still and see that you don't get yourself, or me, into any more difficulty.'

The General hung up and shook his head. 'You know, La Brousse, I am beginning to wonder if I shouldn't beg retirement. We have lost the thread entirely. I have the feeling that everything is coming apart in my hands. We have reports that something is stirring in the Arab intelligence community, especially on the left wing, and then nothing happens. We have a couple of brutal murders, and nothing happens. An ignorant bystander becomes the object of attempts on his life, and we can't find out why, or by whom. If it were not for the fact that Brunschwig has been equally unsuccessful, I would believe that it is old age. Perhaps we should get the hell out of here and go back to Paris. I don't think that Hamilton is going to lead us any further, and just in case, we have that imbecile – what's his name – playing nursemaid.'

La Brousse looked up. 'I have never heard you give up before.'

'Give up, you lout! Don't sit there on your damaged ass and make accusations. Give me an alternative suggestion.' The General clamped his teeth on his pipestem. 'Come, then, super spy, what would you do?'

'This is Toulon,' La Brousse began.

'Very perceptive,' said the General.

La Brousse went on. 'I make two suggestions; in the first place, let's get some extra people down here instead of running ourselves to death along with the poor bastards who are assigned to keep Hamilton alive. To keep him alive is one problem, to catch the perpetrator is another. If we had had another agent to watch Hamilton's car, perhaps we would have caught him instead of getting Hamilton all but killed. With anxiety comes mistakes. How many times have you drummed that into my head? Secondly, we have someone here who can do us some good in the interim. That fat policeman, Tombal. He is still burning over the death of his friend, I am sure.'

'What about Brunschwig? If we call on Tombal, he will report it to Brunschwig.'

'I don't think he will. He has no love for him.'

The General tapped on the floor with his cane several times, then began to walk around the table, with his eyes closed almost to slits, puffing away at his pipe. La Brousse had lost count of his laps, when he stopped directly before him and said, 'Well, Cripple, it makes sense. What time is it?'

'Ten after four.'

'Fine. Drag your twisted hulk into the préfecture and get Tombal. No, moron. Not the phone. I can use the phone without you. Tell Tombal I want him here for dinner, at eight, shall we say. Tell him we want ... let's see ... it's a job for perhaps three trained agents ... tell him we need eight of his best plainclothes people. They will work two shifts. We will decide exactly how and where at dinner. Can you remember that?' he asked sweetly.

La Brousse looked upward toward God and left the room. The General took another turn around the table, felt his knee and winced, then sat heavily in the chair. He picked up the phone and asked for a number.

'Hello.'

'Good afternoon, Madame Rhabbouz. This is General Pineau des Charentes. Is your husband at home?'

'Good afternoon, General,' she replied frostily. 'I am sorry, but André is not at home.'

'Could you tell me when you expect him.'

'I'm afraid that I can't, General. He left this morning. He said that he might be out of town for a day or two. I haven't heard from him since.'

'Mes hommages, chère madame. Please tell him that I

called, and thank you.'

Where have you gone, old Jew, now that I need you, he thought. What black deed are you up to, and why don't I know about it?

As they entered the hotel, Aharon said, 'You will take care of registering, Rhabbouz. Tell them that I don't feel well and prefer to go directly to the room. I want to be out of the lobby as quickly as I can.'

Aharon asked for the key at the desk, feigning dizziness. The clerk complied and started the formalities with Rhabbouz as he left. Aharon walked up the short flight of stairs and found the number quickly. Checking left and right down the corridor, he let himself in and shut the door.

He walked into the bathroom, loosened his collar and tie, took off his glasses and bathed his myopic eyes with cool water from the tap. After drying his face, he returned to the room, where a large bowl of fruit sat atop a table. A small envelope stuck out at the top. He picked it up cautiously, feeling at a grainy substance inside. He weighed it tentatively between his fingers, then shrugged and tore it open.

Inside was a small package of salt of the kind one finds on airline trays, and a white card with the Star of David transfixed on a crescent moon. He smiled and took an apple.

After La Brousse left Tombal, he stopped off at Hamilton's office in the Boulevard de Strasbourg.

'May I see M. Hamilton?' he asked.

The receptionist gave him an unfriendly stare. 'He is in conference with the patron. Is he expecting you? I do not wish to interrupt him.'

'Just tell him that Paul La Brousse is here. We are old friends.'

The girl got up from behind the desk, crossed over to a large set of double doors, knocked softly and was admitted.

Hamilton walked out of the door and hugged the surprised La Brousse, kissing him soundly on both cheeks. 'Mon cher Paul, it is so good to see you. How are the children? And your lovely wife?' He took him by the elbow. 'Come, let me take you to my office. You look well, all things considered. Is your leg improving?'

Hamilton shut the door behind them. 'Now, what can I do for you, my much-oppressed life-long buddy? Has the General sent you to suggest that I commit suicide so that you can pick the culprit out of the crowd at my funeral?'

'You certainly have gotten into the swing of things, Mr. Hamilton,' La Brousse remarked dryly.

'The idea of death grows on you after a while, La Brousse. Now what can I do for my favorite shield?'

'Come to dinner at eight at La Tour Blanche.'

'Who else is coming to the party?'

'General Pineau, Commissaire Tombal and myself.'

'And you need a fourth for bridge.'

'Exactly.'

'Am I to be shot, blown up, hung or just maimed? It's really a shame that Marie Jo isn't here, but she's off in Paris studying up on her Sacher-Masoch.'

'I have always admired your sense of humor, Mr. Hamilton.'

'I'll just bet you have, M. La Brousse . . . or shall I call you Paul?'

'Paul, please. Dinner at eight, then?'

'I wouldn't miss it for the world. And, Paul —'

'Yes?'

'Can the watchdog come too?'

'Oh yes. But I'm afraid he's going to have to eat outside.'

La Brousse limped across the lobby and made heavy use of the banister on his way up the stairs. Continuing an even slow pace, he walked to the room and knocked.

'Who's there?' the gravelly voice rang out.

'It's me.'

The General opened the door after a minute to let him in.

'How many times do I have to tell you to identify yourself properly? You could have been some kind of ventriloquist murderer come to kill an old man.'

La Brousse sat down on the edge of the bed, massaging his aching wound. 'You'll never guess who I saw down in the lobby.'

'No, I'd never guess,' the General mimicked sourly.

La Brousse studied his fingernails.

'Well? Are you going to tell me your secret, my dove?'

'I didn't identify myself by name because I was afraid I would be overheard.'

'Fantastic. Now, who did you see?'

'Mohammed El Kaffar.'

'No. It isn't possible. El Kaffar. Here.' He collapsed in his chair and thought a moment. 'Quickly, have Tombal send out the man who does the pickup of hotel registries every night. I want to see what he is calling himself. See if any of the passports are left behind the desk. I want to see them too. What incredible luck.'

La Brousse did as he was told, then hung up. 'General Pineau, do you know why he is here?'

'Of course not, you clown. I have no idea why he is here. It could well be an absurd coincidence. But no matter what reason he is here, we want to know. He has been lost, so far as our department is concerned, for over two weeks. Now we have found him, and, as you might have guessed, I am thoroughly elated.'

Twenty-nine

The Place de la Libération in the center of Toulon is replete with cafes, all of which face outward, affording a view of the entrance of the Grand Hôtel. As a result, Aboussara had been able to spend the day moving from one to the other without being spotted while he ascertained the whereabouts of Arthur Edelman. He had also been able to eat a square meal for the first time in days.

Inside the hotel, matters were moving more swiftly than the most optimistic of the parties had envisioned. After a brief conversation with Hultz, who had been waiting for him in the lobby, Milt Goodrich had called Arthur Edelman and asked to come to his room for a brief chat.

After hanging up, Milt turned to George, 'Do you think that you ought to be in on this? You seem to have worked out a pretty decent relationship with him.'

'No, Milt. I think that you ought to go alone. You're going to have to build a man-to-man relationship with him. The sooner you start, the better off we are going to be. After all, this gentleman is going to end up as a very important cog in the corporate wheel.'

Goodrich took the elevator to Edelman's floor and walked down to his room. He knocked and Edelman admitted him.

'Arthur,' he said extending his hand, 'I've been looking forward to this for a long time. I'm Milt Goodrich.'

Coloring, Edelman took his hand. 'Come in, please.'

'What do you drink, Arthur?'

'Scotch.'

'Fine.' Goodrich pressed the buzzer for the floor waiter. 'I wanted to get right down to things. This invention of yours, it's going to change the industry. But you know that already. We are preparing the fastest introduction program that the automotive world has ever seen. And you're going to be right in the middle of it.'

The waiter knocked and opened the door. 'Deux whisky-soda, s'il vous plaît,' Goodrich said. 'Let's sit down, Arthur, and kick this around. What are you looking for – really?'

Arthur hesitated, then said with conviction, 'Two things. I want to be independently filthy stinking rich, and I want to see that car on the road – with my name on it in chrome.'

Goodrich was still laughing when the waiter appeared again with the drinks. He signed the bill and turned back to Arthur. 'We are going to get along famously. That's about what I would have said. You know that you're going to have to work your rear end off, I suppose, and if it doesn't pan out, all bets are off.'

'When do you expect to be in production?'

'That depends a lot on you, Arthur. How about twelve months to the assembly line?'

'That fast? Is it possible?'

'If we can get the details out of the way, like making you, how was it – filthy stinking rich. And of course getting your name on some contracts. And if it all works as well on the assembly line as it works in lab and on paper, it's possible.'

Arthur nodded, a little dazed. Goodrich got to his feet. 'Look, Arthur, I know that you just arrived, and you probably want to get a little rest. I just came up to say hello and to congratulate you on a fabulous achievement.' He stuck out his hand again. 'See you later, Arthur.' When the door closed behind him, Arthur leaned his back against it, his head spinning dizzily.

Arthur's Swiss lawyers had huddled with him over the weighty document for three hours. The broad premises had been secured: twenty-five million dollars in General Motors stock payable in exchange for all of the outstanding shares of the Edelman Automotive Corporation; the transfer of title of the patents and applications to General Motors; one-half percent of the wholesale value of each unit produced payable to Arthur Edelman, his heirs or assigns for a period of fifty years; permission to write sublicenses on a worldwide basis, provided that the terms of such licenses result in no diminution of payments to Arthur Edelman and that all such vehicles bear, in addition to the name of the manufacturer, the legend Edelman Solar Car. Last, among the major points, was a twenty-five-year employment contract between General Motors and Arthur Edelman, his capacity to be that of Senior Executive Vice President, with the opportunity to be included among the management slate of nominees to the Board of Directors. All in all, it was about the same deal that GM had made for the license to the Wankel engine nearly ten years earlier.

So on Wednesday, September 21, prior to the expected deadline, the lawyers were locked into the offices made available to them, reducing the agreement to writing.

The city was lovely in the dwindling light. The sun was full and red just above the western horizon. La Grange, one of the lawyers from the office in Toulon, suggested that the VIPs take the cable car to Mont Faron, so that they might have a view of the city, and then return to have dinner at La Calanque to enjoy the fine seafood.

The wind had died with the coming of twilight, but the smell of the Mediterranean pervaded the cable car as it softly swayed over the stunted trees on the rocks below. Hultz and La Grange leaned on one side, looking over the hills, while Arthur and Goodrich looked at the city from the other. In the car following theirs, Murchison lazed against the front window, watching. Aboussara, his heart in his mouth, shared the car with him.

At the end of the ride, La Grange suggested a quick drink on the patio of La Tour Blanche to catch a last glimpse before returning to the seashore.

Murchison followed them and sat at another table. Aboussara walked by and around the corner. He strolled into the enclosure where the pool was located and watched two small half-naked children enjoy a last dip before dinner. He glanced up at the small pretty building and stopped dead in his tracks. Afraid that he would be noticed, he walked in the opposite direction, up a little rise, and sat down on the ground. He turned again to confirm his first suspicion. Even in the failing light, there was no doubt that the face in the window belonged to Mohammed El Kaffar, the Foreign Minister of Quahrein. He could see that there was someone else in the room with him but could not make out the face.

Why would he be here? The Colonel must have sent him. But the Colonel is in the desert. Aboussara disliked El Kaffar as devoutly as he deified Ben Kelb. El Kaffar was smooth, polished, educated, not at all a man of the people, a man of the Revolution. Aboussara had never understood why he stood so high, second only to the Colonel.

He weighed orders and discipline against instinct and intuition, and decided that it was in the best interests of his country if he stayed with El Kaffar. At least for the moment. The other one, that fat little pig, would be with all the Americans at the hotel. Eventually, his opportunity would arise. Thus, when Edelman and the people from General Motors left, carrying Murchison with them like the tail on a kite, Aboussara hung around at the back of the hotel.

By a bit after eight, the sun had fallen below the horizon, and darkness had enveloped all but the fireflies of life in the city below. Spotlights struck against the tall upright cylinder of masonry which gave the hotel its name. Someone turned on the lights in El Kaffar's room. Rhabbouz, transfixed in the sudden brilliance, came to the window to close the shutters.

'The Jew,' Aboussara said to himself in a whisper, 'the damned Jew.' He shrank into the darkness and tried to blink away the welter of confusion in his mind. When he looked up, Rhabbouz had gone.

He slumped against the wall. The idea formed slowly, unwillingly. He had been warned that the Israelis maintained an intelligence network in the South of France. Brave, dead

Kareeb, the little man from Cabasse, the man with one foot, had pointed out the leader. It was the man in the window.

The sour taste of bile filled Aboussara's mouth. It is not possible that El Kaffar is their captive, he thought. He has come of his own free will. Aboussara straightened, filled again with conviction and purpose. He had decided that Mohammed El Kaffar was a traitor to the Revolution and to Ben Kelb and to all Arabs, and that he must die.

'Minister,' Aharon said, holding out his arms to El Kaffar.

'My friend. All is well with you?'

'Yes, and with you, Mohammed?'

'All is well.' He held Aharon firmly with both his hands. 'The years of planning and hoping are at an end. It will begin Friday. Ben Kelb will be arrested on Saturday morning on his way to the city from the desert. I will be in Quahrein at dusk of the same day to make my broadcast. New ambassadors have already been posted in the Arab capitals, and will have explained. All except Iraq.'

'Don't worry about Iraq.' Aharon made a fist.

El Kaffar smiled at him reproachfully.

'Yes, Mohammed,' Aharon continued, 'we are agreed. There is to be no spilling of blood, Jew or Arab, unless it is absolutely unavoidable. I know. We are to stay out of it unless you ask us directly.' He turned. 'We are to have room service, is that right, André?'

'It is already arranged. Dinner for two here.' He bowed slightly and left the room.

'And so, now, have we forgotten anything?' El Kaffar asked.

'Not that I am aware. Of course, no one knows anything, except the Prime Minister and the Minister of Defense.'

'What do they think?'

'The Prime Minister said that God would shower blessings on us for saving His people, both the sons of Ishmael and Israel.'

'Inch' Allah.'

Aharon sat in a chair and looked up through his heavy glasses at the dark narrow face, the deep blue eyes sparkling with intensity. 'It has been a century since we first met in Geneva, Mohammed.'

'Not a century, my friend, only four years. But if we succeed in our endeavor, we will have done the work of century.'

'At least we will have made a beginning.' Aharon chuckled softly. 'And to think that my dear dead mother, olav a sholem, said that I could never keep a secret.'

El Kaffar grinned at him. 'I am glad that you have been able to, Samuel. Just one little leak . . . the slightest suspicion . . .' He ran his finger across his throat. 'So, on to business.'

'I am to demand an audience for us with President Smith at eight on Monday morning. We will explain to him what we are trying to do, what our objectives are and how we intend to meet them. We will ask for the continued protection of the Sixth Fleet, and the direct intervention of Secretary Johansson on our behalf with our neighbors. We will request that Smith arrange a Middle East summit conference in New York, under the auspices of the United Nations, with the participation of the Great Powers.'

El Kaffar nodded, his shoulders bowed. 'It all seems so simple,' he said. 'We have done a great deal of planning. Now it seems that we must do a great deal of praying.' He sighed expressively. 'We must hope that Smith will understand. After all, it was I who presented Ben Kelb's demands. I was the mouthpiece of the Revolution, the chief spokesman for the Arab Left.' He put his hands in his pockets and paced nervously. 'But Smith, above all others, should recognize what the elimination of Ben Kelb, and a mutual assistance treaty between Israel and Quahrein, can mean in the Middle East.'

Aharon agreed. 'It means the end of thirty years of hostility and mistrust.'

El Kaffar looked at Aharon's soft scholar's face, and his voice grew stronger as he spoke. 'We will encourage the reluctant and the afraid. The Jordanians, the Lebanese, the

Tunisians will flock to come over to us, all the Arabs. One by one they will all come over. And by our act of faith and trust we will have accomplished in one stroke what could not be done by armed might and hate in all those thirty years. We will have taken the first step toward unity and peace, and we will have created a new power on this earth, with the human resources of our people and the material resources of our lands, and we shall bind them together and build industries and create progress, and we will rise from the ashes of our hatred and we shall be great – and at peace.'

'Omain.'

Aboussara was fortified in his suspicions by the arrival of Hamilton and Tombal at La Tour Blanche. He watched them seated for dinner, then sped off on his motorcycle.

'Good evening, Mr. Hamilton, Tombal. You will excuse me if I don't rise. My legs and my age are against me this evening. Thank you very much for coming.'

Hamilton greeted him cheerfully, 'It's always a pleasure, General. I asked La Brousse what you had in mind,' he lowered his voice and said confidentially, 'hot coals, the rack or just a simple thrust of the dagger?'

'You do me too much honor, Mr. Hamilton. We are just trying to put an end to this nonsense once and for all. And in view of our agreement, I felt it would be helpful if you could join in – with your consent, of course. And La Brousse, pointing out my ineptitude and my old age, felt that we would all be more secure if we were protected by the bastion of modern police science – Commissaire Tombal.'

Tombal was prevented from replying by a mouthful of bread.

The waiter came by and took their order. 'We would like to have two bottles of wine,' the General said. 'In this gay company it will be needed.'

Halfway through dinner, it was decided that Hamilton would go out on the town this evening, and for the next two evenings, until Marie Jo showed up.

'What I am to do,' Hamilton said, 'is to raise a little hell. I'll just go around from cafe to cafe, make some noisy passes at girls and drink too much. I think that it'll be much more effective if I'm really alone.'

The General shook his head adamantly. 'I am afraid you have gotten too much into the spirit of things, my friend. You will be watched by no less than four of Tombal's best people at one time, not to include your faithful friend,' he pointed out of doors at the parking lot, where the disgruntled watchdog sat, eating a sandwich. 'It is our hope that the assassin will oblige us by making one more attempt to free the world from Donald Hamilton. He will, of course, fail.' Pushing himself away from his empty plate, the General asked, 'Well, how does that suit you, Mr. Hamilton?'

'Dandy, especially the part where he fails. But I'm still not sure that we wouldn't get better results if I had less cover.'

'Out of the question, Hamilton. Just follow the plan. I don't want you on my conscience. You still have our little gift?'

Hamilton patted his jacket and nodded.

'Sweet Jesus,' La Brousse remarked, staring across the floor at the man at the hors d'oeuvre table.

Obviously aware that he had been seen, Rhabbouz walked over to the General's party and said, 'I bid you good evening.'

'Well, Jew,' said the General, 'we can have the pleasure of your company, I hope. Waiter,' he motioned, 'bring another chair for this gentleman.'

Rhabbouz sat down and attacked his plate with gusto. Around mouthfuls he acknowledged everyone's presence. 'Particularly nice to see you up and about, La Brousse.'

La Brousse said, 'I want to thank you and Mme. Rhabbouz for your thoughtful gift while I was in the hospital.'

'A pleasure, my friend.' He winked. 'It must improve your relationship with the General, now that you both limp. A matched pair.'

'It is clear,' said the General, 'that they cut off the wrong end of your penis at birth.'

'It was some time ago, I will admit,' Rhabbouz said, 'but there have been those who disagree with you. And you, Mr. Hamilton, how is the All-American bull's-eye?'

'Very well, thank you, and despite the efforts of your friends, still alive.'

'I heard about the incident at the beach. Damn shame, it was a lovely little car.'

'True, but think how much more unpleasant it would have been if I had been sitting in it.'

They all had dessert, then brandy.

'Rhabbouz,' said the General, 'let us two old comrades take a walk in the garden, shall we? Mr. Hamilton, till we meet again.'

'A pleasure as always, my dear General,' Hamilton said.

La Brousse started to get to his feet, but the General stood in front of him. 'Enjoy another brandy, La Brousse. It won't be necessary for you to come along.' He made sure to brush against him, so that he could feel the heavy steel object through his coat.

There was a railing at the edge of the garden near the hillside. They walked over to it, talking in hushed tones.

'What have you got running here?'

'I can't tell you, but is there going to be any noise?'

'There could be. We're trying to set Hamilton up again. We've enlisted Tombal's help. The place is crawling with his people. Hamilton's going downtown, and to have a little fun. You know, get drunk, pick up women, bars and so forth, hoping that our killer will try to set up his car again or to put him away.'

'Merde! That's all I need. Can't it be put off? I don't want to attract attention.'

'I can't put anything off, unless I know what the hell is going on.'

'God damn it, General, I just can't tell you.'

273

'Would it help if I told you that La Brousse spotted El Kaffar in the lobby?'

Rhabbouz groaned and put his hands to his head.

'Come now, Jew, it can't be as bad as all that.'

'It can't? Hah.' He puffed at his cigar. 'Will you keep your word?'

'On what? You are, after all, a Frenchman as well as a Jew, and a security agent besides. What kind of a question was that anyway?'

'All right. El Kaffar is upstairs negotiating a peace treaty with Samuel Zvi Aharon.'

'A what?' in a harsh whisper.

'A peace treaty between the Republic of Quahrein and the State of Israel.'

'Ben Kelb will broil him over a slow fire for eighty days.'

Rhabbouz plunged forward, 'In two days Ben Kelb will be dead – or in the darkest dungeon in Quahrein.'

'A palace revolution within the Revolution. I would have thought it impossible.'

'Quahrein is a small country. Many people are not required.'

'And Israel's position?'

'A peace treaty, a mutual assistance pact.' He laid his hands on the General's arm. 'Don't you see, a real chance for peace, permanent and lasting. Our technology, their oil, their manpower, our schooling. To benefit both equally, a real partnership between Arab and Jew. If it works, the fire will go out forever.'

'A land of milk and honey, eh, Rhabbouz? Dreamer! You are all dreamers. You will all fall on your asses.' He made a quick assessment in his head. 'There is no way that I can think of that France could benefit from the failure of your efforts, and there may be an advantage for her in your success. Remember, Rhabbouz,' he said with conviction, 'that however stupid one generation or another of her children may be, I love France like a woman.' He paused, took a few paces and waved the pipe. 'Two days you say?'

'Yes. It will begin on Friday.'

'And Ben Kelb?'

'He is in the desert. He will return on Saturday morning, straight into the arms of his captors.'

'Do you think that this business with Hamilton has anything to do with El Kaffar?'

'El Kaffar says not, though agrees that it could be an Arab. He says that an American with a yacht in St. Tropez is the dog robber of Ben Kelb. The president of Royal American Oil. His name is Paul Fosburgh. They get all of their oil from Quahrein. He has some sailors from Quahrein on his boat. One or two mean customers.'

'We never searched the yachts, or even tried. Maybe we should visit him?'

'Not now. That would blow everything. Do it Saturday. Do it Sunday.'

The General considered. 'All right, Rhabbouz. Even if our assassin gets away, you shall have your peace.'

'It is no easier for me than for you. Remember Kalman Jacobs.'

They went inside to the table. La Brousse, Hamilton and Tombal were seated amidst the detritus of their dinner, enduring the glare of their waiter. All of the other guests had left.

'Waiter, don't just stand there like an idiot, clear this mess. We want to talk without the benefit of your donkey's ears hanging over us.'

The waiter scurried over, finished his task in the shortest time possible, then asked, 'And the check?'

'Give it here,' the General said, then signing with a flourish, 'it is a shame they insist on adding service without asking the advice of the client.'

When the waiter had left the room, the General leaned his elbows on the table and said, 'Well, La Brousse, we have decided, the Jew and I, that there will be no need to use Mr. Hamilton in our skeet shoot tonight. I know that that will disappoint Mr. Hamilton, who has become fond of our little game. And that certainly Tombal will not be overjoyed to lose the chance to show his trained seals off to good advantage, and you, of course, will never find out whether you are really smarter than I am. However, that is my decision.'

Hamilton stood and stretched. 'General,' he said with some affection, 'I am very grateful to you. You may have saved my life. I'm beginning to like you more and more.'

'Bah!'

'Shall I send my people home, General?'

'Yes, Tombal. Thank you very much.'

'Then I can go?' Hamilton asked.

'That's right. La Brousse will take you home. Please, no protestations, La Brousse. Perhaps you can share a drink, or a woman. Between you, you should be able to handle one. The old Jew and I are going to sit here and swap lies.'

Thirty

Hamilton and La Brousse each took a car, agreed to meet at the bar in the lobby of the Grand Hôtel. They drove down the hill into town and parked in the street. In a gesture of conciliation, they asked the watchdog to come inside and share a nightcap. Thrilled by the idea of leaving his permanent seat, and as anxious for companionship as for the drink, the watchdog agreed. 'You know,' he said, 'I haven't really heard a human voice in a week.'

As they sat down at the table, they noted a rather noisy group in the middle of the room, perhaps twenty feet away, talking and joking in a combination of French and English. They were toasting copiously with champagne – Dom Pérignon, Hamilton was quick to note. The party was obviously being hosted by a distinguished-looking man with graying temples, but the star of the party was an unassuming little man who seemed to glow in the limelight.

Hamilton was staring vaguely at the uncarpeted tile of the floor, following its intricate pattern, when the one-pound cast-iron egg bounced noisily into his field of vision. He leapt from his chair and in one motion scooped it up and threw it across the room at a plate glass window that overlooked the street in an empty corner.

The weight of the grenade and the energy of the throw provided just enough mass to smash the window. At the moment that it cracked the pane, the small powder train which serves as a fuse for the main charge burned to its end. The explosive force burst from its prison, sending the twenty-eight serrated iron castings which formed the case and the three hundred pieces of segmented wire wound within, cascading in every direction. Part of the force was pushed outward through the smashed glass plate, but the rest swirled back through the bar, carrying with it a rain of metal fragments augmented by shards of glass.

Hamilton had thrown high; the bulk of the shrapnel came back well above floor level. He was the only person in the room, save for a hapless waiter, who had been standing.

La Brousse had been forced over backward by the blast; he lay with his legs dangling over the chair. His ears rang and his eyes smarted. Nonetheless, he did an awkward somersault to his feet and pulled his gun, facing into the lobby, from which he surmised that the grenade had been thrown. He limped through the shambles to the lobby door. A woman guest looked at him and fainted. He moved swiftly to the desk, where the clerk stood transfixed.

'Did you see anyone? Did you see who did that?'

The clerk nodded dumbly.

La Brousse struck him sharply across the face. 'Answer me. Did you see who threw that? Did you see anyone in this lobby?'

'No, I was looking at some papers. I only heard the noise.' He gagged slightly, 'Monsieur, your face . . .'

Ignoring him, La Brousse went to the door and checked the street. The baggage man cowered against the wall.

'Did you see anything?'

'Nothing, I saw nothing.'

La Brousse ran back to the desk, his leg almost collapsing in front of him. He grabbed the clerk by the throat. 'Do you see this?' He waved the gun under his nose. 'If you don't wake up and call the pompiers, some ambulances and Commissaire Tombal at the Commissariat, I'm going to beat you to death with it.'

The man moved for the phone. La Brousse went back into the bar, which was a charnel house of groaning injured people, destroyed furniture and still bodies. He took a quick look at himself in the mirror at the door and understood why the woman had fainted. His face fairly dripped blood, though he could feel no pain, except the throbbing in his leg. As he put the gun back in the holster, he noticed a sizable cut on his right palm, but not enough to cause so much gore.

He walked over to the table at which he had been sitting and turned away. The blood had come from the watchdog. A piece of glass about the size of a dinner plate had scissored its way across the room. He was dead and half of his face was gone.

Donald Hamilton lay unconscious, sprawled over the remains of a table which had broken under the weight of his thrown body. His upper chest was a mass of tiny shrapnel cuts, and there was a severe laceration at the top of his right shoulder and his neck. La Brousse tore away the jacket and shirt and held a napkin against the wound. There was no pulsating sensation; if the shrapnel had not punctured some organ, Hamilton might live. The hotel doctor appeared at the door with his black bag. La Brousse motioned him over and told him to deal with Hamilton. As he got up to check on the others, he saw that Hamilton's throwing hand was badly mangled.

La Brousse started at the tables nearest the window and worked back toward the door. The waiter was so much hamburger, a victim both of the blast and flying glass and metal.

The bartender sat on the floor, cradling his head in his hands. 'Are you all right?' La Brousse asked. The man looked up. He had a bad flash burn on his left cheek, and a superficial shrapnel wound in the arm.

A young couple who had been sitting against the wall shielded by the bar seemed unhurt except for severe fright and a nasty bump behind the girl's ear.

There were nine men at the table of happy revelers in the midst of the room. They lay in various states of disrepair, strewn across the floor. A large man with a pocked face had an open wound from the corner of his ear to the point of his chin.

The man who had been the host was struggling to get to his feet. He had a bloody nose from the concussion, and was missing a small piece from the top of his right ear. He put his hand slowly to his cheek and staggered slightly.

The little man who had been the center of attention lay limp and sprawled, his complexion gray, his mouth slack, his eyes slightly open showing white. Blood trickled from his nose and ears.

Tombal arrived at the same time as the firemen and the ambulance. 'What the hell happened?'

'Somebody threw a grenade. If it hadn't been for Hamilton, we would all be dead.'

'How many were killed?'

'A waiter,' he choked, pointing at the disfigured corpse, 'and my man, there, Hamilton's tail.' He wiped his eyes. 'We invited him in for a drink.' He smeared his face. 'That's him I have all over me. I don't know about Hamilton. That little man over there, the party was for him, I think. He must have a skull fracture. Maybe he's dead.'

'Did anybody see anything?'

'No, they were too stunned by the blast. Even in the lobby. Nobody knew anything. Perhaps we can get more when they calm down.' He started, then shivered. 'Oh, dear God, the General. The bastard will go after my General.' La Brousse took one step and fell ashen at Tombal's feet, the blood coursing from the damaged vein in his neck.

Tombal grabbed a young intern from the ambulance and dragged him across the room, then threw him to his knees by La Brousse. 'Fix that,' he said. The doctor worked rapidly with gauze pads and antiseptic. He located the bleeder, near the surface, and clamped it off. 'He needs blood right away. And lots of it. And he needs to go to hospital to have this mess in his neck sewed up properly.'

'You see to it. I'll remember your face, Doctor.'

When Tombal saw that Hamilton was in good hands, he left a duty inspector in charge and went to the telephone. He dialed the number of La Tour Blanche, only to find that the phone was out of order.

As Tombal rushed around the corner to his car, Aboussara

put the wire clippers back into the canvas bag slung across his shoulder. He had not bothered to see the results of his grenade, but he knew that it must have been a success, landing as it did in the middle of the floor. In one stroke both his original target and the man Hamilton were gone. Allah proceeds in miraculous ways.

Avoiding the ring of light cast by the spots on the high white tower, he worked his way silently to the back of the building. Gliding past the pool, he sought a trellis on the wall. He climbed it, flattening himself against the wall to escape possible detection, then clambered onto the roof of the lower part of the building and counted windows. It was just beyond his reach. The strong wooden shutter precluded his smashing through. He tucked his hand underneath the shutter bottom and strained terribly while walking barefoot up the brick surface of the wall. When he was high enough, he ran the blade of the large knife in his other hand between the shutters and gently lifted the latch. Trembling with the effort, he let himself down to the roof again and lay trying to regain his strength. After a moment, he got to his feet and climbed the trellis to the second-story roof. He tied a rope from his bag around one of the cast chimney pots 'and let himself down to a level just above the shutter tops. He paused a moment, then in one motion dropped onto the shutters and kicked them apart with his feet. As they clattered against the wall on either side of the window, he swung out from the wall, then hurtled through the window, throwing both the casements and the panes on the floor.

The two men stood, dumbstruck at the figure on the floor. Aboussara let go of the rope and jumped to his feet before they could move. He was crouching, his legs badly cut by the window glass. In one hand he held a knife and in the other a gun.

'El Kaffar, you are the meat of the pig. You defile the name Arab.'

'Aboussara.'

'Yes, faithful dog Aboussara. But faithful to Ben Kelb, to the Revolution. Not to El Kaffar, lover of dogs of Jews. Seller of his people. The educated revolutionary,' he sneered. 'And you,' he pointed at Aharon, 'did you think that you had escaped the shadow of the oven forever? No, it is here to haunt you. To reclaim you for the fate that you escaped. And so it will be with all of you. We will nail your tongues and the tongues of your women and children to the Wailing Wall, so that you may wail in eternity together. Death to the Jew and the traitor.'

He stood upright and pointed his gun at El Kaffar. 'Cringe, traitor.'

El Kaffar, motionless, smiled and spat at his feet. Aboussara's aim was spoiled by the splintering door. His first shot caught El Kaffar high in the right shoulder, spinning him around into the wall. The second, aimed at the figure hurtling through the door, caught Rhabbouz in the side, smashing three ribs, before passing through his excess flesh.

There was a flash from the door frame. Aboussara straightened, stunned, and fired once more. The bullet passed harmlessly through the old striped terry cloth robe. Balancing the ancient Mauser carefully in two hands, squinting through glasses, with one ear piece missing, General Robert Pineau des Charentes squeezed off one more shot. A gaping hole appeared in Aboussara's forehead, just above the bridge of his nose, and centered perfectly. The light went out in his eyes, and he fell dead.

Thirty-one

The General took a quick look inside of the room. Aharon stood rigid and white plastered against the wall, Aboussara was stretched dead on his stomach, and Rhabbouz and El Kaffar lay leaking onto the carpet.

'You,' the General said, 'who are you?'

'I am Aharon.'

'What do you do?'

'I am the Ambassador for Israel to the United States.'

'All right. Hold this.' He threw the gun to him. 'Shut the door and do what you can to help them. Close the shutters, and don't open up for anyone but me – understand?'

Aharon nodded and obeyed, robot-like.

As the door closed, the General padded down the hall to his room. He shut himself in, leaving a crack so he could hear what was happening in the hall. He dropped his robe to the floor and started to reach for his favorite pair of brogues, then changed his mind and took out a pair of loafers, remembering that La Brousse was not around to help tie his shoes.

He walked back into the hall, which was now full of milling guests in various states of undress and disrepair.

'What's happening?' he was asked by some enterprising soul.

'A window blew in – freak accident,' he answered. Then in a roaring shout, 'What the hell are all you people doing out here? Go back inside. I am Dr. Du Clos. You are interfering with my caring for my patients. Go back to your rooms, you damn vultures. If you want to see injured people, watch television or go to the movies.'

Chastened and mumbling among themselves, the guests

retreated to their rooms. The General continued down the hall, counting to himself. I fired twice, that's two. Rhabbouz once. The Arab three times. That's six in all, pretty close together. Who knows, someone might buy it.

He had just reached the door of El Kaffar's room when Tombal arrived at the head of the stairs. The General quickly put his finger to his lips and pointed at himself. Tombal slowed to a walk.

'Open,' the General said.

Aharon, still white-faced, opened the door. The General and Tombal slipped through and shut it again.

'How are they?' the General asked.

Aharon hesitated.

'This is Tombal, Commissaire de Police of Toulon. Commissaire, this sturdy figure is the Israeli Ambassador to the United States – Aharon by name. Well, how are they?'

'That one,' he pointed at Aboussara, 'is quite dead.'

'I should hope so,' the General sniffed, 'I shot him myself. How are you, Rhabbouz?'

'At least a broken rib, a couple of leaky holes, nothing major. The scars will add to my charm. Nana will kill us both, and it won't matter anyway.'

'And El Kaffar?'

'I don't know.' Aharon turned to the bundled figure in the middle of the room. El Kaffar lay unconscious with his head on a pillow, his feet propped on an overturned bolster from the couch. 'I loosened his clothing and propped up his legs to try to contain the shock. I wrapped his wound as well as I could, but he's bleeding badly.'

'We'd better get an ambulance,' Tombal said.

Aharon, sweating, said, 'No. There can be nothing public. There must be no noise, no publicity.' He covered his eyes with his hands, and was overcome by a racking sob. 'It isn't possible,' Aharon said. 'It isn't reasonable. All this work, this effort, to come to naught. If he cannot travel, or talk, if he dies, there will be a blood bath. A revolution with no leader. There will be war.'

'What war?' the General demanded.

Aharon looked at him and stood silent.

'Rhabbouz, tell him who I am.'

'Mr. Ambassador, this is General Robert Pineau des Charentes. He is the director of the Arab and Middle East Section of the Intelligence Bureau of the French Ministry of Interior.'

Aharon sat on the edge of the bed and looked at the old man. 'Ben Kelb has organized a suicide mission using his air force and the guerrillas that have been planted in all of the oil-producing countries. He has transmitted to the President of the United States a threat to blow up all of his own fields, and those in the Gulf States and Saudi Arabia and Algeria, if the Sixth Fleet is not removed from the Mediterranean, and if all aid to Israel, both military and financial, is not halted forthwith. The deadline is the thirtieth day of September. Ben Kelb has gone to the desert to meditate. We have planned to overthrow Ben Kelb for more than four years – he has forced our hands. El Kaffar will take over the government. Arrangements have been made with the Quahrein regular army to eliminate the extremists who were to make Ben Kelb's raids. There was to be an announcement of a peace treaty and a mutual assistance bond between Israel and Quahrein. While you stand here, the potential for that grand strategy is seeping into the carpet. And if the United States of America does not comply with Ben Kelb's terms, they may risk another world war.'

The General stuffed his pipe and lit it without replying. He asked casually, 'Where is La Brousse?'

He turned to Tombal when there was no answer, continued to light the pipe and raised an eyebrow. 'Do you know where he is?'

Tombal cleared his throat. 'He is in the hospital. This man, at least I think it was he,' he nudged the body with his foot, 'threw a grenade into the bar at the Grand Hôtel. Hamilton picked up the grenade and threw it through the window. Otherwise they would all be dead.'

Calmly, the General asked, 'Is he alive – La Brousse? And Hamilton?'

'Yes,' Tombal replied, 'they will both live. They've been cut up a bit, lost some blood. There were two others killed. Hamilton's tail was hit by a large piece of flying glass. And a waiter.'

The General nodded and puffed at his pipe. 'Rhabbouz, can you walk?'

He struggled to his feet, clutching his side. 'I can walk.'

'Tombal, get him to a phone. Rhabbouz, can you get Levy or some other doctor up here?'

'We have one in Toulon.'

'Good, get him here. Tombal, tell the manager that this room is off limits. Tell him that everything is fine and that there will be no problems. Explain that a window was smashed and that one of the guests was slightly injured. Tell him that you are calling for a doctor who will take care of the matter. Rhabbouz, get me two or three of your toughs. When they arrive, whistle *La Marseillaise* at the window, and we will throw this garbage,' he indicated Aboussara, 'out of the window. Then have them dispose of him.' He turned to Aharon. 'You will go back to your room. It's next door, I believe. Make yourself presentable. We may need you. And while you're at it, you might pray for this man. If he is unable to play his role, I fear that we shall have a real war. And that is not going to be good, for anyone, not even France.'

The General took off his coat and gave it to Rhabbouz. 'Put this on, you look like hell. It will save the guests from seeing you. Ambassador, unaccustomed as you are to work, do you think that you could hurry next door, put on your coat so you look like a gentleman, and come back here to watch El Kaffar, so that we can all get out of here and do our jobs?'

Stung, Aharon left the room to do as he was told. He returned in a moment. 'I am ready.'

'Good. Wait here. Don't open the door unless it is Tombal, Rhabbouz or me. Let's go.'

Rhabbouz and the General walked down the stairs while Tombal took care of the manager. Tombal asked the clerk for a phone and was told that it was still out of service.

'Where do you need to go, Rhabbouz?'

'An apartment house on the Boulevard Dutasta over-looking the park.'

'And you, General?'

'Take me downtown, Tombal. I want to see that hotel, and then perhaps a quick stop at the hospital.'

They dropped Rhabbouz, who was by then wheezing and coughing badly, and continued on to the Grand Hôtel. The Place de la Libération was clogged with fire engines and police cars. The sidewalk on the side of the hotel where the explosion had taken place was cordoned off with ropes.

'You realize, Tombal, that this will have to be a crime by person or persons unknown. Not very good for your record.'

'It happens, mon général. And to better flics than me.'

'Can I be passed off as a senior police official, or better still, just kept out of the way? We don't want the press involved with SDEC.'

'Just stay with me. When they descend on me, drift away. The confusion is great enough so that no one should bother.'

'Especially with a sloppily dressed old man? Right, Tombal?'

Tombal walked the General past the police cordon and into the lobby of the hotel. Several officers saluted as they walked by. A group of men surrounded a harassed-looking uniformed official with a lot of braid on his cap and his jacket. Tombal motioned the General away and walked over to the men.

'Good evening, gentlemen. Good evening, Inspector Le Seuer. May I speak to you for a moment?'

There was considerable grumbling among the gentlemen of the press, but they backed away and let the two cops through. 'Listen, Le Seuer,' Tombal said, 'where are the people who were in this mess?'

'All at the hospital.'

'All right. Keep those vultures busy, tell them anything

they think they want to know. By the way, who were the people in there?'

'We have been able to identify most of them as people from General Motors, the big American car company. One was rather badly hurt. One of the dead men was a waiter who had been here quite some time. The other dead man had no identification at all. The two others at his table – an American named Hamilton and a Paul La Brousse – were banged up badly. There was a young French couple from here in town. And then there was a man alone. He had an American passport, but no wallet or other identification. He hasn't come to yet.'

'I'm going to the hospital. Keep things quiet here. I want none of the press bothering the people at the hospital. By the way, have you been able to get anything out of anyone?'

'The only one who remembers anything is the desk clerk. He said that after the blast, one of the people came out waving a gun and acting like a madman. No one saw anything else.'

'Keep digging.'

Tombal hustled them through the confusion at the hospital and rounded up the doctors who had been on emergency call that evening. The General asked questions and was satisfied that everything that could be done was already in progress. He inquired after La Brousse and Hamilton and was told that both were under sedation, but all right except for some moderate damage. All the others were out of danger as well, except for the pale little man who had had a severe concussion and a slight skull fracture. 'He is in a coma,' the doctor said. 'There might be neurological impairment – brain damage. We can't tell until he comes out of it.'

The General noticed a well-dressed man with a bandage on his ear who was staring at them intently. When the doctors dispersed, the man hesitated and then walked over to him.

'Pardon me, sir,' he said in heavily accented French, 'but

may I speak to you for a moment? You seem to be able to get people to tell you what's happening here. I can't. Some of the people who were hurt work for me.'

The General replied in English, 'Who are you?'

'My name is Goodrich, Milton Goodrich. I was holding a little party for some of my employees when the bomb went off. I'd like to know how they are.'

'What company are you with, Mr. Goodrich?'

'I'm the president of General Motors.'

'My name is Pineau. This is Commissaire Tombal of the Toulon police. I am sure that we will be able to get whatever information you require from the medical authorities. Perhaps you could help us as well.'

'I will be glad to do anything that I can.'

'Let's go to the administrator's office. I've already been told that all of the people involved in the explosion are all right, except for the two who were killed instantly. One of the dead was a waiter and the other,' the General looked for the words, 'the other was also known to us. He was not one of your people.'

Goodrich breathed a sigh of relief.

It was as an afterthought that the General continued. 'Oh yes. There is one poor soul still in a coma. Possible brain damage, they said, concussion and fractured skull.' The General walked on a few steps before he realized that Goodrich had stopped in his tracks. The General looked over his shoulder.

Goodrich asked carefully, 'Which one is that?'

'They didn't say his name, just that he was a small pale man.' Goodrich's tongue struggled against the cotton which had suddenly filled his mouth. 'Could you ask now, please?'

The General looked at his imploring eyes, then called down the hall after the figures in white, 'S'il vous plaît, docteur. Un moment.' The doctor stopped and turned. 'What is the name of the one in a coma?' The doctor thought for a moment and said in a voice loud enough to be heard at the other end of the corridor, 'Edelman, Arthur Edelman.'

Goodrich reached out with his hand to the clammy green wall for support.

'Are you not well, Mr. Goodrich? Perhaps you should sit down?'

He took hold of himself and straightened. 'No. No thank you,' he replied and continued down the hall after the General and Tombal, his stomach seething.

When they were seated in the office and had been served some hot coffee, the General asked, 'Mr. Goodrich, can you think of any reason why such an attack should be made on anyone in your group, and did you by any chance see who did it?'

Goodrich squeezed the bridge of his nose between his thumb and forefinger. His head still rang from the effects of the concussion. From the moment that he had seen the stretcher bearers carrying Arthur Edelman away unconscious, he had felt an unreasoning anger at the strange twist of fate which had placed them in the wrong bar at the wrong time. Now that he knew the extent of Edelman's injury, he was all but unbalanced by the implications. If there was sufficient damage to prevent him from continuing his work, or if he died, could the solar car be completed? Was there enough in the beginnings of Edelman's work to justify the massive investment to which Goodrich had committed General Motors? Without Edelman's personal supervision, would the timetable for production be stretched so out of shape as to make it economically unfeasible? Then beyond that, what of his commitment to the President? It was possible that this insane calamity could change the shape of American foreign policy, and act as a trigger for war. He strained to think of a way to explain to the men before him the need for the best neurosurgeons, the best possible care, the danger and the risk wrapped up in Arthur Edelman's tenuous life, without breaking the vow of silence he had made to President Smith.

'Mr. Goodrich,' the General asked gently, 'are you still with us?'

'Yes, of course. I'm sorry. My head is still jangling. What

was it you asked?'

'About the explosion. Did you see anyone? Do you know why it happened?'

Goodrich took a deep breath. 'I saw a man in a dark sweater in the doorway just before the explosion.'

'Can you tell us anything else about him?' Tombal asked.

'Only that he had a mustache.'

Tombal glanced at the General, who sat impassive.

Goodrich continued in a stronger tone, 'I think that you ought to take responsibility for the well-being of foreign nationals here in France. I want protection for my people. I think that there ought to be policemen stationed outside the rooms of every one of them. In fact, I insist upon it. And I want the best neurosurgical talent in France looking after Mr. Edelman, however you have to get it.' He looked up. Neither Tombal nor the General had moved.

'And the rest?' the General asked.

'What rest?' Goodrich replied, still in an aggressive tone.

'The *why*, Mr. Goodrich. Why was this done? You know, Mr. Goodrich.'

'I don't know any more than I have told you.'

'Mr. Goodrich, I am seventy-seven years old. There is an advantage to great age. There is a limit to the punishments that can be meted out to you. Death has been my companion for years. He waits around every corner for a weakness in an artery, a step that is a little too high, the breaking of a bone that will no longer knit. Retirement holds a certain fascination for me. There is no point in telling me what will happen to my career if you howl indignantly to your Consul or Ambassador. And besides, then you will have to tell him what you are refusing to tell me.'

'I have told you all that I can. I am insisting on proper protection and medical care for citizens of my country, and of yours as well, I might add. They are entitled to that.'

The General lit his pipe and sized Goodrich up once more. This was not just another indignant industrialist. Perhaps if he met him halfway ...

'Mr. Goodrich, do you know the man who saved your life?'

'The man who got rid of the grenade? No, but I would certainly like to know him. He is a very brave man with very good reflexes. He literally saved my life. That thing wasn't five feet away from me when he picked it up.'

'Yes, Mr. Goodrich, he is a very brave man. His name is Donald Hamilton. He is an architect, building a hotel here on the Riviera. The man who threw the grenade has been trying to kill him for some weeks now.' He watched as the idea penetrated. 'It was a case of mistaken identity. For some reason, someone here on the Riviera was marked for death. For a reason we do not understand, the killer mistook Hamilton for him – believed that Hamilton had something to do with his target. In his attempt to kill Mr. Hamilton, he has killed several other people, and last Saturday he blew up Mr. Hamilton's car. At our request, Mr. Hamilton has made himself available to the killer, so that we might catch him in the midst of an attempt. It takes considerable courage to play clay pigeon for a killer, especially when no one knows what he's after.'

Goodrich interrupted impatiently. 'I am a witness to Mr. Hamilton's courage, General. I've seen him in action. But that has nothing to do with me, or the absolute urgency of Mr. Edelman's state of health. It seems to me that you've taken a French police problem and thrust it off on a group of innocent bystanders. If Hamilton hadn't been in that bar, and you hadn't been using him for bait, one of the world's leading technical innovators wouldn't be lying in this damn hospital now.'

The General pursed his lips and nodded. 'Mr. Goodrich, would it encourage you to cooperate more fully and to feel that this French police matter might have something to do with you if I said that the suspected assassins were from Quahrein? Agents of the Quahreinian government, in fact?'

Goodrich looked up, dumbstruck. He stared for a moment, studying the General's face. 'Would you mind telling me who you are?' The General told him the truth.

Goodrich shook his head in acknowledgment. 'Arthur Edelman is an inventor. He has invented a power source. In my opinion it is a revolutionary change in the technology of the world. We are only in the earliest stages of development. His life is vital. His loss absolutely irreparable. Even if he lives, that head injury ... my God.'

'He was working here in the South of France?'

'Yes. He had just finished. We were celebrating the signing of his contract. His work was ... let's just say that it would take a lot of pressure off world petroleum supplies.'

'Why didn't he work in America?'

'He's a very peculiar man. Evidently, he's had some trouble with the law.'

'Is he a thief, a murderer?'

'Nothing so glamorous. He's a homosexual. He's had a couple of scrapes because of ... well ... he prefers, or at any rate preferred, younger people, below the age of consent, shall we say.'

'Wouldn't it have been easier for him to work in a laboratory?'

'Much easier, but he had some paranoid idea about the company trying to steal his work. We never even saw him until a couple of days ago. All of our communications have been through messengers.'

The General leaned forward in his chair, elbows on the table. 'Do you know who these messengers were?'

'No, there were four meetings and three different messengers, but they were always recognized the same way. They were young men, and they had a rose behind their ears. George Hultz, he's one of the men who was hurt tonight, told me that the last one, the one he saw on Saturday, couldn't have been more than fifteen or sixteen.'

'And where were these exchanges of information made?'

'On the jetty at St. Tropez.'

The General slammed his hand on the desk. 'So. It all falls together. I am afraid that you and I are going to have to trust each other far more than we would like, Mr. Goodrich. I want you to know that I may not let you out of this hospital. It is not necessary to kill you, though I can assure you I would if I felt it my duty. I must give you some information imperative to world security. You must in turn tell me what you know, based on the information that I give you. We must hurry, Mr. Goodrich. We have very little time.'

Goodrich took a swallow of coffee. 'I'll try. What do you want to know?'

'First, when was the last communication picked up, prior to this one?'

'Sometime in the last week in August, maybe a little earlier.'

'Good. The messenger was killed. He was stabbed to death with a skewer and his balls were cut off.'

'But why didn't Edelman know?'

'I am sure that he knew. It was all over the papers for two days. But you see, there are many young fags down here who do it for fun or money or both. They are hardly faithful. Arthur probably thought that the fellow had been cheating on him, and that his new lover had carved him up. It's not the kind of thing one volunteers information about, especially while trying to keep a low profile. Hamilton found the body.'

'That's the connection.'

'Yes, in the killer's mind, there must have been some link between the two. That's why he kept after Hamilton.'

Goodrich lit a cigarette, 'But then what they were really trying to do was to get Edelman.'

'Who knew of his existence, who knew when the messages were to be passed?'

'Just me and two of my most trusted officials, one of whom is lying in this hospital.'

'We have one thing in our favor. The killer is dead.'

'Who was he?'

'His name, I am told, was Abdul Aboussara. He was an agent of the government of Quahrein. Unfortunately, he managed to do some more damage – in a small hotel in the hills above Toulon shortly after he left here. He wounded some very important people.'

'Who was hurt?'

'Do you know the name Mohammed El Kaffar?'

Goodrich swallowed hard. 'Yes, I know the name.'

'What I am about to tell you could cost you your freedom, possibly even your life, Mr. Goodrich.'

'Go on.'

'El Kaffar is planning an insurrection in his country. The man who runs Quahrein, Colonel Ben Kelb, is exactly the wild dog the newspapers say he is. He is about to precipitate a major global crisis. In order to prevent him from doing so, to attempt to establish peace in the Middle East, El Kaffar and certain associates plan to unseat Ben Kelb.'

'When do they plan to do this?' Goodrich asked tensely.

'The insurrection will begin while Ben Kelb is still in the desert and out of touch with his allies. It will begin in about twenty-four hours. On Friday morning.'

'I must talk to the President of the United States immediately.'

'Why, Mr. Goodrich?'

'Because the United States is about to make war on the Republic of Quahrein to prevent Ben Kelb from blowing up the major petroleum installations in the Mideast.'

The General laid his pipe on the table carefully. He watched the wisps of smoke waft to the ceiling as he absorbed the idea. 'Do you know when this is to begin?'

'No,' Goodrich replied. 'I only know that it's going to start very soon. Edelman's invention is part of an emergency plan to maintain a level of energy supplies that will maintain the viability of the economy of Western Europe – the whole world really.'

'And if the Russians react?'

'I am in no position to speculate on that possibility. Thank God, I don't have to live with the decision.'

'Of course,' the General pondered aloud, 'a change in government in Quahrein would make all of that unnecessary. Without Ben Kelb, the threat to blow up the sources of oil disappears. The United States loses the motivation, or rather the need, to assert its power militarily, and the cer-

tainty of confrontation and the possibility of war are dissipated. If El Kaffar installs himself at the reins of government,
and the announcement of the Israeli pact is handled with
some diplomacy with respect to the other Arab governments, Aharon could well be right. There would be a basis
for permanent peace.'

'Aharon,' Goodrich asked, 'the Israeli Ambassador?'

'Oh, yes, he's here too. He is evidently the prime mover
on that side of the fence.' The General picked up his now
dormant pipe and began to light it, puffing up enormous
flames with a large wooden match. He rattled the box back
and forth on the table. 'Of course, all of this depends on two
things. El Kaffar must live – and be strong enough to appear
for the show. And the American attack must be forestalled.'

'And Edelman must live,' Goodrich said. 'He must live
and have the use of his mind, and someone must get to
President Smith in any case. But if El Kaffar is dead, then the
revolution will not take place and the situation will remain
the same. The U.S. attack will still be necessary.'

'Quite so, Mr. Goodrich. Tombal, get the Chief of Medicine in here. If he is at home, have him picked up in a car.
In his pajamas if necessary. Have him get on to the Neurological Center at Marseilles Medical School. Have them get
hold of one of the top people – Professor Olmer if possible.
Get one of your people down the hall to have Mr. Goodrich
checked out immediately.' When Tombal left the room, the
General turned to Goodrich. 'I am as concerned as you for
Mr. Edelman's health. If I were the President, not aware of
the coming revolution, and I knew that my trump card lay
dying or with brain damage in a French hospital, preventing
the destruction of those oil fields would become the most
important thing in my mind. The only hope left of doing
that would seem to be by a rapid preemptive invasion to
catch Ben Kelb's men unprepared, before they can throw the
switch. That could mean world war. We need Edelman or
El Kaffar – preferably both. And for the moment, it appears
that we shall have neither.'

Tombal returned to the room. 'It's all fixed. A team is on

its way from Marseilles. The Chief of Medicine is in a police car, and Mr. Goodrich is free to go as he pleases.'

'You should have thought to light a candle, Tombal. Let's get out of here.'

Thirty-two

The General knocked softly at the hotel door.

'Who is it?' Aharon answered.

'Pineau.'

The door opened and the General ushered Goodrich in. The door snapped shut behind them. The hair on the back of Goodrich's neck stood on end as he heard a rustling noise behind him. Goodrich turned and found himself looking into the eyes of a tall husky young man with a Uzi machine pistol – pointed directly at Goodrich's midsection.

Rhabbouz, lying on the couch, said, 'Ariel, put that down. You're frightening our guest.'

An older man, similarly armed, sat on the windowsill. Still another stood leaning over the bed, his back to the room.

'So, Jew,' the General asked, 'how are we faring in our effort to save the world?'

'Ask Lieberman, he is the doctor.'

'Well, Maimonides,' the General said, banging the dead ashes from his bowl on the table, 'how are your patients?'

The doctor made a few last motions and turned to answer. He was old, with a seamy face, and very thin. His hands were steady, but with parchment skin and ropy blue veins.

'No thanks to that dog,' he indicated the still present Aboussara. 'They will live. This one,' he nodded at the bed, 'is watched over in perpetuity by God and an entire legion of angels. He was shot once. The bullet pierced his right shoulder just above the clavicle, missed the apex of his lung by three centimeters and passed through his back about the same distance above his right shoulder blade. You can see it over there in the wall. He should be dead or crippled. Just the width of a finger in any direction. Well, there's no use in speculating. No broken bones. No major organs disturbed. Ugly, but rather moderate loss of blood, now being replaced,' he rang a fingernail against the hanging bottle. 'He is heavily sedated. His arm is going to be rather useless for a while. And he is going to hurt.'

'Will he be able to function tomorrow?'

'Yes, General, given enough morphia, he should be able to manage. I understand that it is important that he be able to travel. If we can avoid unnecessary movement, and the possibility of reopening the wound, there is no reason why he should not be at least a shadow of himself. He is going to be very tired, of course. He could take a few steps later today, but he needs all of the rest that he can get. Naturally, what he really needs is a week in the hospital, and two weeks, minimum, rest at home.'

'Thank you for the analysis, Doctor. I'm afraid he won't have the luxury just yet. And Rhabbouz?'

'Look at him,' the doctor said scathingly, 'look at the old fool. He has three broken ribs and a modest piece of meat missing from his side. He should be put out to pasture, that one. He is too old for this.'

The General smiled broadly. 'You see, Rhabbouz, I have told you many times that you were an old fool. Perhaps now you will tend flowers or carve wooden ships. Being careful not to strain yourself, of course.'

Rhabbouz winced as he raised himself on his elbow. Neat white bandages and tape reaching to his armpits showed through his partly open shirt. 'A pox on you, you heartless wretch. I will be playing tennis and swimming two kilometers a day when they throw dirt on your box. I am fine. How is La Brousse? And the American?'

'All right, Rhabbouz, they'll live. So,' he said turning to Goodrich, 'it appears that our friend El Kaffar will live to lead his revolution after all. Now, I think that we can get your President to stand down on his planned operation.'

Goodrich's face drained of color. He put his hand to his mouth. 'Not without Edelman. And Holy Jesus – the agent!'

The General's head snapped around. 'What agent?'

'The President told me that he was going to have Hultz followed. There must be an American agent here somewhere. If he's reported in, then the President knows about all of this. He might be forced to ...'

'Speed up his plans as we surmised,' the General finished the sentence. He closed his eyes. 'This pig, Aboussara. Where did he come from? How do we know that he did not transfer his information that El Kaffar is here to another party? Is it not possible that the plans for the putsch are now in the hands of Ben Kelb? That there will be a massacre of all of those who might be involved? That all of the oil fields will be blown up and Ben Kelb will justify his actions to the world by pointing to the revolution? And if the fates are sufficiently arranged against the cause of peace, that all of this will be simultaneous with an American invasion, seemingly part of another CIA plot to maintain the colonial status of the Third World?'

'Well,' he said rising to his feet, 'if it all works out properly, we shall probably not live to view the outcome, but then, of course, neither shall anyone else.'

Everyone in the room started talking at once. The General squeezed his eyelids together and shouted, 'Shut up.' In the silence that followed, he continued in a lower tone, 'Look, Goodrich, do you have any idea where this agent might be?'

'No. I am not even absolutely sure he sent one. He did say that it would be better if he did.'

'And how about the leak? There must have been a leak. Who would have been the contact inside your company?'

Goodrich shook his head. 'I don't know. There were only the three of us who knew. It wasn't me, and I know damn well it wasn't Coughtry or Hultz.'

'I understand why it couldn't be Hultz. I don't think that he would have planned to be the target of a grenade attack. But why not the other one?'

'No,' Goodrich said stubbornly, 'not ever.'

'Never is a long time, Mr. Goodrich.' The General paused.

'Listen, Doctor, can you bring El Kaffar around?'

'Are you mad? You want him to travel tomorrow. You want him on his feet. I told you he wasn't mortally wounded. That doesn't mean he is ready to climb the Matterhorn. If you want him later you can't have him now.'

'If he wants his revolution, I'm afraid he's going to have to find the strength. Get him up. Just get him awake.'

The doctor looked first at Aharon and then at Rhabbouz for help. Neither said anything. 'All right, God damn it.' He took a syringe from his case. 'But it's on your heads, not mine. I am a doctor, not a magician.'

He disconnected the plasma bottle after shutting the valve and shot a small dose of stimulant directly into the tube that led to El Kaffar's vein. In a moment, the Arab began to groan, then to move about restlessly.

'You ask him,' the General said to Aharon. 'You're the one that he knows the best. Ask who was Aboussara's contact.'

Aharon pulled a straight-backed chair to the side of the bed, moving the doctor out of the way. He leaned close and asked softly, 'Mohammed, can you hear me? Mohammed?'

El Kaffar's jaws worked painfully without a sound.

'Mohammed, it is important that you answer me. Please. Can you hear me? Do you know for whom Aboussara worked? Who was his contact?'

The stricken man's eyelids fluttered, and it seemed that he was going to go under again. Aharon turned bleakly to the center of the room.

'Let me in there,' the doctor said. He plugged the stethoscope into his ears and listened to El Kaffar's chest. Then, clucking his tongue, took his pulse, eyes intent on his watch.

El Kaffar mouthed a word.

'What?' the doctor asked.

Aharon pushed the doctor back. 'Try, Mohammed. Once more, please, the name. Who was Aboussara's cover? Who was he working for here, his contact?'

Again the mouth moved a bit, a garbled word escaping in a slight whisper. Aharon put his ear almost to El Kaffar's mouth, then looked up from the bed with a puzzled expression. 'He said Glen something. Something about a pool.'

Tombal walked into the room past the guard and sat down on the edge of the couch next to Rhabbouz.

Aharon motioned to the doctor again. 'It's just too much. He's under again.' Then, with some authority, 'That's all. No more. More stimulant and you're going to put him in shock. He has a shallow enough pulse as it is. Don't spoil the luck of an ill-placed shot by asking me to finish him off.'

'Pool? What kind of pool?' Aharon wondered aloud, 'Glen who?'

'Glen Pool?' Tombal asked, then said, '*Glen Pool* is a yacht. It is harbored in St. Tropez. It's been there for a couple of months, on and off.'

Goodrich's eyes opened wide as he gasped, '*Glen Pool* is the name of Paul Fosburgh's yacht.'

The General motioned everyone silent. 'El Kaffar mentioned Fosburgh. What is he to you, Mr. Goodrich?'

'He's a director of my company, of General Motors, that is, as well as the president of Royal American Oil,' continuing rapidly, his voice rising, 'the major concessionaire in the oil fields of Quahrein.'

There was a moment of silence. The General got to his feet. 'Tombal, how fast can you get a search warrant?'

'The juge d'instruction sits nights. Can you get me a national security clearance?'

'Do you need it to get a warrant?'

'Yes. Or we'll be all night answering questions and explaining.'

'I can do that myself. I have identification papers that will satisfy him.' He paused to gather his thoughts. 'Rhabbouz, have your gangsters throw Aboussara into the trunk of a car. Tombal, take me to St. Tropez. Get on the car radio now; use someone you trust absolutely to find out if that American agent is around. If I were he, I would be in the hospital, watching my chickens, or at least outside. Have him held for your return – but not arrested. Just don't let him at a phone until we call in. Make sure that he is told that it is an important security matter, and that we are seeking his cooperation.'

'I'll call Le Seuer. He is competent. I'll wait for you in the car.' Tombal left the room quickly and walked through the deserted hotel corridors into the darkness.

The General turned to Goodrich. 'Do you think that you could identify Fosburgh from a distance?'

'Certainly.'

'It may be possible that there will be other people on that yacht that you will know. Are you willing to come with me? It could become unpleasant.'

'I'll come.'

'Thank you. Rhabbouz, you will stay here with Aharon and the doctor. We want to make sure that nothing else happens to you.'

'I will, like hell. I'm coming. And don't give me a lot of bluff.'

The General smiled gently, 'All right, Jew. Don't upset yourself. How many of these do you have?' he asked, pointing at the armed men.

'There are four altogether. Two more in a car downstairs.'

'We need to leave one here to keep an eye out. Let one of these fellows help you downstairs. Take your car and the other one with him,' he pointed at the body, 'and follow me down to St. Tropez. I want to think a bit. We'll stop at La Foux and talk again.' He turned to Aharon. 'Mr. Ambassador, you will kindly stay here and wait for our call. We will be as speedy as possible. It should take a bit more than an hour at this time of night to get there. It won't be long after that. Please, in the meanwhile, watch over our friend.' Aharon nodded.

The younger of the two men wrapped his sweater around his gun and helped Rhabbouz up from the couch and out the door. The older Shin Bet agent grabbed the stiffening body from the floor and dragged it to the window, propping it seated on the sill. With one hand he opened the shutters, with the other he pushed sharply. Aboussara fell like a rag doll and landed heavily on the path below. Two dark figures threw him unceremoniously into the trunk of the car.

Thirty-three

Murchison wanted to vomit. He swallowed, fighting back the feeling, and opened his eyes. His head hurt. It was very dark. He moved a bit and his head felt worse. He could smell the antisepsis of the hospital room and feel the sheets beneath him. He felt himself with his hand, then moved the other hand, and then each leg. Aside from the headache and a dull roaring in his ears he seemed to be in one piece. He tried to sit up, but fell back dizzy. He waited another minute, gaining in alertness and confidence, then pushed himself up again. After another moment, he pulled aside the covers and sat at the side of the bed. He blinked, accustoming himself to the low level of light, and ascertained that he was, indeed, in a hospital room. Measuring his steps carefully, he walked to the window, which admitted a dim reflected light from the street below. He was high above the ground. There was a small lamp on the table near the bed. He walked back and turned it on.

He checked the two doors in the room. One led to the corridor. After opening it a crack, he closed it softly. The other was a closet. He checked his pockets. All of his clothes and his papers were there. He dressed quickly, suffering slight vertigo when he bent to tie his shoes. He looked at himself in the mirror over the basin. He combed his disarrayed hair. His eyes were bloodshot and he looked a ghostly white. Otherwise, quite presentable. There was a dark stain on the outside of his right jacket sleeve near the elbow. If it was blood, it was not his own. He looked up and down the hall through the crack in the door. It was empty. He slipped out cautiously, spotted the red light that indicated the stairs, crossed quickly to it and descended.

At the lobby level he stopped to catch his breath, then opened the door slightly. There were a couple of policemen chatting by the elevator. Despite the late hour, there was an air of activity. Choosing his moment, he slipped out, walked purposefully across the lobby and out of the door.

Once in the street, the chilly air helped to sharpen his senses. He walked a block or two till he saw a sign on a small hotel. He knocked at the locked door and was admitted by a sleepy porter. He told him that it was an emergency, slipped him a hundred francs and sat down at the phone behind the desk.

'Yes.'

'28-A.'

'Where were you? You were missed.'

'Problems. Someone threw a grenade at the subject and his party.'

'The original or the copy?'

'Both. I was knocked cold. I just let myself out of the hospital.'

'And the others?'

'I have no way of knowing.'

'Can you call back in ten minutes? Or can I get back to you?'

'I'll call.' He hung up.

He gave the clerk another fifty francs to stifle his grumbling, and sat in a creaky armchair with his eyes closed. He checked his watch and called back.

'Yes.'

'28-A.'

'Go back to the hospital. To your room. If you have not been contacted by two this afternoon, call us back. Find out what you can about the others. Do you think someone knew?'

'Knew that the two were under surveillance?'

'It doesn't matter. They knew what they were doing. It was an assassination attempt, pure and simple.'

'All right. Stay put.'

*

Smith tossed and turned. With the first slight flicker of red light and the low-level buzz, he picked up the phone, and was informed of Murchison's call. He listened, answered yes twice and hung up. He slipped out of bed, careful not to disturb the small sleeping form beside him, put on his robe and walked into the hall. The man outside the door snapped to attention when he passed on the way to the dressing room. Once inside he picked up a blue phone. After a moment a voice croaked, 'Yes, sir.'

'Jack, get over here right now.'

By the time he had dressed, Kugel was sitting in the huge chair against the wall.

'So it would seem that the identity of the inventor is no secret. It should therefore be assumed that his project is known. They tried to hit him. If we knew the outcome of their attempt, we could be more sure of what to do.'

'Yes, sir, but at the same time, it seems certain that they know what his importance is. They've gone to a lot of trouble. They're obviously current about what's happening, at least with respect to the car itself, and if not as to its exact significance, then certainly as to what it portends.'

'Do you think that Ben Kelb might jump the gun, Jack?'

Kugel hesitated, then answered, 'Yes. Yes, I do.'

'I called Oscar after I talked to you. He's getting Gaines and Carver over here right now. I told him to meet us in the bunker.'

They had been sitting at the green-topped table less than ten minutes when the three Cabinet members trouped in wearily. The President explained briefly, then asked, 'What is your advice, Mr. Johansson.'

'Mr. President, it seems clear to me that if our plans have not been compromised, as seems likely, then at least our intent is understood. They will no doubt expect some action on our part. They may attempt to preempt us.'

'You mean by blowing up the oil fields now.'

'Yes, sir, that's what I mean.'

The others nodded their heads in agreement.

'You are all agreed that this may trigger an early execution of their threat?'

Walton Carver said, 'I don't see how we can assume anything else. There must be a security leak at the General Motors end. It wouldn't be Goodrich, and he's the only one that knows anything about our military plans. I believe, therefore, that they can only relate to the car itself. If they were willing to take drastic action to prevent the car from being built, isn't it likely that they might go even further on the supposition that we might have it?'

Gaines spoke out, 'In my opinion, the way to look at it, Ben Kelb anyway, is that we're playing them false. That we're attempting to avoid the penalty of the loss of energy so that we can bluff them out. What Ben Kelb really wants is capitulation, not war. Knowing that Edelman is either dead or badly hurt, he'll want to press his advantage.'

'What would you do if you were the President of the United States?'

'I wouldn't wait, Mr. President. It doesn't serve a purpose. It's possible that Goodrich has enough to go forward on the solar car. But what if he doesn't? Then those oil fields become even more important than we had imagined.'

Oscar Johansson stood and folded his hands behind his back. 'I think that that is a correct estimate. Without whatever small comfort we had from the solar car, we are faced with two choices: strike now in the hope of preventing Ben Kelb from blowing up those oil installations, or give in now.'

'And your recommendation?' Smith asked.

'Strike now.'

Smith turned to Gaines. 'How long would it take?'

'One hour to mount the alert. One hour to load the troops. Nine hours air time to touchdown.'

'The chances of being picked up?'

'Twenty-four planes. The Russians will have us an hour from the East Coast. That is, they'll know that we're sending that many aircraft across the Atlantic. If we head them toward Southern Germany, then turn them over the Alps and across, they'll have about forty minutes. But there ought to be enough confusion to mask us for all but perhaps ten minutes of that. We'll have to get our support aircraft up by then.'

Smith checked his watch. 'That would be eleven hours from now, some time after noon, here, and a little after five in the afternoon Quahrein time.'

Gaines added, 'If you want to minimize the casualty loss, Mr. President, you don't have much time. After dark sets in, this is a completely different operation.'

Smith nodded. 'Oscar, what about public announcements?'

'That can be arranged with the networks on an almost instantaneous basis. As long as you speak from the Oval Office, they're prepared to patch you in on a moment's notice. If we gave them, say, fifteen minutes to get themselves together, they would simply interrupt their scheduled programming. I can arrange a United Nations session for the late afternoon. None of the speeches need to be changed, unless you see something ...'

'No, Mr. Secretary, they're all right as is.' The President picked at an imaginary spot on his suit, then asked, 'Jack, what do you say?'

'We have no choice. We have to go.'

'Walton, how about you?'

'I'm sorry, Mr. President, I don't see any point in waiting. We'll just have to do it on Monday anyway. And if we wait, I don't believe we'll have the chance.'

'Oscar, I want a hot line contact to the Chairman at eleven tomorrow.'

'Yes, sir.'

'Mr. Gaines.'

'Yes, Mr. President.'

'Activate Operation Palm Beach immediately. Please keep me posted on the arranged schedule. Gentlemen,' he got to his feet, 'if you will excuse me.'

They all rose. The President shook hands solemnly with each of them and left. Alone inside the elevator, on his way back to a sleepless bed, William McCandless Smith wiped the tears from his cheeks with the back of his hand.

*

Though his suit jacket was made of wool, and though the slight chill of night was burning away in a rich sunrise, Milton Goodrich shivered in the back seat of Tombal's car. Both Tombal, who was in the front seat next to a plainclothes policeman, and the General, who was beside Goodrich, were sleeping soundly. GM's president looked over his shoulder at the rest of their high-speed motorcade. Rhabbouz was directly behind, slumped in the right-hand seat of his red car, while the brutal-looking young man with the gun drove. As they rounded a curve, he could see the car with the other Shin Bet men not far behind.

He looked forward again. He closed his eyes to the growing light and let himself be lulled by the hum of the motor. He was very tired. His mind wandered to Paul Fosburgh. What if, in fact, he had been the source of information about the solar car? He had suborned someone at General Motors. Goodrich had already closed his mind to speculation on that subject. Well, he thought, has he committed a crime? Possibly. What? Industrial espionage? Not really. He has obtained information concerning a research project of a company of which he is a duly elected and independent public director. It would be impossible to take legal action against him. Security questions? Goodrich did not feel competent to deal with them. In a real sense, of course, he was in the employ of a foreign government. On the other hand, ethical considerations aside, what had he done? Perhaps, from the French point of view, he was an accessory both before and after the fact in the crimes of Abdul Aboussara. But arresting him and charging him would expose a great deal to public view, and would create an international scandal of mammoth proportions. He could very well get away free. Goodrich opened his eyes when the car came to a halt.

There was little activity at the crossroads of La Foux. A dog trotted aimlessly back and forth across the concrete lawn of the service station opposite. No one was in sight.

The driver spoke in French and Tombal started awake. He waited until the two other cars had pulled up behind and halted, their motors still running, before he woke the General.

They both got out of the car and walked over to Rhabbouz, who was swallowing some pills with a swig from a bottle of Evian to dull the tearing pain in his side. In a moment they were joined by the driver of the third car. Goodrich watched them speak for several minutes, the General gesturing with his pipe. Then they returned to their cars and they all started out on the road to St. Tropez.

It was only half past six when they pulled to a halt on the jetty less than twenty yards from the gangway of the *Glen Pool*. The third car had driven on past them to the end of the jetty and then to the left on the Quai Jean Reveille.

'Mr. Goodrich,' the General said, 'you are to stay here. You watch. We are going to roust everyone out on deck. Politely, of course, as is required with important foreign visitors. Look carefully, we will make sure that you see all of them. If you recognize anyone, you will tell us later. Make sure that you are not seen.'

After the General and Tombal left the car, the driver turned and pulled up the little street opposite the *Glen Pool*, then parked so that Goodrich had a good view of the rear deck through the back window.

He watched the General, Tombal and one of Rhabbouz's men walk to the gangway. A sailor who had been sitting at the top of the polished wooden walk watching the strange pantomime came to his feet and went down to meet them. Tombal showed his badge. After a moment of conversation, they were joined by the driver of Rhabbouz's car. The sailor led them up the gangplank and they were lost from Goodrich's view.

'So, my good man, you will now take us to the cabins.' The General pointed with his cane.

'But I must announce you first.'

'You will do exactly as you are told. You will take us to the cabins and we will announce ourselves.'

Hesitantly, the man complied. Rhabbouz's driver stayed behind on the bridge.

The General rapped sharply against the stateroom door with the head of his cane. 'Open up. Police.' He ushered Tombal in front of him.

'What the hell is this?' came a cranky female voice from inside.

'This is the French police. Please come out at once.'

'Paul,' the voice said, 'Paul, wake up. The police are here.'

'Hmmm. What? What police?'

'The French police.'

There were some rustling noises, then the door opened. Fosburgh appeared in a blue bathrobe, his hair hastily combed back. 'What the hell is going on here?' he asked indignantly. 'Do you people know what time it is?'

'Yes, sir. We are terribly sorry, but it is a rather urgent matter. There have been some rather terrible murders committed. We have been told that it could be a sailor from one of the yachts. We would like to have everyone out on deck.'

'You have your goddamn nerve, Commissaire whatever-your-name-is. This ship is private property. There are no murderers on board, just my crew and my guests. And I will personally vouch for them.' He started to close the door.

The General stuck his cane in the jamb. 'I'm afraid you don't understand, Mr. Fosburgh. We intend to go from one end of this ship to the other. Every person will stand on the rear deck. There will be no equivocation. We have tried to discommode you as little as possible. It is very early in the morning, but we felt that you would prefer to have this done while there are only a few fishermen on the dock, rather than to wait until later in the day when the crowds have arrived. We felt that you prefer a little loss of sleep to a major invasion of your privacy.'

'What would you call this?'

'Shall we say that you are being a good citizen of the United States and a helpful guest of the people and the government of France?' The General smiled.

Fosburgh threw his ace. 'Do you have a search warrant?'

The General smiled again. 'You do read French, don't you?' He held the paper out to Fosburgh.

'I am going to talk to the Ambassador about this at my first opportunity.'

'Please feel free to do so. In the meanwhile, however ...'

'All right. We'll be up in a minute. I'll alert the rest of my guests and the crew.'

'Don't bother, Mr. Fosburgh. We'll do it for you.'

They left the second Shin Bet man standing outside of Fosburgh's door and went to the next cabin. Their knock was answered quickly.

Jean was wearing a short black nightgown against which her pendulous breasts protruded. She looked sleepy and cross. The General explained. She turned ashen white, but agreed, and went back inside to change.

It took about fifteen minutes to line up all of the people on the deck. Most of them stood passively in line while Fosburgh paced.

When they had all been collected, the General got up from his small stool and approached Fosburgh. 'May I speak to the captain, please?'

Fosburgh changed tactics. In an icy voice, he replied, 'Naturally, sir. I always cooperate with legal authorities, wherever I go. Captain, if you please.'

The neatly uniformed man, bearded and in his late thirties, walked forward with a military gait and saluted. 'May I be of service?'

'Yes, thank you. Would you mind getting the ship's roster for me?'

He hurried into the bridge and took the book from a drawer, and returned, avoiding the Shin Bet man who was seated, arms crossed, in the chair behind the wheel. He turned to a page marked 'Ship's Company' and handed the book to the General, who looked down at the neat markings, then said, 'Would you please muster your crew for roll call, Captain? Oh, and by the way, I'm sure that you have valid passports for all of the crew and passengers in your safe? I'd like to see them.'

The captain mustered the people on the deck into a straight line, then read through all the names, including

Fosburgh's. All of them answered save one.

'Who is Abdul Aboussara, Captain? Or perhaps you can answer the question, Mr. Fosburgh?'

The captain deferred to his employer.

'Aboussara,' Fosburgh said, 'is a leading seaman. I suppose that you would call him second mate.'

'Is he, as his name would indicate, an Arab?'

'Yes. He is from Quahrein.'

'It is rather odd to find a sailor from Quahrein on board an American luxury yacht. One would think that they were better suited to oil tankers, or perhaps sailing dhows.'

'Not at all,' Fosburgh said patronizingly. 'There are quite a number in my crew. Quahreinians make excellent sailors. And it should be no surprise to find such men on this ship. I am the president of Royal American Oil, the largest operating company in the oil fields of Quahrein.'

'You must be on excellent terms with Colonel Ben Kelb,' the General offered.

Fosburgh puffed with pride, 'Yes, indeed. I consider him to be an enlightened statesman, as well as a close friend and business associate.'

'No doubt. I am sure he thinks well of you too. Shall we get on with this? I would like to look at the people on this boat,' he made a small laugh, 'a little inspection of the troops in ranks, you might say. Before I forget, where is this Aboussara, Mr Fosburgh?'

'Just off on a little errand for me.'

'When do you expect him back?'

'Any time now.'

'What was the nature of the errand?'

'I'm afraid that is a personal matter.'

'Ah, yes. I see. Well, no matter.' He offered his arm, 'Shall we?'

Fosburgh and the General walked down the line of perhaps twenty-five people at a leisurely pace. The General stopped several times to scrutinize one or another of the crew, but continued to chat with Fosburgh. When he stopped in front of the steward, the man began to tremble and to perspire profusely. 'Good morning,' the General said in a conversational tone. The steward's eyes began to roll upward in their sockets. The General put his arm out to steady him. 'Perhaps it is a little early in the morning for him. What is his name, Mr. Fosburgh?'

'Assad,' Fosburgh bit off the word. 'His name is Assad. He is the chief steward. Are you all right, Assad?'

'No,' the man stuttered in reply, 'I mean ... yes ... I am well, Mr. Fosburgh. Thank you for asking.'

'Good, Assad. Very good.'

'Assad,' the General asked, 'do you know Aboussara well?'

Fosburgh, now a little frightened, took a step backward.

'Oh, please don't go, Mr. Fosburgh. There is nothing I have to say to this man that you are not perfectly free to hear. Well, Assad?'

'Yes, sir. I know him well. He is the leading seaman. We are both from Quahrein.'

'Are you? How many others of the crew are from Quahrein, Assad?'

'I think that there are ten in all.'

'You think?'

'Ten.'

'Fine, Assad. Shall we continue, Mr. Fosburgh?'

With an audible sigh of relief, Fosburgh followed him along the deck. The General stopped in front of Madeleine, who was wearing a see-through shirt and bikini bottom. He put out his hand. She took it and he kissed hers briefly and politely. 'Mes hommages, madame. You are truly beautiful.'

'Why, thank you.'

He moved along to the end where Jean Chandler stood, rigid. Her hair was covered by a silk scarf. She wore sunglasses with dark lenses and enormous circular rims. 'My goodness, Mr. Fosburgh, to hide such beauty. Would I be rude to ask that I be allowed to see her face and lovely hair? It would be a blessing to my old eyes.'

'Of course,' Fosburgh smiled in compliance, 'Jean, show the gentleman your face.'

In a single spastic motion, she tore off the scarf and glasses and shook her head defiantly, letting her long flowing hair fall behind her over her shoulders.

'Thank you, Miss. I am rewarded. You are American, aren't you?'

'Yes, I am. How did you know?'

'Just that certain freshness that lovely American women seem to have.' He smiled and turned away. Fosburgh walked behind him to the gangway.

'I trust, Mr. Fosburgh, that we have not discommoded you in any way. It is an unpleasant necessity of my job, sometimes, to discommode people.'

'You mean that's all?'

'Oh, yes. We have seen what we came to see. There is no one here who seems a likely suspect.'

Now magnanimous, Fosburgh said, 'Any time. Always glad to be of service to the authorities.'

Tombal also thanked him, and with the two Shin Bet men, preceded the General down the gangway to the wharf. Almost at the bottom, the General turned back and said in a loud voice, 'By the way, Mr. Fosburgh, if you should see your man Aboussara, you might tell him that we would like to see him.'

'Yes, of course. By the way, I didn't catch your name.'

'Really?' the General asked innocently. He turned and walked down to the jetty and across to his car without looking back.

Goodrich sat in the back of the car, staring morosely into his lap. He did not stir when the General fell into the seat next to him. As though he had forgotten something, the old man said, 'And Tombal, let the next stop be the PTT. No calls are to be put through from here to Quahrein, Libya or Iraq for the next twenty-four hours, nor are any cables to be sent. Can you fix that?'

'Yes, mon général.'

'Also, I want a policeman to walk obviously, and as obnoxiously as possible, up and down the jetty in front of the *Glen Pool*. No more than fifty feet from either side of the gangway. Understood?'

'Yes, sir.'

He turned to Goodrich. 'Cat got your tongue, Captain of Industry? Or did you see something that did not please you?'

Goodrich replied softly, 'The second girl is my secretary.'

'Ah! The thief. The purveyor of information.' Then contritely, 'I am sorry, Mr. Goodrich. Was she close to you?'

'Not really, I suppose. She's been with me for three years. But we never had much to do with each other outside of business matters. A very polite relationship,' he added ironically.

'If I were you, I would check to see how she came to be chosen. I would bet that Mr. Fosburgh, in one way or another, was her sponsor.'

'I dare say, General Pineau. I still don't see how she found out much.'

'Do you arrange your own travel schedule? Get your own tickets? When you want one for an employee, do you call that department?'

'Of course not.'

'Well, there's your answer. Plus a Telex here and there. Possibly a letter or two. Some papers you gave her to put through the shredder. It isn't very hard really. Especially if she was trained for the job, and has any brains. Buck up, Mr. Goodrich. Not at all your fault. It could happen to anyone.'

'Could it happen to you?' Goodrich asked bitterly.

The General patted his knee. 'I am seventy-seven, Mr. Goodrich. It couldn't happen to me. Not anymore. But it did.'

Goodrich brightened a little. 'Really?'

'Chinese girl when I was stationed in Hanoi in the '30s. She was a great fuck, and a great spy. For the Japs, of course. She got quite a bit. Caused rather a furor. We had to change a lot of plans. I got shipped back to North Africa.'

'What happened to her?'

'I shot her in the back while she was going through my

316

desk. Let's go, Tombal, we don't want to lose our momentum.'

'Well, are you going to help me up, you oaf, or shall I just stand here and let the wind blow me to Toulon.'

The helicopter pilot put his shoulder to the General's rump and straightened his back. Between his help and the steady pull that he was exerting on the climbing bar on the side of the ship, the General managed to swing himself awkwardly into his seat. He righted himself, and said over his shoulder to Goodrich and Tombal, who were already strapped in the rear, 'We have done all that we can. Now we must find out from Toulon the condition of Mr. Edelman, and whether they have found this agent. If it is necessary, we can always call Washington. But then, of course, the whole French intelligence apparatus would have to know. It would probably go to the Elysée Palace, and by the time that horseshit was over with, it would be too late. Damn it, young man. Are you going to make this thing fly or not?'

The turbo-jet copter that the General had commandeered through an old friend at the Toulon Naval Base lifted off from the field across from the beach at Pampelonne. In fifteen minutes, they were standing on the landing pad at the harborside.

'Pilot, you belong to me for the moment. You are allowed to piss, drink coffee and smoke, just as long as it is all done within sight of this vile machine. I will need you. Take care of yourself, my health depends on it.'

They climbed the stairs from the pad to the high wall bordering the base and level with the street. Still puffing from the exertion, the General got into the police car that was waiting for them, and sped off through the traffic to the hospital.

A glassy-eyed Le Seuer sat in an armchair in the administrator's office, his head lolling with fatigue. He jumped, startled, when the General slammed the door behind him after admitting Tombal and Goodrich.

'Well, have you discovered anything? Or have you come here for a nap?'

'We found him, General.'

'And you are sitting here?' he asked on a rising note.

'There are two men in the room with him. We haven't left him alone for a minute since he was identified.'

'How did you know?'

'We didn't. We just went through the papers of all of the people who were in the bar. Except for that young couple, they were all still in the hospital. Those two were the only ones who were allowed to go home. He was the only one we could not account for, either through the French or Swiss law firms, or through General Motors. We assumed it was he. We waited till he got up – he was sleeping very heavily, a nasty concussion. We asked him a lot of questions, and told him that he was to be held incommunicado, as a material witness. He howled like a stuck pig. Said that he was a member of the Secret Service, of the Presidential staff itself. He suggested all manner of unpleasant things that he would do to us if we did not release him, or let him get to a phone.'

'I trust that you did not.'

Le Seuer said indignantly, 'I did not. He is still sitting in his room. Fuming. One man in with him. Another outside the door.'

'It sounds good,' the General said. 'But if he has over-powered the man in the room and shinnied out of the window, Le Seuer, you will be on horseback patrol in the Carmargue until the day before your pension is vested; then I will see to it that you are fired.'

But when they entered the room, they found a tight-lipped pale man in his mid-forties seated on the bed.

'Congratulations, Le Seuer. You are still employed. Good afternoon to you, sir. How are you feeling? Not at all well, it would seem. Le Seuer, take your people and wait at the end of the hall.' He waved his hand and sat down in the recently vacated chair. 'This is Milton Goodrich, the president of General Motors. I assume that you recognize him from the bar. Tombal, go outside and call La Tour Blanche and see if you can find out what's going on – and check on our friend down the hall.' After the door had closed, the General continued. 'I don't know what you know. I don't know how much you know. But I will guess. No, please,' he held up his hand, 'don't say anything. You are going to stay shut up here until you either agree to cooperate, or at least until this business is over. So you might as well pay attention. You are in a very important position. You don't mind if I smoke?'

'Not at all,' Murchison said. 'You are the first person I've met here who begins to make sense. Good afternoon, Mr. Goodrich, I remember you from the bar. You weren't hurt, were you?'

'I'm fine. Just lost a little piece of ear. No great shakes.'

'Whatever your name is,' the General began, 'understand that what I am to tell you is for your ears only. Naturally, you will pass it on to the President when you talk to him. I will let you judge whether or not you should tell anyone else. So much for professional courtesy. You have been sent to tail a man named Hultz, a vice president of General Motors.

'A man, who is now dead – I shot him myself – threw a grenade into a room you were supposed to be guarding. No fault of yours, I would like to say. If a man does not care whether he is killed in performing an act, then there is no way to prevent his action. That's the trouble with dealing with fanatics and assorted terrorists. When he left you, he shot a man who is in the process of fomenting a revolution in a foreign country. The intended victim lived nonetheless, and if we help him, he will make his coup d'état.

'At the same time, anxious over the attitudes of the existing government of that state, your President has probably set in motion the wheels of your first real military operation since Vietnam. The reason for that action is about to be eliminated. America can have her cake and eat it too. We must inform the President.'

'So call him,' Murchison interrupted.

'Ah, I will if I have to. That's why I am here. If, in fact, he has not been alerted by you to the possibility of acceleration of the plot against which he is defending himself – we can avoid the risk of exposing the coup d'état. A little confusing perhaps?'

'Not really. If the coup works, then we don't need to intervene. The fewer people who know about the coup, the less chance it will fail.'

'In a nutshell. Our man might have to move up the coup. It's planned for tomorrow.'

Murchison looked at him speculatively. 'Who are you?'

'I'm the head of the Arab Section of French Military Intelligence.'

Murchison nodded. 'I'm afraid it's too late. I called through the security section of our consulate at Cannes.'

'Merde! When?'

'At about four-thirty or five.'

'How did you get out?'

'I got dressed and walked out. Then I walked back in. I figured I needed the rest.'

'So much for security. Look, if I have to use my channels to get through to the President, it will take forever. May I use yours?'

'I can't make that decision. Security section at Cannes will have to tell you.'

'Do you think I should?'

'Have you got this one-man revolution here?'

'Yes.'

'Let me see him and I'll push it through. Deal?'

'It's a deal. Get dressed.'

'What do you mean, you can't get through?'

'It's ruined, Mr. Fosburgh, completely destroyed. Someone has smashed the insides of it completely.'

'Well, fix it!'

'There is no way that it can be fixed – ever. It has to be

replaced. There is no part of it that could be salvaged except the case. Every circuit. The transformer.'

'It must have been those fucking French cops. All right, we'll go and call them on the phone.'

Fosburgh left the ship and hurried on through the early morning shoppers to the PTT building several blocks behind the jetty. He arrived and waited impatiently in line while an old lady counted out her bits of change. When she was finished, he stepped up to the counter. The girl behind the desk looked at him insolently. He forced a smile and slipped a hundred-franc note into her hand. 'This call is very important, please make sure that it is hurried through.'

She looked down in her hand and said, 'I will do my best. It is sometimes very difficult with the Middle East. Please take a seat.' She pointed to the hard worn wooden benches across from her counter. Fosburgh picked up a day-old paper from the bench beside him and started reading.

The innkeeper fawned on the General and Tombal as they entered. 'M. le Commissaire, your orders have been followed to the letter. No one is allowed to disturb the patient. I am grateful to you for keeping this from the press. Matters of this kind often serve to reduce business in an establishment like mine.'

'You have been exemplary in your behavior, my dear monsieur. I shall make it a point to recommend your services to all of my friends when they are in the area.' The General patted him on the shoulder and walked on.

The room had begun to take on a disinfectant smell. Aharon, starved for sleep, answered the door. The old doctor was sprawled asleep in a chair. El Kaffar seemed to be resting comfortably.

'How is the patient, Mr. Ambassador?'

'He seems to be all right. But I'm worried about the doctor. Poor old man, he's exhausted.'

'How old is he?'

'Nearly seventy, I think.'

'The prime of life, my dear Ambassador. Wake the fakir up.'

Aharon pushed gently at the doctor's shoulder. He stirred reluctantly and opened his eyes.

'Now we are all here,' said the General. He made introductions all around. 'Well, Doctor, do you think you can get His Excellency to say hello to our new friend?'

'You are a horrid man, General.' He raised himself from the chair and went to the bedside. He listened with his stethoscope for a minute and checked El Kaffar's pulse. He spoke to him softly, waited and then spoke again. El Kaffar opened his eyes.

'Who are these people? Aharon? Aharon?' He tried to raise himself. 'Prophet of God! My arm.' He fell back again. 'That bastard Aboussara. Where is he?'

The General stepped forward. 'He is quite dead, Your Excellency, gone on to a greater reward.'

El Kaffar winced and managed to turn himself a bit. 'I hope it is as hot as they say. Why am I alive?'

'It was Rhabbouz, Mohammed,' Aharon replied, 'and the General. He shot Aboussara right between the eyes. Rhabbouz caught one – a few broken ribs – but otherwise, no damage.'

'The doctor says you will be good as new in several weeks,' the General said.

'That's not good enough. What day is it?'

'It's Thursday, Excellency,' said the General, 'and you have even less time than you think. You are going to have to make your effort now.' The General explained the situation. El Kaffar looked at Murchison as the General came to an end.

'Well, are you going to let him use the phone, or are you going to help start the Third World War?'

Goodrich interrupted. 'I want to talk to Mr. Murchison.'

'Speak quickly, then,' the General said.

'Not here – alone.' He glanced at El Kaffar.

The General squinted at him and said, 'All right. In the hall. But I'm coming too. And so is Tombal.'

They left the room and walked to the end of the hall opposite the stairs. Briefly, Goodrich explained Edelman's condition to Murchison, emphasizing the possible effects that his fate could have on Operation Palm Beach and its aftermath.

'That is only another reason to stop the invasion,' the General said.

'That well may be,' Murchison replied, 'but until we have some confirmation of Edelman's condition, I am not going to recommend anything to the President, nor let him be influenced without telling him that his hole card may be gone.'

The General turned to Tombal. 'What is the latest news at the hospital?'

'Nothing. He's just the same. They x-rayed him. There is some swelling, some fluid. But until he becomes conscious, there cán be no judgment on his mental condition.'

'Call again – now,' Murchison suggested.

Tombal went down the hall and came back in a couple of minutes. 'No change,' he said.

The General pulled savagely at the end of his mustache. 'God damn it. We can't just sit here and wait for medical bulletins.'

Goodrich, red in the face, said, 'How the hell can you talk about a human being as though he were just a stick of wood? He isn't just an integer in this problem. He is also a person, and a very special person at that.'

'Mr. Goodrich,' the General replied coldly, 'I am fully aware of Mr. Edelman's humanity. But nonetheless, we cannot afford to wait. If, in fact, we cannot prevent your President from invading Quahrein, and the world is at a loss for petroleum, and the alternative offered by Mr. Edelman is unavailable by dint of his infirmity or death, we shall all live, however briefly, to regret his passing, both as a scientist and a human being.' He turned to Murchison, 'Now, do we use the phone or not?'

They returned to the room in stony silence. Murchison said, 'I'll arrange the call.'

'Good,' said El Kaffar. 'Now get me out of this bed and get me dressed. There is much that I must do, and no time to do it. This change in plans could destroy everything. Just hope that Ben Kelb has started out from his wilderness camp. It is better defended than Carcassonne.'

Thirty-four

First one, then another of the helicopters landed in the flat field in Super Cannes. The police cars led the way to the American Consulate. The now sizable group waited in the hall as Murchison disappeared into the Consul's office. Tombal stood looking at the floor. Goodrich paced nervously, his mind more and more occupied with a vision of Arthur Edelman, his mouth slack, the light of genius extinguished from his eyes. El Kaffar sat silently in a chair, wrestling with pain and the immensity of the task before him.

Murchison opened the door and asked them to enter. Once inside the paneled room, Murchison guided El Kaffar to the head of the table, careful of the arm strapped to his chest. The General sat to his right, Murchison to his left. Goodrich seated himself near the head of the table. Murchison cleared his throat and looked at Goodrich. 'Your inventor, Mr. Goodrich.'

'Yes.'

'He asked if anyone knew where the briefcase with his notes were. He woke up about a half hour ago, while we were on our way here.'

Goodrich covered his eyes with his hands, rubbed hard, took a deep breath and sat erect against the chair back. 'Thank you, Mr. Murchison,' he said simply. 'Thank you very much.'

El Kaffar looked back and forth quizzically. Murchison turned to him and said, 'I will talk to him first, then turn the phone over to you, Mr. El Kaffar.'

After a moment the phone rang. Murchison took the receiver from the cradle and waited, then said, 'Yes, sir. Good morning. I'll try to explain as best I can.' He talked for about ten minutes, pausing from time to time to answer questions. 'Yes, sir. He's right here.' He turned the phone over to El Kaffar.

'I understand that you've been injured, Your Excellency,' said the President. 'I hope that you will recover. But I'm sorry to report Murchison's call came too late. We have already started the wheels in motion.'

'You must see that it is imperative that you stop those wheels, Mr. President.'

Smith answered thoughtfully, 'I have no way of knowing whether or not you are, in fact, telling the truth, Mr. El Kaffar. Our relations in the past have not been of the best.'

'I have the Israeli Ambassador sitting next to me,' he said desperately, 'he will tell you himself. You will certainly believe Mr. Aharon.'

'I might believe that he is telling me what he supposes to be the truth. I cannot act on his suppositions. If the coup d'état were a fact, I would be tempted to go along with you. Under the circumstances, I cannot.'

Perspiring heavily, El Kaffar asked, 'What must I do to convince you?'

'Make your move. Start your revolution – and succeed.'

'How long do I have?'

'Five hours. You are about an hour from Quahrein City.'

'But the planning, it could throw the entire operation out of phase.'

'Mr. El Kaffar,' the President said firmly, 'I will call off this operation when I have confirmed that you are in power in Quahrein and that Ben Kelb has been deposed.'

'It took you from 1775 to 1781 to make your Revolution. You want me to make mine in five hours. And this way, if in fact I do manage to do it, it will be said all over the Third World that I was backed by the CIA and American imperialism. Which I am not! You will have destroyed me before I begin. The Iraqis will fall on me like wolves. If you deign to protect me, I have put my people in bondage to you. If you do not, there will be a B'aathist colonel just like Ben Kelb in the Presidential Palace. Those are not attractive choices, Mr. Smith. I would have been better off if Aboussara had not missed.'

There was a lengthy pause, then the President said, 'I will make a compromise with you. I can land the force in West Germany. I will leave them on the runway. They will be refueled. You will have until dawn tomorrow, your time. That's twelve extra hours.'

'I can do it. We shall be grateful to each other for this, Mr. Smith, even if we are adversaries.'

'Will we be adversaries, Mr. El Kaffar?'

'Only time will tell. But there will be peace.'

'Then there will be competition, and conflicting viewpoints, and even harsh disagreement, Mr. El Kaffar. But if there is peace, there are no true adversaries.'

'You will be notified as soon as possible. I am mindful of your need to know. Till tomorrow, then, Mr. President.'

'Till tomorrow.'

El Kaffar slumped in the chair as he hung up the phone. The fine film of sweat that covered his pointed face shone in the artificial light of the room. 'May I have a glass of water?' he asked. Murchison gave him some from a carafe on the table. He drained it. 'I am terribly hot.'

The doctor, looking concerned, got to his feet and brought his bag with him. 'I hope that it is not infection. You will be useless to your people if you are dead. You have exerted yourself overly.'

'Nonsense,' said the General. 'What is the next stop, Mr. El Kaffar? You have much to do.'

El Kaffar swallowed a handful of pills with another glass of water. 'I must get to Quahrein.' He smiled wryly. 'The kind of welcome that I get will depend on whether Aboussara alerted Ben Kelb or his people.'

'Somehow, I don't think that that is likely, Your Excellency.'

'I am glad you have faith, General. You wager very freely with my life.'

'Have you a regular way to get back to Quahrein? Something already arranged, I mean?'

'Yes, General Pineau. If I may use a phone in private. It would not do to compromise my own intelligence here in France.'

'I suppose not,' the old man grumbled, 'it seems that everyone has a network that operates in the South of France. All I have is poor old broken-down La Brousse.'

As they got up to leave the room, Murchison said, 'Mr. Goodrich, I am going to have to ask you to stay. We will see that you get your transportation back to Toulon, or wherever you want to go. You needn't worry about Edelman and Hultz. They are being well protected at the hospital.'

'Of course, Mr. Murchison. Just so that you see to it that I get some sleep in the near future. I'm not as hardy as General Pineau.'

'Nor as young, Captain of Industry. It has been a pleasure to meet you.' The old man shook his hand warmly.

El Kaffar, his slight frame leaning against the doctor, put out his hand as well. 'Goodbye, Mr. Goodrich. Or rather, au revoir.'

'Au revoir?'

'I think that perhaps we shall meet again.'

'It will be my pleasure, Your Excellency.'

'Perhaps, Mr. Goodrich, perhaps.'

Shortly after he telephoned, a small black car came to the front door of the Consulate to take Mohammed El Kaffar to his fate. The old doctor was put in one of the helicopters and sent back to Toulon, Aharon with him.

Tombal and the General shook hands with Murchison and Goodrich again and left in the car which had brought them. 'Tombal,' said the old man, 'one wonders what reception he will receive when he arrives. Seventeen hours to make a revolution. Americans remain unchallenged as the kings of optimism.'

Fosburgh sat for almost an hour. When he had read every article and every advertisement in the local newspaper, he rose and tapped on the counter. 'Are we making any progress?'

'It will be just one minute more, sir,' the sullen girl replied. As if by command the phone rang. She took it from the cradle, listened, argued a little and shrugged. 'I am sorry, monsieur, there will be no calls to Quahrein for at least twenty-four hours.'

He slapped at his forehead in frustration. 'Where may I phone to Paris?'

'That is automatique. There on the wall, or those booths in the corner.'

He walked rapidly to a booth, took some change from his pocket, checked a number in his wallet and dialed the number. After a long series of clicks and whistles, there was a ringing noise. A polite recorded voice explained that he had reached a non-operative number. He gritted his teeth and tried again, with the same results. He banged the phone down on the hook, regained his composure and dialed the long-distance operator. He sat in the stuffy booth for ten minutes before she called him back.

'Je suis désolée, monsieur. That number will be out of service for several days.'

'But why?' he shouted in exasperation.

'There has been some digging in the streets. Evidently that address is without telephone or electricity.' Having explained, she rang off.

A tight smile formed on Fosburgh's mouth. Too many coincidences. My radio is smashed. The phone lines to Quahrein are out. The Quahreinian Embassy has no phone, the power has been cut so that the radio will not work. But if I steam for twenty-four hours, I will be in Quahrein. And no one will dare stop me.

He ran through the streets back to the berth. Once on board, he called for the captain. 'Pay the port charges and release the berth. Then get under way.'

'What shall I give the port captain as our next port of call?'

'It's none of his business. Tell him Greece. Tell him what

you like,' he snapped.

'But where are we going, Mr. Fosburgh?'

'To Quahrein.'

Within a minute after he heard the heavy diesel engines start and saw the bustle on the decks of the *Glen Pool*, Rhabbouz struggled from the car and walked across the jetty to Le Gorille to use the phone. The call served to rescue the General from the clutches of Rhabbouz's raging wife.

'Why can't you pick on a younger man? You are enough of an old fool. You don't need to make one of my husband. You should have been dead years ago, with your spying and shooting and killing. If anything else happens to my husband because of you, I shall kill you myself with a bread knife!'

'But I assure you, madame . . .'

'Nothing you say would assure me, you old cheat. You scare everyone else with your blustering and shouting – but not me.'

Tombal was sitting transfixed in a corner, waiting for an explosion which never came, when the phone rang. She answered it, and started to sob uncontrollably. Tombal said, 'My God, something must have happened to him.'

The General shrugged, 'Not at all. That means he is just fine.'

When Nana had finished crying, she began yelling, 'And as for the divorce, you can have it any time. I will be well rid of you.' She turned on the General, holding out the phone, and said venomously, 'Here, he wants to talk to you.' Then she flounced out of the room.

'Thank God you called,' said the General, 'she was working herself up to mayhem. What's happening?' He listened attentively. 'Aha! We were right. They didn't reach Ben Kelb.' Then in an aside, 'You see, Tombal, what it is to work with a genius. All right, Jew, you say he went to the PTT. He was there for two hours, you say?' The General laughed. 'He tried Quahrein, then the Embassy. Now he knows if he wants to bring a message, he'll have to go in person. What's that? Oh yes, he could always go to Italy. Certainly, but with their phone system, especially to the Mideast, he could swim faster. His plane? Oh, I'm sure he tried that too. It's undergoing a Ministry of Aviation inspection. There are bits and pieces of it all over Nice Airport. Yes, old Jew, you are right, Aboussara never had the opportunity to call. El Kaffar will have a quiet reception. Look, I want to see La Brousse and Hamilton. Wait for us at the landing field. We will all have dinner together. We can watch the returns. I have never watched the returns from a revolution before. We will know by morning. El Kaffar has until then. I will explain later. If it doesn't work, we will be vaporized with full stomachs.' He hung up, motioned to Tombal and started to sneak out of the door.

'I see you, you old reprobate. You make sure that nothing happens to my husband.'

'I will, chère madame, you have my word.' He shut the door behind him.

When the sailors started to pull the gangway back onto the rear deck of the *Glen Pool*, the officer who had been marching back and forth on the jetty came to a halt and walked directly toward them. He said something to the sailors and Fosburgh's heart skipped a beat. The policeman stood staring but said nothing more as the gangway was pulled on board and the heavy mooring lines were cast off. The engines changed their pitch; the chain from the heavy forward anchor clanked into its bin. Without apparent effort, the *Glen Pool* began to glide forward from its berth, and then, gaining speed, moved into the harbor and around the point of the Quai Jean Reveille toward the open sea.

Fosburgh remained in his chair looking out over the stern at the dwindling French coast for half an hour. He looked up at the bright sun, stretched, heaved a sigh of relief and asked the captain, 'Are we past the twelve-mile limit?'

'We have been for several minutes, Mr. Fosburgh,' he replied.

'I think that I shall have a sunbath.'

Fosburgh walked forward down the companionway,

watching the great yacht trail a white wake through the calm sea. An awning of bright red and yellow stripes jutted out from the superstructure, hiding the forward deck from the bridge.

Both Jean and Madeleine lay naked, their eyes closed, on colorful mattresses on the deck. Jean's hand was resting casually on Madeleine's belly, her fingers trailing lightly through the pubic hair. Fosburgh stripped to the buff and stretched himself out on the third mattress. In a moment, exhausted from the early rising and the ensuing tension, he was asleep.

The intercom buzzed twice several hours later, arousing him. The steward announced lunch in half an hour.

Fosburgh hung up the receiver and walked to the edge of the awning, looking out over the stern. They were out of sight of land.

'All right, ladies. Wake up. It's time for lunch.'

Madeleine leaned on one elbow and looked around sleepily.

Jean blinked up at the bright sun, rolled over and got to her feet. She stretched luxuriantly and yawned, then walked to the railing. Looking down into the water, she made her way slowly toward the prow. She looked up for a moment and then down again, put her hands over her eyes and began to scream.

Both Madeleine and Fosburgh ran to her. 'What is it,' he said, 'what's the matter?'

Jean's piercing cries filled the air. She trembled uncontrollably.

Fosburgh shook her shoulders violently, but she did not stop. Finally, in exasperation, he struck her sharply twice across the face. She subsided into heavy sobs.

'What is the matter? Control yourself,' he said.

A small trickle of blood ran from her cut lip to her chin. With visible effort she pulled one hand away from her face and pointed over the rail.

'So? What is it? Talk. Say something.' Fosburgh raised his hand as if to strike again.

'The anchor,' she sobbed. 'The anchor.'

He turned from her and walked to the rail. He looked out over the side and downward.

The body of Abdul Aboussara dangled from the ring at the top of the anchor, held there by several lengths of wire around his neck. The eyes were open and staring opaquely. The edges of the gaping hole in his forehead were tinged dark blue. He was naked, and his genitals had been cut off. Fosburgh vomited violently into the sea.

Thirty-five

Several young Air Force officers had hustled El Kaffar off in a car after his jet had landed in the heat and dust of Quahrein Airport. He was delivered to a small turreted house in the ancient quarter of the city. Once behind its thick masonry walls, he was revived by the dark and comparatively low temperature. A doctor was waiting. He changed the dressing, gave him another injection of antibiotics, and under protest, a couple of stimulant tablets.

El Kaffar dressed in a plain tan uniform, wincing as he put his right arm through the shirt. The doctor adjusted the sling around his neck, and El Kaffar walked out to the car, gritting his teeth against the pain.

The guards at the gate of the Presidential Palace snapped to attention. He stepped down and walked directly through the Moorish architecture and decorations to Ben Kelb's office. He opened the door. Ben Kelb's military aide looked up in surprise as he walked into the room.

One of the Air Force men who accompanied El Kaffar said, 'You are under arrest. Please come with me.'

The man behind the desk reached for the drawer. There was a soft thud, and he pitched over backward. A smell of gunpowder filled the room. The officer put the pistol, with its grotesque silencer, back into the waistband of his trousers.

El Kaffar opened the door of the inner office and snapped on the light. It was empty and the drapes were drawn. The air conditioner whirred in the box on the windowsill.

He sat behind the desk. 'Has the operator been changed?' he asked.

The officer who had done the shooting replied, 'As soon as

you touched down.'

'Put him in the closet,' El Kaffar pointed to the dead man, then picked up the phone. 'Get me Captain Hassan.' There was a pause. 'Hassan, this is El Kaffar. Have you been notified that we are moving ahead of schedule? Yes, now. That's fine. Make sure there are as few left as possible. Do you think you know where they are? Yes, all of them. That's right. As little bloodshed as possible. Every death is the death of a brother. All right, see to it that all of the phones are out of order. Are there any Embassies with private generating equipment? Good. In,' he looked at his watch, 'ten minutes, kill all power in Quahrein City.'

He rose from behind the desk. 'Who is to stay here?'

'Captain Mahdani.'

'Is he here?'

'I'll get him.' The officer left the room and returned in a moment with a younger man.

El Kaffar said, 'You are to deal with the radio. We will broadcast in four hours. You understand your instructions? You know what you must do?'

'Yes, sir.'

El Kaffar left the room, accompanied by the other officers, and went back to the car. 'Take us to the military airport.'

The car roared through the gate. Two new guards had taken the place of the others, who sat bound hand and foot under a spreading tree.

The car arrived at the airport gate, which was open. They passed through. El Kaffar bit his lip. There were three bodies stacked behind the tiny guard house.

They pulled up at a rusting abandoned quonset hangar, which had been built by the Italians during the war. El Kaffar walked through a door in the back. A group of men in battle dress sat in a circle on the floor. Three jeeps and a truck were parked near the huge front door.

The officer in charge got to his feet, snapped to attention and saluted.

'Are you ready?' El Kaffar asked.

'Yes, sir. We will try to take them in the barracks.'

'No shooting unless necessary. You are to try to explain.'

The man saluted again, gave some orders and got into the truck. Half of the soldiers followed him silently. The remainder mounted the jeeps. With squealing and clanging, chains brought up the front door, and the truck sped out onto the field toward the pilots' barracks. El Kaffar went back to the car. In ten minutes he heard several shots. He leaned forward to the driver. 'Go out in front where I can see.'

There were several more shots. He could see from the car that the dismounted men from the truckload of his supporters were rounding up a few soldiers outside the barracks building. Suddenly, a car roared out from behind the barracks and headed toward the line of Mystère IIIs on the runway. The soldiers from the truck fired at it, but it continued without faltering. At the line of planes, it stopped and several men jumped out and ran to the aircraft. The fire from the men in the truck was now being returned by the ground crews loyal to Ben Kelb near the planes.

El Kaffar stuck his head out of the window and yelled into the hangar, 'Move the jeeps.'

They rolled forward. Two were mounted with .50-caliber machine guns, the third with a 106-mm recoilless rifle. The soldiers from the truck were charging now; the chatter of small arms fire filled the air. El Kaffar saw some of his men drop under the withering hail from the planes. He heard several engines whine into life. Two of the planes started to move slowly from the line toward the runway.

The jeeps followed them, then stopped. There was a puff of smoke and a brilliant flash of light from the breech of the anti-tank gun, followed by a thunderous clap of sound. The first of the planes exploded in a gout of flame and smoke. The second plane halted in its tracks, and began to turn away from the holocaust. The staccato burst of the heavy machine guns echoed over the field; the one-ounce slugs stitched the silvery fuselage and ricocheted from the Plexiglas canopy. The plane started to pick up speed, then slewed to one side. The undercarriage buckled, there was a shower of sparks, and an explosion.

The soldiers from the truck lined the ground crews and pilots in front of the jeeps, and marched them off toward the barracks with their hands on their heads. The officer stood on the hood of the truck and waved his arm.

'That's that,' said El Kaffar. 'Take me to the Royal American pumping station at Wadi Gua Limone.'

After receiving the phone call, the man walked out of the Jiddah Hilton into the broiling Saudi Arabian sun. He got into his car and drove for a few minutes. Then he took his briefcase and walked into a yard, where some children were playing among the debris. Chickens pecked at scraps on the ground. He pulled a string on the briefcase and threw it under the steps. The children did not look up as he left.

Inside the house a woman hummed as she rolled dough for bread. In another room a man worked studiously over a kitchen clock and some batteries. The stained fez was pushed to the back of his head. A map lay on the table. A small x marked the location of his target, the main Aramco pumping station, some twenty miles distant in the sand. The man in the suit was already walking back to the bar at the Hilton when the house blew up, shattering such windows as there were for ten blocks around. The bodies of the man, the woman and the children were charred beyond recognition.

The refinery outside of Homs in Syria was working at capacity. After the Israeli raids of the Yom Kippur War, there had been years of effort at rebuilding it. It smelled sulfurous, as it poured millions of gallons of petroleum and products through the pipelines.

A man on a donkey, leading still another, watched it belching the residue of progress into the sky. Then he dismounted, walked to the wire guarding the right of way and pulled out a pair of pliers. He cut the strands and led the donkeys through the gap. He walked to the valves sil-

houetted in the sky twenty feet above his head. With in-
finite care, he removed a small black box from the ground
between them. With a screwdriver, he disconnected wires
from terminals. He removed four heavy packages from the
valve junctions, loaded them on the donkeys and walked
away.

Fifteen miles away, in the city of Homs, a man was
tripped and fell headlong under the tires of a heavy truck.
It passed over him and he died instantly.

Crates marked 'Drilling Equipment' and 'Drill Pipe' were
strewn about the sand floor of the black camel's-hair tent.
Two of the three men were piecing the breech block to the
barrel. The third man was arming the fuses of the incendiary
shells, wrestling the heavy shapes about with practiced efficiency. In the background, across the desert, the thrum of
equipment could be heard. The pumps, sometimes in unison,
sounded like the beating of a heart. The Atlas Mountains
stood out white-capped in the distance, like a mirage in the
shimmering heat.

Seven men, dressed as Berbers, rode camels to the tent.
The three men heard them and went outside, fingering their
side arms. They exchanged polite greetings. The leader of
the mounted men touched his forehead, and they moved on.
Relieved, the men from the tent watched the Berbers go,
then went inside. The three Berbers who had gained entrance
during the brief discussion slit the men's throats. One went
outside and blew a whistle. The riders returned, loaded the
contents of the tent on their camels, buried the shells that
they could not carry, and left.

El Kaffar sat huddled in the jeep, which stood on a short
rise above the massive oil-producing complex of Wadi Gua
Limone. Derricks dotted the sand to the horizon. Pumps
rocked up and down, drawing sustenance from the sand. A
smudge of smoke rode hazily into the sky a few miles to his

immediate front, marking the only charge set by Ben Kelb's agents which had not been discovered in time. The resulting fire had been quickly extinguished by the engineers of Royal American.

El Kaffar's troops had eliminated the few pockets of resistance at the field and were loading into trucks several prisoners, a number of corpses and a sizable amount of demolition equipment from the abortive attempt to destroy the Quahrein Field.

Satisfied that this portion of the exercise had been a succes, El Kaffar instructed the driver to return to the city. Once within the range of the short-wave radio in the jeep, he called in to the Presidential Palace. Algeria was secure, and Qatar and Oman. More news was expected. He replaced the microphone and winced as the jeep hit a bump, jarring his arm.

Once free of the sand and on the highway, the jeep made good time to the Palace. Despite his physical discomfort, he strode energetically into the office, to be greeted by much clicking of heels and saluting. He sat at the desk and was informed that the operations in Syria and Saudi Arabia had been successfully executed. Over the next hour came specific news of this mission or that. He checked his mental calculations against the operational plan on the desk and scrawled a few numbers. Better than ninety-five percent of the oil sources which had been targeted for destruction were now safe. He looked at his watch, then through the west window at the declining sun. He pushed the intercom button, 'What of the armored column? What of Ben Kelb?'

'Nothing, sir.'

A film of sweat shone on El Kaffar's forehead. He looked at his watch again, imagining the giant transports lined up on the German airstrip, like birds of prey.

Thirty-six

Ben Kelb was twenty miles from his desert camp when the radio jeep accompanying him received the message. An agent at Wadi Gua Limone had called, spoken quickly and then disappeared from the air. Ben Kelb, dressed in traditional desert garb and mounted on a camel, swung his force around and headed back to the camp at breakneck speed. Just as he arrived, the first vehicles of El Kaffar's armored column appeared at the crest of the hill overlooking the fortress.

Ben Kelb climbed to the top of the wall and shouted orders. The small carefully trained garrison responded with dispatch. About a dozen tanks were already in formation over the crest and on their way down the hill. Several armored personnel carriers appeared behind them. Three 155-mm howitzers at the rear of the camp roared. Explosions rocked the crest of the hill. After a momentary adjustment, the howitzers fired again, splattering dirt and shrapnel in front of the lead tank. The target was bracketed. The third salvo blew up two tanks. But the remainder of the formation, scattered across the hillside, turned and gained the crest without further damage.

Ben Kelb waved a scimitar at the top of the wall. 'Dogs! You dare! You challenge my right to rule a United Arabia!'

The commander of the lead tank dismounted and ran to a truck at the rear of the column. He hopped through the door, startling the operator who sat amidst the blinking panels of communications equipment. 'Get me El Kaffar. Hurry!'

El Kaffar, awash with perspiration, tore the phone from the hook. He listened carefully to the tank commander, then said calmly, not wanting to impart his own growing sense of panic, 'Then what's holding you up is a few pieces of artillery. Yes, yes, I know you have lost two tanks. No, not at all. I have the most complete faith in you.' The officer spoke again for a moment. El Kaffar looked at his watch, then replied, 'I'm sorry, but that will not do. I don't have the time for you to circle behind the camp. We don't have three or four hours to waste. Frontal assault is out of the question with the artillery? All right. Hold on a moment.' He put his hand over the mouthpiece and shouted. An officer appeared at the door. 'Find out how long it will take to knock out some artillery at Ben Kelb's desert camp. Call the airfield, I want everything that they can throw. Let me know immediately.' He took his hand from the mouthpiece and continued in a reassuring voice, 'I am arranging some air support. You'll have it in no time. Just hold on for a minute.' El Kaffar was overcome by a fit of violent coughing. When it stopped, his head ached. He looked desperately at the watch. The officer he had sent for the planes appeared at the door. 'They're on the way,' he said. El Kaffar nodded in acknowledgment and relayed the message to the tank commander. 'Keep me informed. Remember, speed is imperative.'

Elmo Wright took the helmet liner with its single shining star from the desk of the operations shack and placed it carefully on his head. He stubbed out the smoldering butt in the ashtray, measured the distance between the forward edge of the headgear and the bridge of his broad nose with two fingers and stepped out into the evening air. He spoke briefly to his driver, who saluted and drove off. He put his hands behind his back and rested them, crossed, against his carefully tailored and starched fatigues. He watched the flickering of cigarettes among the men on the grassy strip next to the giant transports on the runway. One by one, his unit commanders appeared at the shack for their final briefing.

*

341

Calm night surrounded the *John F. Kennedy*. Admiral Thurston sat relaxed in the command chair, soothed by the gentle motion of a ship at sea. He looked over his shoulder at the chronometer on the bulkhead behind him and straightened up. 'Flag officer.' The man stepped up smartly. 'Make to Sixth Fleet that we are in a go status. Final steaming orders in sixty minutes as per instructions. Get me the flight officer.'

The Admiral's adjutant disappeared and was shortly replaced by a tanned fortyish Commander in flight gear. 'All right, Charley,' the Admiral said, 'wind 'em up.' In under two minutes, Admiral Thurston noted with satisfaction, the peaceful night was torn by the persistent wail of warming engines.

Ever since the tanks had fled his camp Ben Kelb had merely maintained a full defensive alert, with all men armed at their posts. He had ordered several salvos thrown behind the hill just to keep them honest. He knew that if he could maintain his position for a short while, he would be able to get help from his neighbors in Libya and Iraq, and this nonsense would be at an end. Then there would be time for vengeance.

It was some time before he heard the whistling of the fighter planes overhead. There were six of them. They made two brief runs. As they sped away the camp erupted in a boil of flame which licked at the night sky. Ben Kelb was thrown rudely to the floor as the stacked artillery shells exploded in sympathy to the bombs from the planes, hurling the howitzers and their incinerated crews through the air like matchsticks.

The tank commander led his column over the hill and toward the camp as skirmishers, in a single line to bring all of his firepower to bear simultaneously. Small arms fire crackled in the air. The protective wall at the front of the camp crumbled under the withering fire of the tank cannon.

Ben Kelb leaped to his feet and mounted his camel, swinging the sword over his head. 'Form your units. Charge!' Hesitatingly, the remaining men in the garrison began to follow his orders. The armored column drew to a halt to his front, not firing. 'Fire,' Ben Kelb shouted. 'I said fire!' First one, then another of his men cast their weapons to the sand.

From the lead tank, about two hundred yards away, the commander spoke into a megaphone. 'I have been ordered by El Kaffar to offer brotherhood and peace to all of you who wish it. You will not be our prisoners, but our brothers.'

At first, no one moved. Then, as a body, Ben Kelb's men began to walk forward unarmed toward the tanks.

'Cowards! Sons of whores!' Ben Kelb trotted his camel forward and struck first one and then another of the men with his sword. Then he wheeled the camel and charged the tank, brandishing the blade above his head. 'Pigs! I will move mountains. I will kill you with my bare hands.'

When he was about fifty yards from the tank, the commander shook his head in disbelief, looked once more at the frantic figure rushing at him and squeezed the trigger.

Colonel Ben Kelb disappeared forever in a burst of flame and shattered steel.

El Kaffar sat in his office with the lights out. Moonlight bathed the otherwise darkened city. He had ceased looking at his watch some time ago. He moved restlessly in the chair when he heard the planes return to the airport from their strike, but resisted the temptation to press the intercom button. He measured time by the throbbing of his wound.

The door burst open, admitting a flood of light. A young officer appeared beaming. 'He is dead. It is over. Ben Kelb is dead.'

El Kaffar breathed deeply several times, then rose to his feet. 'Quickly, open the line for the American Embassy. I am going there now. I need to use their phone.'

They drove rapidly through the empty narrow streets and

halted at the Embassy's back door. A startled servant ran to fetch the Ambassador.

When he appeared, El Kaffar said, 'Mr. Ambassador, I must call President Smith from here immediately. He is expecting my call.'

'But why?' he said, surprised.

'To call off an invasion.'

General Wright adjusted the combat pack on his back, checked the time, took one last drag, then stomped out the cigarette. He picked up the loaded M-16 and cradled it in his arms, strode forward toward the lead plane and stood where the MATS pilot could see him. He swung his arm in an arc over his head twice and walked around to the cargo doors to emplane. The engines spurted into life, each of the planes in line following in sequence.

Wright walked up the aisle between the rows of helmeted combat-ready men toward his seat at the front of the cabin. They were at twelve thousand feet when the radio officer came for him.

He returned the headset to the radio man and gave curt instructions to the pilot. Gracefully, the formation wheeled in the sky, turning back across Europe and the Atlantic toward Nebraska.

In response to direct orders from the flag, Charley Adams caught the distraught Russian reconnaissance planes by surprise. Adams's heavily laden fighter-bombers, which had been circling ever more narrowly near the Quahrein coast, suddenly broke out in vee formation and streaked, afterburners blazing, down the Mediterranean toward Gibraltar. At the Pillars of Hercules, they executed a neat one-eighty, and returned to their carrier bases. The Sixth Fleet steamed away from the Quahrein coast and into a familiar patrolling pattern.

*

El Kaffar sat behind the desk in the small studio, a bit fresher for some hastily applied makeup, crossed flags behind him hiding the white mark on the wall where Ben Kelb's picture had so recently hung. The red light went on.

'People of Quahrein, my brothers. Today a drastic but necessary step in the evolution of the Middle East has taken place. With the support of political and business leaders and of our armed forces, I have proclaimed a new government. It is a government whose concerns are the welfare of the people and the peace of the world. We have before us a future which carries only the good or evil that we bring to it.

'The riches of oil have placed at our disposal all of the facilities of the modern world. We have in the past chosen to buy war planes rather than to build schools, to train soldiers rather than engineers, to learn the arts of war rather than the arts of peace. Quahrein has been filled with the cry of Jihad. Our birthright, the fortune that our oil brings to us, has been despoiled in a vain attempt to develop Quahrein as a military power, to establish and entrench a military dictatorship. I forsook my teaching and my training and encouraged you to risk your lives in the revolt against the King, only to find that we have traded one form of tyranny for another.

'That tyranny is now at an end. Quahrein will be returned to the people. For the next ninety days, you will be governed by a military council composed of Major Kheffi, the Minister of Petroleum, Harim el-Shabbaz, the former chancellor of the National University, and myself as Chairman. At the end of ninety days, there will be the first general election in the history of our country. It will be your choice as to who is to govern you. I am confident that you will choose wisely.

'Our freedom has not been achieved without some bloodshed, and some death. I must announce to you that Colonel Ben Kelb died last night. But today we have peace. It is our prayer that from that peace will grow the strength and self-respect that can never be gained by force of arms.

'Do not stay home, huddled to hear of what will befall you. Go into the streets and run and laugh and cry. Go to your jobs and work. And pray that Allah shall grant us the continuing gifts of peace and prosperity.'

Thirty-seven

The General cursed and shouted. 'Vampires! Ghouls! Fate will repay you for your ill treatment of the sick.' He waved his cane menacingly. 'You intend to have them poisoned by the monsters in the kitchen, when they could dine at their ease among friends. Your lack of feeling and compassion adequately matches your incompetence.'

The older of the two doctors, a calm-looking man in his forties, said, 'You can carry on until you're blue in the face, General, but the answer will not change. You cannot take those men out to dinner tonight. If they feel better and are masochists enough to want to walk around like rag dolls, sewn together as they are, and are willing to come here or to another hospital for daily treatment for at least a week, I will consider releasing them at lunchtime tomorrow.'

'Quack! Malingerer! Assassin!'

'If you do not stop exciting them, I will not let them have any visitors. And by the way,' pointing at Rhabbouz, 'why isn't he in a bed? He looks like hell.'

In a more reasonable tone, the General said, 'If you insist. I shall not disturb them. But tomorrow, before lunch. Is that agreed?'

The doctor acceded with a nod of his head.

'And don't worry about the old Jew, here,' the General grumbled, 'he is made of cast iron.'

He took Rhabbouz by the arm and walked off toward the room in which Hamilton and La Brousse had been placed together at the General's request. At the door, he stopped and asked, 'You are all right, aren't you, Rhabbouz?'

'I feel terrible. My ribs are killing me,' he replied.

'Always whining about this or that,' the old man snarled

as he opened the door.

The room was brightly lighted and large. The window was open halfway, and a pleasant breeze had washed the chemical smell from the air. La Brousse was trying to read a magazine with one hand, the other arm was strapped to his chest. There was a bandage around the hand holding the magazine, and he managed awkwardly.

Hamilton, stripped to the waist, was swathed in bandages to his armpits. His right hand was in a cast that reached halfway up his arm. When he heard the door he looked up. 'Well, look who's here, La Brousse. People from the old folks' home come to visit the wounded veterans. Have you any fruit and candy for us today, Granny?'

'I see that your mouth was not damaged in the blast. How is the rest of you?'

'I got off cheap, General. They picked a small pile of metal odds and ends out of my chest, mostly with a tweezers, I understand. I am afraid I will not be playing the violin soon, and I will have to take a secretary, because the cast will stay on for three months. Nothing permanent. My hand does hurt. They shaved my chest, not very good for my pride.'

'I assume you will survive. And you, the bull's-eye of my department, will you live?'

'That's what I am told.'

'You look pale, La Brousse.'

'Rhabbouz looks worse than I do.'

'Certainly, he has three broken ribs. He says he feels terrible.'

Rhabbouz sat in a chair in the corner resting his eyes.

'Well, General, what's going on?' Hamilton asked.

'We came to celebrate the end of the world. Unfortunately, the bastards won't let you out tonight. They said you could leave tomorrow. Do you feel up to it?'

'La Brousse had two pints of blood. They nicked a vein in his neck. I feel fine, except for the hand. What do you mean, the end of the world?'

The General told them the story. By the time he had finished, Rhabbouz was fast asleep in the chair.

'That's it in a nutshell. If El Kaffar fails, the Americans land, and then ... well, you take your pick. War or peace. I thought that we could celebrate this momentous occasion by having a good meal. I would like to be dismembered and fried with a full stomach.'

'What happened to the assassin?' La Brousse asked.

The General prodded Rhabbouz with his stick. 'Tell them what happened to Aboussara.'

Rhabbouz opened his eyes for a moment. 'After the old man killed him, we cut off his balls and hung him on the yacht's anchor.' He dozed off again and began to snore.

The General put his hand in his pocket, pulled out some papers and searched through them. He picked up the phone on the nightstand and asked for a number.

'Hello, Doctor. This is General Pineau. Yes, I am well. I think that Rhabbouz could use a night in the hospital. Would you mind dropping over here to take a look at him. With me? Oh, yes, he's been with me all day. We are in room 708.' He hung up the phone while the doctor was still shouting.

'Terrible disposition, that man,' the General observed. 'He thinks Rhabbouz should have gotten more rest. This is nasty business, my friends. Soon we shall know the outcome.'

The doctor arrived in ten minutes. 'What are you trying to do, kill him? I thought that we agreed that he was to get some rest after that meeting this morning?'

'He didn't want to miss any of the fun. Besides, he was not finished with his work.'

'More of his work will finish him.'

He woke Rhabbouz and examined him on the edge of Hamilton's bed. 'You are going to spend the night here, Rhabbouz, and get some rest out of sight of this madman.'

The General said, 'Well, if you are all going to be cooped up, I might as well go to the hotel. We shall have our celebration for lunch tomorrow. I shall order in advance. I must tell you that I do not take kindly to being left alone like this in my old age.' He rose and went to the door, then turned back, 'I want you to know, La Brousse, that I miss your help and your presence. I am absolutely unable to tie my shoes without you, and these loafers are killing my feet.' He sniffed and walked out.

'The old son of a bitch,' La Brousse chuckled.

The General toddled down the hall, feeling very old and very tired. He dozed in the car during the short trip back to the hotel. He went to his room, threw his clothes on a chair, fell on the bed and dropped off to sleep.

Only a minute later, his phone rang. 'Yes.'

'It's Tombal, General.'

'What is it?'

'I just got a call from the police in St. Tropez. They found the last messenger. Just a kid. Cut up like Lambert. His face was all burned as well. It is good that Aboussara is dead.'

'It is good that he had his balls cut off too. Come to the hotel at noon tomorrow. We are having a lunch. You are part of the team. You would be missed.'

'Thank you, General. I'll be there. Oh, Colonel Brunschwig has been all over my back about yesterday. He wants to speak to you.'

'No doubt. What did you tell him?'

'Not much. Just that we were in the process of apprehending the perpetrator.'

'Was he satisfied?'

'Yes. He says that it proves that you were wrong. That it was a plot by the Communists to assassinate the president of General Motors.'

Thirty-eight

By nine o'clock the following morning, the *Long Beach* and the *Ticonderoga* had been directed to rejoin the body of the fleet, which was speeding toward Gibraltar in a routine formation. The Russian reconnaissance planes buzzed about in confusion.

General White's bone-weary troops had been unloaded from Arlo Hunsacker's giant MATS aircraft back in Nebraska.

Cut off from the world, except for a scratchy transistor radio which played whining Arab music when it played at all, the *Glen Pool* steamed into the Quahrein harbor proudly displaying Colonel Ben Kelb's personal pennant. It dropped anchor near the private docks, the tender was let down, and Paul Fosburgh, dressed in a white linen suit and shirt and tie, was brought ashore.

When the port captain sighted the familiar craft, he called the Presidential Palace. El Kaffar was sleeping, drugged and exhausted. The duty officer considered his alternatives, then reluctantly approached the doctor who was sitting in a comfortable armchair at the door.

'Doctor, a ship has arrived in the harbor. I think it is essential that the Minister be informed.'

'You are certain?'

'Yes, sir. I think it would be a mistake not to tell him.'

'I'll wake him. Wait here.' The doctor went into the room and gently shook El Kaffar's shoulder. 'One of your men wants to see you.'

El Kaffar opened his eyes and raised himself slightly from

the pillow. 'What is it?'

'He said something about a ship in the harbor.'

'Tell him to come in.'

The officer snapped a salute. 'It's the *Glen Pool*, sir. Flying Colonel Ben Kelb's personal banner.'

El Kaffar smiled. 'Then Fosburgh does not know. Sink it.'

The officer stood dumbstruck. Then said, 'Sink it?'

El Kaffar laughed. 'Never mind, Lieutenant. Tell Captain Hassan to get down to the port as fast as possible. I want Fosburgh brought here with the signal honors due a man of his stature. But tell him nothing. Have Hassan talk about the weather. Anything but politics. Bring him here to me.'

El Kaffar swung his legs over the side of the bed. 'Doctor, give me a hand getting dressed. I am going to enjoy this beyond your wildest imagination.'

Within the hour, Fosburgh to the accompaniment of the usual bowing and scraping had been brought to the Palace and to the grand Moorish hall. When he was brought into the office, he found himself alone there. He fidgeted for a moment and then looked at the wall behind the desk. The life-size picture of Ben Kalb had been removed, leaving a contrasting rectangular mark.

El Kaffar stepped into the room. 'Good morning, Mr. Fosburgh. I'm glad you arrived. We have a great deal to talk about.'

Five hours later, in Washington, William McCandless Smith splashed like a whale in his huge bathtub. Steam from the water had misted the mirror and coated the walls with a fine dew. There was a knock at the door.

'Jack, that you?'

'None other.'

'Come in, pull up a stool.'

Kugel came in, looking bright and relaxed.

'What have you got for me this morning, Jack?'

'Praise from the press. They applaud El Kaffar and cautiously state that this indicates a movement of Quahrein away from the extremist camp.'

'How about that, Jack?'

'It beats hell out of World War Three. What did Oscar say?'

'He asked if he could take a week's vacation. Carver and Aufritz were relieved and disappointed, especially Aufritz. I have the feeling that no one ever gave him a whole economy to play with before. Carlton, of course, has been a bug on self-sufficiency from the beginning.' Then he continued more seriously. 'He's right, Jack. We can't ever find ourselves where we were again yesterday. We can't afford it. There are just so many El Kaffars in anyone's life.'

'Who would have believed it? He must be quite a fellow.'

'Never fear. We'll be hearing from him shortly.'

A week later, a limousine carrying Arthur Edelman, Milton Goodrich and George Hultz pulled into the airport at Hyères in time for a flight to Paris. Edelman and Hultz were going to New York, Goodrich to Washington at the request of President Smith.

The driver stepped out quickly to help Edelman, whose head was still heavily bandaged. Goodrich and Hultz each took one of Arthur's arms, and they walked together slowly toward the plane.

The General stood watching them at the cyclone fence with La Brousse. 'Thank God. Now perhaps we can get some rest.'

A limousine picked Goodrich up at the private terminal of Washington National and whisked him to the White House. The President awaited him.

'Good morning, Mr. Goodrich. Is that bandage a result of your adventures?'

'Yes, sir. I lost a little piece of ear in the process. Nothing serious.'

'Please sit down. I guess that you and I both have lived through a couple of near misses in the past few weeks.'

'It's not the kind of thing that you'd want to do twice.'

'How's our Mr. Edelman?'

'A little unsteady on his feet as yet, and pretty worn out. But his mind is sharp, and he's anxious to get to work.'

'Incredible. With the kind of tension he's been living with, it's a miracle he can even think of his work. Frankly, I'd like to go relax over a game of golf myself. Mr. Goodrich, I asked you to come down here to thank you for what you've done. But I'd like to impose on you a bit further, if I may. I must ask you, confidentially of course, what your plans are with respect to the Edelman car at this point.'

'We intend to develop it for commercial use. Though naturally at a slower pace now. More consistent with the realities of running a business.'

'I hope that that doesn't mean the back burner. It isn't that I don't appreciate all you have done already; I wish the country could know how much you risked in its service. But it seems to me the solar car is almost a national resource. It's your property, but the country needs it, and I would hate to see its potential bottled up for years.'

'I've been thinking on that, sir. It seems to me that a compromise can be struck.'

The President leaned forward, chin in hand.

Goodrich continued. 'We own the worldwide rights to the patents. If we are allowed a head start, that is, if we can make a commercial success of it before we are forced to sublicense to others – say, for two years – I think that I can talk the board into going forward at a pretty rapid clip.'

'What does that mean in terms of when we would have solar-powered cars?'

'In the normal course of events, even taking into account some acceleration in writing off old equipment for conventional cars, I'd say it would be a maximum of three years to production.'

The President leaned back in his chair. 'And during that time, the oil tap is turned on and off, and the industrial world chokes. Do you think that will do, Mr. Goodrich? The figures haven't changed. The crisis is over, but the problem has not disappeared. We are a nation in motion. Currently, the key to that motion is fossil fuel. Oil. We've had some success in beefing up techniques in various recovery methods, but seismology and drilling and pumping still account by far for the largest margin of discovery and production. Restraint by the public has helped too. I'm not asking for a miracle. I've learned that there aren't any. I'd guess you could call it jaw-boning, but I want all the help I can get. The closer you come to producing this car, the closer we will have come to a real sense of independence. Don't give me an answer now.' He chuckled. 'I don't want you to pull me to pieces for exerting undue pressure, and I don't want to be accused of mixing in the affairs of private enterprise. But I would like to know that you will think carefully about what I've said, and that you will consider it when you do make a decision.'

Goodrich stood and put out his hand. 'I shall, Mr. President.'

Thirty-nine

On the day before Christmas, Mohammed El Kaffar was elected the President of the Republic of Quahrein. On the eighth of January, he flew to New York to make an address to the General Assembly of the United Nations.

The delegates applauded politely as he made his way up the broad aisle to the rostrum. He arranged the papers neatly before him and began to speak.

'In my first address to my people as head of state, some three months ago, I spoke to them of the opportunities offered by peace. In the tense world in which we live, it would be less than realistic to expect that one could dismantle unilaterally the entire defense capabilities of a country. But as has been said from this rostrum many times, even the smallest step is a step toward a true and lasting peace. We believe that we have taken such a step. I have asked for this opportunity to address this august body to announce, with the permission of the government of Israel, the termination of the state of hostilities that has existed between us and that nation for so many years.'

The room was alive with buzzing.

'I would like, further, to announce the signing this morning, at the Quahreinian Consulate in New York, of a formal treaty of mutual technical assistance between the State of Israel and the Republic of Quahrein. We are both small countries in a troubled area of the world. We have set out on a course which we hope will succeed in enriching the people of both our countries. Forthwith, certain technical items made in Israel will be licensed for manufacture to both private and public companies in Quahrein. The Republic of Quahrein has in turn signed a sales agreement covering the provision of petroleum and petroleum products to the State of Israel. This contract is to include partial ownership of retail distribution in Israel by the government of Quahrein, or Quahrein share companies. Most important, it is my great privilege to announce that the Hebrew University and the National University of Quahrein will henceforth operate as one great center of learning, with the two campuses benefiting from an exchange of both students and teachers, that we may share both our knowledge and the love and the trust of our young. It is my fervent hope that this small step will be for our troubled area of the world a beginning of the ascent to the freedom which is peace. In a separate paper I will deliver my detailed program for dealing with the problem of the Palestinian refugees. All I wish to say now is that there is room in my country for these people. Not in camps, but as full citizens.'

He stepped down from the podium to thunderous applause. He nodded his head from side to side in thanks, his face serious, but his eyes smiling. He felt a twinge of grief as he approached his seat, watching the delegates of Iraq walk stiffly before him, and through the door into the damp cold outside.

Two days later, the board room of General Motors filled with the men who govern the world's largest industrial enterprise. After some initial milling and chatter, each took his appointed place around the huge table, set with yellow pads and pencils and dotted with carafes and glasses. One of the items on the printed agenda was the solar-powered car, another the annual meeting to be held two months hence, and the proxy statement which was to be filed and distributed to shareholders. The chairman, who had been Milton Goodrich's predecessor as president, called the meeting to order. In rapid fashion, they moved through the order of business.

'I think it would be appropriate to move on to a discussion of our plans for the solar-powered car. Mr. Goodrich, would you addresss yourself to that subject, please?'

'Gentlemen,' Goodrich began, 'you have before you, as addendum to this agenda, as well as the minutes of the last meeting, a financial outline for the development of the Edelman Solar-Powered Car. This proposal is unusual in that the lead time with which we are familiar has been sharply reduced. The reduction serves a variety of purposes, but is not without cost. The solar-powered car is not a final solution to our problems, nor of anyone else's. But is, in fact, a departure in the direction of momentum toward the future.

'It is the considered opinion of our research staff that the solar-powered engine will be, for the foreseeable future, a limited-use vehicle, restricted to lighter passenger cars. It is, as you have already been made aware, a highly efficient machine in a certain range of uses. I envision it not as an extension of our historical dominance of the American motor vehicle industry, but rather as the beginning of our entry into a whole new industry of worldwide scope. I have Mr. Edelman and Mr. Hultz, as well as Mr. Coughtry, to address you on the subject. With your permission, I will ask them to come in.'

In a little less than an hour, Hultz packed the slides he had used in the presentation and walked away with Coughtry. Edelman was asked to remain.

One of the directors, the president of a large Midwestern bank, asked, 'Then what you are suggesting, Mr. Goodrich, in short, is a substantial increase in the research budget to accelerate production probabilities. Is that not so?'

'Yes.'

'The return in the first three years is not up to our normal admissible standards, I am sure you are aware.'

'Yes, I am aware of that.'

'Is it your opinion that the long-range implications are sufficient to permit this deviation from our generally accepted policies?'

'Mr. Woods, I think that it will remake the image of General Motors in the eyes of the public and provide us with a whole new horizon of competence. We risked a great deal with the high-mileage engine and were rewarded. Here our rewards will be of a higher order.'

After further discussion, the resolution was adopted by the board. The Edelman Solar-Powered Car was to be a reality by the fall, and a year hence available to the public.

After the lunch break, the subject of directors and proxies came up for consideration. Before the agenda was followed, Paul Fosburgh, who was attending his first meeting in months, asked to be recognized.

He got to his feet. 'I am aware that this is an unusual request, gentlemen, but I have an announcement that I would like to make to this board. I intend that it should be made publicly later today, or tomorrow. I have worked for many years as a member of this and many other boards. It has been my privilege to serve as president and chief executive of Royal American Oil for over fifteen years. Despite my affection for the business community, and my long-standing friendship with many of you at this table, I have decided to withdraw from all corporate affairs to devote myself to a variety of charitable causes. I would like, therefore, to ask that my name be removed from the list of directors standing for reelection. I would also like to announce that as of this afternoon, effective 5 P.M., I have resigned my position with Royal American Oil, and will not stand for reelection to that Board of Directors. Thank you for your friendship and for your attention.'

There was polite applause, and a brief hum around the table.

Milton Goodrich spoke. 'Mr. Fosburgh, I am sure that I am not alone in thanking you for your splendid efforts on behalf of this company. You have given unstintingly of your time in the pursuit of our affairs, and I want to be among the first to recognize that fact.'

Fosburgh smiled coldly and nodded in acknowledgment.

It was determined that Paul Fosburgh's place on the Board of Directors would be taken by Arthur Edelman, as per agreement. All business having been concluded, the meeting ended.

*

359

Goodrich chatted for a moment with several of the directors, and then very much satisfied, went back to his office. His secretary caught him at the door of her office and put her finger to her lips.

'Oh, Mr. Goodrich, I am so sorry. I just didn't know what to do. I don't even know how he got onto this floor. The security people must have let him through. He said that he didn't have an appointment, but that he would wait. He said it didn't matter for how long. He said that he knew you were in a board meeting. I didn't want to have him thrown out.'

'Don't worry about it. Did he at least give you a name?'

'No. He said that you knew each other intimately, and that he wanted this to be a surprise.'

Goodrich shrugged, puzzled, and walked into his office, shutting the door after him.

El Kaffar sat comfortably in a corner of the couch reading *Business Week*. When he heard the door he put down the magazine and rose. 'I think that sharing the risk of death qualifies as intimacy, don't you, Mr. Goodrich?'

'Hello, Mr. President. Congratulations. First on your election, and secondly on your brilliant speech.' He held out his hand. 'No bodyguards? You came alone?'

'Not exactly, there are a couple of them downstairs in the lobby, waiting for me. But if you can't be safe at General Motors,' he shrugged his shoulders, 'then where can you be safe?'

'You hinted that we would meet again. What brings me this honor?'

'Business, Mr. Goodrich. We have business to discuss.'

Goodrich looked at him blankly. 'I don't think that I understand you.'

'Mr. Goodrich, I want you to meet the largest shareholder of General Motors.'

'M. Dassault? But I've had the pleasure.'

'No. He was, but is no longer. Don't look astonished, he has not divested himself of a single share so far as I know. Are you aware that during the summer and fall the price and volume of General Motors were inordinately high, when compared to other Dow Jones stocks?'

Much amused, Goodrich said, 'Father of His Country and market analyst too. Yes, I was quite aware and not a little concerned. Strong, scattered buying was the report I got. Why?'

'Because directly and beneficially, the Republic of Quahrein owns six point seven percent of the outstanding common stock of General Motors. We have, as the saying goes, bought our piece of America.'

'You're kidding.'

El Kaffar laughed. 'Mr. Goodrich, if I had a picture of you now, I think I could blackmail you till eternity. No, Mr. Goodrich, I'm not kidding. Would you say, offhand, that that size block deserves board representation?'

'Deserves it, Mr. President? Demands it. How long have you been in this position?'

'Several months. I do want to name two nominees to the board. I am sure that you will find them palatable. One is Harmon Copeland, the new president of Royal American Oil, and the other is a senior partner of a New York law firm who represents certain of our commercial interests in the United States. I am sure that you are acquainted with him.'

Goodrich looked at him narrowly. 'And that's all?'

El Kaffar laughed again. 'You are clever, Mr. Goodrich. Oil means a great deal right now, Mr. Goodrich. But, as some wise man has pointed out, trees don't grow to the sky. When there is a need, it is filled. Entropy is the nature of the universe. Energy is needed. It exists in the form of oil, in the hands of a very few small nations. The hard currency that they gain from it serves no purpose, for the most part, other than to create horrendous inflation. There must be a useful outlet for money, otherwise it just builds up the prices for non-useful merchandise. We have discovered a useful outlet for our money. Investment in the largest business enterprise of all. We intend to use that position to improve our own industrial capabilities. In short, we can't live on oil forever.

We have plenty of labor available. You would be amazed to find out how much of it is trained or trainable. We want you to build a plant in Quahrein. We will give you the same favorable terms for foreign investment that you would get anywhere. We will train the labor, or rather pay the training costs for them to be trained here in America. We want an interest in the plant. We'll pay for it, and extend excellent credit facilities as well. Your return will be as great as that of any project you have now.'

'This is overwhelming, Mr. El Kaffar.'

'Would you be less overwhelmed if I sat by and watched the depletion of our oil resources and the waste of our income on gold bars or jet planes to exterminate the Jews? Oh, no, Mr. Goodrich. That's why I made the revolution. That kind of thinking must become extinct, or most certainly we shall. Combine the ability of the peoples of the Middle East with American know-how and productive power. Use untapped Arab manpower, unused Arab genius and skills, combine it with a history and tradition of four thousand years of education and Israeli business acumen and technical capability, add to that the mastery of modern production techniques, and you are talking about the foundation for a great jump into the future for a very large slice of mankind. And it certainly beats guerrilla raids, airstrike reprisals and growing piles of dead and maimed children.'

'What kind of a plant do you want to build? Automobile accessories, refrigerators and home appliances?'

'Not at all. I want to be a licensee for the Edelman Solar-Powered Car.'

Goodrich shook his head. 'You should have been the president of a company, not a country. I can't guarantee you that. But if you make a proposal to the board through your representation, it will be considered. We can certainly negotiate in good faith any reasonable proposal. The desideratum here, Mr. President, is the well-being of the stockholders as a whole. I think that there is a whole field of discussion to deal with. If you will send representatives with your proposals, I will have them carefully studied by our staff, and I myself will help where I can. Then we will be in a position to negotiate seriously.'

'Agreed, Mr. Goodrich. I cannot ask for more.'

'Just one other thing, Mr. President, did you have anything to do with Paul Fosburgh's retirement?'

El Kaffar smiled slyly, 'The day after the coup he showed up on his yacht flying Ben Kelb's personal flag. I suppose he hadn't heard. I just made a few timely suggestions to him. He told me that he was cut out for a life of charitable endeavor in any case. And besides, I think that the last visit convinced him that the climate in Quahrein is not at all good for his health.'

Forty

M. de Quatremain, the manager, fussed over every detail. Every carnation on every table, every candle in every luster, had his personal seal of approval.

He straightened the swallowtails of his coat and prepared to receive the first of the guests to the Inaugural Ball of the Hôtel La Boudrague. The low elegant buildings sparkled white in the starlit June night. A soft breeze blew and St. Tropez glittered brightly across the gulf.

M. de Quatremain was justly proud of the ornamental arrangements that graced both the terrace and the ballroom – the subtle indications that the function was one of dual purpose, not only to inaugurate the lively hotel but to celebrate the marriage of one of its architects. A delightful man, de Quatremain thought, just delightful.

His reverie was shattered by a loud noise.

'What do you mean, I can't have a drink? Get out of my way, you bumbling oaf, before I break this stick across your empty head and charge your misbegotten employer with damage to my personal property.'

De Quatremain hurried over to the bar. There were two men standing in front of the bartender, who was pouring the drinks as requested.

As de Quatremain approached, one of them turned and said, 'What do you want, you little pansy?'

De Quatremain looked at him, the blue eyes under the beetling white brows seemingly growing. He swallowed, and without a word went back to the terrace.

'How do you do that?' La Brousse asked.

'Competence, personal magnetism. You wouldn't understand.'

Shortly before the guests were to begin arriving, Donald and Marie Jo appeared from the lobby. He was in a white jacket, flushed and fit. She wore a white soft halter-topped gown.

They spotted La Brousse and the General and walked over to them.

'It's a shame we had to leave after the ceremony. I would love to have watched. You didn't just shower and change, did you?'

Marie Jo eyed him appraisingly. He ducked his head and made a sour face. He was dressed in an immaculate black smoking jacket and brilliant white ruffled shirt. His patent leather shoes gleamed. His chest was covered with ribbons collected over a lifetime of service. Around his neck hung the Distinguished Service Cross, brightly polished and with a bright new tri-colored ribbon. Marie Jo reached out to straighten his bowtie.

'God damn it, stop fumbling with me.'

She continued what she was doing. 'Stop being such an old bear. You don't scare me anymore.'

'Bah, just because you have big tits you think you can push men around like so much dirt.'

'That's right.' She finished with the tie, kissed his forehead and danced off laughing to greet a friend at the door.

'Ah. Look who's here,' said the old man. 'Do you think that you can move your poor crippled body to the other side of the room?'

'Yes, sir.' La Brousse, who had gotten over his limp months before, dutifully followed the General as he shuffled his way to the door.

The General bowed as deeply as his stomach would permit, took Madame Rhabbouz's hand in his own and kissed it lightly. 'You are ravishing tonight, chère madame.'

'Liar!'

'By no means, madame. Mere understatement. And you, M. Rhabbouz. I think you look remarkably well for a man your age.'

Rhabbouz shook hands, smiled and walked by, following

his wife. Just loud enough to be heard the General added, 'Especially for an old Jew.'

At approximately ten o'clock, a bellboy came to seek Donald out. 'The gentleman said it was important that you bring Mme. Hamilton as well.'

They excused themselves from the table and followed the boy to the front door, and thence into the driveway. A man stood before a strange-looking car. It was bright red, save for a silver panel on its trunk lid. Its interior was of polished dark wood and white leather.

'Are you Mr. and Mrs. Donald Hamilton?'

'Yes,' Donald answered, 'what can we do for you?'

'Nothing at all.' The man handed Donald the keys. 'These are for you. They belong to this car.' He reached into his pocket. 'There's a note that goes with it.'

Marie Jo opened the envelope and read aloud. 'To Donald and Marie Jo Hamilton, without whom this machine might never have existed, nor its grateful donors lived. You are now the proud owners of the eighteenth existing Edelman Solar-Powered Car by General Motors. Good luck and God bless you. Signed Milton Goodrich, Arthur Edelman and George Hultz.'

'Let's go for a spin,' Donald suggested.

'Later, this party is partly for us.'

They went back inside and danced until three. When the orchestra finally gave up and went home, along with the remainder of the guests who were not staying at the hotel, one table held out, champagne flowing. The General and Rhabbouz were telling war stories. La Brousse had a be-wildered smile on his face; for once he had drunk too much.

A boy came up to the table and asked if there was a General Pineau in the party.

'What do you want of him?'

'He has a telephone call.'

'Who is it?'

'He said his name was Brunschwig, Colonel Brunschwig.'

'La Brousse, you drunken cripple, deal with it. I won't be

disturbed.'

Donald and Marie Jo came to the table and wished them all good night and thanked them. 'Especially, the best man,' patting the General's shoulder.

As they walked down the steps toward the car, and toward the secluded cove and the soft sand behind the headland of St. Tropez, they heard La Brousse pick up the receiver and say quite distinctly, 'That is correct, Colonel Brunschwig. He simply won't talk to you now because he thinks you're an asshole.'